C000253099

THE W... ...MILY

The Courage of ...
The Swimming Pool S...

ALSO BY SAMANTHA TONGE

The Christmas Calendar Girls
The Summer Island Swap

THE WINTER WE MET

Samantha Tonge

An Aria Book

First published as an eBook in the UK in 2020 by Aria,
an imprint of Head of Zeus Ltd.
This edition first published in the UK in 2021 by Aria.

A CIP catalogue record for this book is available from the
British Library.

ISBN (PB) 9781800246461
ISBN (E) 9781800241664

Typeset by Siliconchips Services Ltd UK

Printed and bound in Great Britain by
CPI Group (UK) Ltd, Croydon CRO 4YY

Aria
c/o Head of Zeus
First Floor East
5–8 Hardwick Street
London EC1R 4RG

www.ariafiction.com

For the care workers who've been working
so tirelessly during this year's Coronavirus pandemic.
You are superstars.
With special mention to Afton and all the
staff at Westoe

1

It was a misunderstanding that started it. I sat in the wrong row. The air steward said it didn't matter. The flight wasn't full and so I stayed there, by the window. We were about to take off.

I was travelling back to England after attending one of the many toy trade fairs that ran throughout the year, this time in Germany. I managed a shop called Under the Tree. It was the end of October and I was thinking ahead to next year's must-have products. I yawned. It was an obscenely early flight.

Before heading to the airport I'd bought a little Bavarian cuckoo clock. I bent down and took it out of my hand luggage, put it on the seat next to me for a moment and grinned, imagining my plain-speaking gran's face as the wooden bird flew noisily out of its door.

'Must be a great joke.'

I looked up at the lofty frame, red jumper and eyes that laughed with me. Hastily, I put the clock back and removed my woollen bobble hat. He put his big rucksack and anorak into the overhead cabin and offered to lift my bag up there as well. Then he settled into the seat next to me and put on his seatbelt.

'Sorry. I haven't introduced myself. I'm Nik.'

He had an accent, it took me a moment to place it. Australian. He held out his hand and long fingers enveloped mine.

'Jess,' I said, unable to look away from those eyes, surprised by their startling blueness – and the tingly feeling spreading across my palm.

He glanced down at our hands and humorously raised an eyebrow. Blushing, I released him.

'Sorry. Premature jet lag. I've been at a trade fair for two days and feel as if I could sleep through to next year's.'

'Me too. Nuremberg by any chance?' he asked, and we chatted about how busy the fair had been.

'So you manage a toy shop?' he said, then really listened as I replied. His eyebrows moved up and down as we chatted. He was interested, paid attention.

Not everyone did that. It made me feel seen.

The plane vibrated as the engines started and Nik ran a hand through thick hair that was streaked with white. It was unusual for someone in their, what, early thirties, and contrasted with his tanned, smooth skin. He looked distinguished. At twenty-nine I'd not had my first grey hair yet.

'What about you?' I asked.

'My family owns a toy manufacturing business in Sydney and I've been keeping track of the competition.'

The plane turned onto the runway – normally my cue to lean against the window and try hard to relax.

'Do you like flying? You must be used to it, coming all the way from Australia.'

'Love it. Night-time is best, with winds dying down

along with thermal turbulence so that you just glide through the air, with stars coming out, realising Earth is just another spherical mass... it kind of gives you perspective, right?'

'True. It's so easy to believe that the world revolves around *us* – until we leave it and realise we are nothing but a tiny cog in a huge machine.'

'Not that cogs aren't important. Cogs have needs. Cogs have feelings – even teeny tiny ones.' He caught my eye and we laughed. He stared at my hands again, which were clenched together. 'Statistically, this is the safest form of travel,' he said in a soft tone.

'It's still fairly new to me. I only started flying abroad a couple of years ago, with my flatmate Oliver. I never had foreign holidays when I was little.'

'If it's any consolation, I threw up the first time I flew. I was seven. It was Easter and I'd secretly scoffed a huge chocolate egg before boarding. The turbulence didn't agree with my digestive system.' He gave a wry smile. 'Nor did its contents with the passenger in front. The poor woman was wearing white shoes. The whole cabin stank afterwards.'

Laughing loudly, I became aware we were up in the sky. Nik leant in as the air steward trundled towards us with a jingling drinks trolley. The aroma of coffee energised me and we each accepted a cup, both taking no milk and just one sugar. The two of us sipped and gave a contented sigh before chatting about Nuremberg. My shoulders relaxed as the conversation flowed. There weren't any awkward silences and we had plenty of laughs. I'd heard people talk about it before – meeting someone you felt as if you'd known for years. That instant connection, like... I glanced down at my lap… like two halves of a seatbelt clicking together. I thought I'd had it once before.

Not wanting to think about that now, I bought a large bar of chocolate from the duty-free list, wishing I'd had time to grab breakfast. I shared some of it with Nik before we lapsed into comfortable work talk again about how his family's company favoured making traditional products.

'I loved that wooden clock you were holding, when I boarded,' he said.

'It's for my gran. She used to collect wooden ornaments and would always look for unusual decorative ones for our Christmas tree when I was younger. She's a huge fan of the festive season. Gran's a keen reader and would read all of the new children's festive releases with me. We spent many a cosy December Saturday in the library.'

'Do you see much of her now?'

'Yes, but we no longer live together. She moved into an assisted living facility four years ago. She still enjoys Christmas to the full, though. Every December they hold a huge Christmas Eve party. The residents start preparing for it as early as January, buying in cheap craft materials during the sales and, as the months pass, testing out new festive recipes in the communal kitchen for the buffet they put on. They also research different themes. Then in early November a meeting is held to vote for the best one.'

'Why leave it that late to decide?' he asked.

'So that it ramps up the excitement in the weeks before the big day… Last year's theme was a masquerade ball. The year before a Downton Abbey one.'

'It sounds ace. Christmas really is the best time of year. My family and I are often too busy to go to parties, going into overdrive completing the production of extra orders of toys that no one predicted would be quite so popular. Not that I mind. It's worth it if I'm out and spot a kid playing with one of our products.'

Before I could answer the pilot announced we were about to land. How had that happened? Nik had turned hours into minutes. We tightened our seatbelts and I stashed the remainder of the chocolate into my handbag. I gripped the arm rests. Nik pulled a funny face and I couldn't help grinning. Eventually my rapid breathing slowed as he went on to tell a really bad joke, me shaking my head when he delivered the punchline. Relief surged through me as I realised the plane had touched down. When we came to a standstill, a whistling Nik passed down my hand luggage from the overhead cabin, slipped on his anorak and grabbed his rucksack. The air stewards beamed as he thanked them for a great journey. We disembarked and walked into the large, impersonal terminal, hit by the hustle bustle and flight announcements over the intercom. My stomach rumbled as I followed Nik who navigated the crowd easily as he stood a good head above anyone else.

'Are you going to another fair?' I asked, once we'd collected our pull-along cases, needing to leave but not quite wanting to say goodbye. Nik was good company.

'Sure. Tomorrow – one in London just for manufacturers. Then I'm... taking a break for a few weeks. A friend of the family has gone away on business for two months and said I could have his flat for as long as I wanted, in a place called Islington.'

'Nice. But a break? At this time of year?'

'Mitigating circumstances,' he said. 'And I can't think of

a better country to spend time in. You've reminded me of how much I like England. I've really enjoyed meeting you, Jess.'

My stomach did a little flip as he said my name. It caught me by surprise. 'It's been great meeting you too.' I looked at my watch. 'It's only ten o'clock. What have you got planned for the rest of the day?'

'Nothing much. It feels like a waste, to be honest. Guess I'll just head to the flat and stock up on food. If I was sensible, I'd get some sleep.'

'Do you fancy having something to eat together first? My stomach is calling out, literally, for eggs and toast.'

He smiled. 'There's me thinking that noise was the weather gods welcoming me into London with a roll of thunder.'

We managed to find ourselves a seat in one of the airport's crowded restaurants. Despite the early hour, a group of young men sat at a nearby table downing beer and flicking drinks mats, their raucous chat revealing they were heading to Amsterdam for a stag party. Nik and I both ordered a full English breakfast and sat nursing mugs of tea.

'So, you've been to England before?' I asked and took a sip.

'Yes. It's only the last few years or so that I've been going to the trade fairs on my own. I joined the company straight from university and Mum and Dad have been teaching me the ropes ever since, taking me on work trips abroad.' He ran a finger around the mug's rim. 'They brought me here as a teenager though, on holiday to see the sights. Mum and Dad went backpacking during university holidays and always said there was nothing quite like travel for broadening the mind. They liked discovering unusual places. We travelled the length of the country, from Newcastle to Bournemouth.'

'Wow. Any favourite places?'

'Stonehenge was amazing – so atmospheric. And we rented a cottage in the Cotswolds for a few days, in a quiet little village. It looked like a picture off a chocolate box and ducks visited the back garden – Mum fell in love with it. Manchester was pretty cool with trendy independent coffee shops and warehouse stores. We had to visit the Cavern Club in Liverpool as Dad had always been a massive fan of The Beatles and we also took a wonderful steam engine trip through Norfolk. We only spent one day in the capital so I don't really know London.'

'It sounds as if you've seen more of my home country than I have. So what got your parents interested in toy manufacturing?'

'Mum was studying a degree in arts and Dad a design degree with modules in consumer engineering. He was left some money from his grandparents – enough to start the business. Also both of their families are big and even in their twenties, between them, Mum and Dad had lots of nephews and nieces and loved entertaining them, and Grams and Grandpa – Mum's parents – would often talk about how Mum was always making her own toys as a child out of food packaging and scraps of materials or plastic.' He smiled. 'She encouraged me as a boy. I used to love crafting with the week's leftover cereal boxes and plastic butter tubs. I guess that passed the passion onto me.'

'My gran used to be more of a chef and we'd make a new recipe up from leftovers each week,' I said. 'A friend of hers owned an allotment and we'd bake all sorts of crumbles and concoct different pasta sauces with vegetables. Our pumpkin spaghetti became a favourite.' The waitress delivered our breakfast and I looked down at the plate. It had a small pot of baked beans, fried eggs, bacon, tomatoes and mushrooms, plus slices of buttered toast and a hash brown. 'Gran would love this. When I was younger, she'd do me a fry-up as a treat every Friday, before school. There's nothing like waking up to the smell of bacon.'

'So how did *you* get into the business?' he said, offering me the salt before shaking it across his eggs.

'Angela, the boss of the toy shop where I work – Under the Tree – went to school with my mum, therefore she knew Gran and heard how I wasn't sure what to do after my A levels. She said there were worse careers than working in retail, and that she couldn't pay me much to begin with, but would I be interested in a job in a new toy shop she was setting up.' I shrugged. 'Angela gave me a future, a purpose, and I was grateful, working hard to prove her trust wasn't misplaced.' A comfortable silence fell for a few moments. I popped the last bit of toast into my mouth. 'What do you eat for breakfast in Australia?'

'Similar to this if I've got time. Or I grab a bowl of cereal.' He closed his eyes and made a satisfied noise before opening them again. 'I hadn't realised how hungry I was. Thanks for suggesting this, Jess. I feel like a new man. Well... almost. My legs are still aching from being squashed behind that seat in front.'

'Not a problem I have, at five foot three.' I cut through an egg, sunshiny yolk spilling across the plate. 'Although next to Gran I'm practically a giant. She must be only four foot something now.'

'Grams shrank too during her final years.'

'Oh. I'm sorry to hear she isn't with you anymore.'

'It was a huge shock when she passed – even though it had been foreseen for a while.' He stopped eating for a moment and his voice became quieter. 'Grams didn't always know who I was, at the end, but sometimes she'd wink or pull a comical face and we'd laugh.' His mouth quirked up. 'But then she'd always been a joker. Grandpa was the serious one and saw it as his duty to teach me the things he'd grown up doing, such as fishing and tying knots. Whereas Grams and me would dance in her kitchen, hand in hand, singing to her favourite folk music. He always did say he wouldn't last long if she went first.' Nik dug his fork into a mushroom and a sheepish look crossed his face. 'Jeez, sorry, I'm getting way too serious this early in the morning.'

Don't apologise. Your openness is refreshing.

'You get on well with your grandparents?' he continued.

'My granddad died before I was born. He got hit by a stolen car. But yes, Gran practically brought me up. I don't know how I would have managed without her.'

Nik nodded. 'I used to love listening to stories from when my grandparents were younger and whatever problem I faced, they had some experience to draw on that they'd share with me and it would help.' He wiped his mouth with a paper napkin. I pointed to the corner and a splodge of yolk. He grinned and wiped it again before pushing his plate away and giving a contented sigh. 'I don't feel like moving now.'

I groaned and looked at my watch. 'I hear you but I've got to drop into work. It's almost twelve and I promised to help out this afternoon. I'd better get going.'

'Is it in the centre of London?'

'God no – I couldn't face the daily commute. I live in a town called Amblemarsh and Under the Tree is in a neighbouring village called Springhaye which is also where Gran's care home is.'

'It sounds quintessentially English, I'm picturing meadows and wildflowers.'

'It boasts a river with canal boats. The village is quite quaint. There's a brilliant pub next to Gran's place and the shops are very unique. There's a bookshop that also sells art, and a shop that sells nothing but handcrafted umbrellas.'

'No!'

I grinned. 'A needlework shop sells everything you could imagine connected to embroidery, it's next to The Corner Dessert Shop that serves the best ever puddings. Next to Under the Tree is a camera shop called Smile Please. The owner, Mr Wilson, begrudgingly sells the mod cons to do with digital photography but his heart is in the old school trends and he stocks quite a collection of film cameras – some you could practically class as antique. It's a family business, like yours, and has been handed down over two generations and still offers film processing.'

Nik sat up. 'There's only one vintage camera and film processing shop I know of in the whole of Sydney.' He reached into his rucksack and lifted out a clunky old-fashioned film camera. 'I'm a huge fan myself and have even got my own dark room at home – yes, hands up, I'm a bit of a photography nerd,' he said. 'There's nothing quite like the excitement of developing your own negatives.'

'Then you'd love Mr Wilson's collection – almost as much as he'd love showing you around. Since the proliferation of phones with cameras their shop is often empty and certainly the only young customers he has are photography students.' I paused. 'You're most welcome to tag along, as I head into work. Springhaye is about forty minutes on the train from here and it would take you just half an hour from there to get back into London later. It stops at King's Cross which isn't far from Islington. You could pop into Under the Tree afterwards. I'm sure my colleague, Seb, could cover whilst I have a quick coffee with you in the staff room before you leave. Although I imagine you must be tired, so please feel welcome to pop in any other day, if you prefer.'

'I'd love to come with you, if you're sure you don't mind! That breakfast has re-energised me and I've nothing else planned.' His face broke into a smile. 'Thanks, Jess.'

2

The door's bell rang and I turned around as Nik wheeled in his suitcase. The lunch hour rush had just passed and the shop only had a couple of customers. Winter sunrays poured indoors with him.

'Welcome to Under the Tree.' I beamed.

Nik put down his rucksack.

'Was Mr Wilson as pleased to see you as I thought?'

Nik let out a low whistle. 'What an amazing shop – he's a real gent and let me study all the vintage cameras and wanted to take a look at mine. I've never seen such a range of analogue equipment. I could have spent hours looking at the range of lenses and he had a beautiful camera with a chrome and leather body. Its focal length lenses are really interesting. It's one of the more reasonably priced ones as well. I've only seen it online before and am really tempted. It's just come into stock and I've wanted a Pentax for ages.'

'You'll have made his day.'

Nik looked around.

'That's the reading area I was telling you about,' I said. I couldn't help feeling proud as I pointed straight ahead, past the till, to a section of the shop with red carpet and cushions on the floor alongside open picture books. Nothing pleased me more than seeing little ones ensconced in there, on a dark, wintry afternoon. Surrounding the square of red carpet was a wooden library of stories for older children. In the centre of the shop's main floor was a table covered in pocket money priced toys. On the walls were shelves full of board games and plushies, building bricks, dolls and drawing equipment – plus one area dedicated to merchandise from well-known brands based on television series. The floor was beech laminate and the walls magnolia. The ceiling was eggshell-blue with white clouds painted on, along with yellow sunrays projecting out from the front right corner, above the door.

'Love that,' Nik said, pointing to the corner opposite, diagonally. A huge Christmas tree was painted on the wall, with sparkling baubles and a fairy on top.

'The shelf projecting out from under the lowest branches features our toy of the week. The current one is a kit to make your own insect house.'

'The whole vibe here is really cosy.'

'You can say small if you want to.' I grinned.

'I don't mean that, Jess. What I'm saying is... I can see this place has got soul. Some shops I visit are sterile and clinical with staff wearing crease-free uniforms and plastic shelves full of regimented stock.'

'No chance of us being that tidy here.'

His eyes crinkled at the corners and made me want to joke again.

'There's nothing better than a toy shop that feels like home,' he said.

'Jessie! Finally it's quiet enough for a proper chat. How was Nuremberg? Did you try any German sausage?'

I smiled at my assistant. His eyes flickered with amusement.

'No, but the apple strudel was excellent. This is Nik. His family own a toy manufacturing company and he was also in Germany. Nik, please meet my assistant, Seb.'

'Ah sorry, I thought you were a customer browsing.' Seb reached out his hand, biceps bulging in his tight shirt.

Nik shook it enthusiastically. 'Great to meet you.'

'How about I get three coffees, Jess, and you can tell me all about the trip?'

I gave him a thumbs-up. Nik wandered off towards the reading area, picking up a child's dropped beaker as he passed a buggy. Seb moved closer to me.

'So… you had a good trip? I'm glad. You deserve it.' Seb jerked his head towards Nik. 'How? When? Where?'

'We were on the same flight. Earlier this morning. Above the North Sea.'

'It's great not to be given your usual answers of online, late last night after drinks and Tinder.'

'That was only once and taught me never to trust a profile picture again.'

'That's ageist, Jess. You've got to take your hat off to anyone in their eighties trying to get a date.' He glanced at Nik. 'Clearly this time you've nothing against white hair.'

'This is business. Pure and simple.'

'Really? Given half a chance I'd—'

'Coffees please, Seb. Don't make me use my managerial voice,' I said, trying to keep a serious face.

Seb had joined the team five years ago, whereas I'd been selling toys here since I was eighteen. I'd even come up with the shop's name, which was meant to give the sense of it being Christmas all year around. There wasn't one toy I disapproved of selling – they all had an important place in a child's life, regardless of whether they were produced to educate or just share cuddles with. I'd never received many gifts as a young child. Somehow, over the years, working here had compensated.

I told Nik more about my job as we sat in the staff room. Seb had offered to man the shop as we had an unexpected rush of customers.

'Angela's brilliant,' I said. 'Over the last eighteen months she's worked hard towards opening another shop and has started to pass more responsibility to me.'

'That's great.'

'It is and I'm really excited to have been given this opportunity to prove myself…'

'I sense a *but*…'

I drained my cup. 'I'm just being silly.'

He leant forwards, eyebrows raised, encouraging me to explain.

'This trade fair was the first I'd been to. Angela came and spent the first day with me – before going to Munich to stay with friends for a few days. She's back after the weekend. I have to admit – I felt completely out of my depth.'

'But wasn't it exciting, leaving your comfort zone? My company has got complacent and that's why I'm doing this trip. We need to challenge ourselves. I've had an idea of how we might do that but need to research and I feel more fired up about work than I have for years.'

'True. I can't deny the thrill I got from researching the direction our stock might take next year and to be given the opportunity to attend seminars such as the one about current market trends. My hand ached afterwards, I took so many notes. I felt so comfortable talking to other retail managers.' It was still sinking in that little old jet-setting me had spent the last few days hobnobbing with fellow industry types and had been taken seriously as a contender. 'But I'm worried about letting Angela down. The sheer size of the fair, with the thousands of products and visitors… and I don't think I saw nearly enough of the technological toys promotion area nor—'

'Me neither. But we aren't superheroes and can only do our best.'

'That's exactly the sort of thing my gran would say.'

'My Grams too. She was a fantastic sounding board, if I didn't want to worry Mum or Dad. I knew she loved me to bits, but being one step back from actually bringing me into the world, with that little bit of emotional distance that parents don't have, she was able to give me real perspective.'

'I know what you mean. Even though Gran brought me up from the age of nine and we're really close, I've always felt she could mentally take a step back when it came to my problems and offer logical solutions.'

'Is she happy at her care home?'

'Willow Court is great. The warden, Lynn, treats residents like family and does her best to make everyone as happy as they can be, whatever their challenges, whether it's with dementia or mobility. I don't know how she finds the energy, each year, to help organise the Christmas party. But it means so much to Gran and her friends. Lynn makes sure they all have their part to play and everyone is still talking about it well into the New Year.'

'She's made good friends there?' he said and accepted a third biscuit.

'Oh yes. Flamboyant Pan is her closest. Then there's Alf – he's a lovable rogue. And Nancy is always so cheerful despite the challenges of recently having to use a wheelchair.'

'It sounds like a lovely place.'

'I'm visiting tomorrow after work. You're welcome to join me,' I said in a jokey tone.

Seb's head appeared around the door. 'Sorry to intrude but things are getting busy out here – it's as if the whole of Springhaye suddenly thinks Christmas is in two days and not two months. And there's a phone call for you, Jessie.'

Nik looked at his watch, stood up and shot me an apologetic look. 'Sorry, Jess, I'm getting in the way.'

'Not at all – it is my day off but I really ought to help out. Unpaid hours – now there's a perk of moving out of your comfort zone.'

We both smiled and he followed me as I hurried out of the staff room and went to the phone by the till.

'I won't be a minute,' I said to Nik as he picked up his rucksack and gripped his pull-along case. I put the receiver to my ear, surprised to find it was Gran. My mobile was still on airplane mode so she'd had to ring the shop instead of my personal number. Her voice sounded all choked up. I turned away from the shop floor, heart racing as she kept on talking. Feeling sick, I eventually ended the call and turned back but all that was left of Nik was his business card on the counter.

3

Gran read out the email she'd received over the phone that evening. Oliver saw my expression and insisted on accompanying me to visit the next day. As did Buddy – for him the words *Willow Court* meant countless tickles and dog treats. Gran's hooded eyes met my gaze as soon as I walked in and rushed over to hug her. I'd never get used to her being smaller than me.

'Que sera, sera,' she said in a resigned tone. She clutched a tissue but her cheeks were dry. I couldn't ever remember seeing her cry. Stiffly she lowered herself into a brown armchair that she'd covered with a colourful throw. I sat on the bed. Oliver joined me after kissing her on the cheek – a kiss that would have normally pinked up her face. Even though he frequently beat her at cards, Gran always said what an appealing young man he was, with his athletic build, tawny crew cut and caring attitude.

Or rather, on the quiet, with a mischievous grin she'd tell me he was *a right sort* – and I'd tell her she had to stop picking up new words from *Love Island*. However, I had to agree and often wondered if it was normal to admire your flatmate… your friend… when he came out of the shower with nothing but a towel around his waist. I concluded it was. It didn't mean anything. I thought Seb was good-looking. It didn't mean I fancied him.

Gran's room was furnished in a welcoming way, with warm laminate flooring and floral curtains. Photos of me and her last dog, Buster, stood on the windowsill, along with a higgledy-piggledy stack of books – Gran was supremely grateful for the mobile library. The room had a spotless ensuite bathroom and she still saved leftover bits of soap to make new bars.

'But why... I mean... how...?' I shook my head and pulled off my hat and scarf. Outside, clouds tried to crowd out the ambitious sun. 'I can't believe it – Willow Court... closing down for sure?'

'They couldn't even give you a date or tell you in person, with a relative at hand for support?' Oliver shook his head. 'But don't you worry – we'll see you through this, Alice.'

Gran stroked Buddy's cheek, running a hand across the Labradoodle blonde curls that Oliver joked matched mine. His chin rested on her jogging bottoms and her forehead smoothed out as those brown doggy eyes stared lovingly into her face.

'Lynn didn't want to worry us,' she said eventually. 'But since the summer we've all heard the rumours of financial problems. It's tough for her too, losing her job as warden. Perhaps she was in denial. They're saying the money troubles got worse over the last few weeks and the owners now find themselves in a pickle. Apparently some of the facilities are considered outdated, as well, and they just haven't got the money to re-equip the place to the necessary standards. A hotel has put in an offer and they've snapped that up. In a few months' time some fancy, schmanzy business type could be enjoying my view.'

Gran glanced out of the window. It always looked grubby lately. She focused on the river, just as rain began to fall. Long grass edged its banks, sprinkled with the delicate colours of wildflowers in the summer. Willow Court was an attractive building – red brick and sprawling like a ranch, all the rooms being ground floor. It was dual-registered, meaning it was a residential care home but had a nursing care wing as well. Some rooms were paid for publicly, other were self-funded, depending on a particular resident's circumstances. Cash-strapped Gran had been lucky to get a place here. A barge glided past bearing jolly flowerpots and then went out of view behind a huge weeping willow. She often waved to holidaymakers. One time a man responded with an impolite gesture. He lost his balance when Gran sent back the same. When she'd told me about him falling into the water, we'd both laughed until it hurt.

It took a lot to upset her. Or it used to. It was hard observing the change. When you're in your teens and scolded for not eating your greens you never imagine that, one day, the lines of dialogue will be swapped over.

'Let me read the email again,' I said and took her phone. 'Honestly. It's not good enough. They should have at least tagged me in.'

'Lynn was furious,' said Gran in a flat voice. 'She said there was no protocol for this kind of situation but it was just common sense and compassionate to involve relatives.'

My eyes scanned the words. 'Right. So the council is duty bound to find you another place, seeing as they pay for you to stay here. We'll be given a directory of homes and can research them ourselves and visit, and express a preference as to where you go although that can't be guaranteed – and any choice mustn't cost more than Willow Court... blah blah... Your mental and physical health will be reassessed...' I looked up. 'Of course, I'll be with you every step of the way, Gran, at all the appointments and we'll arrange visits together – that goes without saying.'

'You're a good girl,' she mumbled.

Oliver took the phone and skim-read the screen. 'We should ring that helpline.' He clicked on the link. 'Its website says that closures at short notice are rare but...' He shrugged. 'They happen.'

'Come on. Let's go down to the dining room. I smelt fish on the way in.' I laid my coat on the bed, next to Oliver's, and stood up.

'Not hungry,' muttered Gran. 'I hardly even noticed when my breakfast was late this morning. But before you say it, Missy, I know things aren't going to feel better on an empty stomach. Isn't that right, Buddy, my handsome boy?'

He barked.

'I'll tell you all about a very nice man I met on the aeroplane yesterday. He's from Sydney.'

Oliver gave me a sideways glance. 'That Nik you couldn't stop talking about last night?'

My ears felt hot.

'That's more like it,' said Gran and she visibly brightened. 'You know I'm addicted to *Neighbours*. I hope you've got stories about surfing and beach barbecues.' She pushed herself up, shaking off Oliver's offer of help. She ran a hand over the top of the armchair. 'It all makes sense now. The dining room tables have looked knackered for months, with scratches, and legs wobblier than mine. Last year Lynn said new ones were arriving but we got new table cloths instead and they didn't make them tables look any younger than if you'd tarted me up in a crop top and mini skirt. Then the seated exercise teacher stopped coming in the spring and we no longer have our fortnightly still life painting class.'

'That's a shame. You never did get a nude model,' I said.

Gran managed a laugh. 'Good thing too. I can't think of anything more likely to put me off my dinner. You know, I found it hard to get used to the busyness when I first moved here – all the chatter and wandering residents, the singing sessions and bingo nights... the staff doing goodness knows what with hoists and catheters... but the noise grew on me, like a favourite radio station. Yet lately it's been quieter than a morgue some days.' She defiantly pushed the tissue up her sleeve. 'Leaving our home in Cressmead Tower... my stellar neighbours... that was wrench enough. But I got through that and I'll get through another move. And... and we'll have to choose a really special theme for this year's Christmas bash, seeing as it will be Willow Court's last one.'

'We'll help you make it the best ever,' said Oliver.

'Nancy and some of the others have started to talk about the festive food they'd like to cook, to contribute to the buffet. Back in January, in the sales, Pan, me and some others picked up a bundle of cheap craft materials like glitter and foil to make our crackers and decorations. Alf, who trained as a calligrapher when he retired, has been writing the invitation cards for us to fill in. He's leaving the date of the party blank at the moment, until it can be one hundred per cent confirmed. They look right professional. He's a diamond, the amount of time he puts in.'

Gran pushed her feet into comfy, wide trainers. She'd splashed out on ones with rose gold stripes, saying if she had to wear them all the time she wanted to feel less Paula Radcliffe and more Kim Kardashian. I slipped an arm around her shoulders. Gran slipped an arm around my waist and we headed left, along the corridor, Oliver walking behind with Buddy. Lights automatically flicked on as the sky outside darkened. It was quieter than usual for midday, without the clatter of cutlery and lively banter. We walked past reception and into the dining room area with buttercup walls and a pine floor. The decor had looked a bit tired this last year. A handful of residents sat at tables. Seeing as he was so well-behaved, Lynn always let Buddy in.

'Salmon with hollandaise sauce,' I said and breathed in. 'Followed by crème brûlée by the looks of it.'

'We had stewed apples and custard yesterday – your mum's favourite,' said Gran wistfully.

I wouldn't know about that.

'Woo hoo! Alice! Darling!' called Pan. Despite the time of year, she wore her favourite rainbow-coloured sunhat. Large gold hoops hung either side of her cheeks. Long red nails beckoned us over. 'Jess! Oliver! How lovely to see you! It's been ages.'

The three of us looked at each other but said nothing. Pan might have looked dynamic but she wasn't always on the ball – she'd had other things to worry about lately.

We headed over and she stood up. After she'd greeted Buddy we all hugged.

'Did you get that email this morning?' asked Gran. We sat down, around the rectangular table.

'What email?'

Gran reached across the patterned tablecloth. 'About this place hitting the duffers.'

The smile dropped from Pan's face as torrents of rain broke through the cloud. 'Yes. I... I forgot for a moment – at least there's one upside to this blasted diagnosis. I haven't told my boys about the closure yet. They've been harping on for me to move in with them, ever since... I won't be a burden. I can't see us moving out until the spring. That gives me the chance to make other arrangements.'

Gran squeezed her hand. 'One thing reaching this grand old age has taught me – you never know what's around the corner. Maybe there'll be a last-minute rescue plan and we won't have to leave at all.'

'I doubt that very much,' said a crisp voice. Glenda approached us slowly, in her court shoes and smart, starched slacks, looking as if she'd just walked out of a board meeting, even though she was approaching eighty, had a limp and the top of her spine bent forward slightly. She may have left her highly paid, well-travelled executive past but she hadn't retired her appearance. Her flawless makeup and co-ordinated clothes were admirable – all top brands, of course. She still fitted the trouser suits and skirts she used to wear to work. Glenda was a woman who believed in herself. In that sense, she reminded me of Gran – although in other ways she couldn't be more different.

'I've just cornered Lynn and demanded more details. She said it wasn't fair to give out information that wasn't concrete. I said it wasn't fair to keep us in limbo – especially for those who are self-funded or have no family to help them with the onus of finding a new home.' Her narrow eyes brightened as if powered by obtaining secret knowledge. 'The deal with the hotel has gone through and the developers are keen to start work as soon as possible.' Glenda rubbed her hip. 'It looks as if we'll be thrown out in the middle of December.'

'That's outrageous,' gasped Oliver. 'That's, what, six weeks from now?'

'Such a shame, isn't it,' said Glenda in a voice that implied the opposite, 'that we'll have to cancel this year's Christmas party?'

4

I stared at Nik's business card, my finger hovering over my phone.

'I wonder if I should contact him,' I said, thinking aloud. 'I felt a bit rude about not being able to say goodbye before he left the shop.'

Oliver and I sat on the sofa in our flat, in front of the television as the credits went up. Ever the diplomat, in between both our feet Buddy snoozed on the floor. I'd needed to put on my pyjamas and chill with Chinese takeout after a busy day at work. One week into November and the Christmas rush had begun. Angela had made me responsible for ordering in this year's festive stock with minimal input from her, and for the last few months I'd had sleepless nights wondering if I'd chosen the right products. Yet it gave me such a buzz to follow my instincts and see a customer buy a toy I'd chosen. Seb had been brilliant, coming over for dinner so that we could discuss the options.

Oliver had picked up dinner after his shift. It was almost eleven. Gran would have had something to say if she knew we often ate at this hour. But then it was Friday night, even if we did both have to be in work tomorrow morning.

'Sorry, I didn't hear what you said,' asked Oliver. '*I was

concentrating on the last episode of the *final* season of the show we've been avidly watching. Did you like the ending?'

'Um... yeah... it was good...' I snuggled under my blanket. Oliver never seemed to feel the cold and would laugh at me each night, hugging my hot water bottle despite the heating being on.

'Jess! How would you know? You've been swiping your phone since swiping that last prawn cracker. Buddy probably has a better idea of what happened.' Oliver stood up and went over to the window. We were one floor up and west-facing which meant enjoying glorious sunsets during warmer months. Oliver drew the maroon curtains closed. They matched the sofa and the rug on the oak laminated floor. The walls were painted a nutty white. The coffee table was made from glass. Working nine 'til five in a colourful, cluttered toy shop made me err towards simplicity with my own interior design.

Our landlord had let us redecorate and we'd added personal touches. A bookcase to the left was filled with Oliver's thriller novels, along with my miniature Buddha and a small lotus flower ornament. On the coffee table sat one of my scented candles. It was burning and smelt of nacho cheese. Oliver had bought it for me as a joke so I forced him to suffer the extremely creamy fragrance. We'd also hung a vibrant watercolour print by a local artist who painted riverside wildlife. The local waterway ran straight through Amblemarsh and Springhaye.

'I couldn't concentrate and I was so looking forward to it.'

'Honestly, you remind me of my parents,' he said with what I could tell was forced cheerfulness. 'Time together was always interrupted by their phones and them muttering *it's work.'*

I tossed the phone onto the cushion next to me, got up and went over. I put my hands on his shoulders and stared into his face.

'Fine. You have my full attention. I'm all yours.'

He stared back into my eyes for a moment and his shoulders relaxed. 'Too late,' he said after a few moments, with a superior air. 'The episode is over.' Oliver strode over to the open plan kitchen and switched on the kettle.

I followed him to the breakfast bar. 'Don't be grumpy,' I said, poking him in the ribs, my finger pushing against muscle.

'Stop it,' he said and reached for teabags.

I could tell he was working really hard to keep a straight face and poked him again. He roared, turned around and tickled the air with his fingers. I bolted over to the window and hid behind the curtains. Buddy barked and claws scrabbled on the wooden floor.

'It is safe to come out?' I asked in muffled tones, failing not to laugh. 'Why don't you tell me how the series ended? You can even have some of those chocolate chip cookies I baked.'

'I'm already eating them.'

A curious nose snuck through the gap in the curtains and nudged my pyjamas.

I stroked Buddy's ears and left my hiding place. Sure enough, Oliver was back on the sofa in front of two mugs of tea and an open Tupperware box. I headed over and collapsed next to him. Our shoulders rubbed comfortably together as I pulled up my blanket once more.

'You're nothing but a big bully, Oliver Hart.'

'And you're nothing but a scaredy cat, Jess Jagger – although you are a fantastic baker.' He offered me the box and I pulled out a cookie. Then another. We sat munching.

'Were your parents really that bad?'

'Time with them was rare enough but even when they promised a family night in I never got their full attention.' He smiled. 'But I'm over it.'

I slipped my hand into his and squeezed, aware of the bravado underneath, the boyish smile reminding me of the one time we'd kissed. It was shortly after he moved in and had too many bubbles to celebrate. He'd smiled at me like that and one thing had led to another. I took my hand away, cringing at the memory. Not so much at the kiss that had warmed me from head to toe, that had got my heart racing and my fingers running through his hair... no, it was our mutual embarrassment when we'd sobered up and drank coffee together the next morning. He'd acted as if nothing had happened. I'd felt a little wounded that he felt so mortified, at least I'd been prepared to joke about it.

I stared at the little Christmas tree in the corner, by the window. Multi-coloured lights twinkled and hid the straggly branches. Oliver had picked it up for half-price, the second year we lived together, before we both got pay rises at work and could have afforded something bigger. Oliver put it up every year on the 1st of November and religiously bought me an Advent calendar on the 1st of December. His face was a picture the first time I'd bought him one too and each morning he'd excitedly shout out what the picture was behind the door. After too many mulled wines he'd once mumbled about Christmas never being celebrated much when he was little. It was then that I'd begun to realise our very different childhoods actually had common ground in buckets.

'Blissful silence,' said Oliver and he stretched as he did every day when he got in from a shift of shaking cocktails and cleaning tables. My days were visually overcrowded, with dolls and bears and electronics whereas it was Oliver's ears that took a beating due to his job in Misty's, a music bar a twenty-minute walk away from our flat.

'Do you think we're weird?' I asked eventually.

'Definitely.'

'I'm serious. We're both thirty next year. Neither of us has settled down. We're living the carefree life of a pair of twenty-year olds. Work aside, I'm only responsible for looking after Buddy and a couple of cacti. The most concrete personal commitment either of us has made is buying a second-hand car each with long-term payment plans. Most of my friends have kids now – or at least a forever partner. Usually a mortgage and—'

Oliver put down his drink and turned to me. 'What's brought this on? We're both doing fine. Some might say commitment is overrated, in business or life.'

I studied his face. As usual, he gave nothing away when we neared the subject of any kind of past relationship in his life.

'But maybe if I had a partner to put down roots with, then I'd be able to look after Gran.' My voice wavered. 'I wish I could take away all her upset. As I've become more senior at work Angela's been very fair about raising my salary, but I'm going to have to save hard for several years to have my own place. If only I could afford to buy…

I don't know... a bungalow, especially adapted for her needs. I'd rent a room to you and—'

'Jess,' he said gently, 'even that wouldn't work. She needs someone around the whole time. As it is, you and I struggle to make sure one of us is here most of the time for Buddy. Increasingly Alice struggles to get dressed and washed. On bad days she wouldn't be able to make herself lunch. With your frequent phone calls and visits you already do the very best you can.' He rubbed my arm. 'Don't worry. We'll sort this out, the three of us together.'

I liked the way he rubbed my arm. Oliver's reassuring presence had filled a gap in my life when I'd moved out of Gran's.

'You're very good to me.'

He took another biscuit. 'Yes, just don't take advantage. It's still your turn to clean the toilet this weekend.'

I shuffled and sat straighter. 'Did you know in Australia they call an outside toilet a dunny? And we're currently enjoying a choccy biccy. I could change careers and get a job as a garbo, chalkie or milko. Facebook is Facey.'

'You've been researching Australian slang? This Nik really made an impression.'

'I'm just curious. I've never really got to know an Australian and we really hit it off.'

'Anyone would think you fancied him,' said Oliver and took a large mouthful of tea.

'What would be the point of that? He lives on the other side of the world for a start.'

'You could always keep in touch via Facey...'

'Ha ha.' I picked up the business card again. It was basic and didn't even mention the name of his company. 'But he is around for a while, on some sort of break. Maybe I'll ring and see if he fancies meeting up. It must be lonely, not knowing anyone here. I feel bad that I've left it this long.'

'It was Bonfire Night last night and Remembrance Sunday this weekend – why not take Nik to a fireworks display? Or you could meet him in London – take him to see the Cenotaph.'

'I'm out to work early in the morning, like you, although Angela texted to say I could just do until three tomorrow, if I wanted, as she's going in to look at some paperwork and can cover. I think she appreciated me going straight to Under the Tree from the airport last Saturday. But Nik may not want to come all this way for a couple of hours, just for coffee, before I head to Gran's at five. And I can't cancel her, not with the shock of Willow Court closing. Even if I could there's Buddy to think about.'

Between us Oliver and I managed to stop Buddy from getting lonely. The fact that Oliver worked shifts helped, and sixteen-year-old Immy next door loved to spend time with him after school. Eventually I insisted on paying her when she offered to let herself in and take him out for a walk.

'I know… I'll text him. That way it's easier for him to duck out, if he's actually really busy. He left his business card – I don't want to come across as unfriendly by not contacting him. At least this way I've made the effort.' I picked up my phone and added Nik's number to my contacts list before typing.

Hi Nik. Jess here – we met this time last week, on the plane from Nuremberg. Sorry I had to take that call. Hope you got to Islington okay.

A message pinged back almost immediately.

Hi there Jess! I was just thinking about you and how you shared your chocolate with me. I thought you'd appreciate this joke:

What do you call a wooden toy that likes chocolate?

Pinocchi-cocoa.

Mentally I gave myself a hug and grinned before replying.

Love it! How about telling me some more of your bad jokes in person?

5

Red anorak. Khaki trousers. Feet planted on the grass verge at the front of Willow Court. I almost forgot to turn the car as I stared at Nik. There was something compelling about his smile. I waved as my battered old hatchback headed into the car park and he followed. We'd agreed to meet at Willow Court and go to The Corner Dessert Shop before I visited Gran. I'd nipped home first to pick up Buddy. He'd been jumpy what with fireworks going off all week. I smoothed down my curls after I'd climbed out of the car although there was little point as one touch of the dusk dew would instantly unleash the frizz. I'd sprayed my favourite perfume across my hair, as well as on my clothes. I had as many bottles as I had candles.

'Hey, Jess, how you going? Great to see you again.' Nik opened his arms and we hugged briefly, a spark of electricity making its way down my spine. He bent down to stroke Buddy. 'And who's this handsome fella?'

'My other flatmate, Buddy,' I said with a smile. 'Great to see you too – although I don't flatter myself you came all the way to Springhaye for a couple of hours with a woman you met on the plane. Did you get it?'

He put his rucksack on the ground and delved

inside, pulling out a box that he opened. Out of that he gently pulled an old-fashioned camera. It had a chrome and leather body just like he'd described, with the word Pentax printed above the lens.

'I've been thinking about it all week. You texting prompted me. I rang Mr Wilson first thing this morning to see if it had been sold. I asked him to put it aside until I dropped by this afternoon.'

Carefully he put it back in its box and into the rucksack. We crossed the road and headed down the high street, passing Under the Tree. I wished I'd worn gloves as the tips of my fingers turned red. Nik looked in and waved at Mr Wilson as we passed Smile Please. The Corner Dessert Shop was next to the bank. It was bright and modern with white furniture and matching walls, decorated with silver frames filled with tempting photos of sweet treats. It was a welcome contrast to the clouds outside darkening the winter afternoon.

We went in and found a table for two, on the left. Like many of the food and drink establishments in Springhaye, dogs were allowed as long as they were under control and didn't climb on any of the furniture.

'I don't think I've been to a dessert shop before,' said Nik as Buddy collapsed at my feet.

'They've become really popular over here in the last couple of years. You won't find a wider choice of sweet treats. All they sell is desserts and puddings – huge ones as that's all the meal consists of, without any savoury dishes. Then there's a range of soft drinks, teas, coffees and mocktails.'

Nik took off his anorak and scanned the menu. 'Wow.'

'I know! I couldn't believe my eyes when this place first opened up last year.' I glanced through the choices of sponges, waffles, pancakes and ice cream dishes, the cakes and cookies, the tarts, the macaroons and muffins... Nik focused on the page of traditional English puddings. I knew it well. Gran and I often came here and she always had trouble choosing from her old favourites, including apple and blackberry crumble, sticky toffee pudding, custard tart and jam roly-poly. He glanced at a neighbouring table where a couple were eating and his eyebrows shot into his hairline.

'Shall we share one? I've got a sweet tooth but it's not Jurassic-sized.'

'Thanks goodness you said that. Gran and I always do. You choose.'

He ran his finger down the menu and looked up, eyes shining. 'Bread and butter pudding. I've always wanted to try that.'

I called over the waitress and we ordered. I always thought a person's choice of dessert said a lot about them. Nik's was straightforward and simple, whereas Pan came with me and Gran once and ordered a colourful sundae sprinkled with strawberries and hundreds and thousands. Our pot of tea for two arrived and I poured.

'How was the fair you went to last week, for manufacturers?' I asked.

'Interesting but I didn't feel inspired the way I wanted to. I'm hoping I'll get that more from visiting toy shops and markets. What I need is inspiration to pass onto our design team.' He stirred his drink. 'Were toys a big part of your childhood? I was never much of an outdoorsy sort and preferred staying in with my books and puzzles or plastic safari animals.'

'I didn't have many when I was really small,' I said briskly. 'Just Teddy and some Barbie dolls from the charity shop. Then I moved in with Gran. I felt like I was living in Aladdin's cave with the Lego, and play food, the bowling and skittle set...' We chatted about current trends and how the toy market had changed over recent decades. 'You should hear Oliver, my flatmate, talk about the toys his parents bought him – he even had an electric BMW for kids in the garden that he could sit in and drive at five miles per hour.' I sipped my tea. 'Sorry I didn't message earlier. It's been an especially busy week.'

'No problem at all. I've been settling in. So, it's full steam ahead for Christmas at work?'

'Getting there... but there's also other stuff. The phone call I got, when you left... it was my gran. She'd had a bit of bad news.' I told him about Willow Court closing.

'Oh, Jess, I am sorry to hear that. I feel for... Alice you said she was called? It's more than a care home, isn't it? Or rather, the opposite, that's actually just what it is – her *home*. I can't imagine what it must feel like to be uprooted but with you by her side I'm sure Alice will get through.'

Suddenly I felt warm from tip to toe.

'Was your Grams in a care home, at the end?'

'Yes. Grandpa looked after her when the Alzheimer's started. They still had a happy life. It wasn't advanced and medication helped. But he died, out of the blue, with a heart attack.' Nik paused for a moment.

'You don't have to go on,' I said gently as he bent down and stroked Buddy's head that was now resting by his legs.

'It's okay. I find it's better to talk rather than hold things in.' He smiled. 'My grandmother taught me that. There were no secrets between us. Mum and Dad wanted Grams to move in and we managed to persuade her. Grandpa's death seemed to fasten the pace of the Alzheimer's and after a couple of years, as a family, we found it too difficult to cope. We were lucky enough to find her a wonderful place. The staff felt like family, by the end.'

'Willow Court's like that.'

We sat in silence for a moment. It was ended by Nik's gasp as the bread and butter puddings arrived. Regimented triangles of baked bread covered a dinner-sized plate, crisped to perfection on the outside and sprinkled with juicy raisins and cinnamon. Baked in custard, there was a generous dollop of vanilla ice cream on one side, and whipped cream on the other. The waitress came back with two pots, one containing a Clementine drizzle, the other made from lemons.

Nik's eyes widened as he raised his spoon and we dug in, not speaking much until the plate was clean and then we compared the best meals we'd ever had out in our lives.

'In Canada,' I said. 'With Oliver, on a hiking holiday.' I was so unused to foreign travel that walking through airports always made me feel like a celebrity. Oliver couldn't get over my excitement at simply checking in our luggage. 'We were advised to order Caesar cocktails for brunch one morning. It didn't sound very filling but the waitress winked and said to trust her.' I shook my head. 'The drink was just like a Bloody Mary, with a celery stalk in it, but the other garnishes sticking out of it were unbelievable... fried onion rings, slices of roast chicken, and an actual cheeseburger in a bun. It was fantastic!' But not just because of what we were eating. Away from England, Oliver seemed somehow less tense. We'd got a bit tipsy on the vodka and tomato juice, and as we left the café he took my hand. It felt natural and made me feel toasty warm despite the stiff breeze. I'd almost wondered if we were going to share a tipsy kiss again, like when he first moved in. It was silly really, to think that about a well-established friend. In fact, we'd soon sobered up once we were outdoors, and his fingers slid away. Despite the cheeseburger and chicken, that had left me with an emptiness I couldn't explain.

'I'd have loved that! Nothing beats a burger. I had an amazing one in Germany the other week, stacked with avocado and bacon, and topped with a fried egg. I didn't think I was going to be able to eat for a week afterwards.'

I groaned. 'I feel like that at the moment. Thank goodness we shared that dessert.'

'Grams wouldn't have approved,' he said, a twinkle in his eye. 'Grandpa had high cholesterol and she became fanatical about low-fat baking. It's amazing what she could do with a banana… I mean…' I chuckled as his eyes crinkled in that appealing way again.

I looked at my watch. 'Where has the time gone? I'd better get going, Gran will wonder where I am. I imagine you're itching to get back to your flat and properly examine your new camera?'

'It's certainly a beautiful piece, yes – although the block of flats I'm staying in is very quiet.'

The waitress came over and Nik asked if I minded him paying – a way of thanking me for helping him find the camera he'd been coveting for a long time. We finished our drinks and headed back outside into the cold. A wind had got up and Nik turned up his collar. Easily chatting, we made our way back up the high street, stopping for him to gaze thought he window of the umbrella shop. We stopped at the junction, Buddy's tail going into overdrive as he recognised Willow Court.

'Right, well, I'd better get to the station,' he said.

It was only five o'clock. I felt sorry for him going back to an empty flat.

'This might sound odd, but you're more than welcome to come with me. Gran and her friends love visitors – but I completely understand if not. In fact, you could probably find a fireworks display near you, I can look on my phone or—'

'Would it be odd if I said yes? I'd love to, Jess. Thanks. For me travel is as much about the people I meet, as the places, but only if you're sure – I don't want to intrude.'

'Not at all – but I warn you... Gran will expect a scene by scene description of the latest developments in *Neighbours*.'

We smiled at each other and crossed the road, me feeling excited in a way I hadn't for a while.

6

'You managed to find the camera shop okay, then,' I said as we reached the other side of the road.

'I asked for directions at the station.'

'Real human contact?' I grinned. 'I'm impressed. Most people use Google Maps.'

He reached into his pocket and pulled out a small flip phone. Tiny. Basic.

'I can only phone or text. I'm not a fan of social media. I leave Junior Magic's staff – that's the name of our company – to deal with our online platforms.

I gasped. 'Haven't seen one of those for years.'

'It's on loan from a museum,' he said, eyes dancing.

'Well, they do say size isn't everything,' I said, loving the banter. 'How on earth do you manage without the weather app?'

'Rain or shine, it doesn't bother me. I like both.'

'The calculator?'

'I'm good at maths.'

'And obviously you prefer real cameras instead of phone apps.'

'That way I get to put photos in albums. My nephew has

got heaps of shots on his phone. Over a thousand. Yet he never looks at them.'

I tilted my head. He was only in his thirties yet his ethos was similar to Gran's. We rang the buzzer and Lynn let us in. She straightened her glasses as I introduced her to Nik. He shook her hand whilst I signed us in.

'I haven't had time to talk to you Jess, not properly, since that email was sent out,' she said. Her dark eyes looked sunk into her normally sunny round face. As well as working all hours she had a little one at home. 'It was nothing to do with me. If I'd had my way I would have told each of the residents face-to-face, separately and with relatives present, and—'

I rested my hand on her arm. 'No one blames you, Lynn and I know it's not easy for you, either, losing your job.'

Her eyes glistened. 'Yes. Like family, they are, your gran and the others. Some nights I've not slept for worrying over their future. But in some ways… it's a relief. We've had real trouble, over the last few months, recruiting quality staff. It has meant standards have slipped further. Those of us who love it here can only do so much. Without investment in Willow Court's facilities and team over the last couple of years this place just hasn't been hitting the mark, especially in the nursing wing.' She sighed. 'And not just there – Betty got served fish fingers with beef gravy a few weeks ago, in the canteen. She didn't mind but that's not the point. Then I had to get rid of a new member of the team who would leave Phyllis in her room for too long and she missed her lunch several days in a row. Our mantra is that dignity and respect should be at the heart of everything. Anything less simply isn't good enough.

'And I'll miss Alice, that's for sure.' She pulled her ponytail tighter. 'The closure is out of my hands so all I can do is focus on making the next few weeks feel as normal as possible for everyone whilst they plan for the next stage of their lives. Stress won't do any of the residents any good. And it's about giving them as big a say as possible about their future. The ones with dementia problems...' She bit her lip. 'This whole process could be especially distressing for them, if it's not handled properly. That bloody email wasn't a great start.' She gave a wry smile. 'Sorry for my French but I'm still fuming about it.'

'That's one thing I've treasured about this place,' I said. 'You've always worked so hard, Lynn, to consider people's feelings.'

'It has a lovely atmosphere,' said Nik, looking around.

'Some of my colleagues, like me, have worked here for nigh on twenty years. In many ways it's become like a home from home. We've talked about what's happened and reckon the problems started when we moved from being just residential to the extension being built. The owners were ambitious – too ambitious, perhaps – and the council just didn't come through with the extra funding that was needed to support their new nursing ideas so the company cut corners.' She sucked in her cheeks. 'You just can't do that when it comes to the people with more complex health needs.'

'It sounds like you've been soldiering on for a while,' said Nik.

'It must have been tough – the solution being out of your hands,' I added.

Colour flooded into her pasty cheeks. 'Thanks for being

so understanding. Not everyone's relatives and friends are. Today I'm emailing out links to the directories for local homes for residents and their relatives to trawl through.' She rubbed her forehead. Another member of staff called her name and she left us.

I smiled hello to familiar faces in the lounge, to the left. The dining room was to the right. In the middle were a reception desk and the office, plus a small huddle of residents. Betty stood, as usual, wearing her raincoat and carrying her handbag, with fluffy slippers on her swollen feet.

'It's not fair,' she said and glared at us. 'They're letting you strangers in but won't let me out. I've got things to do – my Jim will be waiting for his dinner, after a hard day in the video store. And the kids need bathing and bed.'

Nik studied her for a moment. 'Count yourself lucky,' he said conspiratorially, 'it's cold and damp out there.'

Betty's face softened for a second, and she stared up at him. Then she reached into her bag. It was empty apart from a doll. She took it out and tucked it under her arm. The staff had given it to her to see if it helped. Betty hadn't been without it since. With a blank expression she wandered into the dining room, telling no one in particular that strangers had been let in again and turning back once to glance at Nik. He and I walked along the corridor, to the left, past artificial plants and colourful paintings. We reached Gran's room. I knocked gently and we went in. The carpet could have done with a vacuum and a shelf on the wall looked dusty. Things hadn't been quite as spick and span as normal, throughout Willow Court, this last year. Gran was asleep in her chair, by the window. Nik and I laid our coats on the bed. I squeezed her arm. She twitched and woke up.

'Gordon Bennett, I must have dozed off.' She noticed Nik and sat more upright. 'Jess, you could have warned me you were bringing a friend! I'd have at least put on a slash of lipstick and my smart striped blouse.'

Nik leant downwards and grasped her hand. 'Great to meet you – and I love those red trousers. It's my favourite colour.'

'You're Australian? The passenger Jess sat next to on the aeroplane? Just what this place needs – a good-looking sort who can tell us all the gossip about our favourite Aussie soaps.'

Relief infused me. Her smile had returned. She'd looked even frailer since Willow Court's closing date had been announced. I'd checked with Lynn who said she'd not been eating so I'd called in with her favourite chocolates, but spied them on her bedside table unopened. We walked along to the dining room, nearing the nostalgic school dinner smell that always hung there. Gran waved at Pan and went ahead to join her friends at one of the rectangular tables. Betty accosted Nik.

'It's not right that you've been let in. I've got things to do out there.'

'How old are your children?' he asked and gently pulled up the strap of her handbag that had slipped off her shoulder.

She scratched her spiky, cropped grey hair. 'Ten and eight. A right pair of rascals, they are. I need to get them bathed and to bed.'

'They are lucky to have a mum looking after them so well,' he said. 'What are their names?'

'Lily and Roger. No one's children look smarter than mine, in their Sunday best...' She stared into the past, smiling, rocking to and fro on her heels. I left to say hello to Pan. Alf and Glenda were on Gran's table as well. Nik was chatting to Lynn now. I couldn't wait to introduce him to everyone and beckoned for him to come over.

'Alice tells us you're from Australia,' said Alf, interested eyes peering upwards. He squinted and ran a hand over his bald head, noisily breathing. 'Your ancestors all convicts, then?'

'Alf!' Gran gave a glare harder than Betty's and I waited for Alf to spout the Flat Earth theory that Australia didn't really exist. Pan couldn't help laughing. Glenda tutted.

'Some people say those convicts never arrived and were really murdered,' Alf continued.

'Alf's a fan of conspiracy theories,' I said to Nik in a low voice.

'I heard that, young lady,' he said. 'You make that sound like a bad thing, when the alternative is to believe that codswallop that man actually walked on the moon.' He shook his head.

I'd learnt the hard way not to argue these points. He'd done his research and the detail of his viewpoint could go on for hours. A friend of his visited a couple of weeks ago and said Alf had always been interested the popular conspiracy theories, like the ones surrounding the murder of John F. Kennedy, and that his interest in theories had got much stronger since his wife had died.

Nik sat down opposite Alf, to the left of Gran. I sat at the end of the table, in between the two men, my leg accidentally brushing against Nik's. For some reason I felt very aware of his physical presence.

'In answer to your question, Alf,' he said, 'no, not convicts

– my very law-abiding grandparents, on my mum's side, emigrated from Finland.'

'That explains your Viking height,' said Glenda coyly.

Glenda flirting?

'Probably, although there's Greek heritage going right back. Must be why I love olives.'

'I went to Australia once, with work,' said Glenda.

'What was your line of business?' he asked.

'I was personal assistant to the owner of a shipping insurance company,' she said proudly. 'Our client there lived in the famous Eureka Tower. The view was quite spectacular.'

'Very exclusive. Lucky you.'

'But Finland's beautiful,' I said. 'All those lakes and forests... why did your grandparents want to leave, if you don't mind me asking?'

'Grams hated the cold. Winter temperatures can easily drop to minus thirty. A good summer's day might hit twenty – low by even the UK's standards. She was always catching colds.'

'I had the pleasure of working with Hugh Jackman once,' said Pan, in her Received Pronunciation tone. 'He had a lovely accent like yours.' A firework went off, outside, and Buddy jumped. Pan stroked his head and murmured comforting words. He'd settled at her feet. Buddy always seemed to know which residents were most vulnerable. He'd only just stopped going straight over to Alf each time we visited, as if sensing the widower had gradually become stronger. Alf had moved here after losing his wife eighteen months ago.

'Couldn't function after my Maisie went,' he'd said one

day, when Pan was talking about her late husband. 'I swear, overnight, my heart failure got worse. She helped me get dressed on the days I was feeling dead tired and breathless. And she was a bloomin' good cook. But most important of all, Maisie was the best company and I loved the bones of her. I'm man enough to admit I get lonely, but she and I always had an agreement – we'd never be a burden to the kids. So moving here was a non-brainer...'

'Hugh was a gorgeous chap. So friendly,' said Pan.

She meant Hugh Grant. Am dram had always been a hobby of Pan's and once she'd been an extra in *Love Actually*. She'd got muddled since *The Greatest Showman* became her new favourite film, but it was kinder not to correct her. Since the diagnosis she felt unsure enough about her life as it was. She didn't need other people constantly making her feel as if everything about her world was wrong. Gran had caught her crying after her hospital appointment. Something had been wrong for a while and now Pan didn't know which was worse – the knowing or not knowing.

Nik asked the others where they'd grown up. Pan was from Hertfordshire, Glenda from West London – Gran and Alf the East of the capital. Dinner arrived and Lynn asked if Nik and I were hungry but I explained about the bread and butter pudding we'd had. He asked her to bring over a few glasses. She didn't seem surprised by his request. The food was easy to manage in the evenings, when residents became tired. Each plate had a small stack of sandwiches without the crusts, a mini pork pie, neat cubes of cheese and several plum tomatoes.

Nik glanced at the laminated menu, standing in the middle of the table. 'Lasagne and garlic bread tomorrow lunchtime, followed by panna cotta.' He looked up. 'How disappointing! I was expecting Yorkshire pudding and steak and kidney pie, jam roly poly and spotted dick – all the classic English meals I've heard about over the years.'

'A pub meal it is tonight, then, to remedy that, if we can manage any more food,' I said. 'My treat. We'll head to The Silver Swan after here.'

The pleasure on his face gave me an injection of happiness.

'Nice to see a young meat-eater. Everyone's bloody vegan these days,' said Alf. 'Fashionable nonsense. It'll die out, you'll see.'

'Not if our planet dies first,' said Glenda sharply.

'I enjoy a good barbecue, I must say,' said Nik. 'Steak, sausages…' He grinned. 'Perhaps crocodile for those feeling adventurous.'

Alf looked quietly impressed.

'But I mix it up with vegetable skewers and plant-based burgers. After all, we'd be living off nuts and berries as well, if we lived in the wild. You look like a man who's brave enough to try anything, Alf. You should try a veggie burger next time you're out.'

'Rabbit food for a strapping lad like you?' Alf cocked his head and looked suspiciously at Nik.

Lynn arrived with the glasses. Nik winked at everyone and delved into his rucksack. He pulled out a curved brown bottle with a shiny yellow label.

'What's Apera?' I asked.

'My favourite drink in the world. It used to be called Sherry. Producers back in Australia changed its name – it comes from the word Aperitif. I bought it as a present for you, Jess, but maybe it's better to share it here?'

'Absolutely!' I said.

'I'd have thought beers on the beach was more your style,' said Alf.

I sent Nik an apologetic glance but he burst out laughing.

'Sorry to disappoint, Alf, but I just love Apero's buttery, caramel taste. Although believe me, I've been teased about it enough in Sydney, when all my mates are drinking beers. I always give my heritage as an excuse. Smoked reindeer and sherry soup is big in Finland and—'

Gran raised her eyebrows. 'That animal is sacrosanct. No one should eat the symbol of Christmas.'

'Alice, darling, don't upset yourself, it's no different to venison,' said Pan. 'I do so love a sherry. My parents used to let me have one with Sunday dinner, when I turned sixteen. I felt so grown-up and would drink out of the pretty crystal glasses pretending I was Grace Kelly in *High Society*.'

'Fantastic actress, wasn't she?' said Nik. 'I loved her in *Rear Window*.'

'Me too!' Pan's eyes sparkled. 'I always knew I could never be as good an actress as someone like her.'

'I'm not a drinker,' said Glenda and cleared her throat, 'but I have been suffering with indigestion lately and sherry is supposed to be good for that.'

'Try sleeping on an extra pillow, as well,' Nik said with a wink.

Glenda actually blushed.

'I had a discreet word with Lynn,' said Nik as he poured out the golden, velvety liquid. 'A couple of glasses won't meddle with anyone's meds – although you can only have a small one, Alf.'

'Better than nothing,' he said. 'I can't remember the last time I drank alcohol.'

Nik raised his sherry. 'Cheers! Great to meet you all.'

'What brings you over to Blighty?' said Alf, after a well-savoured sip. Tight wrinkles around his eyes had softened. In fact, all four pensioners looked somehow brightened by Nik's presence. More relaxed. Engaged. Or was it the alcohol?

'Work,' he replied. 'And a break from work – it's complicated…'

I could have changed the conversation, but was curious too.

'The business, Junior Magic, is in trouble… my family is a toy manufacturer and sales have continually dipped over recent years. I'm taking a couple of months out to see what competitors are doing across Europe, especially around Christmas, so that we can really raise our game next year. I've also got a fledgling idea that might work as a side project, but I need to consolidate it. I visited Belgium and Switzerland before going to Germany last week. I'll try to fit in France – apparently there's a fantastic toy shop called Si Tu Veux in Paris. I might swing over to Ireland for a couple of days, as well, but now I'm in London I intend to visit Hamleys of course, and Covent Garden – then there are plenty of festive markets around the capital, in November.'

'Don't forget Harrods,' chipped in Pan.

'Good point. We need a fresh approach. I'll be looking for materials that we haven't tried yet.' He shrugged. 'I prefer what's considered a more old-fashioned approach to toy-making… puzzles, quality soft plushies, family board games. But we might need to compromise our ethos to stay afloat. Toys using artificial intelligence is an ever-increasing growing market... My right-hand man, Lachlan, is flying over this way in a week or so and doing the southern Europe leg, starting off with the South of France and then Portugal and Spain. Italy after that. Neither of us have had time for a holiday these last few years but have been saving up for the travel we both love – it kind of kills two birds with one stone.'

'Never known the likes of it – a job where you can just take a month or so off,' said Alf. He'd removed his rimless glasses to clean them and put them back, as if to take a better look at Nik.

'You must have a very creative mind,' said Gran.

'Sure, although I don't do much of the nuts and bolts design – I haven't got the computer or mechanical expertise. But I research the competition and consumers. My ideas may or may not be taken up. I'll write a report on my European trip. Share my thoughts. It might mean making some changes to our design team. Hopefully a few new prototypes will come out of it – perhaps a whole new line. And I'm excited to experience a Christmas with weather how it should be – cold and twinkly, even snow if I'm lucky. Perhaps that will get the creative juices flowing.'

'There's no point me getting creative.' Gran sighed. 'I'm really going to miss making all the decorations this year.'

Pan's face fell. 'Yes, getting ready for our party used to remind me of Christmas when I was little, with me and Mum making paper chains out of strips of newspaper. Dad would loop them across the lounge ceiling.'

'I decorate my place with sprigs of holly, wedged behind

picture frames,' said Nik. 'And I've never bought any baubles. As a boy I'd make my own out of foil and glitter. Now my nephews and nieces do. The tree is covered. And the business runs a competition on our website – we sell our products directly too – for children to make their own and post in. The top three get our bestselling toy of the year and I put their entries on the tree in our reception area.'

'What a wonderful idea,' I said.

'There's something about you that sniffs of a bygone age,' said Gran. 'I like it.'

'Show them your phone.' I giggled.

Nik took it out of his bag.

'Even mine's more modern than that,' said Alf, crumbs of pork pie pastry tumbling from his lips. He looked from Nik to the small mobile. Back to Nik. 'I don't think I've seen anyone your age with anything but a smartphone.'

Nik smiled. 'So tell me, why won't anyone be making Christmas decorations this year?'

'Because of this place closing,' said Gran and she slid her half-eaten plate away. 'Tomorrow was going to be a busy day after the morning's bus trip into town, for those who want to go to the Remembrance Service at St Martin's. In the afternoon we were due to have the brainstorming meeting where we choose the party theme. I always look forward to that. We play Christmas music and eat warm mince pies...'

'Perhaps it's just as well,' said Glenda tersely. 'From what I've heard people had been struggling to come up with a new theme. The rumours about his place have distracted them – plus we've done so many now and anyway... we should all be focusing on where we'll be living at the end of this year.'

I'd never really understood why Glenda lived at Willow Court, often keeping herself apart from communal activities. She must have had a beautiful home, what with her fancy job. She could have hired live-in help to assist with her needs due to her osteoporosis, and stayed there.

Nik shrugged. 'I'm lost. Tell me again exactly why aren't you holding the party?'

'Because this place will be closed on Christmas Eve. No one will be living here,' I said.

'Then have it a couple of weeks early.'

'We couldn't do that,' said Gran.

'Why not?' He leant back into his chair. 'Let me tell you about Christmas in July, back in Australia.'

'I've heard of that,' I said.

'Me too,' said Pan. 'Don't you have two Christmases – a proper one in December, which happens to be your summer and then an extra one in July, when the weather's better suited? It's also the name of a wonderful American comedy, filmed in the forties.'

'Great casting,' said Nik. 'And Preston Sturges was a brilliant director.'

'How have *you* seen that?' asked Alf.

'I love old movies. And you're absolutely right, Pan, in Australia we have an early Christmas celebration. In July, our winter, we can really enjoy all the festive things that make up a fantasy, white Christmas, like an open fire, eggnog and mulled wine...You just don't fancy those things so much in the summer. We save the present swapping for the proper time of year but Christmas in July – it's a fun, midwinter event that in lots of ways feels more traditional.'

'It sounds very commercial to me – even more so than the actual event,' said Glenda and straightened her spine as much as she could before peering over the top of her cat-eye glasses.

'It can be. Retailers love it during what is, traditionally, a quiet month for sales. But it's also a great opportunity to spend time with family. It's something to look forward to during the darker, cold months.'

'What has this got to do with our party?' asked Pan. She took off her sunhat and then put it back on.

Nik sat upright and stretched his arms around me and Gran. His fingertips rested on Glenda's shoulder. She leant in. 'If us Aussies dare enjoy the festive period twice, with an extra Christmas six months before, what's to stopping you guys have a festive celebration just a couple of weeks early?'

7

'No one will be in the mood,' said Glenda.

'You're only saying that because you've only ever tolerated our parties,' said Pan. She still had her sunny tones. I'd never heard her say a single word that didn't sound friendly, even when she disagreed with someone.

Glenda put down her plum tomato. 'Yes, because in my opinion Christmas is commercialism gone mad... it's about fake feelings and fake well wishes in cards to people you never even bother visiting. And like I've said – haven't we got bigger things to worry about?'

'Perhaps a distraction is exactly what you need,' said Nik.

'I spent my working life watching decisions being made to maximise chances and profits,' said Glenda. 'I took notes on sound plans being made to secure the future. So, like you Nik, I've got a business head. Surely you agree with me – we shouldn't condone us all sticking our heads in the sand about what's about to happen? We need to focus on moving forwards.' She wiped her mouth, stood up before he could reply and rubbed her hip before slowly leaving, shaking her head.

My stomach twisted slightly. I didn't like any sort

of confrontation. It always reminded me of living with Mum.

'Apologies,' he said and looked around. 'I didn't mean to offend. I hope I haven't upset her with my idea. She seems like a lovely lady.'

'I think she does have a good heart underneath her... cool exterior. Glenda doesn't much value our friendship,' said Pan. 'No one's close to her here, so she's likely the happiest out of all of us to start pushing forwards with plans to leave. Alice probably knows her best.'

Gran shrugged. 'She's not a bad sort. Just runs hot and cold. She always remembers my birthday and helps with my shopping but never talks to me about her past and she hates Christmas.'

'*Hates* Christmas?' said Nik.

'Is that so hard to understand?' said Alf. 'When I was younger, some years I was damn lucky to get a satsuma, walnut and coin – and those things meant the world. Parents these days, you see them out gift and food shopping, buying pigs in duvets of all things – I saw them last year – and God knows what rubbish, looking more stressed than Alice if she's late down to an episode of *Neighbours*.'

He and Gran smiled at each other.

'These folks have got more money than good sense,' said Alf warming to his subject. 'And others who can't afford to spend end up with disastrous credit card bills or problems with loan sharks. If Santa existed he wouldn't want that. Although...' Alf looked sheepish. 'I don't mind the festive season, myself.'

'What do you mean *if* Santa existed?' said Nik with a grin. He stared after Glenda as he drained his glass. I followed his gaze. She'd stopped to smooth down the collar of Betty's raincoat before patting her shoulder and disappearing around the corner.

The residents asked Nik questions about Australia – was it really sunny all the time? Had he gone onto the Sydney Opera House? Their faces dropped when we announced it was time to go. As we left Nik made sure he said goodbye to Betty.

'The atmosphere here is so welcoming and warm – it's a real credit to you,' he said to Lynn.

She looked as if Santa had just given her the biggest parcel ever. 'I have a great core team – it's not all down to me. I love my job and will have lots of personal notes to pass on to people looking after them, wherever they all go next. Take your gran, Jess – if her appetite's off I know she'll always at least fancy a bowl of cold baked beans. And if Betty has bad dreams, during the night, singing nursery rhymes calms her down. There's no doubt the next few weeks are going to be a challenge, but I'm blown away by the loyalty of my long-term colleagues. They've all agreed to work right until the end. I've heard some horror stories over the years of care homes closing and staff leaving as soon as, to start new jobs. I'll do everything in my power to keep things normal here for as long as possible.'

'She's a star, isn't she?' Nik said, on the way out.

'It's clearly her vocation, working in the care home industry. She's always got a smile and buckets of patience.'

I took Nik on a tour of Springhaye, citing Buddy needing a good walk as a reason but really it was to build up an appetite for dinner, after the humungous bread and butter pudding. The cold air and brisk pace achieved my goal and an hour later we went into the pub, glad for the warm. Nik and I raised another glass of sherry to each other in the pub, after the barman had raised his eyebrows at our drinks order.

Nik carried the tiny glasses over to a circular mahogany table. They looked comically small in his large hands, as if we were actors in a movie called *Honey, I've Shrunk the Glassware*. The pub was full of weekend drinkers enjoying pints and spritzers. I'd often treat Gran to lunch here on a Sunday. Oliver came too and was a big fan of the carvery. He'd always remember to bring a packet of cards and we'd play Gran's favourite game of Rummy. When he was small his nanny had been a big fan of traditional games, even though his parents bought him all the latest technological gadgets. The shiny mirrored bar contrasted with the worn tables and scratched, dark laminate floor. A collection of gnomes sat on the rafters. You'd miss them unless you looked up. The landlady, Kath, used to have them outside but got tired of Saturday night revellers hiding them around the village.

'You shouldn't worry about Glenda,' I said. 'She'll have something different to moan about tomorrow – the indigestion that doesn't stop her eating cake or the pneumonia she thinks she's caught. She'll attend the meeting about the party... despite her reservations each year, for some reason she begrudgingly takes part. And I'm glad. I reckon she secretly gets a degree of enjoyment from it.'

He picked up his menu. 'What can have happened for her to dislike Christmas so much?'

'I... I haven't always been a fan myself but as I've got older I've grown to love the festive season, even though I get a little bored of the music after listening to it all day, every day in the toy shop. Gran used to make these amazing fruitcakes with, literally, inches of royal icing on top. We'd stick on plastic snowmen and reindeer from the pound shop, and she made the marzipan herself.'

'It's the details of a childhood Christmas people remember, isn't it?' he said. 'Running upstairs to read a new comic annual or watching the cat hide under piles of discarded wrapping; the smell of roasted meat sneaking into every room and talking of food...' He studied the menu again. 'Steak and kidney pudding? Perfect. It sounds like a main and dessert rolled into one.' He grinned. 'Never thought I'd order anything that stodgy ever again after our snack this afternoon.'

I had bangers and mash. Nik wanted to know if that dish was anything to do with fireworks. The barman overheard and explained that during World War One there was a meat shortage, so sausages were also filled with cereal and scraps and that made them explode whilst cooking. Afterwards Nik and I ordered a bowl of apple crumble between us. He was very polite and let me have the last mouthful. Unlike Oliver – we'd fight over the last chunk of brownie or scoop of ice cream if we ever shared. It was worth it to laugh at the wounded expression he'd pretend to wear afterwards if my spoon scooped quicker.

Nik gave a contented sigh as the barman appeared to remove our plates, and asked him to pass on to the chef that the meal had been second to none.

'No idea why everyone says English cooking is bad. That food was fit for a king.'

'People like stereotypes. They're familiar. Unthreatening.

I'm not sure Alf will ever recover from the fact that a "strapping lad" like you drinks sherry and eats plant-based burgers.'

Nik grinned. 'He's quite a character. I like Alf. He calls life as he sees it, just like Glenda. And she may not be the only resident who needs persuading that bringing their Christmas celebration forwards is a good idea. In fact, an overload of carbs has helped me brainstorm the party – would you like me to share my thoughts?'

'Oh, yes please. It's going to take more initiative and effort than ever if we're going to pull this off on time. Any outside help would be appreciated.'

'Ace! I do love a project.'

His youthful enthusiasm made me feel half my age. 'Hold on.' I rummaged in my handbag and pulled out a pen. I reached for a napkin. 'Okay. Let's go.'

'Isn't that a bit old school for you?' he asked, in a teasing tone. 'I'd have thought you'd punch notes into your phone.'

'The battery's gone.'

'I'm saying nothing,' he said and laughed, attracting appreciative looks from a group of young women at the bar. 'Okay. Why not contact the local press? I think it's a story that suits the residents' generation – a stiff upper lip in the face of adversity. Readers will love that. And going public might make the event extra special – give your gran and her friends the attention they deserve. I help out with various local charity initiatives, back in Sydney, and press coverage is also great for getting help.'

'What do you mean?'

Nik sipped his coffee. 'You've got a couple of weeks less

than normal to organise this event. Glenda's right – people who are straight-talking often talk sense…'

I loved how Nik saw the good.

'…everyone *will* be distracted by the priority of sorting out where they are going to live when Willow Court closes. So the coverage could also be about asking the community for help – caterers, any company with spare decorations… why not go big? It's the last one.'

'You're good,' I said, pressing the napkin flat with one hand whilst I scribbled.

'Last winter I helped renovate a homeless shelter. There was a fire just before a cold front was due – not cold by British standards, but still, no one deserves to sleep outside on an empty stomach at any time of year. The community really pulled together –the local paper advertised for help and joiners rebuilt shelves and units without charging. Electricians mucked in for free. I was part of a team that helped redecorate and a restaurant donated a cooker they were about to replace. It was hugely satisfying to see it all come together.'

Nik told me about other charity work he'd done – a sponsored hike in a nearby national park… and every Christmas Junior Magic ran a shoe box appeal for impoverished children in our locality.

'That's amazing. Where do you find the time, with work? I feel wholly inadequate.'

'Don't be. Your life's no less busy. You look after your gran – and Buddy. I've only got myself to worry about.'

By the time we'd finished talking, the white napkin was covered in scrawl on both sides. I waved for the bill. Nik tried to pay when the waiter came over, but I got there first.

'This meal is a thanks from me,' I said, 'for breathing cheery, warm Aussie air into Willow Court this afternoon, at a time when the residents need it most...' A lump formed in my throat. 'It was good to see Gran perk up. I'm really worried about what's going to happen. She's been so happy at Willow Court and a bit of excitement around the party, keeping busy... that would soften the blow just a little.' I folded up the napkin and put it carefully in my bag. 'I'm grateful, Nik. Your input will really make a difference.'

I'd been watching a couple at another table. He'd snapped at her several times and talked her down every time she'd tried to respond before going back to scrolling down his phone. Now she sat in silence, simply drinking her wine. I wanted to go over and tell her she deserved better.

Aside from Oliver, I hadn't met many men as thoughtful or kind as Nik. My mum's boyfriends were usually bad choices. Talking about Christmas reminded me of one with her then-boyfriend, Dave, who hardly spoke to me at all. I was eight. Mum couldn't be bothered to cook vegetables and hadn't had enough money to buy turkey. So I'd had my usual – chicken nuggets with baked beans and oven chips. I didn't mind but could have cried when she said the Christmas puddings had been too dear. I'd wanted to see blue flames on the top that my friends had told me about. She'd switched on the telly and told me to watch what I liked – she and her latest were off down the pub.

I could have been one of those children Nik did his shoe box appeal for.

I shook myself, determined not to dwell. I'd always worked hard not to let my past define my future. I had Gran. An amazing job working with toys. Buddy and Oliver and now a lovely new friend. Nik passed me my coat, cleared our cups and took them to the bar. Buddy pushed close against my legs as we stood outside and breathed out white air. As a child I'd sometimes pretend to blow out smoke when it was cold, trying to be like Mum. She'd noticed once. Asked what I was doing and why. When I replied she'd burst into tears. I'd never seen her like that before. In between sobs she told me never to dream of being like her. I didn't understand. I thought she'd be pleased.

Annoyed at how these flashbacks popped up now and again, I pushed the memory away.

'You're really worried about Alice, aren't you?'

'Yes,' I said, smarting at the cold air. 'But Gran's one for getting on with things and not wallowing. I've just got to do my best to make this party the best one ever.' I bit a fingernail. 'I really hope I can pull it off.'

Nik zipped up his red anorak. 'Sounds to me like you could do with all the help you can get, at this meeting. Look… I love a challenge. How about I come along tomorrow – for extra moral support? Although please tell me if that's too much, I—'

'You'd do that? You'd really help me? But you must be busy researching for work.'

'Sure… but there's no tight schedule with that,' he replied vaguely.

'What about other things you want to do – that trip to the Cenotaph, for example, that I mentioned, or what about the London Eye and—'

'My mate who owns the flat I'm staying in, gets on well with his neighbour, Rob, who knocked this morning to check I'd settled in okay. He happened to mention the

Cenotaph as well. His grandfather died during the war. I can get to Whitehall from Islington on the tube in half an hour, with a couple of changes. Apparently there is a service at eleven. To get a good view you need to get there as early as possible. Rob said, if I liked, I could go with him. But I'm at a loose end in the afternoon. To be honest you'd be doing me a favour.'

'I look forward to hearing about it. My Sunday morning is brunch with Oliver and Buddy – I know it must sound silly, but it's one of Buddy's favourite times of the week. I take him out for a long walk when Oliver heads off to work, late morning. The rest of the week we're both rushing around and too tired to play with him much in the evenings. If it wasn't for that I'd have suggested us meeting tomorrow instead of today.'

'It doesn't sound silly at all.'

'I'm off work Monday. I could meet you in London then, if you wanted, and show you around. But honestly, don't feel obliged about tomorrow afternoon...'

Nik offered his elbow and after pausing for a second, I slipped my arm through it as we headed out of the pub's car park, part of me feeling like skipping.

8

'But you hardly know him,' said Oliver as I approached the breakfast bar. He'd turned on the Christmas tree fairy lights even though it was daytime. Brunch was almost ready. It was utter luxury for me to have tomorrow off, as well as today. Consecutive days away were rare at Under the Tree. I poured orange juice whilst the kettle boiled for coffee. Oliver served poached eggs onto toast topped with mashed avocado and sprinkled freshly chopped parsley on top. It was one of our healthier meals. Well, almost – he sat down with me and shut his eyes whilst I performed the ultimate insult and squirted the whole of mine with tomato ketchup.

'Finished?' he asked in a solemn voice.

I giggled my reply. He opened his eyes and we started eating.

'You can't ever get married, you know,' I said and wiped avocado from the corner of my mouth. 'I'm not sure how I'd function without this once a week.'

A strange expression crossed his face for a fleeting second. He caught me looking.

'I'm sure Nik makes a better breakfast,' he said and rolled his eyes.

'Meow!'

Buddy barked from his place on the sofa.

'Seriously though, Jess. You hardly know the guy yet now you're taking him along to the residents' Christmas party meeting?'

'I do know him. He runs a toy manufacturer called Junior Magic. He's from Sydney. His grandparents were immigrants from Finland.'

'That's quite a rundown.'

I put down my knife and fork. 'What's ruffled you? He's just a nice man trying to help out.'

Oliver stared at me for a moment, sighed and took a swig of orange juice. 'It's just... I don't want to see you hurt. Working in a bar... so often I see supposedly nice men behaving like real jerks, all charm and *let me buy you a drink* until they realise they aren't going to get what they want. More than once, every weekend, we have to deal with angry exchanges or tears... how can you trust this guy? He could be anyone.'

'I'm nearly thirty and hardly some youngster fresh on the dating scene – not that this is a romantic thing. But I think I can recognise a superficial idiot when I see one.' I bristled. 'And growing up with some of Mum's dodgy boyfriends I reckon I've got a pretty good gut feeling for these things. Don't you trust my sense of judgement?'

'A toy manufacturer travelling during one of the most profitable seasons for their business? And now he can suddenly drop everything and help you?' He shook his head. 'Something just doesn't add up.'

'He's explained all that.'

'Precisely. I think you should be careful. People aren't always what they seem.'

I snorted. 'Whatever's made you so cynical?'

He broke eye contact and I felt insulted that he was treating me like some helpless damsel. I finished my brunch in silence, headed into my bedroom and shut the door. I only lasted half an hour during which my stomach tied into knots and I sat on the bed, hugging my pillow. Oliver and I never argued. Perhaps he was jealous of Nik – owning a business, travelling the world... yet Oliver wasn't the jealous type and always said how much he loved his simple life. I got the feeling that was due to his past but Oliver so rarely opened up about his jobs prior to London. He'd only recently moved down from Birmingham when we first met and if I asked any questions he'd change the subject.

I opened my door. Oliver's was closed and I couldn't hear anything. The lounge was empty. He must have gone to Misty's early. Buddy lay asleep on the sofa and I went over to the kitchen. Oliver had washed up and tidied away, apart from... I let out a huge sigh. He'd left out a dinner plate and in the middle was a large red kiss drawn with ketchup.

'Friends again?' said a voice behind me.

'You made me jump, I thought you'd gone out,' I said, swinging around. His bedroom door was now open.

He ran a hand through his tawny crew cut. 'I couldn't leave – not with an atmosphere between us. I- I do trust you to look after yourself, Jess, and know you don't need me for that.' He opened his arms and came forward, enveloping me in them. I nestled there for a moment feeling warm and safe. Eventually his arms dropped and he opened his mouth as if to say something, but then changed his mind. Oliver looked at his watch.

'Right, I'd better going. Honestly, breaking and making up is exhausting.'

'Thanks,' I said, 'for making the first move.'

He took my hand and shrugged. 'My parents never used to admit they were wrong. I swore I'd never grow up like that.'

I squeezed his hand encouragingly before he took his away.

'I shouted at them once.'

'What about?' I asked.

'I was a hot-headed ten-year-old and they'd missed my Christmas play yet again. I asked them how come no one else's nanny went, feeling furious with myself as tears ran down my cheek, me stamping my foot and saying they didn't care.'

I rubbed the top of his arm.

'They said I was ungrateful and that they worked all hours to provide me with the best education. I never shouted at them again. I didn't want to give them the satisfaction of knowing that I missed them.' He gave a lopsided smile before taking my hand to his lips and kissing it. Then he grabbed his coat and hurried out of the front door. I gazed after him, wanting to follow and hug his heartache away.

Any doubts Oliver had planted in my mind about Nik were extinguished as soon as I pulled up into Willow Court. He was already there, helping Glenda – she must have been to the shops and dropped her bag as he'd squatted and was picking up a couple of apples. I hurried out of the car and gave a big wave. By the time I reached them the tarmac was clear. He stood with an arm around Glenda, holding her bag, complimenting her navy coat that had gold buttons down the front. Buddy tugged at the lead, keen to see his friends.

'I've just been explaining that any bowling would be far better indoors at this time of year.' Nik scratched Buddy's head. 'And that really, for a decent game, apples are a bit small.'

I'd rarely seen Glenda smile like that, with her cheeks plumped out.

It was almost two o'clock. Most of the residents, including Gran, were already in the lounge, drinking cups of tea. It wasn't only the central heating and smell of warmed mince pies that welcomed me as I walked in, but the terracotta curtains, the sage walls and fern leaf patterned armchairs, each with a drinks tray attached to one side. The whole room had such a conservatory, sunshiny feel. Paintings hung on the walls of scenes from bygone times – an old-fashioned sweet shop with colourful jars, a horse and cart in front of a farm and a classic car driving down a narrow street. Lift music played in the background and was cheerful, unobtrusive and somehow comforting.

Nik chatted to Betty who paced in and out of the room, in her usual raincoat, holding the doll. He asked her about her children, Lily and Roger. As the creases in Betty's forehead momentarily smoothed out, it touched me that he'd remembered that detail. She talked about her 'wonderful life' with them but those sentiments only lasted briefly before she was transported back to the present and complained to Nik that strangers were being let into Willow Court whilst she wasn't being let out.

I turned left into the lounge and headed over to Gran, stopping to hug Pan who was dressed from head to toe in animal print and then Alf who always acted as if physical contact was embarrassing, yet never seemed to want to let go. Gran grunted and pushed herself up. I passed the dog lead to Nik who'd come over.

'Let's get this meeting started,' she said.

'First, I hope you don't mind – but I couldn't help buying you this,' said Nik. He set his rucksack on the floor and pulled out a slim paper bag. 'I passed a bookstore today. They had a whole section dedicated to Christmas. During our meal last night Jess mentioned that you used to enjoy reading festive novels with her when she was younger and are the mobile library's keenest customer. The store had a special sale on. Apparently this new detective novel is selling out. It's about a series of murders that all relate to a Christmas party in a haunted mansion.'

Gran's mouth fell open as she pulled out the book and ran her hand over the cover. 'I don't know what to say. You hardly know me.' Her eyes gleamed. 'I love cosy crime – although Alf always tells me off for reading the last page first. Thanks, Nik.'

They smiled at each other and a warm glow enveloped me. I took off my hat, scarf and coat and draped them over the back of her chair. Nik sat down next to Alf, wiping mince pie crumbs from his chin. Buddy collapsed at their feet. Arms linked, Gran and I made our way to stand in front of a hatch, behind which was a small area where residents could make coffee or tea and cook snacks. Nik winked and my stomach felt topsy turvy.

'Right everyone,' said Gran, taking her hands out of her

cardigan pockets, 'as I've already told most of you, our Australian visitor has come up with the brilliant idea of having our party a couple of weeks early. If Nik's home country can celebrate Christmas six months before, there's no reason why us lot should be shy, right?'

They looked at him and some raised eyebrows. Others shrugged. Alf stopped feeding Buddy treats.

'I'm afraid there is,' said Glenda with a feisty tone. She folded her arms after pushing herself up. 'I know Nik means well but it's going to be a load of frivolity and nonsense at the very time we should all be focusing on the serious business of planning our futures.'

'Perhaps organising a party is just what Willow Court needs to lift everyone's spirits,' said Nik and not for the first time I admired his appealing tone. It was like comforting cocoa on a stormy night, or a hot water bottle warming a bed.

'Glenda's got a point,' piped up Fred, a former firefighter with, appropriately, an unlit cigarette in his mouth. 'I've given no thought to the theme of our bash because all I can think about is where am I going to live in the New Year.'

'But couldn't an earlier party double as a way of saying goodbye?' I said.

'That would be nice,' said Nancy. She sat at the back, in her wheelchair. Her voice wavered. 'I'm going to miss everyone so much – staff as well. If we don't have a party... a formal date where we all come together... I'm worried everyone will disappear in dribs and drabs and I won't get a chance to tell the people that matter how much they've meant.'

'That's an excellent point,' said Nik. He stood up and

looked around the room. 'It's a last chance to celebrate your friendships. And getting the local press involved, I'm sure, would bring in lots of help. It's a way of... of giving you closure, over this closure.'

'We should do our bit,' said Gran. 'I read the papers. More care homes than ever are closing because of lack of funding. If we spoke to the local rag about our knees-up, they could tell the personal story behind what's happening to the rest of folk like us, around the country.'

Some of the residents perked up at this. Good old Gran, knowing that appealing to the higher cause might raise more interest.

'But what would the theme be?' asked Alf. 'I've not thought about it much either – not with fielding calls from my son and daughter insisting I need to move in with one of them...' He tutted.

'Problems some of us would be glad to have,' mumbled Glenda.

Nik shot her a sympathetic look and she turned away as if she'd been caught off guard.

'All I came up with,' Alf continued, 'was a Vegas Christmas. We all dress up fancy. Have a roulette table. Poker. Cocktails.'

'There's little Christian sentiment in gambling,' said Glenda in a stiff voice.

'It's an excellent starting point,' I said brightly. 'I'm sure we've all got different ideas about the meaning of Christmas... anyone else?'

Silence.

'That's it... I've just remembered my idea,' said Pan eventually. 'How about a dazzling 1920s Gatsby Christmas, with gold foil curtains, ostrich feathers and champagne glasses?'

'I don't feel especially glamorous at the moment,' muttered one woman. 'Drinking champagne? That feels like taking the celebrations too far this year.'

Pan looked crestfallen.

'Wouldn't that make for a fun birthday party?' said Nik and gave her a thumbs-up. He looked thoughtful for a moment as the air held nothing but the Michael Bublé Christmas album Lynn had put on. 'In fact... the idea of basing your get-together on a movie and something Betty said about her children has given me inspiration, along with my trip to the Cenotaph this morning. We want to celebrate your friendships but... the party, what with everything that's happened, I'm guessing you guys want a kind of... a comforting feel?'

'Cut to the chase, lad,' shouted out Fred.

Lynn came in and sat down at the back.

Nik came up to the front, next to me and Gran. He shot me a look and I nodded. 'Okay. What about a party based around... *It's a Wonderful Life*?'

Gran's face lit up. It was one of her favourite movies.

'Jimmy Stewart?' said Alf.

'It was nominated for five Academy Awards, you know,' said Pan. 'It was super, that line about an angel getting its wings every time a bell rang.'

'Donna Reed was certainly easy on the eye.' Alf sat up straighter.

'Never seen it,' said Fred.

'Goodness, how is that possible?' said Pan and her jaw dropped.

'That's a sad state of affairs,' said Gran, shaking her head with disapproval.

Nik rubbed his hands together. 'Okay. For those who haven't, here's a quick synopsis. George Bailey is feeling unfulfilled with his life in Bedford Falls, having never been able to pursue his glamorous dreams of travelling but staying to run his father's building and loans business instead. He's also thinking of ending it all because of a misplaced loan, so an angel is sent from heaven to show him, with flashbacks, just how much worse off local people would have been without him – just how much his life *has* mattered. Clarence, the angel, succeeds and duly earns his wings. He's shown George that...' He looked around all the residents. 'Despite all the hard times and disappointments, it's still a wonderful life. And at the end the community comes together to help George with his money worries.'

'We could make decorations in the shape of, well, angels for a start,' I said.

The residents looked at each other.

'It's such a perfect idea,' said Gran, eventually. 'We could play Forties music.'

'And snow. We'll need lots of icy decorations,' said another voice.

'Glenn Miller,' said Betty, lucid for a second before wandering out of the room again.

'Oh yes,' said Pan dreamily. 'There's nothing quite like Big Band tunes to get people *in the mood...*'

'There's a theory that Glenn Miller never died in a plane crash, you know,' said Alf. 'Strong evidence suggests he was captured and killed by the Nazis.'

'Alf, really.' Glenda rolled her eyes. 'Why are most of your theories so unpleasant?'

Gran returned to her chair whilst Nik and I circulated the room. It seemed to be a universally loved movie that made residents feel nostalgic and secure. Even Glenda approved of the sentiments behind the story. Several times I stole looks at Nik as he chatted easily to the residents.

What a genius!

Liver-spotted hands rested on his arm. Behind thick lenses, wrinkled eyes returned his smiles. The familiarity and warmth of *It's a Wonderful Life* was just what Willow Court needed. It even got approval from the contingent of movie-goers, amongst the residents, who loved the modern Marvel comic films and romantic comedies. Nik had brought a notepad and wrote down people's initial thoughts.

'As you might know,' he said, '*It's a Wonderful Life* was released in the mid-1940s. Visiting the Cenotaph this morning really makes my generation think about how everyday life must have been for ordinary families during the hard war years. It must have felt fantastic, in the late Forties, to go to the cinema and escape into a film.'

'What did you think to the service?' asked Gran.

'Very moving.' Everyone stopped to listen. 'I've never seen a queue like it. We got there early at eight. Time flew until the service at eleven, soaking up the atmosphere, talking to people.'

'I imagine with your height, lad, you got a great view,' said Alf.

'It was great seeing the veterans' parade. I couldn't see Prince Charles lay the wreath, but the Queen, William and Kate were on the balcony at the Foreign and

Commonwealth office. I took some photos I'll eventually show to my neighbour, Wanda, back in Sydney. She loves The Duchess of Cambridge – has her on a mug, a plate, a tea towel and even her phone cover.' His voice softened. 'Seeing those veterans, it really makes you appreciate what people went through in both of the world wars – losing comrades, family and friends...'

'I was four when the Second World War ended,' said Glenda. 'Never saw my dad – and he never saw me.'

I didn't know Glenda and I had that in common.

Nik reached over to her chair and squeezed her shoulder.

'That's the way it was for many children,' she continued. 'Mum did her best afterwards and eventually married his closest friend.'

'I remember Dad going off,' said Alf. 'I've always liked St Martin's Remembrance Service and it didn't disappoint this morning – it gives me the chance to really think about him.'

'Didn't he come back?' I asked.

'His body did,' Alf said gruffly, 'but his mind was never the same. He was forgetful, suffered from tremors and headaches, and he couldn't stand loud noises. For years he'd suffer a panic attack on Bonfire Night. Shell shock they called it back then. I wish I'd understood better, when I was a lad, but I found it scary and just kept out of his way.'

'You weren't to know,' said Pan. She studied her nails. 'I remember my grandmother. Determined she was, that the war wasn't going to stop her love of fashion. She always wore nail polish – it was the one affordable cosmetic, at that time, and she said it helped ease the horror of having to wear her overalls in the munitions factory.' Pan smiled.

'She'd paint on her nylons using gravy juice. As a little girl I couldn't think of anything more disgusting, but as I got older I understood.'

'Like Jimmy Stewart's character in *It's a Wonderful Life*, Wanda's dad couldn't do service in the Second World War due to deafness in one ear,' said Nik. 'She said the feeling of inadequacy never left him. A little girl once gave him a white feather – she'd heard stories about a white feather campaign where women gave them to so-called cowards who wouldn't go off to fight.'

'That's so sad,' said Pan.

'But *It's a Wonderful Life* is a celebration of all the ways people are brave and kind and help each other – often without even realising,' said Nik. 'I can't think of a better theme for a Christmas party.'

'This is all very well,' said Glenda. She'd been consulting her phone. 'But has it fully sunk in with everyone that today is the 8th – the *8th* – of November? When are you thinking of holding this party? I've just been looking at an online calendar. We've been told to move out by Tuesday the 15th of next month. This get-together can't be at the last minute. That means Sunday the 6th would be the most sensible date. That is only four weeks from today.'

Everyone looked at me and Gran, even Buddy.

'She's got a point,' mumbled Alf. 'And some of us are bound to have left by then.'

'I… I hadn't really thought about that,' I said. Of course. It was Bonfire Night weekend. Remembrance Sunday. I should have been more aware of the actual dates.

'We've got application forms to fill in. Phone calls to make. Meetings with relatives or social workers and occupational therapists. All of that on top of our usual appointments with health professionals.' Glenda smoothed down her jumper even though there were no creases. 'That last week or so will be spent packing. It's just not possible,' she said with a satisfied smile.

'Willow Court is doing everything to see if you can all be transferred somewhere together,' said Lynn, dark circles framing her eyes.

Glenda gave one of her snorts. 'Over thirty people live here. Any residential home with that amount of free places can't be very good.'

'Hear, hear,' swept around the room like a slow Mexican wave along with comments like 'there's just no point celebrating this year'.

Nik and I crouched by Gran's chair.

'Perhaps it's best to forget it,' I said. Gran's eyes looked watery and I passed her a tissue. 'I hope you aren't coming down with the cold that is doing the rounds.'

She sniffed and took it. Nik and I stood up.

'Perhaps we're expecting too much,' I said to him.

Nik stared at Gran. 'I hate to see Alice so upset.'

Her watery eyes were due to a bug, weren't they? Gran never cried. Not over her arthritis. Not over losing her home here. Not over the fact that her only child – my mother – never contacted either of us anymore. She certainly wouldn't cry over a Christmas party. I glanced down and my eyes pricked as she dabbed hers. Pan had come over and stood the other side, patting Gran's shoulder. I thought back to previous Decembers and the jollity of the yearly celebration. It was always the one time of year Gran seemed to completely forget her stiff joints, dancing if she got the chance, albeit with a walking stick, handing out buffet food and clapping vigorously as everyone sang carols.

Who the hell did Glenda think she was, trying to ruin our plans just because *she* hated Christmas? Before she'd launched in with her calendar comments the residents were getting excited. I glanced back up at Nik. He looked right into my eyes and I experienced that sense again that we understood each other completely.

'Four weeks isn't long,' I said in a loud voice, and a hush fell. 'But look... the legacy of *It's a Wonderful Life*... I know it's only a movie, but art – doesn't it reflect life? That film's about how we keep going and make the most of our situation.'

'Jess is right,' said Nik. 'Surely what we can take from the story is that however tough life gets, it's worth battling on? This party has always meant so much to Willow Court. Let's put up a fight. Let's make it one to remember. I mean...' His cheeks flushed. 'That's if you'll let a particular Australian bloke muck in. I'd be happy to help with the organising, in between the occasional business meetings, and sightseeing trips to London.'

'You'd really help out?' stuttered Gran.

'Sure – the alternative would only be to sit alone in my flat. And you know what? It's kind of fateful, the idea of having a Christmas party early and choosing the theme of *It's a Wonderful Life*, because that very snowy, wintry movie was actually filmed in the summer. It came about early too!'

Surprised faces looked at each other. Alf sat scratching his head and staring at Nik.

'Any residents who've already moved out could come

back for that day. I'm sure we could arrange that,' I said and looked at Lynn who nodded.

Nik grinned and draped an arm around my shoulder, his long fingers curled around the top of my arm. Sparks of electricity travelled down to my fingertips; I wasn't expecting it and for a second, I felt a little giddy.

'Let me help make this an awesome party, one that no one will ever forget,' he said. 'Now... where are those mince pies?'

9

Days off, I was discovering, weren't exactly that when you moved into management but I wasn't complaining. I knew how lucky I was to have a job that made getting out of the bed every day easy. There was something magical about walking into Under the Tree. The ring of the door's bell was like a click of the fingers that transformed the problematic adult world into a little happy oasis, with the bright colours, the squeals of delight from children and cheerful background music. I was grateful for the extra responsibility – even though, with Christmas approaching, it gave me sleepless nights.

It was Monday and I'd be showing Nik the sights of the capital. We'd had to delay meeting up by an hour or two to later this morning as Seb had messaged first thing to say his car wouldn't start. He'd be an hour late due to having to take the train. Not that I minded. I loved work plus the prospect of spending time with Nik added an extra dimension to the day ahead. Oliver put his fingers in his ears at my whistling that not even the boiling kettle could drown out, but that only made me whistle louder.

What's more, it was a special time, first thing in the shop, a bit of tranquillity before Springhaye sprang to life and I could wave to the card shop owner on the left, as she pulled up her blinds, and the greengrocer who often threw me a free apple. I'd savour my second coffee of the day whilst putting money in the till and refilling any shelves we hadn't had time to re-stock the night before. A small thing, but I also really enjoyed being the one to turn the shop sign around, from closed to open. The thrill never left me. That one act symbolised that I was providing a service and that mattered. I wasn't wasting my life, I was getting out there and earning money, I was helping people and spending my days constructively.

A woman passed by outside and I held my breath for a second. She looked just like Mum with the slumped shoulders and wild curly hair. She was the same height, the same build... I went closer to the window as she crossed the street and caught a clearer look of her face, confirming she was a stranger. For some reason I always felt the need to do that.

The bell went as the door opened and heavy breathing entered the shop.

'Jessie, you're a star. I managed to get here quicker than I expected. The train service has really improved since the last time I used it.' Seb took off his coat.

'I have a dilemma,' I said.

'Happy to lend you my wisdom. Shoot.'

'Do I or do I not tell you that you've put your jumper on inside out?'

We grinned at each other.

'So, you're meeting up with Nik today? Business or pleasure?' he asked as he put it on the right way around.

'Business, I'd say – it feels right, being hospitable towards a fellow member of the toy industry. And he's been so kind to Willow Court's residents.'

Seb snorted and was about to talk when the bell went again and he hurried to hang up his coat. A man around the same age as me came in with a toddler, probably just having dropped off an older child at school. We had a run of parents come in after nine who'd browse the shop and perhaps read a couple of books, before heading to the coffee shop opposite. He yawned and lifted up a bottle of water, wedged into the collapsible cover of the buggy. The toddler kicked her feet, screaming to be let out. Her dad had deep black circles under his eyes. I nipped behind the till and came back with a cow puppet on my hand. I bent down in front of the little girl.

'Mooooo,' I said and wiggled my fingers. 'And what's your name?' The girl stopped crying, choochie cheeks red and blotchy, before giving a toothy smile.

'Tilly,' said the man.

'Well, Tilly, would you like to read some books with Mrs Cow?' I said and looked up. Her dad gave a tired smile. Interacting with customers was my favourite part of the job. There was nothing more rewarding than seeing a child's face light up. Seb tapped my shoulder and, out of sight of the girl, pulled the puppet off my hand.

'Go on, get mooing, boss – I mean moving. Me being late mustn't stand in the way of true love. Nik will be waiting.'

Nik and me? I rolled my eyes and went to protest but Seb had already bent down and was singing about cows jumping over moons. I fetched my things and squeezed his shoulder before heading onto the street. Half an hour later I was sitting on the train opposite a man who was playing Christmas music so loud that, despite him wearing earphones, I could hear every word.

I was almost at King's Cross. Nik had suggested we spend our lunch brainstorming the Christmas party. Tomorrow we'd meet at Gran's in the evening. I could get there by five. Most residents congregated in the lounge after their tea. Being an assisted living facility, as opposed to a full-blown care home, it meant not everyone there was ill. Residents like Betty were catered for but also those who had simply lost a bit of mobility or no longer wanted the responsibilities that went along with living alone. So whereas Oliver and I slumped in front of our telly at the end of the day, Gran and her friends often sat together chatting, doing crosswords, swapping magazines – and watching dating shows, even Glenda, apparently, although she'd sit at the back and pretend to read a novel.

For a change tonight, though, Oliver and I *would* be staying out late. We'd *had words,* as Gran would say, again this morning. He'd been at Misty's late last night so it was the first chance I'd had to tell him the news...

He'd put down the bread knife. '*What?*'

'Nik – he's offered to help organise the party.'

'Why would he do that?'

'Not everyone does something just because they might profit. He's got a good heart.'

'How can you be confident of that after knowing him for such a short time?'

'Haven't you ever had that instant connection with someone? Felt like you've known them for years; that you share the same values?'

'Sure,' he said and coloured up. 'But that doesn't guarantee

85

a happy ending. I have to be honest, Jess – it's laudable to think the best of people but I think you're being a bit naive.'

My palms felt sweaty at the possibility of an argument brewing.

'It's plain *weird*. You know that I think you're amazing – it takes some people a whole lifetime to hone getting out of emptying the food recycle bin as often as you do…'

'Idiot.' My stomach relaxed.

'But if I was, say, in Sydney for a month, I wouldn't be sidelined into helping organise a party, when I had the chance to spend my days sampling the sights and night life of that city. I don't think that makes me a bad person. It makes me normal.'

'No such thing as normal,' I said. 'We're all different.'

'True, but doesn't his behaviour strike you as the slightest bit odd? Even… creepy?'

'What a horrible thing to say. Can't you be a little more welcoming? He's not here for long. I'm sure you wouldn't feel like this if you met him, so the sooner that happens, the better.'

Buddy's ears had gone flat at my sharp tone. He never heard raised voices in our flat – not unless he stole a chicken nugget or scratched the furniture. But I felt defensive of Nik – he'd breathed a gust of optimism into Willow Court. Gran texted me today and said she and Pan agreed Nik felt like a friend already.

'Sounds like a good plan,' said Oliver and gave a thumbs-up. 'You know I'd expect no less of you if you thought my latest Tinder meet sounded dodgy.'

'I can't remember your last date.'

'Maybe I'm getting choosy in my old age…'

'Tonight. Misty's, seven o'clock. Hold on, I'll check with Nik.' I texted him, and after a quick exchange, Nik and I agreed we could finish our day out early and he wasn't bothered about the short train ride back to London afterwards. Oliver didn't start his shift until midday, so Buddy only would only have the afternoon on his own until Immy next door came around for a couple of hours to play and take him out for a walk. That would set him up for the evening without me or Oliver.

'Done,' I said and put away my phone. 'There's no going back now.'

Oliver came over and took my hand. 'I don't like it when we disagree, it's just... guess I feel kind of protective... I mean, we're good mates, right?' he hastily added. 'I feel the same about Buddy.'

'Wondering if that's a compliment,' I replied, smiling.

'It is.' His hand dropped away. 'Sometimes I imagine Mum and Dad being much older... I ask myself if I'll ever feel protective towards them, given how they've always been so distant.'

'And what do you conclude?'

'I've no idea.' He shrugged, pursed his lips and went back to slicing bread...

'Is it posh then, this flat?' I asked Nik as we sat on the tube together, after meeting at King's Cross, on our way to Big Ben. He was keen to see that and Buckingham Palace this afternoon.

'It's certainly very fashionable – I'm not sure I fit. My flat in Sydney is colourful and cluttered – with French doors opening onto a balcony full of flowerpots and bees sneaking in. The only orderly part of it is my dark room. Whereas this is all streamlined appliances and oatmeal furnishings and artificial carefully placed plastic plants. I wish I could be more on trend but I never seem able to muster the enthusiasm.'

'Me neither.'

A cosy, cluttered feeling filled my chest – cluttered with thoughts about how Nik and I were so much alike. Life right at this moment, just for this second, would have been pretty much perfect if it wasn't for the recent arguments with Oliver. When I returned to my flat every night, it felt like home, not just because of my belongings but because he and Buddy were there, even though he left his wet towel on the bathroom floor and always forgot to put the extractor fan on when he fried meat. And he'd always leave the cutlery drawer open and put empty jars back in the fridge. That last one really niggled. It was something Mum used to do.

The clouds were kind and held onto their rain as if to annoy the forecasters who'd said it would be torrential today. We chatted non-stop and within the hour were walking on the Albert Embankment, along the south side of the River Thames, with Big Ben and the Houses of Parliament across the other side, in the distance. It felt romantic which was ridiculous. Nik was a visitor, soon to return to the other side of the planet. A trader walked past, pushing a trolley selling plastic snowmen that danced when you wound them up. I'd told Nik about how the last couple of years there'd been scaffolding around the clock, meaning it didn't look its best.

'But it's the flaws that are more interesting in life, don't you think?' he said, those blue eyes mesmerising me. 'Back home, I love taking snaps of people. Those at the two ends of life – kids and oldies… their faces are the most natural. Everyone else in between is trying too hard to look their best. There's nothing like a close up of someone utterly relaxed with who they are.'

I slipped my arm through his and shivered as he pulled me close whilst we walked past a living statue – there were many along the Embankment, in between the plane trees planted there, I'd read, because they are especially good at soaking up pollution. This one was dressed in a suit, with a top hat and glasses. He stood on a plinth that said Scrooge. His skin and the whole outfit were sprayed to look like bronze and it was hard to tell he was human.

I looked up at Nik as we walked and chatted more about his photography, how he found a bare winter tree as fascinating as one in full bloom. How ruins were far more interesting than shiny skyscrapers. From anyone else those comments would have sounded pretentious, but there was something so genuine about him.

It felt special, a friendship where you plunged straight into deep conversation. I'd only ever had that with Gran – and Oliver.

We stopped by a rough sleeper and both put change in the takeaway coffee cup in front of him, on the damp pavement. Nik reached into his rucksack and took out a bar of chocolate. He broke off a chunk for me and himself and then handed the rest to the man. Nik took out his camera and photographed the Houses of Parliament and then shots of me holding onto the elegant dolphin lamppost near us, *Singin' in the Rain* style. He shook his head and muttered the word *beautiful*. The hairs on the back of my neck prickled.

We walked further along the Thames past a small group of political protestors, who were claiming several recent aeroplane crashes around the world had been orchestrated.

'As you might remember, Alf loves conspiracy theories, including the Flat Earth ones,' I said.

'Yes – what was that about not believing Australia exists?'

'The idea was once mooted that creating the idea of your country was a hoax to cover up the biggest mass murder of all time, namely that British convicts supposedly sent there were actually drowned. And that pilots are in on it and fly people to other islands that are nearby, telling them it's Australia.'

Near to St Thomas's hospital now, we sat down on one of the swan benches, featuring cast iron swan panels and arms. The clouds finally broke.

'Alf really gets passionate about his conspiracy obsessions, arguing for and against the evidence. I reckon it keeps him going. His heart failure can make him very tired, but just the mention of the Illuminati or Elvis supposedly having been spotted is enough to get him firing on all cylinders.'

'I don't think there's anything wrong with people believing in things that can't be explained, as long as they aren't hurting anyone,' said Nik. 'Not even if he believes my country doesn't exist!'

'I think Alf's got over that one – especially as he's just as keen on *Neighbours* as Gran. But he's always coming out with a new one he's discovered, about real events or mythical creatures... do you have the tooth fairy in Australia?'

'Sure do. So, has Alf got reservations about Santa, like Glenda?'

'Yes but he's like a kid who's just worked out Santa isn't real but doesn't want to admit it and spoil the magic. He loves Christmas, especially the rich food which is a shame as he's only allowed to eat a little of it. Talking of which, let's find somewhere for lunch.'

Nik pointed to a takeaway stand to our left. 'How about we stay out here and eat fish and chips? I can't go back home without trying them.'

'Aren't you cold outside, what with being used to warmer climes?'

'No. Must be my Finnish genes. Of course, if you'd rather eat indoors then—'

'I think it's a great idea.' Insisting on paying, I headed over. The fried, savoury smell wafting my way from the stand was mouthwatering. I stood for a moment once I'd paid, holding two cones of fries and cod goujons. That smell... I felt warm and fuzzy inside for a second, but it was tinged with sadness. The fried aroma reminded me of fish and chips with Mum, eaten on the village bench when I was little, just the two of us – one of rare times I got her full attention.

Nik wolfed his down and patted his stomach. 'I could do with losing a few kilos but not on holiday. Not in England.'

I couldn't see what he was worrying about. I found his solid frame appealing. What with that and his white streaked hair and sherry habits, he was nothing like the type of man I usually went for. When we finished he threw the containers into a bin. Back on the bench he slipped an arm around my shoulder. We sat in silence, for a moment, admiring the riverside view, away from stresses and strains. I could have sat there for days.

'Was your job in the toy industry your first?' he asked.

'Apart from a paper round, yes. Same for you, I imagine, what with it being the family business?'

He nodded.

'Was it always your lifelong goal? Is there anything else you'd love to do?'

'No. I'm pretty much perfectly happy.'

'No other dreams? I could never leave the toy business but fantasise about opening my own shop somewhere like Paris. I'd live in a quirky flat and spend my days reading and seeing the sights.' I thought back to a conversation we'd had on the aeroplane. 'You love flying, haven't you ever dreamt of being a pilot or...' I glanced at his legs. 'Becoming a professional basketball player.'

His laugh bellowed out. 'Hell, no, Jess. I haven't got the discipline for any sport. No, I'm totally satisfied.'

In such a go-getting, material world his attitude was refreshing.

'Although there is one tiny thing...' His expression turned serious. 'I wish I had more time for my shoe box work and could make a real difference on a national scale, evening out the balance between the kids that had nothing and those, like me, who had so much. Of course that's unrealistic but I'm really hoping, one day, we can help the wider community of Sydney and not just our locality.' He took his arm away. 'Anyway, enough of enjoying ourselves, we've a party to plan. I've brought my notebook. So is there more than one local newspaper? Which do you think would be the best to contact?'

'The *Amblemarsh Gazette*. It covers Springhaye and everyone in the area gets a free copy through the door. If we want to run an ad for a sale at Under the Tree that's the publication we always use.

'Perhaps I should take a photograph of the residents? The paper will be more likely to run a story if it involves less work and expense for them.'

'Good point. I'd never have thought of that.'

'Tomorrow night we need your gran to take stock of the craft supplies they have gathered during the year and then we can brainstorm exactly which decorations to make.'

'Perhaps we should run a viewing of *It's a Wonderful Life* – for Fred's sake and to refresh everyone's else's memories,' I suggested.

'That's a great idea – it will really get people in the mood. A cinema screening… we must have popcorn.'

I was the same as him – any event I was planning, the food element was always important. I took a deep breath and put my hand on his. He stopped writing. I stared into his eyes.

'I'm so grateful, Nik, for all your help and for putting some spring back into Gran's step. I… I'm lucky to have met you on that plane.'

'Me too.' He wrapped his arms around me. I smelt fresh aftershave with hints of… orange and clove. It reminded me of Christmas. He leant back, tantalisingly still holding on to the outside edge of my hand. I felt such a magnetic pull to this man.

'I love travelling but the bit that interests me most is getting to know people. I can see the palace or London Eye on a postcard – but seeing inside someone's life… It's been an honour to meet you and your gran, Jess,' he said softly.

As he spoke a car backfired in the distance which must have explained why my heart was pounding.

Misty's had a glass front with the name written as a dusky pink neon sign. Next to it was a poster advertising the upcoming themed Christmas events. Condensation ran down the inside. It always got steamy, what with there being a small dance floor.

'Monday is Eighties night.'

'That was a big decade for UK-Australian relations,' said Nik. '*Neighbours* aired for the first time over here and then *Crocodile Dundee* was a massive hit.'

'Yet what a let-down you are,' I said in a jokey tone and pushed open the door. 'You don't use Australian slang nearly enough. I haven't heard you say *fair dinkum* once.'

Despite the relatively early time of seven o'clock, the bar was crowded. A two-for-one cocktail hour was responsible. I took Nik's elbow and led him through the throng, towards the bar, looking forward to a drink and relaxing after an afternoon travelling to see the outside of Buckingham Palace and watching a thrilled Nik take tens of photos. The room was dimly lit with neon spotlights dotted across the ceiling. Oliver had a metallic shaker between his hands and was laughing with Greg, a colleague. Oliver caught my eye and that sense of home infused me. I could just be myself, good or bad, and we always got over our little fallouts – although this one about Nik was the biggest we'd ever had.

'Hello there, Nik,' he said loudly and reached across the bar. The two men shook hands. 'I'm Jess's flatmate, Oliver. What'll it be?'

'G'day mate. Great to meet ya. So what do you recommend?'

A few heads turned at the accent which seemed stronger than usual.

'Leave it with me,' said Oliver and he pointed to a table, against the left-hand wall, with a reserved sign on it. It was one in a row of pink tables, with slate-grey upholstered poufs on the nearside, opposite a long couch, on the other, with plush pink cushions.

It wasn't a big room but the window front and glass along the back of the bar gave it a sense of space. On the other side of the bar was a small dance floor. Music blared out after six, with a jukebox providing atmosphere before that. People travelled from other towns for its top-quality cocktails and stylish bar snacks, including spring onion and butter sandwiches served with vintage cheddar crisps, or the bowls of gourmet popcorn such as the Camembert one drizzled with redcurrant sauce.

'Thanks for a great day,' said Nik as we sat down together, on the couch. 'I really enjoyed visiting Her Majesty this arvo.'

I slipped off my coat. He did the same. Today he wore a red checked shirt.

'Cool place,' said Nik. 'Is Misty the owner? She must be one talented Sheila to decorate the place like this. It's glam but simple. I love it.' He unbuttoned the top of his shirt and I couldn't help noticing his smooth tanned chest. Oliver appeared with a tray bearing three cold cocktails. He set them down and slid the tray under the table, sitting on the pouf opposite.

'You little ripper,' said Nik. 'They look ace.'

They did. But I was distracted. *G'day mate*. Great to meet *ya. Arvo. Sheila. You little ripper.* They look *ace*. I looked at Nik and his eyes twinkled as if to say is this Australian enough? Suppressing a chuckle, I picked up my drink, which was bright orange and had a sliver of circular citrus fruit floating on the top.

'Thanks, Nik.' Oliver rolled up his grey shirt sleeves. He had nice forearms. I'd always thought that. 'They're clementine martinis.'

Nik gave a thumbs-up. 'Chrissie can never come too early.'

I gave him a pointed look and, out of sight, gently punched his thigh. The light in his eyes flickered. 'Cheers,' he said and sipped it. 'Mmm. This certainly isn't a let-down.'

'Enough,' I hissed at him and we both started laughing. I looked at Oliver. 'Sorry. Nik's just being silly. This cocktail really is delicious.'

'Nothing to do with me. The clementine juice is freshly squeezed here and Misty sourced the fruit from an organic grower.'

'Misty is a real person?' said Nik, his Australian accent back to normal.

'She's been running this bar for years now – used to be an actress but never got the break she wanted. All those years of waitressing, though, to pay the bills – it paid off;

taught her what she needed to know about the drinks and hospitality business. She bought this place with her wife.'

'Pan would love to meet her, wouldn't she, with her drama background?' said Nik.

I looked at Oliver. *See. He thinks of other people and remembers details about them even though they've only just met.*

'Unusual name,' he continued.

Oliver swigged back a large mouthful. 'It was popular in the 1960s apparently. Her parents chose it because they went on a cruise for their honeymoon and the sea was often foggy...'

'That's so romantic,' I said. Mum could never remember why she'd chosen Jess – she said something once about it being the name of the handsome doctor who helped deliver me.

'Jess?' Oliver lifted up a small bowl. 'Your favourite.'

I still wasn't used to the little ways Oliver showed that he cared. I took a stick of honey-roasted sweet potato and dipped it in the Punjabi orange pickle, put it in my mouth and closed my eyes. When I'd finished chewing, I opened them. Oliver was staring at me, a smile on his face.

I passed the bowl to Nik. 'Try this. It's a slice of heaven.' Thinking I should leave the two of them alone for a moment, I muttered something about powdering my nose before heading off. I actually did powder my nose and refresh my mascara. I even zhuzhed up my hair. It wasn't like me to wear makeup and it felt good to want to make the effort. It had been a while since I'd been on a night out that I'd felt excited about.

I came out of the toilets and started to cross the dance

floor but walked straight into a man who was shouting at anyone who would listen. Accidentally, I stood on one of his feet.

'Watch where you are going, you stupid bitch,' he slurred, deep lines in his face, the reek of alcohol hitting my face. I froze, heart thumping louder than the bass beat as he staggered towards me. Like watching a film I saw Oliver appear out of nowhere, a furious look on his face. He dragged the man out of the door by his shirt collar and onto the pavement. Moments later he was back and took both my hands. He led me to a quiet corner, by the window. I couldn't breathe.

'Inhale and exhale, inhale and exhale,' he said gently. 'It's okay, Jess, you're safe. You're a grown-up now. You're the one in control.'

Mouth feeling dry, I nodded. He rubbed his thumbs over my palms and it felt so reassuring. My breathing slowed.

'Thanks,' I whispered.

'You did it yourself,' he said and kissed me on the forehead before following me back to Nik who was chatting to a couple behind our table.

He looked up and grinned. 'Everything okay?'

'Never better,' I said took a large gulp of my cocktail.

'Oliver and I were just talking about the Christmas party, before he left to sort out some trouble. I was just telling him how much the residents think of him. Alf said he wished he was generous enough to let his good friend Oliver actually win at dominoes for once, and Pan told me he looked just like Brad Pitt... which you do, of course, mate,' he added.

Oliver smiled but concern etched his face. Perhaps he

was worried that man would come back in. I picked up the last chip. At least he and Nik were getting on.

'You okay?' said Oliver when Nik left to buy more drinks.

'Yes,' I snapped. 'Just leave it.'

He leant back. I put my hand on his knee.

'Sorry. I... I just feel stupid that's all. Disempowered.'

'The man was a jerk. And Jess Jagger is one of the strongest women I know.'

I gave him a hug.

'Right... anyway...' Oliver said, 'it sounds as if you've thought about the Willow Court Wonderful Life bash in detail.'

'Nik's made loads of notes and come up with some brilliant ideas. I've rung Gran and told her to warn everyone that he'll be taking a photograph of them all together, when we pop in tomorrow night. He reckons it'll make our pitch for some coverage by the *Amblemarsh Gazette* even stronger if we've done a bit of the work for them.'

I dipped my finger in the pickle and sucked it. Oliver shook his head and pulled away the plate.

'You and Nik had a good chat?' I asked

'I asked him about his business, Junior Magic. I was going to Google it but—'

Nik appeared with three cocktails that were frothy and white with a thin, shiny slice of orange rind on top of each of the glasses' rims.

Oliver studied it. Lifted it to its lips. 'This is a new one on me.'

Orange... lemon...

'It's a popular one back home called London Calling,' said Nik. 'I like it because it contains—'

I raised my palm. 'Sherry!'

Nik opened his mouth to say yes but a new song came on. 'Men at Work! Oliver – do you mind? I just have to dance to a song about Down Under.' He held my hand tightly as he led me onto the dance floor and we found a bit of space. His rhythmic moves caught my eye, yet what stood out most was how he looked after me, guiding my feet around a spilt drink and my body away from other dancers' over-enthusiastic arm movements. Oliver sat at the far side, staring, and I waved. Half-heartedly, he waved back. He must have got fed up, night in, night out, having to deal with rowdy customers.

When Nik and I returned Oliver asked him about Sydney. And Finland. The two men chatted easily and laughed about a comedy film they'd both seen recently. Reading was also common ground, both of them being fans of detective stories, although Oliver liked edgy thrillers and Nik preferred cosy crime, like Gran. As they talked, I went through Nik's notebook. We had a lot to discuss tomorrow night with the residents. I got up to buy another round but Nik insisted he had to leave. By the time he got back to Islington it would be morning in Australia and a good time to ring and check on the business.

'And I'm visiting Hamleys tomorrow,' he said. 'I rang ahead. The manager sounds pretty decent. He's agreed to meet me briefly, and share his thoughts on the new trends that might appear in his store over the next couple of years. So I'm going to need to get up early.' He beamed at us both. 'Great to meet you, Oliver.'

Oliver stood up and held out his hand. 'You too. I hope your trip proves productive.'

I couldn't wait for tomorrow evening now, the three of us together, with Gran and her friends, sharing our exciting plans for the party and hopefully cheering everyone up, despite the uncertainty of the next few weeks.

'Thanks for a great day, Jess.' Nik hugged me, put on his anorak and disappeared into the crowd.

'One last drink for the road?' I asked Oliver. 'Club Tropicana' by Wham! had just started playing. 'How about a Pina Colada?'

'No thanks. I've had just about as much sweetness as I can stomach, for one night…'

Strangely, this didn't stop him having a hot chocolate when we got home.

II

I nipped home to pick up Buddy after work, before heading to Willow Court. I also applied a quick squirt of perfume. I put on lip gloss as well and changed into a red blouse. I pressed the buzzer to be let in and yawned, still catching up from being late out at Misty's last night. Betty glared at me as I smiled. I said hello to her and one of the care workers. I signed in and, pulling off my hat, headed into the lounge. Oliver was already there, playing dominoes with Alf at one of the tables, near the window. It took a while to reach Gran. Everyone wanted to say hello to Buddy and his chin lay on many knees for a cuddle, before finally settling on hers. He'd known to avoid Glenda's smart trousers and in any case, she'd warned me to keep clear. She was sure her sniffle was turning into a chest infection. I bent down and kissed Gran.

'Gordon Bennett, your cheek is freezing.' She tutted. 'Let me make you a nice cuppa.'

'It's okay, Gran, I'll—'

'I'm not completely useless yet, young lady. Come over to the hatch when you're ready.'

I grinned at Pan. That was more like it. The gran who cleaned sick off my fake Ugg boots, the first time I ever got drunk. The woman who told me, after every romantic break-up at school, to make sure I grew up never relying on anyone else for my happiness – dogs excluded. Oliver caught my eye and pulled a face. I went over as they sorted out the dominoes to start a fresh game.

'You beating him again, Alf?'

Crow's feet deepened as he winked. 'I just can't help it.'

I blew on my hands. 'Honestly. It's arctic out there.'

Alf scoffed. 'I keep telling you, Jess, this climate change guff is all rubbish. Your red fingers prove that – this winter is as cold as any other. Anyone with half a brain can work out global warming is just one big made up conspiracy, so that leaders and worldwide organisations can exert control.'

'Over what?' I asked.

'Now don't get Alf started,' said Oliver amiably.

'Where we can fly. How often. What we do with our rubbish. Which light bulbs we use. What sort of bags we use to go shopping. Which countries we should buy our food from. I tell you – it's got bugger all to do with our planet and more to do with politicians staying in power.' He rolled his eyes. 'Talk about a nanny state.'

'And what do you reckon to the bush fires, back where I live,' said Nik, cheeks as red as my fingers. I hadn't noticed him come in. Betty was hovering behind him. He hugged me, nodded at Oliver and shook Alf's hand.

'I read about the truth behind that,' said Alf. 'Many reckon it was a government conspiracy to clear land so that they could expand the high-speed rail system.'

'I agree, sometimes there's a story in between the lines,' said Nik.

'Exactly,' said Alf.

'Although the death of over one billion animals... that's quite a price to pay for faster travel.'

'Well, some say... I mean...' Alf shrugged. 'Yep. I agree. I saw those poor koala blighters on the box. Not sure even the most hard-hearted of politicians could take action to cause that. I, well, I didn't mean to offend, lad... I just believe in not taking things at face value.'

'That's very wise.' Nik held out his fist for a fist bump. Alf had no idea what to do so I showed him. 'Right,' said Nik, 'let me get you a fresh cuppa, Alf, whilst I get myself one.'

Oliver's jaw dropped and I was just as surprised that someone had actually made Alf stand back from one of his eccentric theories.

'Quite something, isn't he, our Australian guest?' said Alf, staring after him. 'He gets on with everyone.'

'Too good to be true,' said Oliver brightly.

'He's all the residents can talk about at the moment,' said Alf. 'It's almost... not natural.'

'Let's not start a theory saying Nik is a robot. Or a vampire like... who was it you were talking about last week?' I said.

'The actor in that dark future film I liked – *The Matrix*.'

'Yes. Keanu Reeves – because he never looks any older, right?'

'It's not just me who thinks that, you Buddhist missy.'

I pulled a chair over and sat down. Alf and I grinned at each other. Any observer might think I was constantly giving him a hard time over his theories, or laughing at him, but the two of us knew the truth. I'd learnt a lot about Buddhism in my twenties and it really helped. I'd gone through a rough patch – it was my twenty-first. Mum had hardly visited during the teen years and slowly, as I got older, contact petered out. I'd got it into my head she would at least reach out for my big birthday. It didn't happen and that's when my interest in Buddhism began. Alf couldn't get his head around the philosophy I'd discuss, like thoughts not being who you were and how important meditation was. We respected each other's right to a different view – that didn't mean we couldn't tease each other about our beliefs.

'How was work today?' asked Oliver as he lined up his domino pieces. 'Is the Christmas madness well and truly underway? I'm practically out of our organic clementines this week already and festive tunes are all anyone is playing on Misty's jukebox. I swear, if I hear "Last Christmas" one more time…'

'I feel for you. I already know every Bing Crosby song off by heart and this afternoon we sold our last Lego gingerbread house and can't get hold of anymore.' I should have made the initial order bigger. I occasionally wished Angela was a little more hands-on, but then she believed in throwing people in at the deep end and I rapidly learnt so much when I started working for her. I'd never forget my first day, it still made me smile. She insisted I go on the till and I ended up charging ninety-nine pounds instead of ninety-nine pence for a packet of fruit-shaped erasers.

We turned towards the hatch. Gran was knocking a teaspoon against the side of a glass. She beckoned to me. Nik stood next to her. I headed over and she pointed to my cup on counter. I collected it.

'Do you want to sit down, Gran,' I said, 'whilst Nik and I share our notes?'

She nodded and went back to her chair.

'Although first,' said Nik, 'we could listen to ideas anyone else has had, since we decided on the theme a couple of days ago?'

Of course. Why didn't I think of that? He had his notebook at the ready. I bit into a shortbread round. Nik was just so thoughtful. It was strange to think I'd never have met him if I hadn't changed seats on that aeroplane. The residents went quiet and glanced at each other. Finally Nancy adjusted the cushion behind her back in her wheelchair and moved forward a little.

'I've got my old record player – still use it,' she said.

'I know. I regularly hear Tom Jones,' said Glenda with a grimace.

'I found an old Duke Ellington's Orchestra album,' continued Nancy, blushing. 'I could bring my player down here.'

'Great idea,' said Nik and wrote it down.

Lynn put up her hand. 'My brother plays the saxophone. I'm sure Geoff would love to come and play some Big Band solos.'

'I've been thinking about American food,' said Gran. 'We could make cookies for the kids.'

'And try to find some cheap red and white candy canes,' said Nancy. 'They're American, right?'

'I've mulled over an idea, too,' said Oliver, his face brightening. 'How about I set up a little bar? I've got a special recipe for eggnog that I use at Misty's at this time of year.'

'And a jolly important idea it is too,' said Fred and he grinned as a tangible wave of enthusiasm was washing across the room.

'We thought perhaps Saturday afternoon we could all watch *It's a Wonderful Life* right here – I've got the day off,' I said. 'Oliver finishes his breakfast shift at two and Nik is free. The three of us need reminding of the movie as much as anyone else and I know Gran's got a DVD of it somewhere. She forced me to watch it every Christmas, when I was younger.' I pulled a face and everyone laughed.

Pan clapped her hands. 'A private screening. How exciting.'

'I'll bring some of Misty's popular gourmet Apple Pie popcorn,' said Oliver.

Nik and I explained about the ideas we'd had then he put down his notebook. Everyone had been told about the photo for the pitch to the newspaper and looked suitably smart. We moved around a few chairs and left some at the front for people who had trouble standing. Nancy was positioned there as well. Gran sat in the centre, Buddy and Lynn by her side, with a couple of the other care workers. The residents insisted Oliver and I were included too. Also at the front sat a few residents who were much further into dementia than Pan.

'What's that lady with the lovely grey curls wearing?' asked Nik, as everyone tidied themselves. 'I love the bright yellow colour.'

'That's Phyllis. It's an activity apron. Lynn is always updating a range of items for those with dementia. If you look closely it's perfect for restless hands, with the loops and zips and beaded plaits attached to it. Poor Phyllis had always been a very busy lady, she ran boarding kennels for dogs, and like Betty she finds it difficult to settle.'

'What a fantastic idea,' he said and studied her for a moment. 'Right. Here we go.' He bent forwards, looking through his camera. 'Say Chattanooga Choo Choo.'

'My dentures will fly out if I try that,' protested Fred but despite this he and the others were soon singing the words.

Nik took his shots then the residents relaxed and started chatting. I went over to him but Betty got there first.

'Take me home, Jim,' she said. 'I've been waiting for you to come for me. We mustn't leave the children alone for long.'

Lynn walked past at that moment and stopped. She and I exchanged glances but Nik didn't miss a beat. He curled a hand around Betty's arm, the one that wasn't carrying her handbag.

'They're fine,' he said. 'We should enjoy ourselves. Let's go for a little stroll.'

Her face almost broke into a smile. Around the room they walked, Betty staring at his face. They stood by the window, looking out onto the lawn. Then they went over to where Fred and Alf were sitting before Betty went off on her own. Lynn and I went over.

'Betty wasn't this ill when she first arrived,' said Lynn apologetically but Nik waved his hand. 'She showed me family photos once. Jim was very tall, like you. Perhaps that has triggered something.'

'Has her husband been gone long?' he asked.

'Six years. He looked after her the best he could at home, but had a stroke and couldn't manage. That's when she came here. It worked well as they were locals and he visited as often as he could. The book shop on the corner of the high street, just before you turn left for Springhaye Forest – that used to be the video store he ran. Their children have moved away but they see her as regularly as they can. Lily travels abroad a lot, with work, and Roger has a son with special needs so it's not straightforward – but both of them also video call her once a week. We help with that.' Lynn smiled. 'You know, right up until she got ill, Betty ran a blog, reviewing the latest films and videos. She first set it up just before her husband retired and over time modernised it, reviewing DVDs and television shows online. She and Jim were huge fans of the big and small screen.' She patted Nik's arm. 'You visiting, the party… maybe it's a good thing for her.'

'This meeting has been such a tonic,' said Fred. 'Downright depressing it's been, ploughing through the directory that you emailed us, Lynn, with my daughter. It's impossible to tell from the list which homes might be most suitable.'

Alf nodded. 'A blasted pain, it is. My son's been ringing them one by one to find out if there's a waiting list or if the rooms have an ensuite bathroom and what the other facilities are.' He shrugged at Lynn. 'Not that it's your fault. You've been a real brick. We'll just have to muddle through.'

'Gran and I have found the same,' I said, glad that most of the residents had family to help. It felt like a mammoth task. I really hoped we found somewhere she liked and the council agreed to fund her preferred choice.

'That photo of yours was a great idea, Nik,' I said when we were alone, a few minutes later. 'It will be a fantastic way for the residents to remember all their friends.' I sighed.

'It's so sad. No one should have their home broken up like this at their age.'

Nik put his arm around my shoulder. Alf and Oliver were standing apart, but both studying us. Alf's head was tilted, his brow wrinkled. Oliver turned away as soon as I made eye contact.

12

I looked at the Peter Rabbit clock. Half past eleven. The shop phone rang and as he was by the till Seb picked it up.

'Angela,' he mouthed and I hurried over. Seb passed me the receiver and I moved to one side as he served a customer.

'Hello,' I said.

'Jess. Glad I caught you. I'm hoping you wouldn't mind working through your lunch today.'

'Oh. Actually, I've arranged to meet a friend.'

'Can you cancel?'

'It's a little difficult as my friend is coming all the way from London especially.'

She sighed. 'I see, fair enough. It's just I passed the shop early this morning. I actually went on my speed-walk for once. The new window display…'

'Do you like it?' I asked eagerly. 'Seb and I worked late last night to finish it.'

She paused. 'I'm sorry, Jess. It still needs a bit of work. It's too much like one we made last year. The key to good business is continuing to innovate. Some customers will visit the shop year in, year out, throughout their kids' childhoods.

They won't be pulled into the shop by something that seems over-familiar.'

'Right…'

'It's okay to make mistakes, you're still learning but… be a little bolder. You could… I don't know… do a food one with those plastic Christmas grocery kits and perhaps order in some gingerbread men stickers for the front window, or…'

My self-confidence dwindled as she continued brainstorming.

'If I'm to expand the business I need you to not be afraid of taking initiative. That's what makes a good manager. You need to put your own stamp on the place, Jess. Be brave.'

I nodded down the phone. She must have sensed it.

'Right. Well I'll leave you to it and drop in, in a couple of days to see what you've come up with. Enjoy your lunch but, what with the festive season upon us, it might be useful if you didn't make any more formal arrangements during working hours that can't be changed at the last minute. You know I'm all for being flexible with staff's hours, but we just need to be careful until we're through the January sales.'

I put down the receiver and rubbed my forehead, excited by the challenge but not wanting to disappoint again. I smiled as a leopard-print buggy was wheeled in. After receiving a nod of approval from the mother who wore a stylish pair of sunglasses, I offered the toddler a chocolate lollipop in the shape of a reindeer. One of the toy suppliers had given us a jarful as a freebie for stocking their light-up plastic reindeer. Following a prompt from mum the boy said 'Fank koo'. I put the jar back on the glass counter, by the till, and then crouched down and took off the purple and green foil wrapper. Chubby fingers grabbed the white stick and pushed the chocolate between grinning lips. He told me his name was Ben. I always asked the children what they were called. It gave the shop a personal touch. Ben and I were clearly kindred spirits when it came to anything made with cocoa.

I stood up and stared around the store, as sunrays poured in. We'd been blessed with another gorgeous winter's day, with frost twinkling on the pavement early this morning.

'Seb, could you refresh the pocket money counter this afternoon?' I asked. 'The last of those leftover Halloween stationery items aren't going to sell now. It's time to swap them to fit with the rest of the Christmas stock.' Now that the euphoria of deciding that Willow Court's party would go ahead had subsided I needed to be mindful of how I'd juggle organising that, along the extra hours that would be needed to keep Under the Tree ship-shape at this busy time.

'I'll get onto it straight after lunch. Fancy eating together? Angela must have called in really early this morning and dropped off doughnuts. She left a note saying she'd provide a weekly Friday sugar hit during the coming demanding weeks.'

'Much as I'd love to see you stuff your face with the sugar you swore off on Monday...'

'It's been a stressful week,' he said airily. Then his face became serious for a moment. 'Although in comparison to your gran... how is Alice doing? Any luck with finding her a new pad?'

'We're just sifting through all the possibilities. The warden, Lynn, is asking around and reckons personal recommendations are best. The local mobile hairdresser goes into all the homes. Lynn is going to ask her opinion. She'll have a bird's eye view of the things that really matter like how caring staff are and the employee turnover in each place, plus how much one-to-one attention residents are given and whether they are truly treated like individuals. We'll get there,' I said, hoping by telling myself that it would come true.

'If there's anything I can do...'

'Just keep me laughing in your own inimitable way.' I smiled. 'We'll have to share a sugar hit another day.'

'Well, it won't stop me gorging. I'll pump it off at the gym and am going super healthy next week, for sure. Tim and I have just bought a juicer and I've joined a new exercise class.'

'What's your latest obsession?' Seb followed all the new fitness trends. Last year was cycling karaoke and laughter yoga. This year, so far, he'd taken twerk classes and—

'Bondage zumba,' he said, with a straight face. 'The strips of theraband are really good for working pecs and glutes.'

'Sounds like something out of a Jackie Collins story.' Seb was a massive fan and had shed tears when she'd passed away, before embarking on a marathon re-read of every one of her thirty-two novels.

'Go on... just one wee doughnut won't harm...'

'Sorry, I've got a date. I mean, a meeting with a friend,' I added hastily.

Seb led me into the reading corner. Its busiest time was early morning, after the school run when parents with toddlers came in. Then it would fill up again after three, if older children wanted to relax with books and spend their pocket money in the shop – especially on their pay day, Friday.

'No one says *date* as a slip of the tongue – especially if their usually bare work face is sporting mascara and lip gloss and you are wearing your industrial-strength musky perfume that you save for nights out.'

'It's just lunch,' I protested.

'Then clearly you want more.'

'You don't know what you're talking about.'

'How long have you known him?'

'Who?'

Seb folded his arms.

'Around two weeks,' I said casually.

'Ah. I should have known. You're talking about the very lovely Nik. And what does Oliver think to him?'

'If you must know he's kind of suspicious.'

Seb frowned. 'Why?'

'I'm not really sure. Modern times have made us cynical, I guess. But you've met him – Nik is such a refreshing kind of person and as far as I'm concerned, what you see is what you get.'

'Your trusted flatmate's doubts haven't changed your mind? Interesting. Must be serious.'

I snorted. 'Nik said he had exciting news to share that couldn't wait until tomorrow when we had the matinee screening of *It's a Wonderful Life* at Willow Court – he's being such a help with the party. I offered to meet him in London tonight, instead, but a neighbour he's got to know, Rob, had already suggested a trip to the pub. This meeting is about Gran and the other residents – that's all.'

'Julia Roberts once got married after three weeks,' he

continued. 'Okay. Here is the acid test of whether you fancy him or not.'

'Seb, this is a waste of time. I'm not some teenager who develops romantic feelings overnight.'

'There's nothing juvenile about love at sight,' he said firmly. 'I knew the second I met Tim he was the man for me. Okay… let's be logical about this and see how many details about him you've soaked up in just fourteen days. Answer these five questions…' He rubbed a hand over his chin stubble. 'Number one – the most important… is he married?'

'No.' I recalled Nik's words about only having himself to look after himself.

'Two – what's his favourite colour?'

'Um, red,' I said and shuffled from foot to foot.

'You already know that?'

'Well, he always wears—'

'Obviously I need to dig deeper. Okay, number three – what… what is his secret dream?'

'Are you serious?' I threw both hands in the air.

He stared at my arms. 'You've already discussed this with him?'

'Of course not! Well, maybe… look, it just kind of came up… he runs this local charitable Christmas shoe box scheme for children and he'd love to expand it to at least help all children in Sydney.'

Seb shook his head. 'I don't think I knew about Tim wanting to write a novel until we'd been dating for six months… okay… number four – and it's really important that you answer this one without hesitation. What was the first thing you thought about this morning, when your alarm went off?'

My mind flashed back. The sun hadn't yet risen. All I could hear was Buddy's snuffly breathing and then... 'Sudden, cheerful birdsong,' I said. 'It reminded me of Nik shooting happiness into dark moments. I mean... not really... it's just...' I gave a nervous laugh and swallowed.

'Jessie Jagger. I've never seen you like this. Not that I need to ask any more questions, but just to be sure... Number five – choose one sentence to describe how being near him makes you feel.'

I stared at the ground as certain words came into my head.

Gently, he lifted my chin. 'It's only me.'

'But it sounds stupid. He only walked into my life a couple of weeks ago. I can't have feelings for him. Not proper ones.'

'Why not? Hormones don't run by stopwatch. Love doesn't schedule itself alongside a calendar. Cupid's dart can hit you at any time. It doesn't mean you're immature or have lost your senses. It means you've been lucky enough to be swept up by a bit of magic and that's what life is all about.'

'Is that a line from a song?' I mumbled.

Seb smiled. 'No. For once I'm speaking from the heart.'

I took a deep breath and whispered, 'When he's close it's as if I've been showered with pixie dust.'

13

'What did your colleague mean by *I'm quite a fan of pixies myself?*' asked Nik as we sat down at a table by the window in The Silver Swan. He put down two cokes. 'He gave me an intense look when he said it.'

I laughed brightly. 'Oh, that's just Seb, he… he often stares through people when he's thinking about work. We'd just been discussing some… some new merchandise based on fairytales.' And fairytale nonsense it was. I knew Seb meant well, encouraging to me to spout spontaneous random thoughts from my head, but perfect Prince Charmings didn't really exist, let alone ones that swept shop workers off their feet. 'Anyway… don't keep me hanging… what's this news that couldn't wait?'

If looks could kill, Seb would have been dead on the spot. I was already regretting mentioning pixie dust. As soon as I'd said that he'd taken out his phone and Googled for a few minutes.

'Right,' he'd said. 'Practicalities first and you need to act fast. There is a cut-off age of thirty for getting a working holiday visa for Australia. If you get one of those, you can work there for twelve months. I'm sure, after all these years of dedicated service Angela would keep your position open, but if things went to plan—'

'Stop. This is madness.'

'Why? There is nothing rational about true love.'

But being rational was a good thing, I'd learnt that at a young age. When Mum went to prison I understood I had to live with Gran. It hurt but I'd tried looking after myself, the times Mum was out with a boyfriend, and it didn't always turn out well. Like when I accidentally left the gas hob on. The kitchen smelt funny. Mum shouted a lot when she got back. I knew it made sense to move in with someone else even though I wanted to stay with her.

Nik lived on the other side of the world. My gran, my life, both were here on a much smaller island. I had a great friend in Oliver, and Buddy. A lovely boss.

Any suggestion of a romance was nonsense.

And yet as Nik smiled and his eyes crinkled in such an appealing manner, it felt as if it were midsummer and not winter outside.

'I emailed the editor of the *Amblemarsh Gazette* on Wednesday, attaching the photo I took and, as we discussed, I asked if he'd consider running a piece on us. He didn't see it until yesterday afternoon and rang me immediately. What a great bloke. His dad is in a care home and he knows how distressing it was for everyone there when it was under threat of closure. He said community stories go down especially well at this time of year so he was completely on board. At the bottom of the piece he'd print your email address for people to contact you with offers of help – I didn't think you'd mind…?'

'Nik, this is fantastic.'

'His dad's favourite movie is also *It's a Wonderful Life* and alongside the piece on us he's offered to run a giveaway of the DVD and a Christmas cookie hamper. To enter, people have to email the newspaper with an idea of how we could make this party the best one ever and he'll pass those onto you.'

'That's brilliant. The more brainstorming the better.'

'But here's the thing…' He looked at this watch. 'We've got one hour to come up with around two hundred words copy. He needs it today if the coverage is going in next Friday's issue. As it's late notice we've got to send him the basics so he can quickly tweak it.'

I didn't reply.

He frowned. 'Have I overstepped the mark? I didn't mean to take over.'

'No… no, not at all. You're… you're so brilliant. Why would you do any of this?'

'I like you,' he said, in his transparent, honest way. 'I like Alice and her friends are great. A better question might be why *wouldn't* I?'

It meant so much to be sitting face to face with a man I could trust. A lump rose in my throat. How I'd struggled with dating during my twenties. I'd got close to guys and even went out with one – Connor – for a whole year. However my relationships always ended in the same way… I couldn't fully commit. Not emotionally. When Connor arranged to spend the bank holiday weekend camping with mates, and didn't tell me until the week before because he'd been busy at work and forgotten, I ended it. I couldn't go back to that childhood feeling that I didn't matter; that fear that I'd grow up like Mum, letting men treat me badly.

However, getting close to considerate Seb had given me hope and then thoughtful Oliver had confirmed for me that some men were honourable. It sounded like such an old word but the concept was new to me. When he moved in I hadn't expected to feel so valued.

Nik pressed the top of his biro. 'Let's get cracking before our ploughman's lunches arrive.' He grinned. 'It sounds like such a manly dish. Alf will approve of me eating it.'

My phone vibrated for the second time in the back pocket of my jeans but I ignored it. This hour was too precious. Nik started writing as I dictated. He gave me his full attention when I talked about what we should include, nodding, tilting his head, asking me to explain further, expressing approval. I felt like I was the cleverest writer in the world and my confidence grew as he wrote down every sentence.

Is that what true love felt like?

I pushed away the thought.

Nik went back and suggested edits, before writing the last couple of lines and passing them over for me to read. Our lunches arrived promptly and made me realise how hungry I was as I gazed at the plump plum tomatoes, the crusty white bread, perfectly round pickled onions and unapologetic slab of cheddar cheese. Lettuce, a dollop of pickle and a mound of crisps completed the feast. I started eating straightaway. We were halfway through my lunch hour. When I'd finished I grabbed the notebook and made some final adjustments.

'Your surname is Talvi, isn't it? I'll mention your name in full.'

He nodded.

I checked through my writing one last time and then pushed it over to Nik so he could read the final version.

A Midwinter Night's Dream

After months of rumours about financial problems, Willow Court Assisted Living, in Springhaye, has finally announced its closure in the middle of December. The new owners, Amblemarsh Property Development, plan to turn it into a thirty-bedroom hotel. Shocked residents were given just six weeks' notice and gave up on their dream of holding one last Christmas party. However, visiting toy manufacturer Nik Talvi, from Sydney, told them about Australia's early Christmas in July celebrations and suggested they simply move the party forwards. So delighted residents will now host their party on the night of Sunday 6th December. It will provide them with an opportunity to say a proper goodbye. This year's party theme is the much-loved movie, It's a Wonderful Life.

But they can't do it alone! With just three weeks remaining from today's press, this is a call for donations for the buffet, for hands to help make decorations and voices to sing carols... anything that brings this American-themed celebration to fruition at a stressful time when the residents also have to find a new place to live.

Let's help them make this a party to remember!

Please message Jess, on the email below, with your ideas.

'Something's missing...' He crunched a pickled onion and swallowed. 'I know. Why not ring Alice? – Ask her how much this party means. A personal quote will make the piece resonate more with the community.'

I rang her straightaway. Luckily for us she was running late for lunch and hadn't gone downstairs yet. I scribbled notes as she spoke and after I'd hung up, re-read what I'd written.

'Okay. What about this? *Seventy-eight-year-old Alice Jagger says, "We're a right mix of sorts, here in Willow Court, but we feel like one big family. The move's going to be tough. We may have been ill whilst living here and some dear friends have passed, but we've still had wonderful times. This bash will celebrate that."'*

Nik pushed away his plate. 'It's a belter. Like you. It's awesome the way you look after your gran.'

For a few seconds I felt as tall as him. 'She looked after me growing up. It's only right that I return the favour now. Mum... had problems, you see, and my dad was never around.'

Nik nodded.

'She had me young and hardly knew my dad. When he found out she was pregnant he panicked and ran. Apparently he came back, but Mum was with someone else then and told him to get lost. He sent money for a while but we moved house and it stopped.'

'Jeez ... that must have been hard on you, growing up.'

At least Mum never badmouthed Dad, not even when she went on one of her rants about men. Gran had met him once. Said he seemed immature but not a bad lad. Mum simply shut him out. I didn't know why. That was one of the hardest things about her not wanting a relationship with me now – the lack of answers about my father and about why she found life so difficult.

'I consider myself lucky, having my gran; it could have been so much worse,' I said, as my phone vibrated again. 'She acted as two parents. She certainly vetted my boyfriends as passionately as any father would have. She even grilled Buddy when they first met!'

'Grams was like that,' he said. 'Mum and Dad were more laidback but she'd badger me to meet every new girlfriend and bring them to hers for coffee – even in my early twenties, before she got really ill.' He smiled. 'She always said there was no rush to get married but I'm not sure she'd approve of me still being single at thirty-four. If only she were still here, I could tease her that it's all her fault for scaring off any decent prospects. I could always tell how much she liked someone depending on whether she offered them a second slice of cake. But Buddy... that reminds me... I love markets and after a bit of research visited the Brick Lane one.'

'In the East End?' I said. 'Near Aldgate East tube station?'

'Yep. Cool place! I'd read about some alternative toy stalls there and it didn't disappoint. I found one that sold nothing but eco-friendly toys. Junior Magic hasn't gone down that path yet and it's really made me think – apart from... I don't know... a kind of moral duty my family and I are starting to feel, environmentally aware products could really pep up the business. This stall sold cards and jigsaws made out of recycled cardboard and plastic toys made out of recycled water bottles. Also themed games to do with cleaning up beaches or building conservation areas for jungle animals...'

'That's so interesting. We stock drawing books made from recycled paper but that's about it. I'll mention this to Angela. But what has this got to do with Buddy?'

'It also sold craft packs. I bought one to look at the quality for the price.' He pulled something out of his pocket. 'It's a charm friendship bracelet. The pack contained a choice of five different coloured bands made from woven embroidery threads and lots of little charms that you sew in, made from recycled plastic. So, I chose a...'

'Lotus flower, a book, a dog and a heart,' I said.

He slipped it onto my wrist. As his fingers brushed against the surface of my skin it tingled. 'This bracelet is about you – the lotus flower – you told me you're into Buddhism, right? And the book represents—'

'Gran?'

He nodded. 'The dog is Buddy, of course...'

I hardly dared ask. 'The heart?'

He gazed at me with those piercing blue eyes. 'Maybe you've got a secret admirer.'

I felt as light as if I were filled with helium and might float away if someone didn't pull me back to earth.

As if the universe was answering my imagination, a figure loomed at our table. Oliver? What was he doing here? It was almost two o'clock. He should have just been arriving at work.

'Jess,' he said, trying to catch his breath. 'Seb and I have been trying to ring you. It's Alice.'

14

Oliver's car was waiting outside. He dismissed any suggestion that he go back to the bar – said he'd cleared his absence with Misty. Nik stayed behind to pay the bill and type up the copy we'd been working on, before emailing it to the editor.

'Tell me again what happened,' I asked, voice shaking. All I could picture was Gran covered in bruises.

'Lynn tried to ring you and then the shop. Seb called me when you didn't reply to him either. Alice was drinking coffee in the lounge. She got up to take a photo of Pan with her phone, to send to her sons, who've been more worried about her than usual. She muttered something about everything going black, before fainting.'

'Is the doctor on his way?'

'No, Lynn called an ambulance. Even though Alice collapsed backwards and the chair broke her fall, she still hit the floor with a thump and when she came around complained of a sore back. Wait, I've just felt a text come through.' He rummaged in his duffle coat's pocket and passed me his phone.

'The ambulance is already there. Lynn says to meet them at them at Amblemarsh General. You need to turn around.'

My throat caught. 'Hospital... that means it must be bad, right? What if...?'

Oliver glanced sideways at me, indicated and turned off the main road. He parked up, in an avenue under a horse chestnut tree and undid his seatbelt, and mine too.

One of the tree's large leaves tumbled down past the front windshield. Gran was great at planning outings and used to take me conkering. What a thrill every time I opened one of the prickly casings. She was on a budget but always fitted in a yearly week's holiday in Margate, and trips to the cinema would cost less because we'd smuggle in our own drinks and snacks.

'Why have we stopped? We need to get going.'

Oliver pulled me towards him and placed his hands on my shoulders. 'It's going to be all right, Alice is made of tough stuff – and so are you. Because of her age, the paramedics probably just want the doctors to check her over. Let's just sit here for five minutes, you've had a shock – we both have.'

'I... need to hold everything together for Gran. I don't know what I'd have done without her all this time.'

'You'd have managed, somehow,' he said and took his hands away.

I studied his serious face. 'Did you love your nanny? Like you loved your parents?'

'I used to ask myself that as a child,' he said and grasped the steering wheel. 'God knows I saw her much more than them. Weekends as well.'

'Did she ever say anything about the way they were?'

'Just that they were working so hard and travelling with their jobs to give me a great upbringing. It didn't feel like that. When you're a kid you don't appreciate any benefits of private schooling, you just want mates and as little homework as possible. But you see – like everyone else – Nanny was in awe. Not everyone's boss worked for the Foreign Office. It was as if she felt their status rubbed off onto her. I never felt like that. Their time mattered more to me than money. I wanted an everyday family life with a dog and messy cooking, with walks jumping in puddles and bedtimes stories with hugs.' He gave a wry smile. 'I guess some might say I was ungrateful, but the new toys, the latest top-of-the-range gadgets, honestly, they didn't mean much.'

I was always surprised by our common ground, despite us growing up at opposite ends of the wealth spectrum. He switched on the engine and we fastened our seatbelts. Oliver turned back onto the main road. I thought about the bracelet Nik had made and I wondered what sort of charm could represent my flatmate. A cocktail would be the obvious one – if the craft kit were for adults. Or a car – he loved tinkling with the engine. I looked at his strong hands gripping the steering wheel, dependable, just like him. A rock – that's would be the perfect charm because Oliver was always there.

Like the time I lost my purse and couldn't get home from London. I'd gone shopping to buy an outfit for a friend's wedding. I only had a little charge left on my phone and wouldn't have enough battery to sort out things using my banking apps. For some reason Oliver was the person I felt like ringing. I'd missed the last train and was stranded at King's Cross, in the dark, about to be turfed out by the station guard.

He rang through to book and pay for a room at a

nearby Travelodge. The hotel was great and let me use their telephone to contact my bank's helpline and get my cards cancelled. They looked up the number for me, online. I was due into work the next day so Oliver came in early on the train, met me for breakfast and then bought me a train ticket home. We travelled back to Amblemarsh for nine. Gran and I told him how amazing he was. He'd shrugged it off and said that's what friends were for.

Oliver was one of those people who was hard to get to know, but once you broke down the barriers his loyalty knew no bounds. Me, Misty, Gran… and of course Buddy – it was as if, since moving to London, he'd created a new family of his own.

I felt a little shaky as we approached Amblemarsh General. I told Oliver to drop me off – that I'd get a taxi back, but he rolled his eyes and parked up. We hurried to the A&E reception and I gave Gran's name. A nurse took us through to what she called the Clinical Decisions Area and we were taken to one of the bays, the curtain pulled halfway around it. I rushed forwards. She looked so small, propped up on huge white pillows, hair ruffled. I gave her a hug.

'What are you doing here?' she scolded. 'There's no need. It's all a fuss over nothing. I want to go home.'

Lynn moved to the end of the bed. Oliver sat down by Gran and held her hand.

'Thanks so much for staying with Gran,' I said in a low voice. 'What have the doctors decided?'

'The doctor – a nice man, he really took his time – reckons the stress of the move might be taking its toll,' said Lynn. 'And that's perfectly understandable. Just before she fell—'

'I got an email on my phone,' interrupted Gran. 'And you can stop talking about me as if I'm not here.' Her cheeks were pale.

'A shock makes the blood pressure drop. That slows the pulse,' explained Lynn. 'The result is less blood – and oxygen – to the brain and that makes you faint. The nurse did an ECG and we're just waiting for the doctor's verdict. But I'm sure the test will come back normal, and he'll say that, coupled with the fact she's never fainted before, it's almost certain that an underlying condition isn't responsible. However, her back's hurting.'

Gran shuffled on the bed and winced. 'I'm having an X-ray in a minute.'

She could have fractured something.

'Who was the email from?' I asked.

'Social Services. My assessment for the move is Tuesday.'

'Try not to worry,' said Lynn gently. 'The council is duty-bound to offer you somewhere else to live and Jess is helping you try to find one that's just perfect.'

Her voice wavered. 'That email… it all seems more real now. What if I end up somewhere away from you, Oliver and Buddy, Jess? What if none of my friends move to the same place? I… I don't feel like I've got the energy to start over. And…' She stopped.

'What?' I asked.

She fiddled with a button on her cardigan. 'Nothing. I'm being silly.'

'Join the club, then,' said Oliver. 'I spent a good ten minutes asking Buddy what he thought was causing the bathroom fan to rattle, this morning, and then it dawned on me that he couldn't help.'

She managed a small smile. 'I buy the newspapers... The staff at Willow Court are the bee's knees, they treat us with kindness and nothing is too much trouble. But occasionally you read about horror stories of places where residents are abused and online I've watched the secretly filmed videos. I may have no choice if everywhere is full and I don't want to see out my days being...' She gulped. 'Being treated like a nuisance – or even worse, like a child.'

Her eyes filled and not for the first time anger swept through me about the speed with which this closure was happening.

'That will *never* be the case, Gran, and you know those cases are very few and far between. Newspapers just love to blow up a shocking story.'

'Several of my colleagues have relatives in care homes and they can't speak highly enough of the attentive staff; they say they are real heroes – just like the ones where you live,' said Oliver and I shot him a look of appreciation.

'I know. They are true stars – and you're both so good to me. I don't like to make a fuss. But I love my view of the canal. My room's so cosy...' Her voice broke. 'I'm trying to put on a brave face, but the truth is... I'm scared. Scared I've got no control over this decision. Scared of having to rely on people who... who might not be quite as understanding as the staff at Willow Court. And of being alone – Willow Court runs lots of lovely activities. We have a laugh. What if I'm left in my room a lot? My arthritis is only getting worse. I'm going to lose the little independence I've got left as I lose my mobility.' Her chest heaved and she put a hand over her beaded necklace. 'That list of directories... it doesn't tell us the things that matter, like what the food is like and do the staff know how to have fun.'

Oliver stood up and let me have his seat. Firmly, I took Gran's fingers. 'Now, you listen to me, you're not moving anywhere until we give it a thorough once-over. Together we'll visit and talk to the staff and the residents. You aren't going to be made to live anywhere you don't want to.'

'Jess and me both have cars – wherever you go, nothing will stop us visiting as much as we do now,' said Oliver. 'It won't make a difference.'

'What if they don't let Buddy in?' she croaked. A tear ran down her cheek. 'Some men turned up with a van today. They took the paintings out of the lounge. Betty got really upset and called them thieves. She didn't understand. Then they came back in and tried to take—'

'Don't upset yourself, Alice. I gave head office short shrift when I rang them, believe me,' cut in Lynn, face flushing red. 'I've made it quite clear any removals will have to wait until the last resident has moved out.'

Gran wiped her face. 'It's as if our home is being dismantled before our very eyes.'

'I've always got my ear to the ground about other facilities,' said Lynn. 'I won't let a single person move anywhere that I've heard a bad word about. If it's any comfort, I've rarely heard a negative word about any of the care homes in this area. For a lot of the people who work in the care sector it's a real vocation. And I'm talking to the mobile hairdresser I mentioned tomorrow.'

Gran sniffed. 'It makes you think how upsetting all of this must be for someone on their own, like Glenda and perhaps... perhaps she was right about the party being too much.'

★

Oliver fetched us chocolate from a vending machine before driving himself and Lynn back to work. The X-ray was done and the doctor eventually came back with all the test results. As Lynn suspected, the ECG was normal. So was the X-ray but Gran had slightly bruised her tailbone and it would take a month or so for the pain to completely go. Plus her blood pressure was sky-high so the doctor decided he wanted to keep her in for observation.

I went to bed early, before Oliver got back from Misty's – after I'd paced around the room for almost half an hour, up and down, over to the window then back to the bed. Seeing Gran like that, vulnerable and afraid, the future a vast unknown, reminded me how I'd felt when the police turned up to arrest Mum, saying something about dealing, me wondering if I'd go to jail too. Gran had got me through that unsettled period. Now it was my turn to get her through this – and do everything I could to make the last Christmas party the best ever was a good starting point. That's if it went ahead. Maybe Gran would think it was too much work for her to help organise now.

But if that were the case, I'd take over her role. Angela was putting the pressure on at work and we had to find Gran a new home but somehow I'd fit it all in. The Christmas party was more important than ever now.

15

Silence fell in the lounge at Willow Court as I stopped the DVD and switched off the television. In the corridor Betty walked past, muttering to herself. Nik came up to the front and stood by me.

'What a movie,' he said.

Nik, Oliver and I had turned all the chairs to face the hatch and set the television up on its shelf. Sleet started to fall outside, just as the opening credits rolled. We'd dimmed the lights. Even Glenda stopped moaning about her indigestion. It didn't seem right watching it without Gran. I dropped into the hospital to see her at lunchtime and the doctor didn't want to release her yet, not until her blood pressure evened out and her back was less painful. Gran insisted we watch the film without her; told me not to visit, that she just wanted to rest. She'd seen *It's a Wonderful Life* a million times before so wouldn't be missing out and as for the party... Gran just didn't sound bothered.

Oliver had brought a range of gourmet popcorn from Misty's, the promised apple pie flavour, along with a new one supposed to taste of mince pies and a savoury option that tasted just like a Christmas turkey dinner – Buddy did his valiant best to try to snaffle a portion. Nik had brought a bottle of sherry. We'd hurriedly come in, shutting the reception door behind us, wanting to shield the residents from the fact that despite Lynn's indignant call to head office, the pretty wooden benches from out the front had already been taken.

'What was everyone's favourite scene?' asked Pan. 'I love the one where George and Mary are children and she whispers into his deaf ear that she'll love him until she dies.'

'For me it's when the dance floor opens up into a swimming pool and George and Mary carry on doing the Charleston in the water and then everyone else jumps in,' said Alf. 'It reminds me of a dance I went to, back in the Forties. I snuck out in Dad's smart shoes that were a size too big for me. I came out of them whilst me and my Maisie were doing the Jitterbug.' His eyes shone. 'But I carried on. She'd thought that was the funniest thing and always said that was the moment she decided I'd be the man she'd marry.' He got lost in thought for a moment. 'As the cancer finally started to take her, I'd hum our favourite old tunes. I hope she found that comforting.'

A collective pause was taken by everyone as they shot him sympathetic glances.

'I love when George is with his daughter Zuzu and she's won a flower,' said Nancy, stroking Buddy's head. 'When the dead petals fall off and he pretends to make the flower as good as new.'

'It's the ending for me,' said Glenda crisply. 'Everyone singing "Auld Lang Syne" and the community rallying around to help George with his money problems. I do like a film where all the ends are tied up neatly.'

'And the bell rings to let us know that the angel Clarence has got his wings,' said Pan.

'Just to let you know, Nik's been brilliant and the photo he took on Tuesday has been accepted by the *Amblemarsh Gazette*, along with a few words,' I said. 'They'll be running the piece about Willow Court this coming Friday the 20th.'

'Good work,' said Fred, his usual unlit cigarette hanging from his mouth.

'Before her fall Gran talked about making dough decorations painted white. She'd make them when working as a nursery assistant.' When I got old enough to get myself to school she took on an early morning cleaning job as well, plus she stuffed envelopes at home and delivered leaflets. I got my newspaper round as soon as I was old enough.

'Flour, salt and warm water is all you need,' I continued. 'Then you knead the dough and roll it out ready for cutting. We could poke a straw through the top of each shape and then they go in the oven for one hour. These could provide themed tree decorations – angels and bells sprayed different glittery colours would suit.'

'Not that angels actually exist,' said Glenda with a sideways glance at Pan. 'I always found the film preposterous from that point of view.'

'Who knows?' piped up Alf. 'What with the American government hiding aliens in Area 51 there could be a secret angel bunker in Whitehall. Lots of people believe a falling white feather is from their guardian angel.'

Fred shook his head. 'Aliens and angels, for real? What a load of bunkum.'

'We could spray pine cones white as well,' said Lynn hastily. She'd just walked into the room. 'I always think of

It's a Wonderful Life as the snowiest film I know. I could take a group of you walking into Springhaye Forest. We could collect twigs and holly and spray those as well, to build on the idea of a wintry scene.'

Everyone talked amongst themselves about ideas for the American-themed buffet and the music that could be played. Nik went to pick up popcorn that had been dropped but Oliver rushed to beat him to it. Then Nik and I mingled whereas Alf and Oliver went to a table by the back window and chatted together in low voices.

'Just one idea I had, before I have to go,' said Nik, moving to the hatch again.

'Won't you be joining us for tea?' asked Glenda who looked at Lynn.

'You're more than welcome,' said Lynn.

'No. I have a date,' he said.

Whilst everyone made teasing noises my heart lurched.

'With my bed,' he said. 'A neighbour took me on a pub crawl last night. I agreed to spurn my sherry for once and try various different types of English beer. I think the last pint of Guinness was drunk around three o'clock this morning...'

'That's more like it, lad,' said Alf.

Nik yawned. 'Chatting now about memories of family and mates... watching the film in black and white... it's got me thinking – I thought guests might enjoy seeing a collection of your old photos. I'm sure all of you have got old shots passed down to you from parents. Photos from the Forties and Fifties would be brilliant, showing people you loved, shots of family life and yourselves when younger. We could make a collage using Blu Tack, or simply spread them out on a table. It would really bring to life the era of the theme of the party.'

'I've got photos,' said Pan. 'Oh, the fashions back then – woolly tank tops and tailored suits for the men... knee-high, tight-waisted dresses for women. And the hats, the updos and pin curls... I've got a shot of my mum, looking ever so glam. She was a whizz with a needle. In fact, she still looks great now. Maybe I'll invite her to the party.'

A couple of the residents exchanged glances.

'She sounds like a talented woman,' said Nik easily and he beamed. 'I'm very much looking forward to meeting people's relatives. You have your sons and grandchildren to invite as well, don't you, Pan?'

'My sons... yes, yes, they must come first of course – they've been so good to me lately.'

'I've still got some of my parents... Dad in his favourite felt fedora hat and high-waisted trousers,' said Nancy.

'I've got some old snaps too,' said Fred. 'Reckon that's one reason I went into the fire service, not that I can see them clearly now – damn glaucoma. Dad was a dispatch rider, Mum a nurse. My gran often looked after me and my brother. It made a big impression on me as a kid, seeing them go off in uniform, and then looking at the photos as I got older.'

A warm glow of nostalgia spread across the lounge as if happy times from the past were giving the residents a hug. They recalled their childhoods and the cherished photos they had, stashed away, like those of babies in voluminous white Christening gowns, of beach shots with women in modest swimming costumes that looked like short dresses... of

Austin cars and street parties... of relatives dressed in their Sunday best.

Not for the first time Nik had brought the place alive and I couldn't help but stare at him.

Neither could Oliver and Alf.

Glenda had been unusually quiet. Nik seemed to pick up on that as he turned to her.

'Have *you* got any old photos?' he asked.

Glenda shrugged. 'I have some lovely shots from the farm I grew up on – my stepfather owned it. I can say lovely now. At the time it was a tough, physically demanding life and that's why I was determined to move to the city when I got older, and work in an office. But I suppose I could rustle up some photos I'm sure any visiting children would enjoy looking at, of our animals, if we're really going ahead with this party.' Her brow softened. 'I think I've got one of my favourite cow that I used to milk, Nettie. She used to love a belly rub and scratch behind the ears. She'd always welcome me with a loud moo.'

'Great,' said Nik and he went over to her and crouched down. Her face flushed bright pink. It amused me a little – Glenda was usually so no-nonsense... yet at the same time I felt pleased for her. She'd never had a boyfriend or companion as long as I'd known her, nor ever been married, nor spoken about a previous partner.

'It's obvious to me,' said Nik, 'that with your organisational skills you're the perfect person to bring this idea to fruition.'

'Me?' Glenda's mouth fell open. 'I've not got time, what with moving... and this party... as far as I'm concerned—'

'For someone with your administrative experience it

would take up no time at all.' He placed a hand on hers. 'It's obvious from the smart way you dress that you've got a flair for presentation and an eye for detail.'

She gave a nervous laugh. *Glenda* unsure of herself? She looked away and picked an imaginary piece of fluff off her turtleneck jumper. 'Well, if you really think...'

He squeezed her hand and stood up.

'Everyone, get those photos ready, and over the next couple of weeks Glenda will come knocking on your doors to take a look and pick the ones she thinks are most suitable.'

Glenda sat up with a jolt, as if she'd just come out from being under a spell. 'Now wait a minute, I didn't agree to—'

He gave her a thumbs-up. 'You're a real sport for offering, Glenda.'

'Here's to Nik – for saving our party,' said Pan. 'I don't know about everyone else, but I feel excited about it now and that's a much-needed chink of light in what has felt like a dark time.' She tentatively started singing 'For He's a Jolly Good Fellow' as if she felt she might be doing something wrong. Buddy barked and her expression eased as Nik gave her a wink and everyone else joined in – apart from Oliver and Alf.

'Thanks heaps,' he said when they'd finished. 'Although we've still got a lot of work ahead of us, to pull this off. Don't sing my praises too soon! And none of this would be happening without Jess, Alice and Lynn, they're the people you should really be thanking.'

'This party means a lot to you, lad, doesn't it?' said Alf. 'Why? We're just a bunch of old codgers – why should you give up your time?'

Everyone looked at Nik – Oliver, intensely so.

The skin around his eyes developed red blotches. 'This is a business trip but also, last week it was the ten-year anniversary of my grandmother's death,' he said in a faltering voice. 'I miss her advice and laughter... and the way she'd always be on my side, even when I got into trouble.'

The residents nodded.

'Ten years on... I don't know... the business has been floundering, and whilst she was my cheerleader, she always told me if she thought I needed to buck up my ideas. Our toy company badly needs to become more dynamic and relevant and this trip is partly because of her. It's what she would have suggested I do.'

'She sounds like my Maisie,' said Alf.

Nik's voice sounded strained. 'I loved her very much.'

My throat ached at his openness, at the raw emotion and how he wasn't afraid of sharing his feelings.

'That's why I'm more than happy to help. Grams' care home was first-class and this is just the sort of thing the staff there would have organised. It's my pleasure to lend a hand and in some small way it kind of makes me feel close to her again.'

'We can do it,' said Nancy and she punched the air.

'Sod the damn move – let's make this party one to remember,' said Fred.

With a vibrancy that had been lacking of late, the residents got up to make their way into the dining room for sandwiches, with workers in their aqua blue uniforms helping those who couldn't manage. I wished Gran was here.

Nik yawned again, looked at his watch and put on his anorak.

'You did well to rope in Glenda,' I said in a low voice.

'Normally I wouldn't push so hard but I didn't want her to feel left out. Everyone seems to have children or grandchildren who'll be attending – she doesn't. Perhaps being forced into one-to-ones with everyone will make her feel more like part of this community.'

'And well done for putting Pan at ease,' I said. 'She's never said anything about her mum being alive before.'

'All the time I spent with Grams... I know how stress can make memory problems worse and Pan – like everyone else – is having to cope with a lot of upheaval at the moment.'

'Your gran... it was lovely what you shared with the residents. She sounds like an amazing person.'

'She really was.' He leant forwards and kissed me on the cheek. 'Right, I'll be in touch. Must go now otherwise I'll fall asleep on the train. I want to have a look around Pollock's Toy Museum tomorrow, and some quirky toy stores in Camden.'

Betty appeared by his side as I ran a finger over the skin his lips had touched. 'Are we going home, Jim? My bag's all ready. If we hurry no one will notice.'

He took her hand. 'I want the house to look spick and span for you, Betty. I need a bit more time to tidy it.'

She stared for a while. Nik held her gaze. Eventually, she nodded and walked away. Nik left.

A shiver crossed my back as, once again, I thanked the heavens for sending this man into my life. Oliver must surely realise, now, that he was a great person through and through. I turned to face him, to suggest we get takeout tonight. Not cooking would give me more time to ring the hospital and find out how Gran was doing, and send her a cheery text explaining everything that had been discussed this afternoon. However, I was met with folded arms and the deepest frown as he gazed through the back window at Nik hurrying away in the darkness.

16

'You've hardly spoken since we got home,' I said. Oliver hadn't turned on the Christmas tree lights like he normally did as soon as he got in. Not even when I told him the great news that I'd rung the hospital and the ward sister said Gran's back pain had eased off a little and to ring at lunchtime tomorrow after the consultant's rounds. I was hoping this might mean she was going to be discharged.

Oliver, Buddy and I were on the sofa, a cinnamon-scented candle lighting up the coffee table. I was in my pyjamas, Oliver in a jumper and jeans, and Buddy was wearing his widest puppy dog eyes, despite knowing he had very little chance of getting one of the sticky Chinese pork ribs. It was our Saturday night in. Takeout. A dance reality show on the telly. A cheap bottle of wine. We should have been in our element, arguing over who was the best contestant and which of the three of us had snuck the last prawn cracker.

'I'm tired that's all. Playing Alf at dominoes – it takes all my concentration to keep up. I'm hoping one day he reveals his secret.' He took a glug of wine. 'It reminds me of my nanny – our all-time favourite game was called Rummikub. She didn't believe in letting people win, not even children, but she always encouraged me, taking time to explain the tactics she used. I'll never forget my sixteenth birthday – I went out with my mates at the weekend, but on the actual day Mum and Dad were away on business so she and I had a games night. I beat her for the first time.'

'That explains why you never let me win at Super Mario.'

'We both know you could thrash me if you put the practice in. Your reflexes are the quickest I've ever seen with card games like Snap or Ming.'

That was one of the first things I'd ever noticed about Oliver – the way he built me up.

'You never kept in touch with your nanny?'

'There was an argument… Mum and Dad tried to blame her for me not wanting to go to university. She'd always told me to follow my dreams whereas my parents focused on the future being all about getting a high-paid job. She was devastated, having looked up to them all those years and left under a cloud of their making. But I still visited her on her birthday and would drop by at Christmas.' He gave a wry smile. 'I never got used to calling her Julia. In the end she got cancer.'

'I'm so sorry.'

'I was grateful to be there right at the end, in hospital. She didn't have any relatives to speak of – said something about a fallout years before.' He shrugged. 'One thing I've realised, getting older – there's no such thing as a normal family.'

We watched television for a while.

'So tonight… you're just tired?' I ventured, in between dancing contestants.

'Exhausted.'

Living with Gran had taught me never to dodge asking

difficult questions. She would always answer mine. Like the time I caught her crying on Mum's birthday. She said she felt sad – like she'd failed as a mother. I gave her a big hug. In return she'd ask straight out why I was irritable if I was having a bad day and we had open discussions about periods and boyfriends. Most of my friends hated it when their parents asked about things like that but I rarely complained. It was nice to have an adult take an interest. Mum had always evaded the truth. After her release from prison, it was weeks before she came around to see me. I'd been nine when she was charged and just turned eleven when she was released. I wanted to know why she hadn't called straightaway and why wouldn't she let me visit her in prison? Why she didn't want to live me with again? She'd said it was hard to explain – that I'd understand when I was older, that we'd talk about it then, but she still kept her distance and now had a husband and stepdaughter.

I turned off the television.

'Oi! I was enjoying that,' he protested.

I took his glass of wine and placed it on the coffee table. I gave Buddy a gentle push and he jumped off the sofa and settled by my slippers.

'What's going on? Your face looked like thunder watching Nik leave Willow Court today. You've met him, had drinks together and shared jokes. Please, tell me you're not still suspicious.'

He picked up the remote control.

'Don't do that. Talk to me.'

'I don't want to argue with you, Jess. Let just watch. The last dance is coming up.'

I sighed. 'You still don't like him.'

'Nik's very… nice.'

'Sarcasm doesn't suit you.'

'What would you prefer? That, like him, I charm every living thing that crosses my path? That I'm always jolly and polite? That I always know exactly what to say?' He put down the remote and picked up his phone. He tapped away for a moment and then showed me the screen. 'I've been searching for Nik's website. I can't find a reference to Junior Magic anywhere. See? All that comes up is a theatre by that name and a magician.'

'Perhaps his company are having problems with the website. Remember when Under the Tree's went down and Seb's boyfriend, computer consultant Tim, kindly offered to look at it? Look, there are a million reasons why Nik's website might not be up and running.'

'But I can't even find any trace of the words Junior Magic on the internet, in relation to toys. You'd think shops stocking his products would list the details on their platforms. It's as if it doesn't exist.'

'For goodness' sake. I've got his business card.'

'Does it mention the name of his company?'

'No. Granted, it's basic, but you've met Nik – he's not a frills person.'

'He looks striking. Do you remember seeing him at the fair in Germany?' he asked earnestly.

'Hundreds of people attend these trade events. Honestly, Oliver, you're being ridiculous. You think he's making up being a toy manufacturer?'

'Conmen are masters of pretence.'

'It's not like you to be so cynical. Remember when Alf first moved into Willow Court and from the off was going on about all his conspiracy theories – no one quite knew what to make of him but you've always been open-minded and made a point of getting to know him first. That's one thing I like about you – you never judge people on appearances or hearsay and won't read celebrity gossip magazines for that reason.'

'Just as well, given the outfit you wore when we first met,' he said, the tension leaving his voice. 'You were practically naked.'

'I was wearing a swimming costume.'

'In the middle of winter, on a London street, it was snowing!'

'As you know, I had good reason. Anyway. Back to the issue in hand – what exactly is it that's bothering you? I saw the looks you and Alf gave each other today.'

'There's something… off about him. I can't put my finger on it. He's said, himself, that his company – if it really exists – has hit hard times.'

'You think… I don't know… that he's after me for money?' I laughed. 'Well good luck to him, with that.'

'Perhaps he's after the chance to start afresh here in England – marriage would give him British citizenship.'

'Honestly, you've read too many catfishing stories and I'm perfectly capable of reaching my own judgements. I've followed my gut in the past. It hasn't often let me down.'

'But what about Alice? And Pan? This isn't just about you. What if he's after their savings? Why else would he be interested in helping out a bunch of pensioners when he could be seeing the sights in London?'

My stomach felt increasingly tight. 'He explained about

his grandmother and why he feels comfortable in the care home – why he wants to help with the party.'

'Quite a sob story, that was.'

'Oliver!'

He flushed. 'I want to believe him, Jess, really I do – I don't like thinking the worst. He's just... too nice.'

'That's like saying a sunrise is too pretty or chocolate tastes too good. Surely an abundance of niceness is a good thing?'

'I don't trust his smarmy charm and old-school ways.'

'Is the world really such a jaded place that we now feel sceptical of someone who displays nothing but kindness and goodwill?'

'*Niceness* is different,' he said and picked up one of his Chinese ribs, nibbling off a piece of meat he'd missed. 'It's not always genuine. I'm nice to the customers who toss their money at me or order drinks whilst talking on their phone. Nice is sugary. Saccharin. I'm surprised Glenda of all people hasn't been more careful, he's even sweet-talked her. She's never been married and isn't short of a penny.'

'And she's a good forty years older than him.'

'Pan's well-off too and not in her right frame of mind.' He sighed. 'Look, I kind of get it. I admit there's something... magnetic about his personality. When he walks into a room, when he talks, you can't help but focus on him.'

Oliver felt that too?

'I'm not listening to any more of this,' I said, feeling a little sick as I stood up. 'Apart from anything else, you're speaking as if me and our friends are completely stupid. Nik has brought a ray of sunshine into Willow Court. In fact,

I think as a thank you...' I lifted my chin. 'I'm going to ask Nik around for dinner. Tomorrow night.'

We had a long-standing agreement that was rarely used – if either of us was dating, now and again we could ask for the flat to ourselves. I'd only taken advantage of this a couple of times and was usually relieved when Oliver came back home at midnight and I could ask yet another unsuitable date to go home. There was Jack, a customer, who'd come into Under the Tree to buy a present for his niece. We'd got chatting, hit it off and eventually went for drinks. After a couple of weeks I asked him over for dinner. He made himself at home straightaway, kicking off his shoes and lounging on the sofa whilst I made dinner.

No one is perfect. Jack had lots of good points. He complimented my cooking and asked me questions about myself but he didn't offer to help wash up and switched on the television whilst I did. I was wary of men if there was ever the slightest whiff of them not treating me with respect.

Oliver hadn't taken advantage of our agreement much more. There was Beth who travelled the world with her job and wouldn't have been able to see him regularly. And Grace who I thought was a perfect match – she was interested in cars, like him, and they both loved board games. However designer labels were important to her and just two dates in she was trying to get Oliver to buy more upmarket clothes.

'But tomorrow's Sunday and the first part of that new thriller serial set in Rome is on.'

'We can record it.'

'Jess! You were going to make your amazing pesto pasta and garlic bread, whilst I bought that tiramisu ice cream we both love, and a bottle of Italian red.'

'We'll do it Monday,' I said and walked into the kitchen. 'Nik is spending the day visiting toy stores around Camden tomorrow – he'll feel like a relaxing night in and I'm interested to hear what he found out.'

Oliver turned on the television again. 'Whatever you want.'

I hated this, hated the awkwardness. 'Look, I like him,' I said, truly admitting that to myself for the first time, let alone out loud. 'I don't understand why you can't just be pleased for me.'

He met my gaze. 'I… I'm not sure either, Jess. You deserve to be happy. I want that more than anything.' Hastily, he looked back at the screen. 'I admit my suspicions aren't entirely logical,' he said in a harder voice. 'Let's call it a sixth sense.'

'Well, I'm going to invite him around for seven-thirty. If you could stay out until twelve, I'd appreciate it. Thanks.'

'He'll never get a train back at that time and the sofa's too small for him.'

I tried not to smile and got up to make coffee.

17

Seb sat down next to me in the staff room. I'd just given the hospital a quick call. Angela came in to help out at weekends now that the festive buzz had started. She asked if we wanted to take our break together, during the brief lull when Sunday shoppers rested their feet in cafés or pubs – it was a treat for us to eat at the same time. Despite its moderate size, Amblemarsh was lucky to have a thriving town centre. This was thanks to the council who had taken over an empty department store building, last year. They'd decided to create a community hub with a cheap café and areas you could drop off children to be looked after, or elderly relatives with dementia, for a couple of hours, in order to look around the shops or visit the cinema. I offered him one of my crisps and he passed me a carrot stick.

'How's Alice?' he asked.

'The doctor wants to keep her in for just one more night. If her blood pressure's still okay tomorrow, and she's comfortable enough with her back, she can go home. I really hope that happens because her assessment for moving is Tuesday. The ward sister let me have a quick chat with her.' I popped the carrot stick into my mouth and chewed for a moment. 'I'm worried, Seb. She didn't sound right.'

'She's had a massive shock.'

'Two, in fact – the closure of Willow Court and now this. I'm concerned it's all too much.'

I wished I could talk to Oliver about it. He'd always been a great sounding board. But now there was this Nik thing between us. It was probably just as well I'd not been around for our usual Sunday brunch today, having come in early as the Christmas trade was swelling. What with everything going on, I'd made silly mistakes at work such as forgetting to buy fruit and biscuits for the weekly children's reading club. The thought of Angela forging ahead with her plans to expand the business, and Under the Tree opening another branch, had made every day feel like Christmas during the last eighteen months since she'd first mentioned her dream. I'd pored over the details of potential properties with her, often over a cider in The Silver Swan, both of us brainstorming the decor of the next shop and the target customers for the area. I'd been with the business right from the start and felt proud of it expanding. I didn't want Angela to doubt my commitment now.

I offered my crisp bag to Seb and he took another.

'Has that fur sloth sold out yet?'

'She'll be okay, you know,' he said softly.

Tears suddenly threatening, I smiled. 'So the sloth?'

'Yes. All gone. Sloths and llamas are still really holding their appeal.'

'I think the parents like them even more than children. I'll be lucky to order any more in, at this rate. I think its hammock, with suckers to stick it onto the inside of a car window, have made it a real hit.'

He rubbed his eyes. 'Yesterday was even busier. I'll

need an early night tonight. At least Angela liked the new window display. Dangling cotton wool balls, to look like snow falling onto the top of that cardboard Christmas cake, so that they ended up looking like icing, was a genius idea of yours. In fact, that's given me an idea for a special display the week before Christmas ...'

It had been great watching Seb's confidence grow. As he chatted away I tried to focus but Oliver's comment about Nik missing the last train tonight was distracting me. What if...? My heart hop-skippity-jumped. Nik was just the distraction I needed at the moment to forget about all my problems.

'So what do you think?' Seb asked.

'Huh? Um, sorry. I was miles away.'

He studied me for a minute and grinned. 'With that wistful look on your face I imagine you are indeed thousands of miles away, on the other side of the planet. How is our tall, distinguished Aussie? When are you seeing him next?'

'Tonight, as it happens.'

Seb bit into his wrap. 'Pub? Club? The silver screen?'

'The small screen. I've invited him for dinner.'

Seb suffered a coughing fit and I slapped him on the back.

'I can't remember the last time you invited a man around to your place. You're going to need help.' He removed the square of kitchen roll from his lunchbox and reached behind his ear for his pen. He scribbled furiously and eventually passed the square to me.

'Before Tim, when I was on the dating scene, I was always super organised and wrote lists. You'll thank me for this.

I put down my sandwich and scanned the sheet.

Shave

Nails

Teeth

Music

Lighting

Lingerie

Protection

'Seb, we're simply eating together, not even the menu will be this long.'

'Time's ticking. A month from now he could be back in Oz. What would Jackie Collins do?'

'Kick ass,' I replied automatically. It was an exchange between us Seb always instigated when he thought I needed encouragement.

I was still thinking about that when I got home at five. Oliver had reluctantly agreed he may as well stay out after finishing his shift at six. I took Buddy for a quick walk around the block and fed him when we got back, promising our haste would be worth it because it meant he got to enjoy the company – and cuddles – of a guest for the evening.

I walked past the bathroom mirror and stepped back to take a closer look, chuckling to myself about Seb's list. However, my eyebrows were a little wild. My skin looked dry and a scrub and floss wouldn't harm my teeth. Getting paranoid, I pulled off my socks. The nails perhaps needed a slash of red polish and my fingernails would need to match, and I'd got those lacy bra and knickers that I'd bought on a whim, not realising they'd feel super itchy. I stuffed a hand down the top of my jumper and ran a finger across my armpit. It had more stubble than Seb's chin. I looked at the clock. This was a disaster, I hadn't got nearly enough time to get ready. Thank goodness I'd got up extra early to prepare a cottage pie. I wanted Nik to sample good old-fashioned English home cooking. For pudding I'd thawed out a rhubarb crumble I'd made in the summer. It was Gran's favourite fruit and I'd always make a batch when it was in season, for the days she'd come over for lunch and an afternoon movie.

I switched the shower on full-blast and washed my hair. I shaved and shaved again. Then I moisturised from top to toe once back on dry land. I went into my room and lit a lavender scented candle that was supposed to be calming, before filing my toenails. I was just about to apply the red nail varnish I'd bought once, but never used, when I caught sight of a clear lip gloss on my dressing table. It was a present from Oliver. Coconut – my favourite flavour and fragrance as it reminded me of suncream and holidays.

I put the nail varnish down, rummaged in the chest of drawers pushed up against the far pale turquoise wall, and pulled out the lacy bra and knickers. I recalled the last man I'd brought home for dinner. Max was a high-flying executive. We'd met in Misty's. Seb and I had headed there for happy hour and a chat with Oliver, after a late-night stocktake. For that date, I'd straightened my curls and worn a skirt and high heels. Oliver took a double take when he came through the front door and joked that I looked nothing like my normal self.

His comment got me thinking as he'd grinned and left, warning curly-haired Buddy to watch out if I picked up my straighteners. I ended up changing back into jeans and roughed up my hair – I changed back to just being myself. As it was, Max arrived wearing jeans too – and a guilty conscience. Turned out he had a wife and this was the first time he'd considered cheating. I spent the evening listening to everything that was wrong with his marriage before sending him home early – to her.

I put away the lacy underwear and glamorous polish. I smeared coconut gloss onto my lips and patted sparkly green shadow onto my lids to match my eyes. I defined my curls with some argan oil and slipped into a cream halterneck jumper that always made me feel attractive. Then I sprayed myself generously with my current favourite fruity fragrance and put on my small lotus flower earrings that kind of matched the bracelet Nik had given me.

I went into the lounge and switched on my Christmas jazz playlist, drew the curtains and dimmed the lights. I set up two places at the breakfast bar with a tall white candle in the middle – fragrance-free for once. I moved it to the right, then to the left – then back to the middle.

It was twenty-five past seven. I caught sight of Oliver's favourite hoodie, draped over the back of the sofa. Perhaps he was envious of Nik's career. Yet he'd never shown any interest in being anything other than a barman, perhaps as a reaction to his ambitious parents working twenty-four-seven and Nik didn't show off about being a partner in a family business. In fact, he'd revealed how Junior Magic was currently navigating choppy waters. Perhaps Oliver was just being over-protective. He and I were good friends. Yet he'd never grilled any of the other men I'd shown an interest in, over the years.

I made the drinks, having looked up sherry cocktails online. I'd stumbled across a recipe for Tiojitos – sherry, mint and lemonade. I wasn't going to waste any more time thinking about my flatmate's mean-spirited thoughts. The intercom buzzed and I went over, an adrenaline rush making me feel a little shaky. Was the music too loud? Should I brighten the lights? I hurried into the bedroom and applied another generous squirt of perfume. With a deep breath, I returned to the lounge.

18

Nik wore a smart winter coat, chinos and shiny shoes. A whiff of spicy, woody aftershave wafted over me. I wanted to come across as elegant and seductive but couldn't help laughing as his face was hidden behind a bunch of roses mixed amongst green foliage. The roses were red. I felt a little breathless as he passed me the flowers.

'They are lovely. Thank you.' I stood on tiptoe to kiss him on the cheek. He smelt so good.

'Your Christmas tree is up in the middle of November?' he said as he walked in.

I grinned. 'I don't think it's against the law.'

'I'm not complaining. Mine goes up on the first.'

I took his coat. Underneath he wore a tailored red shirt, the top two buttons of which were undone. I felt an urge to unbutton several more.

'I'll just lay this on my bed.' When I came back he was on the sofa, saying hello to Buddy. I put the flowers in a vase and placed it on the glass coffee table.

'Love your place,' he said.

'It's humble but it's home. I still think about life in Mum's terrace many years ago, with all the space and having a garden – it took a bit of getting used to, moving to Gran's tower block.'

'I get it, living in my flat Monday to Friday – most weekends I head over to the family home in Terrey Hills, a leafy suburb about forty minutes north. There's horse riding and bushwalking.'

'Australia's so vast it makes me think that your family's place must be massive.'

'Sure – there's a tikki style outdoor canopy over decking and a small pool but if business doesn't pick up...' He shrugged. 'I'd hate to think my parents might not be able to retire there.'

'What's your life like in Sydney, during the week? Do you go out much?'

'Not recently, we've all been working overtime, but the bars' terraces are great for heading to after hours for people-watching or, if it's colder, the indoors jazz haunts. And there's nothing like the beachside bars for relaxing. There's something so calming about looking out onto the sea.'

'It sounds very different to London. How was Camden?' I put the vegetables on, my nerves settling a little.

'I could have spent a whole week looking around the markets – at the street food alone. It came from all corners of the earth, there were dirty vegan hotdogs and halloumi fries topped with yoghurt and Turkish chilli, as well as katsu curry and bowls of rice with tofu and pickled vegetables...'

'What did you go for?'

He looked sheepish. 'A bag of the most delicious, freshly made, warm doughnuts.'

That proved my point. Nik was what he was and didn't

care what anyone else thought and certainly wasn't out to impress me like some conman pretending to be sophisticated. I went over to the sofa with two cocktails. Buddy slid onto the floor as I sat down next to Nik.

'Cheers!' He took a sip. 'Sherry? You didn't need to go to so much trouble.'

'It's the least I could do,' I said, feeling encompassed in a warm, fuzzy glow. 'What about the toy shops you wanted to visit?' I shuffled back, into the sofa. Nik did the same. He stretched out his long legs, sliding his feet under the coffee table, then rolled up his shirt sleeves – force of habit, I suspected, living in hotter climes. It made me want to run my hand over his bare, tanned skin.

Concern etched his face as he put his drink on the table and turned to face me.

'If it's okay… can I first ask about Alice? Is she home yet?'

'She's…' I tried to steady my voice. 'I'm worried, Nik. Not about the fall, per se. I think the doctors are just being extra careful keeping her in. But Gran didn't sound anything like her usual self on the phone.'

He hung on each word as if every syllable mattered.

'My concern might seem strange – given the circumstances, why should she – but Gran's a trooper. She always bounces back. I'd say that was one of her strongest characteristics.'

'Perhaps she just needs more time. Even in my thirties I find the things I'd brush off in my twenties hang around longer.'

'Like what?'

'If I feel I've failed over something at work. Or…' He

shrugged. 'A romantic break-up. I just need longer to digest what's happened. Maybe, now, Alice is the same.'

Feeling a release of tension, I raised my glass. Nik picked his up and took a mouthful.

'Anyway, my research day – I found a quirky shop that sells nothing but traditional toys, so I felt quite at home there with the wooden items, magic tricks and board games. But the fact that I felt so comfortable made me realise that for the big sales, to really keep Junior Magic current, I – the family – have got to leave our comfort zone. It's time to attract the more prevalent, modern type of buyer, whilst still staying true to our principles of quality and child developmental value.' He shrugged. 'It was the same at Pollock's toy museum. I didn't want to leave. The old artefacts and toys I'd grown up with gave me a lovely feeling of nostalgia and familiarity.'

'Did you see the Ancient Egyptian clay mouse from around 2000 BC?'

'Sure! With its moving mouth and tail…'

'Keeping the old and bringing in the new… it's a fine balance and one we tread carefully at Under the Tree. Angela is always studying the latest studies on child development.' In fact, she'd started to pass her magazines onto me. The articles were fascinating and more than once I'd stayed up late reading. 'She sees it as her responsibility to offer parents toys that whilst fun, give their kids the best start in life. Apparently neither traditional nor electronic toys can compete with books in terms of teaching very young children language – that's why we have a reading area as well.'

'There are studies that prove the old-fashioned toys

– blocks, balls, crayons, action figures, puzzles – are crucial as they foster interaction between the child and caregiver, in a way that electronics don't,' said Nik. 'Also creativity is paramount. Take how themed Lego kits are now widely available – they often come in packs with instructions on how to build something specific. And those kits have their place but, creatively, it's really important children also play with just random piles of the stuff and build something out of their imagination. That way they puzzle-solve on their own.'

'Hmm, and electronics can be good for, say, developing maths, but for interpersonal skills, for creativity, you can't beat the old ways.'

'That's why I'm thinking the way to modernise our manufacturing business might be to still produce traditional toys but give them a modern twist, perhaps focusing on wildlife and conservation – and to also spend more time developing touchscreen toys. I accept it's really important that children get used to navigating technology. So we'll see.' He smiled. 'If nothing else, this trip is certainly making me think. And I'm really looking forward to my trip to Birmingham tomorrow. I believe the biggest Christmas markets in the UK are there and have opened. I'm keen to look at the toy stalls.'

'Oliver used to live there, yet he hasn't got much of a Brummie accent.'

'Have you known him long?' asked Nik, staring intently at me.

'Four years – around the time Gran moved into Willow Court. He was brilliant from the off, helping me move her stuff – calming her down. Him being here helped me adjust to no longer living with her.'

'How did you meet?'

'Long story. I was half-naked in the snow.'

'I knew you Brits didn't get much of a summer, but having to resort to sunbathing in winter?'

'It was Seb's fault – one of his latest fitness trends... outdoor swimming. He was taking part in a charity event at one of the capital's lidos – a challenging winter one. Somehow I let him persuade me to join in. It was an arctic day, large snowflakes outside. A Sunday, late afternoon, I'd only just got back from work. Seb rang me excitedly and said it was the perfect opportunity for me to get used to exercising in the cold. He ordered me outside to do star jumps and run on the spot. You've seen this road – normally it's quiet. So I headed outside in my dressing gown and when the road was clear, let it drop and jumped up and down in my swimming costume. I took my phone so that he could watch me. We couldn't stop laughing.' I gave a sheepish grin. 'I was only twenty-five and clinging to the last moments of officially being a young person, and Seb is a difficult person to say no to.'

Nik snorted and took another sip of the Tiojito.

'Out of nowhere Oliver appeared. The snow had started halfway through his jog but he was still sensibly dressed in jogging trousers and a fleece and...' Something about him had caught my attention and I'd moved out of the way without looking properly and slipped on the snow. He'd insisted on helping me inside and...

'The rest is history?' he said.

I got up to check the vegetables. What was I doing, going on about Oliver? But as I took the lid off the steamer, I went back to that night. Oliver had been such a gent.

'It looks as if that ankle's twisted,' he'd said. 'Do you live nearby?'

I'd jerked my head towards the building on my left.

'Which floor do you live on?'

'The second,' I'd said and winced.

'Can I help you upstairs? I mean only if you'd like.' He'd held back, a flicker of amusement in his hazel eyes. I'd nodded and he'd picked up my dressing gown and helped me into it first, tightly tying it around my waist whilst I had held onto his arm...

'Let's eat,' I said now and Nik came over to the breakfast table. I put down our plates. Like a Bisto kid he breathed in the gravy smells wafting up from the cottage pie. We looked across the breakfast bar at each other, the candle's flame dancing seductively in between us. He ate with gusto and then polished off the rhubarb crumble and custard. It was ten o'clock by the time we'd finished our coffee and collapsed back onto the sofa, me glowing from his compliments.

'I love your place,' he said, hands behind his head. 'Must be useful having a flatmate – someone to share the DIY and housework with?'

'Talking of which one of my bedroom drawers is jammed. *I* can't work out what's wrong. You're right. Oliver is brilliant like that. You've reminded me to ask him to take a look tomorrow.'

Nik jumped to his feet and held out his hand. 'Show me. Let's see if I can fix it.'

A competitive spirit? He pulled me up effortlessly – in fact, a little too hard and I banged into his chest. We looked at each other and laughed. Keeping hold of my hand, *he* led *me* into my bedroom, where he'd seen me put his coat. Momentarily, my breathing quickened and I fought an impulse to pull back, forcing myself to inhale and exhale more slowly. Letting down my defences scared me and I couldn't control those apprehensive feelings that went back to my childhood, but I'd learnt over time to rationalise that inner voice. *It's okay. Nothing bad is going to happen. This is compassionate, gentle, trustworthy, guileless Nik.*

'Wait a minute,' he said huskily, as I went to turn on the light. He pulled me over to the window. 'I saw it on the way here. Isn't it romantic?'

I looked out of the window, my body brushing against his. We gazed up at the creamy white full moon, Venus dazzling to its right. Venus. The planet of love. Nik and me – tonight it was literally written in the stars. I turned to face him. He looked down at me, moonlight catching his eyes and the kind laughter lines.

'Makes you feel so small, doesn't it?' he said softly. 'And insignificant. Even when you're flying through the sky and closer, it still gives you that perspective. And yet, back on Earth, much smaller things count for so much – like new friends.'

I couldn't tear my gaze away from his face and those soft lips.

The door rattled.

No. He wouldn't. Please, don't let that be Oliver back early. Buddy let out an excited bark.

Crap.

'Honey, I'm home...' called a voice. 'Where are you?' A silhouette lurched into view.

'Hi there, mate,' said Nik.

Oliver switched on the light and stared at us, standing there by the bed.

'Won't Nik miss the last train?' he said in a tight voice.

'Oliver,' I forced a laugh. 'For goodness' sake. Why... why don't you go and put the kettle on.' I shot Nik an apologetic look.

Nik looked at his watch. 'Sorry, Jess, I've totally lost track of time.' He turned to Oliver. 'I'm off to Birmingham tomorrow. You used to live there?'

'Yeah...' he said in a disinterested way.

Nik waited for him to expand but he didn't so he kissed me on the cheek and went to leave.

'I'll text you,' I whispered.

He winked. 'Thanks for the meal. You're an amazing cook. I'll see myself out.'

19

'Great timing,' I said and pushed past Oliver.

'Jess. I'm sorry but I've saved you from making a huge mistake.' Oliver touched my arm. I shook him off and headed into the kitchen area.

'Look...' He began to clear the plates, leftover puddles of gravy on them.

'Leave them,' I snapped. I blew out the candle and switched on the overhead lighting.

'I didn't mean—'

'Yes you did.' I squirted too much washing up liquid into the bowl and eventually bubbles overflowed. 'All I wanted was for you to stay out until midnight. Was that really too big a favour?'

'But, Jess...' He came over to me eagerly. 'I've been in The Silver Swan researching his company.'

'You're unbelievable. This obsession of yours needs to stop.'

'But I finally managed to find the website of Junior Magic. It's such a small business in Sydney, that must be why it was so difficult to track down. It's not a manufacturer. It's a tiny toy shop.'

'Why would he lie about that detail? You aren't making any sense.'

Like I'd mentioned to Oliver before, I had a good gut when it came to judging people due to growing up around the friends Mum chose. I could spot a liar a mile away by the time I left junior school. When one of her boyfriends spoke with his hands in his pockets, that was a dead giveaway. Or if they broke eye contact at the crucial moment of a conversation or shuffled their feet. These were sure signs that Mum, for some reason, would always miss.

Nik was a good guy. I knew it in my bones.

'In a way his lies about the detail are irrelevant,' he said.

'What do you mean?'

'Because the whole story's a load of garbage, he doesn't even work there. I checked the *Meet our Team* page. And it's no family business, that's not what the website says at all.'

Oliver scrolled down his phone and passed it over. I clicked onto the Contacts option of the website. I studied it and then handed the phone back, turning away to carry on washing up. 'I suggest you look at the address again.'

Silence for a few seconds

'Sydney – North Dakota,' he mumbled.

I spun around and threw a hand up into the air, suds floated down to the ground. Buddy came over to investigate whereas I felt an urge to run away, as fast as I could, from the drama. 'Your instincts are about as accurate as a compass in a magnetic storm. You've been incredibly rude to Nik and you've ruined what was one of the nicest evenings I've had in ages.'

A wave of anger washed through me. It wasn't asking

too much, was it, at twenty-nine years old, to have a bit of fun? Oliver wasn't my dad or my guardian angel. I'd always managed fine without both of those things and wasn't about to start needing them now.

'Come on, Jess… he's like Leonardo DiCaprio in *Catch Me If You Can* or Paul Newman and Robert Redford in *The Sting*.'

'And you're acting more like Mr Bean.'

'Take those red roses. It's hardly subtle, is it? He's just too smooth, too much of a cliché.'

'Bringing flowers to dinner is just good old-fashioned manners.'

Oliver sat down at the breakfast bar and fiddled with a wine cork. 'How was Nik's day? Wasn't he visiting that Pollock museum?'

I leant my back against the sink. Hopefully Oliver would drop this nonsense now. 'Yes. He had a good time.'

'Nanny took me there years ago. I still remember its pride and joy, the Ancient Egyptian mouse. I loved looking at the tin toys and the jester painted above the shop front, on the wall, is brilliant.'

My brow relaxed. 'Great place, isn't it? You know, back in the 1850s it used to be—'

'A printer's. I know. Then they turned it into a toy shop a century later. Just amazing.' He stared at me.

'What?'

'I've never been there, Jess. I got all that information off the internet. See how easy it is?'

Heat flooded my face and a sense of nausea backed up my throat. 'What is this? Some sort of power game to make me feel stupid?'

'Jess, of course not – look, you know I trust your opinion more than anyone's, on everything from if a new shirt suits me or whether I've overreacted with an impolite customer at work. You're intelligent and perceptive and that's why you were promoted at work. But romance… it makes all of us do stupid things. Remember that woman I dated and I ignored all the signs she was married and just looking for a bit of fun? I even made up some excuse, in my head, for her wearing a gold band on her third finger. You made me see that I was making a fool of myself.'

'You're being just as foolish again. Honestly, anyone would think you were jealous.'

'What?' He froze.

'Just because there's no romance in *your* life, doesn't mean I have to behave like a nun. Surely you don't begrudge me a bit of fun?'

I felt an inexplicable urge to cry. Four years I'd known Oliver and our friendship had gone from strength to strength. I should have known it was all going to end one day.

'Jess, the last thing I wanted to do was upset you. Look… I've said my piece. I promise to keep my concerns to myself in future. At least let me tidy up.'

I didn't reply.

'I can be a bit of an arse sometimes,' he continued.

'I don't want to talk anymore,' I said quietly. 'Please. Leave me alone.'

20

I pulled on my hat. 'Sure you'll be okay? I can cancel this afternoon off. All that new stock has arrived and…'

Seb came out from behind the till. Several customers browsed the shop, picking up plushies and reading instructions on the back of board games. A mum with toddler twins – Lily and Meg – sat crossed legs on the red carpet, in the reading area, flicking through picture books about polar bears and flying sleighs. Andy Williams crooned about a happy holiday in the background.

'Wednesday is one of the quieter days of the week, even with Christmas coming, and you're in extra early tomorrow, right? To be honest I'll relish having the shop to myself. I get to play my own Christmas music. Motown festive classics, here we come. Little feet will love jigging along.'

'Well, ring me if there are any problems and tomorrow we'll discuss your idea for the window display for the week before Christmas. I've also got an idea I'm impatient to try. We could start setting it up tomorrow afternoon and I'll stay late to finish it off.'

'Count me in too' he said and smiled. 'Any clues?'

'How about one based on books? We've never done that before. Some passers-by might think that all we sell is toys. I've had a look online and seen how you can build an effective looking Christmas tree out of books, by stacking them horizontally. We could also give selected stories prominence in the window, with toys related to them by their side. For example that new book that came in, *A Winter Woodland* – we got a squirrel plushy and electronic rabbit. I'll have a look on my walk in Springhaye Forest this afternoon for other accessories, such as twigs we can spray with that fake snow I got in, if you think the idea has got potential.' I included Seb in a lot of the decision-making like Angela had always done with me. With a new store opening there could be career opportunities for him. The doorbell rang and a man with a scarlet face and matching flat cap pushed past me.

'I'd like to speak to the manager,' he said loudly. The twins' mum looked up.

'How can I help?' I said and took off my hat. I bit my lip, hoping this wouldn't take long. I was joining Lynn and some of the residents to collect material for Christmas decorations. I had to be there by two o'clock and it was almost half past one. I wore my jeans, my thickest anorak, and had my beanie hat and gloves to boot. We had a couple of hours of daylight before sunrays would start to be replaced with frost.

He delved into a plastic bag and pulled out a picture book. It was one of our biggest sellers about a Christmas elf. The front was sparkly and eye-catching.

'It's five quid cheaper on Amazon. This is an absolute rip-off.'

'Is there anything wrong with it?' I asked, politely.

'Yes. The price.' He marched to the till. 'It hasn't been

read. I was saving it to give to my son at Christmas. It's like new.'

I went over. Seb approached another customer who'd waved their hand for assistance. The man thrust the receipt into my hand. He'd bought it almost one month ago. I took the book from him and he folded his arms as I flicked through the pages. I pointed to several chocolate stains, in the shape of fingers.

'I'm sorry, sir. I can't take this back. There are signs of wear and tear.'

'Are you calling me a liar?' He started to sweat and his arms fell to his sides. 'I told you —no one has read it. It must have got dirty here.' He jerked his head towards the little twins looking at books.

'We check every story before we sell it. Is it possible your son found it without you knowing?' I heard my heart thumping.

'Not unless he's grown six feet and can reach to the top of my wardrobe,' he said and sneered. 'I'll take my future business elsewhere if you're going to be difficult. It's a pity as this is one of my son's favourite shops.'

I held his gaze and noticed the deeply set rings under his eyes and the coat that had a small rip on the sleeve.

'What is your son called?' I asked. Uncomfortable as it could be, I enjoyed trying to resolve customer complaints.

'Max,' he said and snorted. 'Why? Are you going to put him in toddler jail?'

I thought for a moment. 'Curly black hair and freckles? He has an obsession with trains?'

The man's jaw dropped. 'How did…?'

'I like to get to know all our regulars.' I went behind the

till. 'I can't offer you a refund but how about a voucher for the same value? It's valid for twelve months.'

We looked at each other, he swallowed and rubbed his nose. 'Cheers.'

The doorbell rang as he left. Seb came over and raised an eyebrow.

'Sorted,' I said and beamed. 'His son, little Max, often pulls his mum in here. They're good customers.' I stared at the grubby book. 'We can afford to write off the loss – just this once.'

'Now off you skedaddle,' he said. 'Motown is calling me.'

I hurried out, whistling as I made my way to my car parked further down the road.

'Thanks for popping in,' said Gran, twenty minutes later, as I caught my breath. She was staring out of the window, watching a barge glide past.

I'd practically skipped into the hospital on Monday, when she'd finally been discharged, however she didn't brighten up when I told her all about the movie screening and how enthusiastic everyone one was. Her back still ached and for the first time ever she talked about getting a Zimmer frame.

I bent down and gave her a hug. She didn't take her eyes off the canal.

'Where's Buddy?' she asked.

'Getting cuddles in the lounge before our walk. I don't expect you've heard back yet from the council yet, following your assessment.' I sat on the bed, next to her.

Gran lifted a cup of tea. It was on a little table on wheels, in front of her bedroom armchair. Wedged by her side, against the chair's colourful throw, was her favourite weekly magazine. It looked unread.

'We only saw the social worker yesterday.' Finally she turned away from the window.

'How do you think it went?'

Gran shrugged. I didn't like talking behind her back but I'd had a quiet word with the social worker, Hazel, as I walked her out and explained that Gran was still feeling the aftereffects of her fall. As it was, the care needs assessment hadn't taken long. Gran still needed help washing and dressing. The only thing that had changed since her last assessment was that her mobility had slightly worsened. Time would tell as to whether her fall was a one-off or something that would happen more often from now on. I'd had to push her to be transparent with Hazel and the occupational therapist. Gran was all for putting on a brave face but that wasn't going to help her get into another care home speedily.

I lay awake last night, worrying about her future. It was about a month now until the residents would be forced to leave. Social Services had reassured us that Gran would be found somewhere even if it was a temporary placement and I'd been making calls to places on the directory. But I hadn't found one yet that was suitable even though the staff all sounded very friendly on the phone. Those that met Gran's needs had a waiting list. Others were mainly for dementia patients or didn't have ensuite rooms. What if it was months before we found the perfect place? What if this current low mood turned into full-blown depression?

'How are you feeling about it all now?'

She reached for the magazine and browsed, even though it was upside down. 'I only got upset in hospital because I was in shock.'

I reached forwards and closed the magazine. 'The social worker... she seemed genuine, right, and seemed to really care?'

'Hazel said I could ring her any time. That meant a lot. One thing I learnt a long time ago – acceptance makes life a lot easier. We can try to fight against things that have happened and can't be taken back, but what's the point? Far better to get on with dealing with them. It is what it is.'

I'd learnt that at a young age, too.

'What do you think of the care home I rang up yesterday? You looked at the link I emailed you? The rooms are ensuite and Upperhyde is only ten miles away. The warden sounded very accommodating.'

'Upperhyde is a busy town and this place... Darkthorn House, it's right in the middle by a busy road instead of a canal.' The corners of her mouth sunk. '*Darkthorn* doesn't sound very friendly.'

'I think it sounds sexy, like a *Game of Thrones* character.'

Normally she would have laughed at that.

'So, I'll book a visit?'

'Whatever you think is best,' said my Gran, never before in her whole life.

I looked at my watch. 'Nik's meeting me in reception. I haven't seen him since Sunday.'

'Oh, he's been here a while.' Momentarily, her features brightened. 'He popped in to say a quick hello and to see how I was. Apparently he's been messaging Glenda about the photograph collection.'

'I didn't even know they'd exchanged numbers.' That was so cute.

'When he was in Birmingham he found a market stall

selling 1940s postcards and wanted to know what she thought to including those along with our photos.' Gran's eyes twinkled. 'You should have heard her talking about him in the lounge. I've never seen her so fired up. She passed his texts around, like badges of honour, and didn't once complain about her indigestion or back... It's kind of sad in a way.'

'How so?' I asked, a warm glow infusing me as she became more animated.

'She's never had photos of a husband or children to show everyone. Her... what shall we call it... sweet spot for Nik – well, I'm seeing her with new eyes.' She glanced at me sideways. 'Talking of sweet spots, how's my favourite barman? He couldn't swap his shifts so that he could go on this jolly with you?'

'I don't know. Now, did you watch that new detective show last night? *The Coffee Shop Mysteries*? It's right up your street. The main character—'

Gran's eyes narrowed. 'What do you mean, *you don't know*?'

'Oliver and I don't live in each other's pockets.'

Nik had hardly texted since Sunday and now he'd turned up early today to visit Glenda on his own, without telling me – this new distance between us was no doubt caused by Oliver's abrupt behaviour.

'Jess? What's going on?'

'Nothing,' I said in as innocent a voice as I could muster and I stood up.

'Well, if you don't want to tell me...' She gazed out of the window again.

'Okay... look... we had an argument.'

'What?' She turned back.

'I can't face talking about it, Gran. Not at the moment. Let's just say I've hardly spoken to him since Sunday night.'

'Oliver has got a heart of gold – like you have. Life's too short for long silences. I often wonder if I should have made more effort with your mum as her occasional visits, after prison, started to peter out... but I didn't want to rock the boat for you.'

'You did your best, Gran, and you and me – we've always had each other.' She drifted away, back into deep thought. I leant over and kissed her on the top of her head before making my way to the reception area.

Nik was in the lounge, crouched down next to Phyllis. He patted her arm as she played with a fiddle muff. It was another of the dementia items Lynn had ordered in and was perfect for restless hands, with a soft small ball attached inside and beads and tassels along its hems. He got up and sat next to Glenda. He laughed loudly with Nancy and I heard him say something about decorating her wheelchair with tinsel. Fred, Pan and Alf stood by the building's entrance doors, along with Lynn and Buddy. The walk was just going to be a slow one. Lynn said a bit of gentle exercise would do them good. Everyone wore boots as the forest was always muddy in places, regardless of the weather. Lynn zipped up her coat and put on thick pink gloves that had sparkles sewn through them. Her woolly hat was crowned by a fashionable fur pom pom. It made a refreshing change to see her wearing something other than her navy uniform. A rucksack stood by her feet.

'I think this walk is going to be what we'd have called

a constitutional, back in the day,' said Fred, a cigarette bobbing up and down as he spoke. He wore a tweed trench coat and matching trilby hat and leant on a walking stick. Its handle was shaped like a duck's head.

'The nice cup of coffee Lynn has got in her flasks and the fruitcake she made,' said Alf, 'that, me old mucker, is the main reason I'm going.'

I went over to Nik to tell him we were ready. Several of the residents were wearing Christmas jumpers. 'Jeez, sympathies, Glenda,' he was saying. 'I had backache once for a couple of weeks and that felt bad enough. What do you think has caused your bad hip?'

'Oh, a fall. It's the osteoporosis. I found out I had it when I broke my wrist in my fifties, falling off a ledge on a hike. It was a team-building weekend with work, in beautiful Somerset and very pleasant apart from that. How did you injure yours?' she asked.

'You don't want to hear that... it was down to me being silly.' Nik gave me a hug.

Thank goodness for that. Oliver hadn't entirely put him off.

She smiled. 'It can't be sillier than me tripping off a ledge whilst I was powdering my nose. I think I must have a mild disorder that makes me perspire more than others.'

'There's nothing silly about anything that makes you feel good,' he replied.

'So, your... well, let's not call it silliness, then,' she said. 'Your *misfortune* – what happened?'

'I've got to go. How about another time?' He tightened his scarf.

I pushed his shoulder. 'Did a kangaroo punch you out?

Or you tripped over a didgeridoo? Did wearing a cork hat mean you couldn't see where you were going?'

Glenda rolled her eyes.

'It was nothing really – a couple of years ago I was buying groceries at the supermarket, down the road from work... some kids were in there, hassling two members of staff. They were still at school but tall and full of bravado and were trying to steal alcohol and cigarettes. One of them grabbed a couple of bottles and bolted. I ran after him and wasn't as fast – no surprises there, turned out he was the son of an Olympic athlete, he'd fallen in with a bad crowd – but I lunged as he turned a corner and managed to catch his leg, falling in the process. I ricked my back.'

Glenda and I exchanged horrified looks.

'He could have had a knife,' she gasped.

Nik's shoulders bobbed up and down. 'I didn't think about that. It probably sounds worse than it was. Honestly, they were just kids and I was happy to help. Anyone else would have done the same.'

'We must tell the others,' said Glenda. 'What a story. What a tremendous thing to do.'

'No... please,' he said and looked sheepish. 'I'd rather not have the attention. I mean... people might expect all sorts from me then. I'm no superman.' He grinned.

By the look on Glenda's face, like me she totally disagreed.

21

Lynn went to pick up the rucksack, containing refreshments, but I beat her to it. Talking of backache I knew she suffered, having spent a lifetime making beds and manoeuvring residents who needed help with personal care. She smiled gratefully and I was just about to put it on, as we all made our way outside, when Nik reached out his hand.

'It's okay, thanks,' I said, having grown up fiercely determined to manage on my own. Only Oliver had chipped away at that, letting me see that sometimes accepting help from men didn't have to end with regrets.

'You'd be doing me a massive favour if you let me carry it,' he said. 'It'll inject some manliness into my reputation in front of Alf – being the carthorse might make up for the fact that I drink sherry.'

I hesitated. 'Well, if you're sure?' I handed the rucksack to him and took Buddy's lead from Lynn. He slipped it onto his back and held the door open to let the residents go through. I held back and indicated for him to follow the residents outside, before me. He gave a thumbs-up and headed out, me behind him wondering what it would feel like to stroke the back of his neck.

Springhaye Forest was a favourite spot with the more

mobile residents during the summer. It was the other side of the canal. The woodland walks were flat and paths had been trodden into shape over the years and before you entered there was a large grassy area, with picnic benches and a car park for people coming from the other direction. On the edge of that tarmac usually stood an ice cream van in the summer. I'd push Gran this far in a wheelchair during the summer months and we'd both enjoy a 99 flake. To get there we turned left out of Willow Court and slowly walked the short distance to the end of the high street, passing some shops that already had Christmas trees in the windows and jolly festive music escaping onto the street whenever it had the chance. There we turned left again, at the book shop that used to be the video store Betty's husband worked in, and strolled over a bridge. The residents sat down at one of the picnic benches to re-energise. I let Buddy off his lead and he followed the trails of various scents leading to holly bushes sprinkled with bright red berries.

'I'm worn out already. Wish I wasn't so jolly unfit,' said Fred. 'I wouldn't be able to lift so much as a fire hose these days, let alone a ladder.'

'What about giving a fireman's lift?' I teased.

'If I had to. If it meant saving a life. No question about that, I'd do anything,' he said gruffly. 'I was thinking the other day about one blaze... all this talk of Christmas reminded me. A young couple had overloaded the plug board with fairy lights in their lounge. They were upstairs putting their little one to bed and a fire started. A right mess it was, afterwards, everywhere black, with melted patio doors and a collapsed ceiling. The full shebang. I never got used to that. Not when a building had been someone's home. Me and my colleague had to pull all three of them out of a top window. Domestic smoke alarms weren't so common back then.'

'Were they all okay?' I asked and glanced at Glenda. The way she was staring up at Nik and pursing her lips I knew she was bursting to talk about the robbery he'd bravely got involved in.

'Damn lucky they were. Of course the whippersnapper was too young to understand that and couldn't stop crying because the Christmas tree and presents had gone up. Me and the crew had a whip-around and bought him a bike. He joined the service twenty years later, just as I was retiring.'

'What a terrific story,' said Pan. She adjusted her purple beret having dressed up for the occasion with a slash of red lipstick and glossy handbag. Even her wellies were leopard print. Gran had bought them for her last Christmas as Pan liked to walk along the canal.

The residents got up and we headed onto the woodland path, Buddy back on his lead. I breathed in the earthy smells of damp soil and rotting leaves. Bare beech trees, oaks and silver birch still looked beautiful against the blue sky despite their lack of leaves. Evergreen pines added fragrance and colour to the landscape and more holly bushes added a festive feel. Moss covered nearby rocks that lay next to a family of sepia-coloured fungi. A squirrel darted up a tree trunk. Alf gave an enormous sneeze and a roost of starlings flapped their wings. Buddy barked. Nik and I looked at each other. Our appreciation of the forest didn't need articulating.

'I love fairy lights,' said Pan. 'I know it's a health and safety matter but I've always wished we could have them in our rooms at Willow Court.'

'Don't worry, we'll have a whole bunch up for the party,' said Lynn as she circumnavigated a puddle.

'I remember visiting Paris one Christmas with my husband, before we got married,' said Pan. 'We'd only been seeing each other for six months and were still in that first flush of love...'

My eyes were drawn to Nik as he helped Glenda over a tree root.

'We found ourselves in a super little cocktail bar, on the... the... this big fancy street in the centre of Paris...' She frowned.

'The Champs-Élysées,' said Nik.

'Yes! And after watching a play in a theatre in Montparnasse. It had gone midnight. We were the last customers. The staff had turned off all the lighting near us apart from twinkling fairy lights across the window. We sat there telling each other those things, those secrets, you only tell someone when you begin to realise that maybe, just maybe you might have a future together. We hadn't realised closing time had passed and apologetically got up to leave. However the manager came over, smiled at us both and put down two coffees and a tray of biscuits for us, whilst he cleaned. I've never forgotten that night.' She stopped walking. 'I hope I never do.'

I went over to her side and we linked arms. 'Look,' I said and pointed at a branch. 'Doesn't that bird look pretty, puffing out his chest? It reminds me of pop-up book we've got in the shop, all about a robin and a worm.'

'His red bib is marvellous,' she said and pointed to a nearby bush. 'Like those little berries.'

'They're called hips,' said Alf. 'That plant is Wild Dog Rose. And don't be impressed – I only know that because the missus knew more about gardening than Alan Titchmarsh. In fact, Maisie saved a neighbour's cat once. Her friend Shirl had been laughing about how her tabby wouldn't stop chewing the Christmas tree and she had no doubt it would have a go at the mistletoe she'd just put in a vase on the cat's favourite window sill. She hurried home after Maisie told her mistletoe was toxic for many pets.'

'Talking of heroes...' said Glenda and she caught Nik's eye. He shook his head very slightly. She sighed. 'I... I watched a new show, last night, *The Coffee Shop Mysteries*, and one character—'

'I was telling Gran about that,' I said swiftly.

Lynn pulled a black dustbin bag out of her pocket and I pulled out a smaller one to collect items for Under the Tree's next window display. Nik and I did the bending down as the others pointed out objects that would make perfect decorations. Fred used his stick to point to the fallen cones he could just about make out as we approached a cluster of conifers. Pan had an eye for small fallen branches that once sprayed, would be perfect for hanging homemade decorations on. Alf spotted more holly and, well-organised as ever, Lynn delved into the rucksack for secateurs. He also noticed a white feather and managed to bend down and pick it up.

He held it out to Glenda. 'Could be an angel looking out for you. Who knows?'

'What a lovely thought,' said Nik.

Glenda looked at Nik and hesitated before taking it from Alf. She put the feather in her coat pocket. Lynn put a finger to her lips and pointed to a rabbit. It stood rock still for a few seconds, then twitched its nose and ran off, giving flashes of its white bobtail. We started to make our way back. Temperatures were dropping.

'I watched a YouTube video about how to make a card holder out of twigs by binding them together into a slatted pyramid shape,' Glenda told Nik as we walked on.

Lynn and I glanced at each other. She'd never offered much input to the Christmas party, in previous years.

'Good idea,' he said. 'In fact... we could build a structure from twigs to hold the photos you're collecting. What do you think?'

Pan, Fred and Alf walked together, Fred squinting and pointing out potential tripping hazards with his stick. Lynn and I brought up the rear. I took the dustbin bag from her even though it wasn't heavy. She couldn't stop yawning.

'This walk of yours was a brilliant idea,' I said. 'I've loved every minute of it, getting fresh air. The toy shop is becoming increasingly stuffy as it gets busier with December approaching.'

'It's done me good too. My head needed clearing.'

'How are you doing?' I asked gently.

Her eyes glistened.

'It's easy for us relatives to forget that you've got to move on as well. You've been brilliant, Lynn; you've really made Willow Court special.'

'I've enjoyed every minute of my time there.'

'Even when Gran first moved in and you overhead her telling me she thought you were uppity?'

'I've always liked Alice's feistiness. It so hard... saying goodbye to residents. Not everyone will be here for the big goodbye at the party.' She kicked a small stone. 'But that's life and I know it's good that some residents have already got plans and are leaving next week.'

'Like Bert? Gran told me his family have found a suitable care home near to another son, up north.'

'Yes. It's a solution everyone is happy with which is great. Decisions like these can cause fallouts between family members. Everyone thinks they know best. And then there's Dora. She's moving in with her family temporarily and they'll see how it goes – her daughter has retired since Dora first moved in here and her mum's physical needs are similar to your gran's. She can bear her own weight and most days her arthritis doesn't stop her enjoying herself.'

'Like Pan, she's only just been diagnosed with Alzheimer's, hasn't she?'

'Yes. Her daughter wants to look after her for as long as possible, now her situation has changed. A move was probably on the cards, regardless of this place closing down. So it won't be a disaster for all residents. That's some small comfort for me.'

We reached the grassy clearing. Glenda let Nik help her sit down even though she was quite capable. Fred, Alf and Pan joined her. Nik stood by another table and put the rucksack on it. Lynn and I went over to him, Buddy running off his lead now. She took out two flasks and clear plastic cups. Nik handed around a foil package containing the slices of fruitcake. Glenda budged up and just as she looked up at Nik, Lynn thanked her and sat down in the space.

Glenda's face was a picture.

'Pity we can't all sit around one table,' I said, heading back to the rucksack whilst Alf fed Buddy dog treats. I put my plastic bag down there. Nik raised his arm and we clinked mugs before I gratefully knocked back a warming mouthful. 'How was Birmingham on Monday?' I asked.

'Overwhelming! Stall after stall and crowds, even though it was midweek and they have only just opened. I walked past crafts, handmade toiletries and jewellery... then pottery, handbags and knitted items. And I could have spent all day just tasting cheese, eating German sausage or apple strudel.'

'Did you have a mug of mulled wine?'

'Along with a hot chocolate and you'll never guess what I found.'

I raised an eyebrow.

'A Spanish stall dedicated to sherry. Dry ones and sweet, with detailed explanations of the soil and landscape the grapes had grown in, and something about the different types of flora—'

'The what?'

'Apparently that's a layer of yeast that can be part of the production process. Needless to say, I bought a bottle, but purely for altruistic reasons.'

'I find that hard to believe!'

'It's true! I got talking to the stallholder, Pedro. He said sherry was a well-respected drink in Spain, with a history and tradition. We got talking about Christmas and then...' Nik chuckled. 'He pulled a face and said the British put it into sloppy trifle. He saw that as sacrilege. But that's why I've bought it. That pudding sounds delicious to me and I'm going to make one for the Christmas party – so the sherry isn't just for me.'

'Sherry, mulled wine, hot chocolate – this was a business trip, right?'

He gave a bellow of laughter. 'Yes – on a more professional note the choice of wooden toys was just incredible. One stall sold vertical stacking puzzles that, when completed, made an object such as a rocking horse. So yes... there was food for thought as well as for my stomach.'

'You could do a practice run of the trifle at my flat if you like,' I said. 'Gran used to make them when I was younger – minus the sherry for me.' In any case, back then, I couldn't bear the smell of alcohol and as I grew up I filled my living spaces with the smells from perfumes and scented candles.

He drained his cup. 'Well done, Lynn. This cake is amazing.' He got up and went over to the other table, resting a hand on Glenda's shoulder as he took another slice.

'Come and join us, Jess,' called Pan. 'Otherwise your second slice will disappear.'

'There's always mine,' said Alf in a morose voice. 'Lynn says I should only have one.'

'Doctor's orders, Alf Talbot,' she said.

He grinned. 'You sound just like my Maisie.'

I got up and went over, not looking where I was going, and stood on a large stone almost tripping over.

'Steady on, old girl,' said Fred. 'Anyone would think you've got my eyesight.'

'Perhaps I should have given that white feather to you,' joked Alf.

But I hardly heard. I looked down at the stone. Of course!

'You'll need that second slice, Nik,' I said, 'Because I'd like to show you Pebble Rock.'

'That's a good idea,' said Lynn. 'You'll get a lovely view as the sun sets.'

'It might be a bit cold,' said Glenda sharply. 'You and Nik should come back to Willow Court and get warm.'

It touched me again how she'd bonded with him. 'How about we take the rucksack with us, to save Lynn's back, and then drop it by later? We'll say a quick hello.'

'It'll be lighter now, with the flasks empty,' said Lynn. 'I'll be fine carrying it.'

'You can't be too careful with your health,' said Glenda quickly. 'Yes, Jess, I think that's an excellent idea.'

'It must be nearly time for lunch,' said Pan. Fred, Alf and Glenda exchanged glances. She looked at her arm. 'Oh... I haven't put on my... my wrist clock.'

Without hesitation Nik rolled up his sleeve. 'Look at my watch instead, Pan,' he said and crouched by her side.

Her face broke into a smile. 'It's got a Mickey Mouse in the middle. His arms are the hands. It's adorable!'

Nik looked sheepish. 'Okay, you've caught me – I visit Hong Kong Disneyland every couple of years with colleagues. Only for work purposes, you understand. I don't enjoy the magic at all.'

We all smiled and said our goodbyes. Nik and I wandered back into the woodland with Buddy by our sides.

22

'I'm excited to be visiting Springhaye's equivalent of Uluru,' Nik said as the path we'd been following started to incline.

'Um, it's more of a small hill – but has an unusual tradition and there's a lovely view of Amblemarsh.'

Pebble Rock was a little steep as you neared the top and Nik offered me a hand. I hesitated before slipping my hand into his, wishing we weren't wearing gloves. He heaved me up and Buddy followed. We stood on the plateau. There was a wooden bench the other side, just before the far edge.

'Wow!' He put down the rucksack and went over to bend over piles of pebbles that lay all around. 'There must be hundreds of stones and so many messages and hearts. Is it okay to touch them?'

'Go ahead.'

He picked one up. '*Sharon loves John, 2016.* They remind me of the padlocks lovers fasten everywhere in Paris.'

'It started on New Year's Eve 1999. Remember how the world decided we were going to fall foul of the Millennium bug? That computers' systems would fail in important areas such as utilities and it would lead to widespread chaos – and some religious groups believed it was the end of times?'

'Yup. I was thirteen, I went to a mate's beachfront house for a barbecue party and we all held our breath at midnight but the lights stayed on and gadgets still worked... talk about a disappointment.'

'A group of teens from Springhaye decided to paint a stone each that they found in the forest and leave it up here – something to be remembered by if the apocalypse arrived and they didn't survive.'

'There's nothing like a bit of drama at that age,' said Nik.

Not for me – although I did remember fitful sobbing when someone told me Zac Efron had a girlfriend.

'Some painted on their favourite pet. Couples dating shared a stone like the one you picked up. The Silver Swan's landlord was one of that original group of teenagers and painted a football on his and wrote Manchester United Forever.'

Carefully Nik searched through the stones. 'I've found a pet. A black and white Labrador, going by the picture. *Patch. Much loved. RIP 2009.* Some of these are beautiful. Have you ever left one?'

I gave him a sheepish look but trusted Nik with my secret that only Oliver knew about. I went over to the pile on the left. I dug underneath it at the back and eventually found a flat bright red stone. I passed it to him.

'*Jess loves Steve 2007.* Tell me more,' he said and handed it back. I returned it to its place, underneath the pile.

'Must I?'

He took my arm and led me to the bench. Buddy jumped up next to me.

'Over the years it became a tradition for youngsters to leave stones here on New Year's Eve. Other people would leave them all year around, when a loved one died or for other reasons but teenagers stuck to that date. All my friends came up here. We were in Year 11. Gran let me go to a house party. She didn't know the parents weren't going to attend and we snuck out. Everyone else had a boyfriend or at least a crush. I wasn't really into boys at that age so felt like the odd one out...' I cleared my throat. 'Steve was our cat. Gran had had him for years. He was named after her favourite actor, Steve McQueen. I told my friends he was a lad who lived in my road and went to boarding school out of the area. I felt bad for lying but in a way the stone told the truth because I did love our cat.' I rolled my eyes. 'Sorry. Waffling. I bet you wish you hadn't asked now.'

'Not at all. Maybe you and I should leave one – we could paint an aeroplane on it.'

My stomach fluttered.

'Can you remember your first love?' I asked.

'Isla. Feisty attitude. Taller than me when we first met. She loved surfing. I loved my books. I never understood why she liked me. We were so different. I was much quieter back then and us getting together surprised everyone.'

'You? Quiet?'

'Sure was. Maybe that's why it doesn't bother me now when I get teased for drinking sherry. I grew up being mocked for preferring books to football and visiting my grandpa instead of meeting in the park to smoke. It... it was hard, you know? Not fitting in – it feels like the end of the world at that age.'

I knew.

'But eventually I gained a tight group of mates who weren't as sporty, like me. We'd hit the beach together at weekends to fish in rock pools. That's when I first met Isla. She strode over one day and offered to take me surfing.' His smile broadened. 'My mum couldn't believe it when I got home. She'd been trying for years to convince me of the fun of her favourite pastime.'

'You knew Isla from school?'

'She was in the year below – said all the boys in her year were jerks. She loved talking about books and had seen me in the library. Isla really brought me out of myself. I couldn't believe my luck, to be honest. I'd started to believe all the comments from other boys at school that I was weird...' He chuckled. 'Wound my grandpa around her little finger. He was as upset as me when we her dad got a new job and she moved to Perth. Even though Isla didn't want to change me, without realising it she did. For some reason, being with her, I felt more as if I fitted in, even though I was the same person. Perhaps I simply gained some self-esteem.'

'She was popular?'

'Yes, but it wasn't that. I think first loves are so special because it's when you realise that actually, there is someone out there who thinks you are just perfect – that just being you is enough. Have you ever felt that too?'

I thought hard. 'No. Not really. Not until... well, I met Oliver, I guess.' Something inside me shifted uneasily as I thought about our recent arguing. 'Not that we've ever dated,' I added hastily.

'He seems like a great guy.' He looked pointedly at me. 'How come you two never got together? Do you think it could happen?'

'Noooo!' I said with feeling. 'We're just friends by mutual agreement. It wouldn't make sense. Why ruin a good thing? We get on so well as flatmates – ours is a practical relationship and always has been.' Apart from that kiss that I remembered, like a guilty pleasure, whenever I had a run-in with an especially difficult customer or just a stressful week; it felt like a cosy hug. 'I could never go out with someone who doesn't like crisp sandwiches.'

Nik laughed and we both gazed out at the view that encompassed Amblemarsh. Our breath began to blow out white. Birdsong had practically disappeared apart from a blackbird's alarm call. Foxes could be spotted here at night. I pointed out the area where Oliver and I lived and a church and mosque. You could just make out the local school and how the canal snaked through with grassy banks either side was the prettiest thing.

'What a gorgeous sunset,' Nik said, stretching out his legs.

Marvelling at the strips of tangerine across the sky, I agreed. My heart skipped a beat as he slipped an arm around my shoulder.

'Thanks for making me feel so welcome,' he said. 'You've given me a sense of… home, on my travels.' A curl had popped out from my bobble hat and gently, he brushed it away, taking my breath as well. 'You're a one-in-a-million-woman, Jess. Alice bringing you up – I know there's a story behind that. It must have been tough. But you've come through the other side a positive and generous person. I can't tell you how much I admire that.'

'It *was* difficult but living with Gran changed everything.'

Nik simply pulled me closer. I liked that. He reined in his curiosity.

'I've been meaning to say…' My breathlessness continued,

wondering if we might kiss. I couldn't ever recall feeling this deliciously nervous with a man, apart from when Oliver and I had snogged, but there was no point thinking about that anymore. 'I know you're only here for a short time but—'

'Jeeeess! Nik!'

He pulled a puzzled face and stood up. Buddy started yapping. Was that Lynn, interrupting us? I gazed up into the heavens. Was the universe determined I should remain single forever? But what if something was wrong with Gran? What if she'd fallen over again?

'We're coming,' I called.

Nik slipped the rucksack on and I picked up my plastic bag. Holding hands we helped each other down the slippery bank.

'Everything okay?' I asked as we reached Lynn, suddenly aware of the bitter cold. Frost had appeared and icy air pinched my nose. Tail wagging Buddy lunged to greet her.

She stroked him and rolled her eyes. 'Silly me, I left my keys in the rucksack. Another member of staff let us in but my shift's ending now and my car keys are in there.'

23

Lynn's timing couldn't have been worse. I wouldn't see Nik until Friday evening now. I was busy at work and he would be visiting a manufacturer of artificial intelligence toys in Liverpool tomorrow. Then during this afternoon's forest walk I'd heard him arranging to go out with Glenda Friday afternoon. He insisted, as she was on her own, that he'd help her go through the directory to look for another home. She'd already rung a handful herself and found nothing suitable. As a thank you she was taking him to The Corner Dessert Shop, having been horrified that he hadn't yet tried scones.

The *Gazette* was out on Friday, hence the evening get-together of the residents in the lounge to celebrate. Then every Sunday afternoon and Wednesday evening from then until the party there would be a meeting during which we'd make the decorations and discuss any offers of help that came in after the publicity. This Sunday was the 22nd of November. Two weeks before the party. That meant four crafting and brainstorming sessions.

And only three weeks until all the residents had to leave.

My chest tightened.

The smell of a scented candle hit me as I went walked

into the flat. Oliver had set the breakfast bar for two people. He wore a smart shirt.

'Have I forgotten a date you've arranged?'

'No. It's a spur of the moment meal thing,' he said. 'Hope that's okay.'

'Do you mind if I stay in my room? Or I can go out to the pub if you want more privacy. Been a bit of a day.' I took a breath, hesitating over saying more and instead asked 'Who's the lucky lady?'

'I don't know if she'll think it's lucky, but...' He put down the tea towel and came over. Oliver held out his hand. 'The meal's for you. Sorry for being an idiot, Jess. Your feelings about Nik are none of my business. As long as you're happy that's all that matters.'

I hesitated again then slipped my hand into his. His fingers wrapped around mine and he pulled me close. My body relaxed and I leant on him for a second.

'I'm sorry too. I've hated the last few days. I can tell you really are full of remorse because you detest that particular candle.'

'Why anyone wants to pay good money for something that smells of... what does the sticker say... ? *Fluffy towels.*'

'It's clean and cuddly.'

'It smells more like toilet freshener.'

Five minutes later I came back in a fresh jumper and jeans instead of the pyjamas that were calling.

'Just dishing up,' he said. 'You take a seat and pour the wine.'

'Oooh, red. Fancy schmanzy,' I said. Normally we got the cheapest white or cider.

'Here we go,' he said and came over carrying two plates

of… pizza. 'I added the veggie topping. I only finished work at six. It would have taken a miracle to shop, get back and cook from scratch. Anyway, this means you can have you favourite accompaniment.' He fetched a saucepan and poured hot baked beans over the top. Oliver knew me so well. 'Cheers,' he said. His glass touched mine. 'How did the walk go?'

'We collected twigs and some lovely pine cones. It was a shame Gran couldn't come but I think it did the others good. Alf picked up a feather and gave it to Glenda, harking back to their discussion after *It's a Wonderful Life* and whether angels exist.' I sipped my wine. 'Contradictory, isn't it, how conspiracy theorists often don't believe in things that have evidence behind them, but do believe in things that are simply based on myths?'

Oliver shrugged. 'Sometimes it's just a feeling you get, I suppose, that you have to follow – an instinct that Mother Nature gave us.'

I didn't react, giving him the benefit of the doubt that he wasn't talking about Nik.

'I mean, I only have to look at baked beans to know they're barely one step up from baby food.'

'Ha!' My shoulders relaxed. 'Remember that time I'd come into Misty's for a drink after work and stayed for dinner? We'd had that random snowstorm during the day. It had melted by teatime. Those Snowflake Martinis you made were so popular…'

I flushed at the memory, having forgotten a detail of that night. I'd knocked my drink onto on the floor. Oliver had dashed over to mop it up. We'd both tried to pick up glass at the same time and as we straightened up our faces were really close. A ballad was playing in the background and I'd sensed us both hesitate for a second before pulling away and me being filled with... with a feeling of regret. Then he'd gently taken my hand as he'd spotted a splash of blood. I hadn't wanted him to let go which was ridiculous.

'Perhaps I should make some of those as well, on Friday night, along with the eggnog,' he said brightly. 'I've been thinking about snacks to put out, as well, and I might put together a drinks menu.'

'Great idea. Anyway, back to that night, I left before you because I was worried about Buddy being on his own as it was October and people had started letting off fireworks. I had a horrible feeling on the way home that I was being followed and ran the last hundred metres. I heard on the radio the next day that a man had attempted to mug a woman.' I shrugged. 'So sometimes, I guess, a gut feeling is a good thing.'

Neither of us spoke for a moment.

'How was Alice today?'

'We discussed a potential residential home I've found, in Upperhyde – Darkthorn House. Gran's agreed to visit but I'm worried about her, to be honest. This fall, it's really knocked her back.'

'If I'm not working I'll go as well... if you want.'

'That would be great.'

'So, if you enjoyed today's walk what's this about it *being a bit of a day?*'

I put down my knife and fork. 'This is great. What's for pudding?'

'Is it to do with Nik? What's he done?'

'Nothing,' I said, trying not to feel irritated. 'If you must know it was Lynn. She interrupted us when...' I wiped my mouth. He'd actually put out napkins. 'Look, Oliver. I like Nik and I won't apologise for that. I don't want to have to tiptoe around you over this.'

'I... I don't want that either,' he said and pushed away his plate. 'I'm here to talk if you want. Honest, Jess. I'll try to put my own feelings aside. I don't want there to be a taboo subject between us. So...?'

'Okay, it's just...I'm just very aware he'll be leaving in a matter of weeks and I can't find the opportunity to tell him... you know...'

'How you feel?'

'Yes. I took him up to Pebble Rock tonight, and it was lovely, but then Lynn came looking for us because we had the rucksack with her keys in.' I sighed. 'He spends more time with Glenda than me.'

Oliver sat a little straighter. 'Really?'

'He's ever so good with her. She's showing a side I've never seen. He's been messaging her privately about the photo collection she's co-ordinating.'

Oliver sat in silence.

'You still think he's some sort of conman, don't you?'

'I don't know, Jess. Conman? His profile doesn't precisely fit that. Most of the ones you read about create a whole new persona to attract women – a glamorous one indicating they've got money, a high-flying life, or they make themselves out to be some sort of hero like... like being ex-army or having saved someone's life.'

I broke eye contact.

'Nik hasn't mentioned anything like that, has he?'

'And what of it? Are you telling me that every hero in the world has made their story up?'

'Of course not. I... I'm just interested.'

'A couple of years ago he chased and managed to catch a kid who'd robbed a shop. He was the son of an Olympian, it turned out.' I shook my head. 'Nik didn't even worry about the possibility of him carrying a knife.'

Oliver got up to clear the dishes and busied himself at the worktop, serving up one of my favourites – black cherry cheesecake. In an animated fashion, he talked about the mini bar he was going to set up at Willow Court's party, and how he was considering offering a clementine mocktail as well. He didn't mention Nik again but his unspoken accusations hung in the air, his lack of faith in my judgement reminding me of Mum's boyfriends making her feel inferior.

He'd never made me feel like that before. We had always been each other's cheerleaders – or so I thought.

Well, I wasn't my mum. I didn't put up with that kind of behaviour. After eating I insisted on doing the washing up and went straight to bed.

24

I stood in the middle of Under the Tree and yawned. Last night Seb and I had stayed late to do the new window display. I'd told him I could manage alone but Seb insisted, so I took him for a curry afterwards as a thank you – and let him play his Motown CD full blast while we worked. How he managed to swivel his hips and gingerly stack books like in a game of Jenga, to create the book Christmas tree, I'll never know. We'd sprayed the twigs I'd collected from Springhaye Forest with fake snow and scattered pine cones. On a second attempt we'd finally managed to construct the book tree without it falling down. Schoolchildren pestered their parents to stop, on the way to school this morning, so that they could peer in. It made all the extra hours worthwhile. And Nik and Glenda had stopped to admire it, this afternoon, before heading off for their visit to The Corner Dessert Shop.

I'd spent the best part of today replenishing stock, ready for the weekend rush. I rubbed my back as a woman came up to me. Seb was tidying the reading area, in anticipation of the after-school customers who'd bundle in after going on their Friday treat trip to the sweet shop three doors down.

I'd try not to stress about sticky fingers flicking through picture books and always had a packet of wipes handy.

'Have you got any electronic dancing llamas?' she asked.

'Like the one wearing a straw hat, featured on the consumer show last night?'

She nodded eagerly.

I braced myself. There was nothing like being on the end of a parent's disappointment. It happened every time a media outlet did a top ten of the must-have toys for Christmas. Some we'd predicted correctly and bought in a-plenty. Other times we hadn't.

'I'm so sorry, we sold the last one an hour ago.'

Her face fell. 'When are you getting more in? I don't want my daughter being the only one out of her friends who doesn't get one.'

'I rang up our stockist first thing this morning, when I realised there'd been a run on this product. They've been overwhelmed with demand and won't be able to tell me until the end of next week if they can fulfil our order.'

She tutted. 'I can't find it online, either. Have you got a waiting list, in case it comes in? Can I put my name down?'

'No. We don't do that, I'm afraid.'

'Why not?' She put her hands on her hips. 'I've rushed here before picking my two up from school. It's not easy for me to just drop in on the off-chance. I work mornings and the traffic is always late at this time.'

'You could ring in,' I said calmly, despite knots forming in my shoulders.

'But that's still no guarantee it will be here when I arrive...' She delved into her handbag and waved a business card in the air. 'You don't even have to write my details down.'

I wiped my sweaty palms down my jeans. 'I'm sorry. In the past we've been caught out by the practice of holding stock back.'

Her cheeks flushed. 'You're saying you don't believe I'd turn up to buy it?'

'I'm saying it's not our policy but please feel free to ring into the store next week and we'll let you know if we've heard anything.' I forced a wide smile.

'Forget it! I'll go to one of those big superstores that you local businesses are always complaining about. Is it any wonder shops like you go under?' She shook her head and flounced outside.

Another customer shot me a sympathetic look. I headed out to the staff room and ran my hands under the cold tap. In some ways, the ruder a customer was the easier complaints were to deal with, as I found it especially difficult when a lovely parent tried to hide their disappointment.

'What a day,' I said to Seb a couple of hours later as I turned the door sign to *closed*. 'Those little ones loved you reading Beatrix Potter. Who knew you could twitch your nose like a bunny and talk at the same time.'

'Tim does. It's what I do when he wears a new aftershave. He has totally different taste to mine and prefers ones that smell woody like decomposting leaves. So, Willow Court tonight? Will he be there?'

'Yes. Oliver still has his suspicions.'

'He's normally so fair and sensible. Remember that university student Misty took on during the summer? You and I went there for a drink after work, for my birthday.

That student turned up late for their shift for the fourth time in a row. That aside, she seemed so polite and hardworking. Oliver was in charge that day and didn't blow.'

'No. He got another member of staff to cover the bar whilst he sat her down with a coffee. Turned out she was working two jobs to help look with the bills since her mum had been made redundant. He had a word with Misty to arrange a little flexibility with her hours.'

'Then there was the time he rang the shop to let you know the emergency electrician hadn't turned up when your freezer broke down. He wanted to check if you'd heard from him. You were, er....'

'A teeny bit annoyed.'

'That's one way of phrasing it.' His eyes twinkled. 'But Oliver said there was probably a good reason and he'd try to find out what was going on. Turned out the electrician's wife had gone into labour and with all the excitement he hadn't thought to ring his customers.'

I frowned. 'I know and yet for some reason he's disliked Nik right from the start.'

'So if you're so sure that he's wrong about Nik, and he's never been like this with any of your friends then this can only point to one thing – the issue is with Oliver and not Nik.'

208

25

Stepping from foot to foot, to keep myself warm, I waited outside Willow Court. Seb was right, but what could be up? I doubted Oliver's job was under threat. He never heard from his parents so it couldn't be family stuff. He wasn't in a relationship, nor had any money worries.

Unless he did. Anyone could be hiding a gambling problem, or debt. Perhaps jet-setting, successful Nik pressed all the wrong buttons.

I relaxed my jaw suddenly aware I'd been clenching my teeth. Lynn waved through the glass door. I shook my mini umbrella and collapsed it before sticking it in my winter coat pocket. I stood by the radiator for a few moments, the warmth relaxing me.

Betty grimaced. 'I want to go outside. It's not right that strangers are being let in.'

'It's raining and cold outside, Betty. A proper wintry evening. I'd stay in if I were you.' I signed in and entered the lounge. The big terracotta curtains were drawn and Lynn had found time to put up fairy lights along the top rails reminding me of the shops in Springhaye and Amblemarsh that were already in full Christmas mode, with windows decorated and staff wearing festive shirts. Nik held court in the middle of the residents, an open newspaper in his hands – it had to be the *Gazette* that had come out today. He was reading out loud with Glenda by his side listening intently to every word. She must have been in seventh heaven, having spent the afternoon with him as well. Oliver had finished work at four and said he'd bring Buddy over. Sure enough Gran's knees were home to the chin of her favourite dog. Oliver was behind the hatch, whistling as he set out plastic cups. He'd prepared eggnog in advance and refrigerated it. Alf stood on the other side of the hatch deep in conversation with him.

Everyone had a copy of the paper. I took off my hat and coat and lay them over an empty chair. Buddy looked up and his tail wagged. I went over and kissed his head as Nik finished. And then I kissed Gran's.

'What about me?' asked Nik, pretending to be hurt.

'I'd need stilts to do that.'

Everyone laughed as he bent down.

'Anyone else?' I said, hoping no one had seen my blushes.

'No, but allow me young lady...' said Fred. I went over to his chair and he took my hand and in a very gentlemanly manner kissed the top. Then he shook his copy of the newspaper. 'Damn fine article, we were just saying to Nik. You two did a grand job. Hopefully the offers of help will roll in.'

'I've just had a lovely email. A local mum from America loves baking and has said she'll make us eggnog pie and spiced rum fruitcake.' I had no idea how I'd manage alone, sifting through all the messages, if we were inundated. Gran still seemed in low spirits.

'I loved the quote by you Alice,' said Nancy, 'talking about how we were one big family.'

'We certainly didn't choose each other,' she said and everyone nearby laughed. I looked around. Where was Pan?

I read the article, along with the hamper competition. 'You all look great in that photo,' I said.

'What does it feel like to be local celebrities?' asked Nik.

Going by the lively chat it felt fantastic.

'I've never been in a newspaper before,' said Nancy. 'Lynn has said she'll photocopy the article for us so that we can send copies to family.'

Everyone pored over the photo, Fred frustrated that his poor eyesight meant he couldn't see the funny expression everyone said he was pulling.

'How was the trip to Liverpool?' I asked Nik, tapping one foot to music from a Christmas CD.

'Awesome. Junior Magic definitely needs to explore artificial intelligence. And it's inspired me regarding the side venture I'm considering. How about dinner out tomorrow night, on me, and I'll tell you all about it? In fact, you could visit my flat, if you prefer, and I'll cook you real Aussie fayre.'

I beamed.

'Who'd like to try some eggnog?' called Oliver in a loud voice. 'I've also concocted an alcohol-free version and I'm happy to take on board suggestions for any favourite drinks you'd like at the party. Here's a cocktail I'll be making – a Snowflake Martini.' He lifted one in the air. The sky-blue liquid looked beautifully wintry with white flakes stuck around the plastic cup's rim.

'Is that sugar around the top?' someone asked.

Oliver shook his head. 'I've dipped the rim in honey and then pressed the cup into flaked coconut. This drink contains Blue Curacao, vodka and a splash of pineapple juice. I've not made the mixture too strong. It's a lovely refreshing drink and perfectly fits in with the party's snowy theme.'

'What exactly is this eggnog stuff?' asked Fred. 'I've always thought it looks damn sickly.'

'I bet Glenda could tell us – she's so well-travelled,' said Nik.

Glenda's eyes shone behind her cat-eye glasses. Oliver stared at Nik for a moment before nodding.

'I did spend one Thanksgiving in New York,' said Glenda. 'My boss and I were there on business. It was just another November day to us and we were going to spend the day in our sister branch in Manhattan, but a client insisted that we go to his. He showed us both how to make it with egg yolks, sugar, milk, double cream, bourbon and what was the spice…? Nutmeg. That was it.'

Alf pulled a face. 'No offence, Oliver, but some things sound like they just never should be.'

'Glenda and I will have one, won't we?' said Nik.

Oliver gave a smile – the fixed one he used with rude customers or when our landlord demanded more rent.

'Snowflake Martini for me, please,' piped up Nancy. 'It looks like it belongs in my granddaughter's favourite film, *Frozen*. I'll take a photo and send it to her, now that she's shown me how to add attachments to emails.'

Drinks circulated the room, along with jokes about how the residents were all living the high life, now that they were famous. The banter almost blocked out the sound of rain pelting down outside.

'This eggnog is fantastically decadent,' I said to Oliver, who'd come around the other side of the hatch and had been scribbling down residents' suggestions, Martini coming up more than once as a favourite ingredient.

'It's the least everyone deserves. I still can't believe they'll all be gone in less than a month.'

Glenda came over, holding a half-full glass. 'This is delicious thank you, Oliver, although I do hope it doesn't aggravate my indigestion.'

'How is it going collecting everyone's photos? I'd love to see them,' I said.

'I forgot to bring them. Nik's just popped to my room to pick them up.'

'You gave him your key?' asked Oliver.

'Nik's so helpful and generous. He made himself quite at home there when he popped in before our trip to The Corner Dessert Shop, to help me with paperwork. He's going through the directory with me. Also I mentioned that I find my finances and visits to the bank increasingly difficult to manage and he's offered to help me set up online banking.'

'He what?'

I kicked Oliver sharply on the ankle as Glenda headed over to speak to Gran.

'What was that for?' he hissed. 'Someone should tell her to be more careful sharing her personal details.'

'Please. Let's not spoil the great atmosphere.' Shaking my head, I walked away.

At that moment Nik came back. He walked slowly, arms linked with Betty. He must have met her in the corridor. It was so good to see her looking relaxed and free from her restlessness for a few moments. I heard a knock on glass. Someone must have been at the front door. Distracted, Betty let go of Nik and went to look. He came into the lounge and helped Glenda spread the photos over the table.

'I haven't called on everyone yet,' she said to the room. 'But thanks to everyone for being so welcoming. Yesterday I was invited into three rooms and Lynn brought hot drinks and biscuits. So far everyone has found several photos each for me to display so we are building quite a collection.'

I went over and scanned the black and white shots. Men in military uniform. Women in floral dresses and hats. Classic cars driving down roads. Scampish children running around, playing with skipping ropes and footballs. Happy times on beaches and outside churches. And some of the residents as young people – Fred in his fireman's uniform with a quiff of thick chestnut hair and Nancy as a young Girl Guide.

Lynn came in carrying a black dustbin bag. She walked more slowly than usual, her normally pink cheeks looking sallow. She went over to one of the tables by the back window and emptied the contents onto it.

'These are the twigs and cones we collected in Springhaye Forest on Wednesday,' she announced in a tired voice. 'I believe Glenda will be using some of them to make a frame for the photos. You might all like to take a look and get those creative juices going. Sunday afternoon we'll start decorating them. I've ordered in spray cans of white paint and glitter. They should get here tomorrow.'

'Perhaps we could draw up a schedule for each crafting session we've planned,' I said to Gran.

'Maybe,' she said vaguely.

'We should focus on a different element each time,' I continued brightly. 'Like one session for making woodland decorations – perhaps another for the dough ones Gran used to make, then there are the paper angels... We also need to factor in any baking we want to do, for those keen to contribute to the buffet and practise making the American cookies.'

'Excellent idea,' said Glenda. 'Organisation, organisation, organisation was my mantra during all the years I worked as a personal assistant.'

She stole a look at Nik who gave her a smile of approval. He'd magically dispelled the grumpiness she normally displayed around festive activities.

'Alf, how are you getting on with the invitation cards?' I asked. Normally Gran would have been chasing everyone up.

Alf had been writing in a notebook. He looked up from his chair next to Fred's. 'I finished the last one yesterday.' He lifted a plastic bag onto his lap. 'Everyone help yourself. Remember there are two each, seeing as we've limited it to sixty guests. I've enjoyed using the old calligraphy skills again.'

'Were you always a calligrapher?' asked Nancy.

Alf took off his glasses and rubbed his eyes. 'No. I was a bookkeeper until I retired. I always loved writing – figures or letters – but saw my retirement as a chance to do something more creative. My Maisie made it clear our retirement wasn't going to be about lounging in front of the box all day...' He chuckled to himself. 'So I took a course and even did a bit of freelance work with companies designing T-shirts or developing stationery headings. Then when my heart problems started, and I got tired from time to time, it became a hobby.'

'Maisie must have loved getting cards from you,' I said.

'She called me a silly soft sod when I incorporated symbols of hearts into the words.' He shook his head. 'I'd do anything to hear her say that just once more.'

'My father won my mother's hand by the way he wrote her name,' said Nik. 'It's Joanna but he always writes it Johanna – says she deserves to stand out as a little different. He sent her stacks of love letters before she agreed to go out with him.'

'Used to drive my Maisie mad when people misspelt her name with a *y* on the end. Not even I would have got away with that,' said Alf.

Lynn walked to the front, by the hatch. 'Everyone, just to let you know I'll be sending out an email to you and your relatives tonight. I've gone through the directory of care homes Social Services gave us, for this area. I agreed with you all – to save time more information was needed about each one before clicking on the links. So I've personally gone on all the websites, picked out the most relevant bits of information and put them by each care home's name of the list. Therefore you only need to click on the one that suits your needs. So, effectively...' She leant against the hatch. 'I've highlighted those with ensuite rooms. Those that have waiting lists or immediate vacancies. Also, I had a long chat with the mobile hairdresser... I haven't passed on any negative comments but if she's spoken positively about a particular home she goes into, I've put a star by that one's name.' She looked around. 'I hope this makes things easier for you all selecting your preferred choices and for considering the place Social Services offers you and... for those self-funded, for helping you decide where to move.'

'Lynn! You must be exhausted,' I said.

'You're a star,' piped up Nancy.

I took my phone out of my jeans back pocket and clicked on emails. I scanned the new list and went over to Gran.

'There isn't a star by Darkthorn House – but that doesn't necessarily mean Julie had anything negative to say. She probably just doesn't work in there.'

'Have you arranged the visit?'

'Yes. Late Monday morning. It's never a really busy day. Seb's kindly swapped the hours it will take, with me. We'll be able to fit in lunch. I haven't been to Upperhyde for ages but seem to remember there's a rather nice tea room... now what was it called... Up The Spout.'

'Whatever you want,' she said, in a listless voice. 'Thanks for arranging it.'

I was just about to ask where Pan was, when she appeared in the corridor wearing her coat. Her face looked drawn and her hair bedraggled. Lynn went over to speak to her and one of her sons, Adam. Pan held her head in her hands.

26

Adam kissed his mum on the cheek before leaving. Oliver strode over there with a small glass of eggnog. Pan hesitated before taking it. She came over and sat down next to Buddy.

'Do you want to take your coat off?' I asked.

Pan looked down at herself. 'Oh. No... no it's okay. I... I must be going out in a minute.'

Gran reached over and squeezed her arm. 'You've just got back, with Adam. You were visiting a care home, over in Bridgeway.'

'Oh. Yes, of course...' She sipped and met Gran's gaze. 'We don't really have to move, do we? Nowhere is going to be as nice as Willow Court.' A tear trickled down her face, leaving a trail in her blusher. 'If I don't agree to live with my sons they feel I should move into a care home that specialises in dementia.' She shook her head. 'It was awful. We went into a room with people in wheelchairs, saying nothing. You should have seen their blank faces, despite carers sitting down with them and talking or singing. The warden and Adam tried to persuade me to finish the tour – she said she had lots else to show me – but ten minutes inside and I couldn't leave quick enough. I just got a bad feeling about it.' Her voice broke. 'What do I do? I've always promised myself I won't ruin his and Stephen's lives.'

Nik stood nearby. He bent down to Pan's level and took her free hand. 'Perhaps they don't see it like that.'

'I'd be like another child eventually – someone else to worry about if they want to go out or on holiday…'

'You've got two sons – I'm sure they would pull together. And how much do you think they'd be worrying if you moved into a new home and they felt you were unhappy?' he said. 'Wanting you to live with them – that's a serious business and I imagine they wouldn't have offered unless they'd thoroughly thought it through.'

Pan sipped her drink again.

'How about you come and look at the photos Glenda has collected?' he said, softly.

She got up. Nik put an arm around her shoulder and guided her over to the table. Oliver and Alf stood together again, by the hatch. Oliver looked as if he'd drunk vinegar instead of sweet eggnog. Alf looked deep in thought like he did when he was reading about a new conspiracy theory and jotted in his notebook again. A sense of injustice swept through me.

Eventually Pan moved to the front of the room, looking at the newspaper. She folded it and turned it around to face her friends.

'This photo…' Her voice broke and everyone hushed. 'It's like it's the only physical souvenir we've got of our time here. It's meant so much getting to know you… but all of a sudden us… this…' She waved her hand across the room. 'It's gone – or it will be in a matter of weeks.'

'At least we've got memories,' said Fred. His face flushed. 'I mean...'

Pan's eyes welled up. 'At the moment. That won't be the case for me at some point – and perhaps not everyone else. Our friendship... the super community we've built... where's the legacy? It should count for something, shouldn't it? The way you've all rallied around me since my diagnosis. How we've helped each other deal with bereavement – like the text we sent to a loved one that never got read or the words we wish we'd said or could have kept unsaid. We all understand how challenging those things are to live with.'

Alf nodded.

'There's the support we've given each other with our aches and pains... be it laughter or a jolly brisk word or just a hug – all those things have been our free forms of medicine...'

Murmurs of agreement spread from chair to chair.

'And the staff...' Pan looked at Lynn. 'They've become genuine friends. Family. Our own mini taskforce who've treated us like their own. But now it's all being broken up. Time will forget the good times at Willow Court and it's like... it's like we'll be forgotten too.'

Buddy wandered over and settled at her feet.

She sniffed. 'B... B... Barry, dear chap, I should mention you too. Best friend to everyone – a real top dog Willow Court wouldn't have been the same without.'

Nik joined her and faced everyone. 'It's only something small but I had an idea during Wednesday's forest walk when I climbed up to Pebble Rock. Most of you have seen it or know what it is?'

Widespread nods.

'How about I collect thirty or so stones and wash them. You've all made me so welcome I'm happy to buy a selection of acrylic pens for rock painting. All of you can do your own – and I'm sure Jess and Oliver, along with myself, will lend a hand for anyone who can't quite manage the fiddly bits. You can paint on anything you want – a symbol of your time here… your name next to a friend's… something that represents you – and then, under calligrapher Alf's supervision of course, I can write on the back of all of them, *Willow Court*. We can do it during one of the crafting sessions.'

'You'd put them all up at Pebble Rock, together?' asked Pan and she wiped her face.

'Sure would. I think I'm right in saying no pebble has ever been removed. You'll all be there together and when people visit and see the stones, they'll remember this place.'

'A stonking good idea!' said Fred.

'I love it,' said Nancy. 'That way our little community will stay as one, forever.'

Pan didn't speak for a moment. 'Yes. Yes, our pebbles together – that will show people that… that whatever stage of life you are at there are always friendships to be made; that there's always love. We could leave no better legacy.'

Nancy's eyes glistened. Fred blew his nose. Gran stared into her lap at a handkerchief. Everyone started to chat about what they'd paint until, eventually, people began to disperse. Medication needed taking and the oldest residents wanted their beds.

'See you at around seven tomorrow, Jess?' said Nik and looked at his watch. 'I'm just popping along to see Glenda before I leave. I'll offer to go through Lynn's new list with her, if she wants – she hasn't got anyone else to help her.' Nik hugged me.

I held him just a little bit longer than necessary, I couldn't help it.

He headed out of the lounge, stopping to pick up Betty's doll. She'd dropped it without realising. Carefully he placed it into her bag, appearing to make it comfortable. Betty held onto his coat for a moment. He stood patiently, smiling and quietly talking, until her hand fell and she turned away, staring into the distance.

Alf wrote one last thing down in his notebook before saluting Oliver. He bowed to me and left. In silence I collected up any remaining cups. I went behind the hatch, as the rain outside started to fall in torrents, and gave them to Oliver at the sink. He dropped them into the soapy water and caught sight of my charm bracelet.

'That's unusual.'

'A… friend made it for me. The charms represent the important things in my life – the lotus flower is my Buddhism. The book represents Gran. The dog is Buddy.'

'Did Nancy's little great-granddaughter make it? I heard her saying she'd just got into beading.'

'No – but this friend is researching craft packs for children.'

Oliver let go of the washing up sponge. 'Nik made it? He's been around for all of two minutes and considers himself an expert on your life? What's the heart all about?'

'What do you think?'

'You and him? Look… I think you need to hear something, Jess.'

'I thought we'd moved past all this? Honestly – I've got

enough on my mind what with work and the party, with visiting Darkthorn house with Gran and now hearing how Pan's been upset, and how finding a new care home may be even more challenging than I thought. Nik is a real tonic for *everyone*. It's as if he's been sent by fate. Why are you doing your best to ruin that?'

'I searched online for information about the robbery you told me about. There is no reference whatsoever to that crime. You said it happened a couple of years ago. Nik was a hero. And wasn't the robber the son of an Olympian? Because of that, the story would have definitely appeared in the local newspaper and probably the nationals. I Googled Nik Talvi and zero came up, just like when I searched for his supposed toy manufacturing business.'

'Didn't it ever occur to you that he might have asked to have his name left out of it, to keep his privacy? He insisted that Glenda and I don't mention it to anyone else.'

'Isn't it at least possible that he's using you, Jess – either for some sort of romantic liaison, so that he can stay in Britain or to get close to the well-off residents?' His voice was steady and calm. 'Just look at Glenda. He's focused on her and has already found a way of looking at her private financial details. He's won her trust with his schmoozing and now she even trusts him with her room key. Glenda's probably the most well-off resident in Willow Court – don't tell me that's a coincidence.' Oliver gazed at me intently. 'Is it really so illogical to think that this isn't normal – not when we've only known about him for a matter of weeks?'

'Have you seen how much more cheerful she is these days?' I said quietly. 'Nik's brought a sparkle into her life. This is a difficult time for her – for all the residents.'

'But this is real life, not a fairytale – Nik's not some wholesome Disney character like the one on his watch.'

I folded my arms. 'Is this what Alf's been writing notes about? Don't think I haven't seen the two of your skulking in the corners.'

'I don't know exactly what Alf makes of him – just that he thinks there is a story behind the smooth veneer.'

My arms dropped to my sides. 'Look, Oliver, are you're miffed that the residents have taken another man into their hearts, because you know—?'

'Of course not.'

'Then is everything all right? I'm always here if you need to talk through a problem.' I did my best to smile but he gave no reply. 'Is it really so difficult to believe that Nik might genuinely fancy me?'

He snorted.

My eyes pricked. I don't know why it hurt so much, Oliver and I had always only been friends, but it ached to find out that he couldn't believe Nik might find me genuinely attractive in the same way it had ached when he'd backed off so quickly, years ago, after that drunken kiss.

'I'll answer that for you, then,' I said, stung by his silence. 'No it's not, because he's asked me to his flat tomorrow night – so I might not be back until the next day and if you can't accept that then maybe... maybe it's time you moved out,' I blurted.

27

I stood outside the block of flats in Islington, having walked past a row of houses with extravagant Christmas wreaths on their doors. It was a beautiful night. The romantic scene was set with a clear moon, devilishly dark sky and sultry streetlamps. I pressed the buzzer confidently – although Seb had worried me when he'd questioned my intentions over lunch in the staff room.

'Number one thing tonight, Jessie – don't make an idiot of yourself.'

'Of course I won't!'

'There's nothing worse than laying your wares on the table to have them rejected. I know. Let's just double-check the evidence to make sure gorgeous Nik feels the same way back.' He grabbed a discarded receipt next to the kettle and turned it over before placing it on the table. He took the pen out from behind his ear.

'How did he act towards you, the very first time you met?'

'I can remember it so clearly,' I said and put down my sandwich as I talked Seb through the things we'd chatted about. 'And he said I reminded him of how much he liked

England. After we parted, when I looked back at him, over my shoulder, he was looking back at me too.'

'And who contacted who first afterwards?' asked Seb. He swigged out of his detox drink bottle.

'Nik didn't have my contact details but one week later I texted the number on his business card.' I smiled. 'He replied straightaway, said he'd been thinking about me and shared a silly joke about Pinocchio.'

'Hmm. There could be a Freudian meaning behind that.' Seb jotted something down. 'How did he react the first time you met again?'

'It was outside Willow Court. As soon as he saw me, Nik opened his arms for a hug.'

'Has he made any big romantic gestures?'

'He's given me red roses – and a charm bracelet with a heart on.' I wiggled my wrist in the air.

Seb put down his pen. 'It's all sounding very positive to me, Jess, and I assume he's ticking all the boxes when it comes to kissing…'

I rubbed the back of my neck.

His eyebrows raised. 'Please tell me that, at least, has taken place.'

I'd sighed. 'It's not for want of trying. We've had a couple of near-misses.' I told him about Oliver turning up at the flat when Nik had come to dinner, and how Lynn interrupted us at Pebble Rock, asking for her keys.

Seb screwed the receipt up into a ball and leant back in the chair. 'From everything you say I conclude that this man is totally into you. As for why he hasn't more openly made his move yet, the answer's obvious.'

It was?

'From everything you've ever said about him – and from what I sensed when I met him briefly – Nik is the perfect gent. So you might need to nudge a bit harder for him to realise exactly how ready you are to take things further...'

Snapping myself back to the present, I pressed the buzzer again. Nik loomed into view, behind the glass door, and it opened. I went in. His arms and aftershave enveloped me. I stood back, admiring the tailored cut of his dark grey shirt with red flowers on it. It complimented his hair and contrasted his warm tan. I followed him along a brightly lit corridor and into a flat.

'You're on the ground floor?'

'It's great. There's a garden.'

'Not much good at this time of year though.'

For some reason he gave a wide grin.

I gazed at the minimalist furniture. The place didn't look lived in, with the immaculate cream walls and furnishings and the sparkling glass tables. It was open plan like mine and Oliver's but couldn't have been tidier. There was a small dining table by the far window that looked out onto the street. Nik had set it up with red napkins and candles.

He took my coat and woolly hat and let out a low whistle. 'What a knockout dress.'

It was tight and short. Not my usual style. A present from Angela who said I didn't make enough of my figure.

'Great place, Nik. It's like a hotel.' I glanced at a small pot, on the floor in the corner, by the front window. 'I should have known there would be a Christmas tree somewhere.'

'You should see the bedroom – it's got a waterbed.'

I tried not to look eager.

'A glass of wine?' he asked after draping my things over

the back of a white leather sofa. 'I've bought a bottle of Chardonnay. I spotted one on your kitchen unit when I came around for dinner, and assumed it was a favourite.' He passed me a glass, filled it a little and let me taste it first. So old school.

'What's for dinner? I can hardly wait.' It was at that moment I spotted flames outside the French windows. I caught his eye. 'You're not serious?'

'I found a barbecue in the utility cupboard. What could be more Australian? And it's oh so cosy standing around those coals.' He pulled the patio doors open and we stood outside. He was right. I didn't need my coat. The glow from the barbecue reminded me of bonfire night. I glanced at the wire rack, the burgers and sausages and...

'Now you're really having a laugh,' I said. 'Brussel sprout and bacon skewers?'

'A classic and delicious topped with grated parmesan. Sausages, burgers, skewers – they are the basics of a good Aussie dinner. I've made coleslaw and a Greek salad and a rather special starter. We often get together at the family house for barbies and my parents are always trying out new recipes.' He flipped a burger and I warmed myself. 'The residents seemed pretty happy about the newspaper article, last night. Apart from Alice – how's she recovering?'

'Slowly. But she seemed to perk up when you mentioned painting stones. That idea was really special.'

'I'm just hoping it makes a small difference.'

'I had a quick look at my emails at lunchtime and guess what? We've already had about twenty replies.' I forced a bright tone, despite knowing I'd have a lot of late nights ahead of me sifting through. Normally I'd have printed them out and asked Gran's opinion on which offers of help we should take up but she needed all her energy, at the moment, to get better. 'I've read a few... a local caterer called The Springhaye Snacking Company, they specialise in finger foods and have offered a hefty discount on buffet dishes. The owner said she'd catered for care homes before so would make sure nothing was too spicy or rich and would include some old favourites like sausage rolls and pineapple and cheese sticks – things that are easy to pick up and eat, yet with a festive twist where possible. A scout group has said it will run a couple of sponsored events to raise money, to help cover costs like that. A Christmas tree farm has offered to deliver us one for free, whatever size we want.'

'That's exciting. We could read more of them after dinner.' He rolled the skewers. 'Almost done. You stay out here and I'll fetch you when our starters are ready – they are something of a surprise.'

More than happy to remain by the coals, I waited, the inside of my chest fluttering as I sipped my wine. Finally he came back and took my glass. 'Don't come in for a minute. I'll just put this on the table.' Seconds later he returned and took my hand. We went in and he stood behind me. I giggled as he placed his hands over my eyes. We walked over to the window, him guiding me. 'Here's the chair,' he said softly. I sat down. He crouched, his fingers still across my face. 'Okie dokes, here we go – one, two, three...' He took his hands away.

I looked down. 'Toast?'

'With Vegemite. I'd be letting my country down if I didn't get you to try that.'

He sat down opposite me, eyes laughing, and I glanced at the plate again. 'How neatly you've cut the bread into four triangles. It's almost worth taking an Instagram photo – almost...' I said.

We both picked up pieces. My nose wrinkled.

'It tastes better than it smells,' he insisted. Slowly, he chewed and then licked his lips. My pulse sped up. Maintaining eye contact, I bit into the bread, briefly savouring the satisfying flavour of melted butter before... 'Do you like it?' he asked. I swallowed as quickly as I could, before gulping back a large mouthful of wine. 'I'll take that as a no?'

'It's just like Marmite, except even stronger, almost bitter. How could you do that to me?'

Nik threw another triangle into his mouth comically and closed his eyes, making appreciative noises as he ate. 'I hope the main course makes up for all the drama. You relax there. I won't be two minutes.' He brought over the coleslaw and Greek salad, and then a burger loaded with pickled beetroot, a slice of pineapple and a fried egg, the whole stack placed in a bun. I picked it up and bit down, yolk squirting onto my chin.

'Oh my God. Nik. What are you trying to do to me? This is paradise on a plate.'

'And the sprouts?'

Mouth full of one, accompanied by crispy bacon and parmesan, all I could do was close my eyes appreciatively and nod. We chatted about favourite childhood foods.

'Living close to my grandparents I grew up on plenty of Finnish meals. Grams made amazing meatballs with mash, heaps of brown sauce and lingonberry jam.'

'I've eaten Scandinavian meatballs in Ikea.'

Nik tutted. 'Good thing my grandpa isn't here. He used to get annoyed whenever anyone assumed Finland was part of Scandinavia.'

'It isn't?'

Nik shook his head and picked up one of the olives. He slipped it into his mouth. 'No. Geographically, determined by the Scandinavian Peninsula, Norway, Sweden and Denmark are the only Scandinavian countries – a subregion of northern Europe. But it gets more complicated from the cultural and historical viewpoints that would require including Iceland and Finland. The latter two would probably refer to themselves more as Nordic than Scandinavian. Grandpa was very precise about these things. It used to make Grams laugh.'

'How was she… towards the end… if you're okay talking about it?' I asked. 'Betty seems angry or sad a lot of the time whereas Phyllis is, overall, more content.'

Nik stopped eating. 'We were grateful that she rarely got upset – even when she didn't know who we were. I remember once, when she was still up to going out, we went to a mall and I took her off in a wheelchair whilst Grandpa went to buy some toiletries she'd run out of. When he came back, she asked who he was. He said her husband. She looked horrified but a flicker of amusement appeared in her eyes. The three of us started laughing – comic tragedy at its best.' He picked up his fork and his eyes shone. 'I treasured moments of togetherness like that, even though they were also sad.' He fell silent for a moment. 'So, what was your favourite childhood food?'

'Pizza takeout,' I said straightaway. 'Cooking wasn't

Mum's thing. Often I just made myself sandwiches but when she suggested pizza I knew that meant she was in a really good mood and that made everything taste so much better.'

He placed his hand over mine. I imagined it running down my spine. 'I guess I was lucky growing up, surrounded by family. I took it for granted at the time. How do you get on with your mother now?'

'I don't know – she hasn't been in touch for years.'

'Do you know where she is?'

'No. Now and again, I felt like calling her but... I know it's stupid... a silly pride stopped me. I gave in just once. I'd just broken up with a boyfriend and was feeling low. I rang her number. It wasn't valid anymore.'

'Jeez, Jess, that sucks.'

'Gran's made up for a lot. She taught me everything I know about cooking for a start.'

'That rhubarb crumble was a top pudding – mine won't come close.'

I groaned. 'Not sure I've got room for dessert.'

'It contains chocolate.'

I put my fingers in my ears but he cleared away our plates and came back with a dish of square, brown cakes.

'Lamingtons. Traditional. Reliable. Honest.'

That didn't surprise me. Nik's simple taste in food seemed to be like his taste for all things in life.

'It's chocolate sponge sandwiched together with jam and cream and then covered in chocolate icing and dipped in desiccated coconut. Traditionalists say there shouldn't be any jam and cream in the middle. It's a bit like the English debate about scones and whether the jam goes on first or not.'

'I suppose just a small one wouldn't harm,' I said, even though they were all the same size. After finishing my third, I groaned and stood up.

'The worst thing after all this food would be lying on the waterbed,' he said. 'Talk about a weird sensation. I couldn't get used to it so have resorted to sleeping on the sofa.'

'I've never been on one. I'd love to try it.' Heat flooded into my face. I didn't mean to be as direct as that. In fact, I didn't mean anything by it – I was genuinely curious.

'Don't blame me if you get seasick. Come on then, bring your phone and we can look at some more of those emails.'

I took my mobile out of my bag and followed him into a room past the kitchen. Like the living area it was mainly magnolia with plain sheets and streamlined wardrobes. Tentatively, I sat down on the bed, next to Nik, leaning up against the headboard. I bounced up and down and couldn't help laughing. Accidentally I fell against him and looked up. He smiled as we gazed at each other.

'See what I mean?' he said.

I nodded, not sure what to say, pulse racing as I straightened up.

The bed calmed down and Nik closed his eyes. 'I'm trying to imagine I'm on my lilo.'

'Do you miss home?'

'Sure. My family. Friends. But you, Jess, and Willow Court have gone some way to filling the gap whilst I'm abroad.'

My throat went dry as I tried to find the words to tell Nik just how much I wanted to get close.

'So, the offers of help that have come in – what kind of things?'

Reluctantly, I tapped on the email icon on my phone. 'Wow. Another five.' I read one quickly. 'Oh. My. Goodness. You'll never guess what someone has offered.'

'A real-life reindeer to ride on? The abominable snowman to liven things up?'

'Idiot,' I said. 'Although you are almost right with the last one – to help set the wintry scene that characterises *It's a Wonderful Life*, get this... a snow machine company called Pro Snow has offered to create the illusion of falling snow outside for us on the day of the party.'

'Love that idea!'

'Does it snow much in Sydney?'

'Now and then. The last decent fall was in 1836.'

'You're joking.'

'Sadly not – it's the price we pay for the ace summers. I can't wait to see some here – even if it is manmade.' He hugged his knees.

'You look like a small child on Christmas Eve.'

'Magic is important, even for adults.'

I shuffled nearer to him. This was it. However annoyingly, at that moment, Oliver popped into my head with all his doubts and unfair accusations. I stared into the distance as something bleeped. Perhaps our friendship, us being flatmates, had come to its natural end. My chest hurt as I recalled the moment I mentioned him moving out. The shock on his face. My shock that I'd actually said it.

'Another email has just landed,' said Nik. He picked up my phone and passed it to me. I looked at the email address of the sender. It was from a woman called Karen.

The skin tightened across my forehead. I couldn't even blink. It was as if the universe had been listening to me and Nik chatting earlier.

'It's from my mother.'

28

I entered the living room and sat down on the sofa. I didn't take off my coat. Or hat. Buddy jumped up next to me and batted me with his nose. He let out low whines, nudging me as I didn't react. I'd made my excuses to Nik as quickly as I could. He walked me to the train station, without asking any questions. In a daze I got into my train, needing to be alone. I hadn't opened the email. This single phone notification had brought back the inner turmoil. Was Mum still married? Had she got another child of her own? Did that mean I had a brother or sister? Perhaps she'd been jailed again. Did she want money? She must have been local to have seen the news article and my email address.

Oliver padded into the kitchen, wearing his Misty's uniform. It had just gone midnight. He couldn't have been in long. He filled the kettle and then went back into his bedroom as it heated up. Seconds later he came out again.

He stood in front of me and I stared past his shoulder. Buddy licked his hand before sliding down to stretch out on the floor. 'I've thought everything through I... I was taken aback that you wanted me to move out, but it's absolutely your call. I've started looking for another flat and will try to make it happen as soon as possible.'

Perhaps Mum was ill. Maybe she'd only got months left to live.

'If I can I'll move out before Christmas. I'm sorry I've upset you so much. I really care about you, but that's no excuse to—'

I'd started to shiver. He knelt down and frowned. 'What's the matter?' He pulled off my woolly hat and took my hand. 'Let me get us a cup of tea.' Minutes later, he was back with two mugs. I sat quietly sipping, in my dress and high shoes. They weren't really me. My heels had blisters. As if he could sense this, Oliver fetched my slippers and swapped the footwear over. 'Do you want to talk about it?' I shook my head vigorously. 'Okay. I'll just keep you company. Let me know if you'd rather I disappear.'

'It's Mum,' I eventually croaked. 'She's got in touch after that article in the *Gazette*. I got an email this evening.'

'Christ.' He took my hand again. 'What does she want?'

'I don't know. I can't face reading it.' I put down my drink.

'You don't owe her anything, Jess. No one would blame you for just deleting it.'

'What if there's a message in it for Gran? I can tell from her occasional remarks that, as she's getting older, the estrangement cuts deeper. I think moving into Willow Court made Gran more aware of her mortality and I expect... I expect she'd like a sense of closure.'

'I expect you'd want answers too. I'd love to ask my parents why they were never around when I was a kid, whether they loved me or not. I know you've moved on, Jess – on the surface. But maybe this will turn out to be an opportunity for you and Alice to find a bit of... of solace.'

'Mum's forty-seven now. She had me when she was eighteen. Since turning twenty-nine I've tried so hard not to focus on the fact that I'm the age she was when she came out of jail and effectively gave me up for a different life.'

'You never said anything.'

'It shouldn't be a big deal.'

'I disagree. I think about things like that. Like last year, when I was twenty-eight. That's how old my parents were when they had me. They let slip once that the pregnancy had been a mistake. I sometimes wonder if they'd even wanted children' Oliver gave a half-smile. 'See – we all mull over this sort of crap.'

I rubbed my forehead. 'I shouldn't be bothering you with all this, you must be shattered, Misty's is always crazy busy on a Saturday night.'

'Do you want me to read the email to you?'

'No. Thanks but…' I wiped my face and sat up straighter. 'I need to get myself together and deal with this – for Gran.'

'You're one brave woman, Jess. You can do this.'

I looked down at our hands. They fitted well together. 'Sorry about what I said about moving out… I didn't really mean… It's just I like Nik and—'

'It's okay. Maybe… maybe the time is right.'

What? My stomach lurched.

'I should have backed off. In fact, it's made me realise… it's unhealthy, my interest in your dating life. I should be focusing on my own.' He gave a small smile. 'So I hopped onto Tinder last night. I'm going for dinner, tomorrow. It's about time I met someone.'

'What's she called?'

'Krishna – or rather, Krish.'

They were already on casual terms.

'She's a businesswoman – just twenty-six and running her parents' coffee shop chain. She loves cocktails and going to the gym. That's about all I know.'

She sounded glamorous.

'Can I see her photo? It's only right I'm as nosy as you've been,' I said and sniffed.

Oliver pulled his phone out of his back pocket and tapped on it for a few moments, then held it up. Long, glossy, black hair. Intense, almond-shaped eyes that drew you in. A friendly smile. She had eyebrows to die for and full lips. Her outfit was sexy yet not too short nor too low. I tried to find something not to like but couldn't.

'She looks lovely.'

'I think so. Look... I meant what I said – I'll move out, Jess, honestly, you don't have to change your mind.'

'I may have moved in here first but after all this time this is our joint home. It was wrong of me to suggest you might be the one to leave. If anyone's going it should be me, but we can work this out, right? I mean, who would scratch Buddy in the exact right spot, under his chin? No one can do that but you.'

'I'm sure he'd find someone who could.' He gave a small smile. 'Invite Nik over again. I promise to keep well out of the way. You think he's great and so does Alice. I have to accept my instincts got it wrong. I... I just want you to be happy. I'll start looking at rentals this week.' He stood up and hurried out of the room.

Oliver moving out of the flat? But this was his home. Our home.

I stared at my phone and tapped the email open. She'd put a mobile phone number at the top and then:

Jess,

I saw Mum's photo in the paper. I had no idea she'd gone into a care home. But that's my fault. I've been meaning to get in touch but the time never seemed right. It's been so long. I'm sorry about that. Really sorry. I don't know what else to say. Life's been complicated.

And you... you look beautiful.

Is there any way you'd consider meeting up, so that I can explain? I know I have no right to ask. And I don't want to hurt you or your gran any more than I already have. If you don't reply I understand. I'll respect whatever you decide.

Please just realise I've never stopped thinking about both of you.

Love from

Mum X

29

Been meaning to get in touch? That was the best she could do? Mum was in for a surprise if she thought I was going to provide a response to that – especially after Gran's recent upsets. Reading this email might tip her over the edge. Seb sensed something was wrong but didn't quiz me – well, not once he'd established my date had gone well and that Nik and I were still a possibility. Instead he kept me supplied with coffee and biscuits.

Nik had rung first thing to check I was okay. With Oliver out on a date I invited him back to ours for takeout, after the planned crafting session at Willow Court.

'Count me in,' he'd said. 'And I'll bring the leftover Lamingtons for the residents to try this afternoon.'

'My waistline says please don't,' I'd replied.

I came off the phone feeling brighter and decided I wouldn't think about Mum's email for a couple of days.

I'd just enjoyed a gingerbread latte from the coffee shop over the road before leaving for Willow Court. Angela had come in to help and try to get through some paperwork. I'd treated the three of us. Seb had swapped a shift again, so that I could leave at two. Angela didn't mind as long as I kept on top of the stock and was on call to drop everything and go in if it got super busy or an emergency arose. Grateful, I'd gone to the shop a couple of hours before opening to get ahead with cleaning and replenishing the shelves. I'd hardly slept so it had made no difference to me to get up before the sun did. And when Angela discovered several invoices were missing, I promised to work through my lunch hour tomorrow and search the little office from head to toe.

It didn't feel like work. I was lucky. Since Angela had started spending less time at Under the Tree I'd put my personal stamp on the office, with a cactus on the windowsill in a plant pot the shape of a Buddha. I'd rearranged the furniture so that there was room for another chair opposite my desk – this made the layout better for when Seb and I brainstormed ideas, away from the temptation of sweet treats in the staff room. I bought a toy aquarium I'd always loved that looked like a live tropical fish tank, to place on top of a filing cabinet. As it needed it anyway, Angela was more than happy for me to give the room a lick of paint and I chose a relaxing pale blue colour. Seb painted motifs of building blocks and teddy bears in the corners, and balloons on the ceiling.

'You're seeing Mr Down Under again tonight?' he asked.

'How do you manage to make so many things sound rude?'

'You've no time to lose,' he continued. 'Isn't the Christmas party just two weeks today?'

Seb was right. I'd turn off my phone, settle Buddy in Oliver's room and I'd send my flatmate a reminder not to come back before midnight – although maybe that wasn't necessary. Maybe Krish would invite him to stay over.

A sense of unease washed over me. She could be The

One. Although that could be a good thing and give me the push I needed to sort out my own life. Oliver and I couldn't share the flat forever. Thirty was looming – a new decade, a time for change. I needed to look at this positively. Oliver couldn't make it to Willow Court today but would definitely be at Wednesday's crafting session. He was at Misty's all afternoon and then heading straight into London to see Krish. We'd cancelled our usual Sunday brunch as I'd wanted to get in early to work, but had met briefly, over bowls of cereal, and he hadn't mentioned Nik or Mum's email. However, he did give me a tighter hug than normal and let me have the last of the coffee.

Nik was already at Willow Court. Lynn had set up tables bearing the forest twigs and cones, and cans of white sprays plus tubes of glitter. Alf was handing out the invitations he'd written to those who still hadn't got theirs. Nancy sat by the window, next to her record player and was swaying in time to a tune by Duke Ellington's Orchestra. I gave Gran a kiss and squeezed Pan's shoulder. Nik was chatting with Glenda.

'Internet banking can seem daunting at first but you'll soon get the hang of it.'

'Having another pair of common sense eyes help me set it up is making it so much easier. You're very kind,' she said, looking especially smart today. She'd dyed her hair a warmer shade of brown and her red lipstick was a little brighter.

'We can carry on our chat about where you move to next. I'd sure love to help. How about lunch out tomorrow, Glennie? My treat. We could go to The Silver Swan.'

Glennie?

'No, *my* treat, darling. I insist.'

Darling?

Nik beamed. 'Okay. It's a date.' He turned to me as Glenda busied herself with the black and white photos. The collection seemed to have grown since just two days ago.

He clasped my hand and gave it a squeeze. 'Hi, Jess. How was work?'

'Great! Although I'm already looking forward to chilling with takeout tonight. Have you thought about what sort you'd like?'

'How about your childhood favourite, pizza? I haven't had one yet, since getting off the plane, and I'm suffering from withdrawal symptoms.'

'Deal.'

'My fave back home has barbecue sauce as a base instead of tomato. And olives.'

'I love ham and pineapple.'

'Swap that fruit for mango and I'm in.'

He and I, along with Lynn, manned the crafting tables although most of the residents were very capable. Another care worker had set up an area to start making the crackers, whilst supervising a resident at the table next to her, Bill, who was fiddling with a mini dementia wooden workbench that had hammers, screws and nails, even a vice. His face was totally relaxed as he busied himself with it. When we took a break after an hour for tea and Lamingtons, Nik sat down and helped him eat some of the chocolate cake before, between them, they hammered in a nail.

Alf kept looking at Nik and writing notes like he had on Friday.

'Another conspiracy theory?' I asked.

He put his fingers to his lips. 'I'll tell you when I've gathered enough evidence.'

I went to the front, near the hatch and yawned. Gran should have been by my side, calling the shots, but she just sat quietly, wearing no particular expression. 'If I could have everyone's attention,' I said. 'I'd just like to fill you all in on the amazing emails I've received, following the article in the *Gazette*.' I'd gone through them in the early hours, as I couldn't sleep. 'I'm really excited about the local mum I've already mentioned to some of you who's American and has offered to make us spiced rum fruitcake and – I'm curious about this one – eggnog pie!'

'It sounds just wonderful,' said Glenda and several people looked at her, eyebrows raised.

I explained about the catering company and scouts and the Christmas tree company that had offered us a spruce for free, and the other emails that had come in this morning – a local choir was going carol singing throughout December and would make sure they called here on the 6th. 'But most exciting of all...' I smiled. 'A snow machine business has offered to create falling snow in the front garden, so that Willow Court really looks like a winter wonderland.'

Pan clapped her hands. She wore bright orange nail varnish that wasn't applied as neatly as usual. The usually smooth foundation appeared blotchy, and deeply set in her wrinkles. That had happened a few times recently. I waited for Glenda to give her usual moans about snow – how it was slippery and mushy and altogether unpleasant, as well as a threat to any pensioner's health if they went out for a walk in it. However, her face looked radiant as she spoke to Nik.

'That must be exciting for you. I remember visiting Adelaide with work, one winter, and getting to know a young woman who'd never seen snow. The following year she visited our offices. The look of wonder on her face when we had a blizzard – I've never forgotten it. She went outside and the snowflakes ruined her styled hair and her mascara ran, but she didn't care one jot.'

'It snows a lot where my family originally comes from in Finland,' said Nik. 'When I was a child Mum and Dad would take me to visit. Much as I love the sun, I never feel more at home than when I'm sitting outside on a porch, in thermals, drinking steaming coffee and looking out onto a white landscape.'

Alf cocked his head, his eyes widened and he wrote something down.

'So I'll see you tomorrow morning, ten o'clock sharp,' I said to Gran as Nik and I prepared to leave.

'Fine,' she mumbled.

'Are we going now?' said Betty to Nik. 'We need to get home. The children will be waiting.'

Nik pulled up the arm of her raincoat that had started to fall down. Over recent months Betty had lost weight.

'They are tucked up in bed, having an early night,' he said softly. 'There's nothing to worry about, Betty.'

She stared at him, her frown lines disappearing for a second.

I sat down next to Gran. 'How do you really feel about visiting Darkthorn House tomorrow?'

'I've just got to make the best of a bad situation.'

'No, you don't. We're not signing up to anywhere you aren't one hundred per cent happy with. I know there's only three weeks to moving out but I promise we'll find you the right long-term fit.'

'Sorry for not being much help lately,' she said. 'I'm just not in the mood for this party. What's the point? And it shouldn't be you worrying about all of this. I should have your mum here to help. You should be out dancing in clubs and partying – not stuck inside with a bunch of old fogies.'

'When did I ever party?' I said, smiling, but my conscience niggled about not having mentioned the email. 'Surely you wouldn't still want Mum around – not after she's kept away for so many years?'

'I don't expect you to understand, sweetheart. You might one day, if you have kids. Karen… she'll always be my little girl. She's made mistakes – flippin' big ones at that. I can't say I don't feel hurt, really hurt—' she thumped her chest '—by her silence but… blood bonds us. She's part of me. Without her around I don't feel complete. She's not been the best mum to you and I can't forgive her for that… but I love her.' She glanced down at the invitation cards Alf had handed out. 'I took these but haven't got anyone to send them to. When did my world become so small?'

Whilst Nik escorted Glenda back to her room I vacuumed the floor and packed away the crackers that had been made, into a box, admiring the ties and brightly coloured foil. I wouldn't think about Mum. I wouldn't let her ruin my evening.

Buddy made everyone laugh by chasing a green curl of ribbon. Alf persuaded Nancy to play dominoes. Lynn left the woodland sprigs and cones, now sprayed and covered in glitter, to dry on their table. They looked so pretty. Betty wandered in and out, clutching her doll. I hoped she found a new home that gave her the freedom to roam and that Bill moved to a place that had special activity toys. Nancy caught my eye and gave the relaxed smile of someone who'd sorted her future – a home near her granddaughter. Apparently, she'd applied there before coming to Willow Court but, at the time, it was full. I told Gran that proved that second choices could turn out well like Willow Court had for Nancy. I wondered what Glenda would do. Money gave her a few extra options and with the degree of her osteoporosis she didn't quite need as much help as say Fred, with his failing eyesight, or Alf with his heart problems that meant some days he hardly had the energy to get out of bed.

Nik and I waved to everyone before heading off. Sleet started to fall as soon as we stepped out, into the darkness. He held out his hand and licked off a sliver of ice. Buddy yapped as he stepped into an icy puddle.

'I will give you a drink when we get to my flat, you know.'

He chuckled. 'When I went to Finland as a kid, we stayed with Dad's parents who'd stayed there, and the boy next door and I would go into the woods to see if we could spot any Arctic hares. We'd see who was brave enough to eat the biggest snowball. Mum never could work out why I used to get stomach ache after playing out.'

We came to my apartment block, having passed a few houses that had sparkling fairy lights up. Nik stood behind me as I opened the door, his hand protectively resting on my back. Buddy charged ahead, pulling on the lead, as we went upstairs. My hands were almost blue. Worrying about Gran's continued low mood, I hadn't been focusing when we came out of Willow Court and must have left my gloves there. Nik took the key as my numb hand struggled to open my front door. I hurried to the central heating thermostat and turned it up, still feeling emotional and walking in reminded me that soon Oliver might be gone.

I spun around, having not turned on the lights yet. The orange glow from the streetlamp outside lit up the room. Nik stood there looking gorgeous, red anorak unzipped. Everything in my life at the moment felt strange and uncertain except for this. I strode over, pulled off my woolly hat and let it drop on the floor. Standing on tiptoe, I shut my eyes and pressed my lips firmly against his.

30

Nik's face jerked back. 'Crikey, Jess, what's going on?'
I took his hand. 'I like you, Nik. A lot. And I think you like me.'

He stepped back. 'You're great – really, but... look, can we turn on the lights?'

Of course, open, sunny Nik wouldn't want to make love in the dark. But I bit my lip. That wasn't what he meant.

'Whatever you prefer.' I went to the wall by the kitchen and flicked a switch, a tide of heat sweeping up my neck and into my face.

'Jess... look... let's sit down.' He moved towards the sofa. 'I think there's been a misunderstanding.'

I couldn't move, wishing I were invisible, wishing a secret door would suddenly appear, headed by the word Exit...

'I'm sorry but I don't think of you in that way.'

... or a sink hole would do because it was sinking in that I'd made a mistake.

He walked back to me and placed his hands on my arms.

'I'm really flattered. Any bloke would be lucky to have you as his girlfriend. I'm sorry if, somehow, I've given you the wrong impression.' 'He took his hands away. 'We've hit it off. Clicked, haven't we? That doesn't happen often in life

– but for me it's just friendship… a friendship I don't want to lose.' He stared at me intently.

'But when you came over to dinner – you took me into my bedroom, to the window, and said the view was romantic. You gave me red roses.' I needed to shut up but I couldn't stop trying to validate myself out loud. 'And at Pebble Rock you said I'd made England feel like home for you.'

Nik looked puzzled. 'And I meant every word.'

'You loved my dress when I came to yours.' It was tight and short.

'It was red,' he said, 'like the roses – my favourite colour.' He slid down into the sofa and held his head in his hands. Buddy padded over and nuzzled them. He looked up. 'Please forgive me. This is my fault.'

Not really knowing what to say, I glanced down at my wrist and the charm bracelet. Nik caught my eye.

'The craft pack – it said friendship bracelets. That's what I made, Jess.'

'I feel so stupid,' I said, my throat tight around the words. 'The heart… I thought…'

'That charm isn't about me.'

'Oh…' I went to take it off.

'Please, keep it – this connection between us… it's important.'

'So you aren't single?'

'I am. Life's been busy. I've put everything into the business. In fact, this trip is making me reassess my life on several levels. Getting to know the residents of Willow Court has made me realise how important family is. That's why I spend so much time with Glenda.'

I sat down next to him. 'Sorry for making you feel so

uncomfortable.' Now my hands covered my eyes. 'I feel so embarrassed but I can't escape as we're in my flat.'

Gently, Nik peeled my fingers away. 'Don't be. You're one hell of a Sheila. We're both blaming ourselves for this – perhaps that means we're even and it doesn't have to change anything.'

My chest felt lighter. Oddly, the rejection was beginning to give me just a tiny sense of… relief?

'Mate to mate, Jessie – I'm a straight up kind of guy, right?'

I nodded.

'If I say you're fantastic, you bloody are. So how about taking a compliment?'

Then why not…? As was so often the case with Nik, I didn't need to say the words out loud.

'You're kind, hardworking, everything any bloke could want, but I've just come out of a relationship that ended badly and the last thing I can think about is dating again. Junior Magic is going through a tough time but I could have done a lot of research at home. I've used my personal savings to travel here. If I'm honest, I needed to get away. Rebekah lives opposite my parents and I always spend the festive season with them. I don't want to run into her. Not yet. This trip is lasting longer than I'd planned, but I can't say I'm unhappy about that.'

If only he'd mentioned this before. 'Sorry to hear that. Break-ups are tough.'

'I deserved it. Rebekah…' He sighed. 'Her ending things made me realise how much I've been working, putting my all into the toy business and charity work – especially at Christmas. She really wanted us to visit her parents in Melbourne last year, just for a short trip, to exchange presents. I said I couldn't leave Sydney in December and I'd said the same the previous year. Glenda's shown me a glimpse of a future I might have. She had a successful career but has faced most of her retirement alone.'

'Most? She's never spoken of anyone close.'

'Not even Gabby?' He smiled. 'You should ask about her.' He stared vacantly at his leather boots. 'Imagine going through the loss she suffered without someone close to lean on.'

'You mean losing her parents?'

'No, the pension fund. Willow Court is great but giving up her lovely lakeside apartment and the live-in help must have been such a wrench, don't you think? She was lucky the council found her such a nice place.'

'Glenda doesn't pay for her room?' I asked, forgetting my romantic faux pas for a moment.

Nik raised an eyebrow and his neck flushed. 'Oh. Me and my big mouth. Just forget what I said. I assumed all the residents knew each other's position.'

'They do, more or less, but everyone thought Glenda was in the money. Wow. Poor woman. This might explain why she's always seemed a little... bitter and acted as if the place wasn't good enough for her.'

'Has she? You wouldn't know from the conversations we've had. She's very fond of Alice and wishes she had a granddaughter like you.'

'But her smart clothes... she always looks so... expensive.'

'They are all from her executive past.'

True.

'But you helping with her finances...?'

Nik looked uncomfortable.

'Sorry. I don't want you to break any confidences.'

'They are just to do with an estate that was left to her by an aunt – small earnings that Glenda inherited. She used to employ an accountant but has been trying to manage herself since losing her big pension. Internet banking will make everything so much easier for her. I see how she can come across as stand-offish but she's a lovely lady when you get under that slightly distant exterior.'

I hung up our coats and fetched two glasses of wine. We leant on the breakfast bar. 'So you and me... we're all right? You want to stay for dinner still?'

'Unless you'd like me to leave.'

I passed him the pizza restaurant menu. 'I could cringe at my behaviour. I just... I've become fond of you. Honestly, with any other guy I would have asked him to go, enabling me to wallow in my humiliation. But no, Nik Talvi has to handle it so well that I'm still charmed and he's staying for dinner.'

'We've all been there and to show there's no awkwardness I hope you'll come over to Sydney, to stay, at the soonest possibility.'

My shoulders relaxed.

We ordered pizza and drank more wine. I even managed to laugh a little. I should have felt morose, a little broken-hearted, but now that a romance wasn't an option I realised, more than ever, that Nik was incredibly good company.

'Good luck tomorrow, at Darkthorn House,' he said at the front door later, as he zipped up his anorak.

'Thanks. What have you got on for the next day or two, before Wednesday's crafting session?'

'Remember the toy shop I mentioned in Paris?'

'Si Tu Veux?'

'Good memory! I've booked a flight for tomorrow. I'll be back Tuesday night. I would have asked you but—'

'Bet you're relieved now that you didn't,' I said and blushed.

'None of that. We've sorted things out, right?'

'I hope so.'

'If it makes you feel any better, I still remember asking a crush out and getting rejected. I felt like an idiot. You shouldn't, but if you do, I know how that feels.'

'Do you still see her around?'

'Yes. She's Junior Magic's office manager. We got over it. These things happen. It didn't mean we couldn't stay good friends. That's how I know you and I will be okay. Steph's a diamond and just so efficient. She texted me yesterday to say the website is sorted and it should be back online now. She's had some brilliant ideas over the years and has really updated us, digitally speaking. Mum and Dad were so wary of the internet when it first arrived, they didn't have an online presence for years and brought me up to be wary of social media. When they finally got a website, they were still sceptical from a privacy point of view. They insisted on stamping all our products with the initials JM so that there weren't too many direct references to the company online.'

'Doesn't that kind of defeat the point of promoting?'

'Yup. It's one of the things we'll be changing. Word of mouth isn't enough anymore. They've accepted that; with the company struggling we all realise a big online presence is the way to go. Steph's been great and has does her best to innovate us, posting videos of children playing with our toys and others showing how to assemble the more complicated ones. Whilst the company's downturn in profits is a worrying thing, I can sense she's excited that she might be given more of a free hand to really bring us into the twenty-first century. Steph's fantastic on the PR front too. That robbery... I didn't want a fuss – she got straight onto the newspapers and kept my name out of it. The lad's Olympian dad used his influence too and that helped.'

'Sounds like she really is amazing,' I said, trying to mean it and feeling the smallest twinge of jealousy.

'Sure is. That doesn't mean she'd have been right for me. Time's let me see that personally we aren't a good fit. She lives and breathes technology with an enthusiasm I just don't have. Also – prepare to be shocked – she doesn't like chocolate.'

Nik bent down with his arms open but then stepped back. 'Sorry. I don't want to...'

I opened my arms. 'I don't want anything to change. I'll get over it. Have a great time in Paris.'

'Thanks. Hey, where's Oliver tonight? At Misty's?'

'On a date,' I said brightly.

Nik pulled on his gloves. 'He's a good guy.'

'You really think so? That night he came home early and you were here for dinner... he wasn't exactly polite.'

'Why do you think that was?'

I shrugged. 'It's not like him, to be honest. It's taken me aback. Normally he's so polite, thoughtful and patient – that's probably why he gets on so well with elderly people.'

Nik stepped into the corridor. He opened his mouth to say something but changed his mind. Perhaps he had his own idea as to why Oliver had been so rude. Nik turned to look over his shoulder as he went down the stairs and gave me an odd look. 'I'm glad you've kept the bracelet,' he said and disappeared.

31

I felt like a party balloon deflating, after its guests had left. Nik and I were never going to be an item. His kindness, charm, his generosity of spirit and humour... once Christmas past they'd no longer be a daily feature. I leant against the breakfast bar, closing my eyes every time I thought of my overzealous romantic behaviour.

Yet I still sensed that hint of relief. I'd made Nik into some kind of Mr Perfect and it was hard admitting that perhaps my feelings for him had been more like a crush. I'd imagined scenarios in my head of us lounging on an Australian beach, cocktails in our hands as the sun set, away from the stresses and strains of everyday life, the responsibilities of work and looking out for Gran, away from the past that had come back to haunt me in the form of Mum's email.

A key turned in the lock and I straightened up, having hardly had time to mull over the strange comments Nik made as he left a few moments ago. Buddy ran to the door and gave an affectionate bark.

Oliver was back. Perhaps Krish was with him. However, he came into view, on his own.

'You didn't stay over, then?' I said.

'Nor did Nik?' he replied and looked around before undoing his coat. 'Everything okay?'

'Sure. Never better.'

'Hot chocolate?' he asked.

'No. I... I think I could do with some fresh air – just once around the block. Fancy coming?'

'Sure, the sleet has stopped.'

Buddy seemed happy to stay on the sofa. We headed downstairs and walked out into the cold. I shivered. Normally Oliver would have linked arms with me. We turned left.

'Fun evening?' he asked.

I smiled at a young couple who passed by. They lived above us. They were laughing and glittery bauble-shaped earrings swung from the woman's ears.

'Interesting.' I glanced sideways at him. 'I'm not saying this to score points, it's just so that you know...' I took off my spare pair of gloves that I'd grabbed from my bedroom and reached for my phone. Sure enough, Junior Magic's website was now visible. I showed it to Oliver and explained that its update was finally finished; that because the family used the logo JM on their products, the company's name wasn't widely visible on the internet. I took a deep breath. 'As for your suspicions about Glenda... he's not after her money.

'How do you know that for sure?'

I explained about the pension, wishing I'd put on an extra jumper. Oliver looked away as I spoke. We turned left again at the end of the road and passed a row of terraced houses. It was dark apart from a few front rooms lit up by people watching television or gaming and several front porches bearing colourful Christmas fairy lights, along with illuminated decorations including a Santa sleigh on a roof and reindeer standing on a lawn.

'Nik's interest in her is innocent.'

'But what about the financial stuff?'

I explained about the aunt's estate. Oliver slipped in an icy puddle and I reached out and righted him.

'I guess almost landing on my arse is karma for all the negative things I've thought,' he said ruefully. 'Nik's just seemed... I don't know, too good to be true. In my experience that's a warning signal. So I guess that seals the deal for you and Nik, now that we all know for sure he's as honourable as he seems on the surface. I... I hope it works out for you.'

'How was your night meeting Krish? What was she like?' I said hastily as we walked around another puddle.

'Easy to talk to and she's got a great sense of humour. She talked a lot about her work.' Our pace slowed as Oliver described the business Krish ran and how coffee shop culture had really taken off in India, in recent years. It had inspired her family to give their UK shops an Indian twist, selling milky chai muffins, coconut barfi and a range of fried rice flour snacks. 'I could relate. Back in Birmingham, for a while, I was in business myself. It was good chatting about my experience.'

My chest twinged. He'd never told *me* anything about that. 'Doing what?'

'In the drinks industry,' he said vaguely. His expression closed down once more.

'So when's your next date?'

'Saturday, although we're going to Skype before then.'

We turned left again and I built up pace, keen to just go to bed and go to sleep. But Oliver held me back, as sleet started to fall again. We stood to the side for one moment as a man passed by with two energetic Alsatians, then started to walk.

'Sorry. Really sorry, Jess,' he blurted out. 'About Nik and causing arguments between us. I should have trusted your opinion more. I was just... well, I know what it's like when you're bowled over by someone, it can make you blind. I'll apologise to him next time we meet.'

My brow softened. 'You don't need to. He doesn't know what you suspected.'

'But I judged him wrongly.'

'If it makes you feel any better, I've got things wrong about him too.' I took a deep breath. 'He's not interested in me. Nik just wants to be friends.'

'Really?' Oliver stopped dead for a moment. 'But I really thought he was acting romantically with you, although...'

'What?' I asked, as he caught up.

'When you think about it, he's full on friendly and caring with pretty much everybody... Alice, Pan, Alf, Fred – they're all taken with him, even Glenda is smitten, and unhappy Betty. Lynn as well. He's got that knack of making everyone feel special. When we were drinking in Misty's he took such an interest in my job, asking all sorts of questions – even with my suspicions I couldn't help warming to him. All that charisma, I found him... mesmerising.'

'You hid that well,' I said and smiled. 'I did notice but I suppose... I convinced myself what he and I had was different.'

He turned to me, sleet landing on his nose, near his freckles.

'Stinks, doesn't it, having romantic hopes dashed?' There was real soul in his voice. 'If there's anything I can do, just let me know.'

We turned left once more, completing the square.

'But you're still friends, right?'

'Yes. He was great about it and has even invited me to Australia. The funny thing is... I don't know – now the shock's wearing off a little, I'm not quite as upset as I thought I'd be. Guess I put him on a pedestal, Mr Sunny Australian, waltzing into my life and waving a sparkly wand over a couple of months that have been challenging.'

'I'm always here to listen, Jess, and I'll do whatever it takes to help Alice. Between us you and I can sort this out, even if we're not living together – and the email...'

'I just don't know what to do about that,' I mumbled.

'Let's go through it again,' he said in a matter-of-fact way. 'What will Alice gain if you tell her about it?'

'Possibly the answers from Mum to questions she's had for years and a chance at a new relationship with her.'

'That counts for you too, right?'

'I suppose. I don't know. It's easier to think of Gran's needs.'

'What if you don't tell her?'

'She won't get hurt again if it all goes pear-shaped.'

He opened his mouth and then closed it.

'What?'

'I can't speak for you and Alice, I can only go by my own experience, but after all this time with my parents, there's always a degree of hurt. It's low key and under the surface but I don't think speaking to them now could make things any worse. The damage has already been done. So if they got in touch I'd reply.'

I hadn't thought of it like that.

'I never got to know either of my grandmothers, you know,' he went on. 'I met my grandpa, on Dad's side, a few times when I was little. He'd wink and pass me a bag of chocolate coins, I've never forgotten that. I heard him arguing with Dad once and Dad saying he visited as often as he could and that he had no control over when any international diplomatic crisis might happen. I always swore to myself I'd visit Grandpa on my own when I was old enough to get public transport, but he died of a stroke when I was fourteen. I've got five cousins, you know. Sometimes I still wonder what they're like. I really wanted to meet them, as an only child. Still do. But as time's passed it's never felt right.'

'Perhaps your parents have reached out to family since retiring last year.'

'I doubt it. They haven't bothered reaching out to me. The last I heard from them was a postcard from the south of France on my birthday. They intend to live there for half of the year, I believe, near Cannes. It's very cosmopolitan.'

I nodded. 'I've never even heard you on the phone to them.'

'They probably assume I'm as busy as they used to be. When things... went wrong for me, just before I left Birmingham and moved south and in with you, I thought that might have brought us closer but they still didn't have the time to chat. I felt like one big disappointment and that puts me off getting in touch.'

We made our way towards the entrance to the apartment block. 'It's been good to chat,' I said.

'You're a great listener, Jess.'

'I don't feel as if I am – I should have been more tolerant of your view of Nik. You were right – I hadn't known him long. You may have been wrong but I should have trusted that you had the best intentions at heart.'

'For what it's worth I think he's mad turning you down,' he muttered.

'Really? When I asked you if it was so difficult to believe that Nik might genuinely find me attractive – when you suspected his motives – you didn't reply. And that's fine but don't say you can't understand why he turned me down when you can.'

'*What?*' he said. The sleet fell more heavily as we escaped into the building. 'It's just us… we always made great flatmates, right? What if we'd dated and things didn't work out? It could have been really awkward.'

The truth was he just wasn't attracted to me. Neither was Nik. But I didn't need a man to validate my life. I manage very well, holding down my challenging job and paying my own bills, going out with friends, spending time with Gran and looking after the best ever dog. That was the difference between me and my mum. I worked hard to be responsible for my own happiness and not seek it from the opposite sex. I had a life – a bloody good one at that. So what if it was time for Oliver to move out? A fresh face moving in might be just what I needed.

In that spirit it was time I got my big girl pants on.

'I'm glad you like Krish,' I said as we entered the flat. 'She sounds like a good match and just let me know if you want to invite her here and I'll make myself scarce. And if you need any help looking for a place to live don't hesitate to ask. Right, and now I really must go to bed. I must be on form, tomorrow.'

'Oh... okay.' Oliver spoke haltingly. He must have been as tired as me. 'Did you want me to come with you and Alice? My shift doesn't start until two.'

That could have worked. We wouldn't be more than an hour at the care home. But I needed some space to digest that Nik and I would never be an item – and that Oliver was moving on with his life.

'It's okay, thanks. I think you've helped me make up my mind – I'm going to discuss Mum's email with Gran.' I wouldn't until we were back at Willow Court but it was the best reason I could think of to reject Oliver's offer.

'Right. I'll take Buddy out for a long walk instead, then. Perhaps I could head into Springhaye Forest and collect some stones for Nik's painting project – do you think he'd like that?'

'That's a brilliant idea.'

32

I'd forgotten just how comfortable Up the Spout was. The little building was Tudor-style and inside there must have been a hundred different teapots lined up on rich mahogany beams. Colourful table clothes were decorated with printed images of suitably themed flowers such as chamomile. There were twenty different types of tea on the menu that was in the shape of a teapot. At the counter was a wide selection of muffins including lemon drizzled ones, vegan ones and a savoury selection including olive and roasted tomato, along with a special turkey and stuffing limited edition, and other types of cakes. Catchy folk music played in the background, against the sound of a gurgling coffee machine and cheerful chatter.

We were shown to a table on the ground floor. The sky was dark and grey outside. The tea room's open fire was a welcome sight, along with its Christmas decorations. A ceramic snowman, with a pipe in its mouth, stood by the hearth.

'How about afternoon tea for lunch? I asked. 'What would you like?' Gran had hardly said anything in the car.

'You decide.'

Normally she had very firm ideas of what afternoon tea should consist of, preferring old favourites. I smiled, remembering one I'd taken her for last year – it was an ultra-modern coffee shop and the afternoon tea platter included fancy canapés and churros with dipping sauces. The waitress came over and I ordered a pot of Earl Grey for Gran. I couldn't resist a festive spiced cappuccino. I asked for ham and mustard sandwiches as well as cheese and pickle. I plumped for traditional scones with jam and clotted cream and two mini slices of Victoria sponge.

'I feel as if we've earned this, walking around Darkthorn Court. It's very spacious and the size of those windows – it's not dark at all.' In fact, the outside was nothing like its name but white and clinical looking, rather like a hospital.

Gran pushed her leather gloves into her handbag. The waitress had hung our coats on a stand near the door.

'So... what did you think?' I said.

She unzipped her fleece.

'The manager was nice, wasn't she, Gran?'

'But no Lynn,' she replied tersely.

'It's too early to say that.'

'So now I can't even say what I want? But then why should I be surprised? I've got no say over having to leave the home and friends that I love.'

I smiled at the waitress as she delivered our drinks. I poured Gran's cup. She added her own milk. She dropped in two cubes of sugar and stirred the spoon slowly. I gazed at her swollen knuckles.

'The ensuite was nice, in the room they said could be yours.'

'That sickly yellow colour leaves a lot to be desired.'

'I thought it was cheerful. As for the view out of the window – how lovely to look onto a children's play park. I bet those picnic tables get used a lot in the summer.'

'Hardly the canal though, is it? Barges passing by all day made me feel as if I was still part of life, still moving.'

The three-tiered afternoon tea stand arrived but I suddenly wished I hadn't ordered so much. Half-heartedly, I took a sandwich and after hesitating, Gran did the same. My phone vibrated and I pulled it out of my back pocket. A text from Nik. He'd arrived in the centre of Paris a few hours ago and had just fulfilled a childhood dream of standing under the Eiffel Tower. He'd signed off by writing *say hello to Alice for me*. I showed the message to Gran. Her eyes brightened.

'This sandwich is very good,' she mumbled. 'Just the right size. Not like the door stops you and me used to enjoy when we were both younger.'

'Don't eat them all,' I retorted.

Gran's voice quivered. 'Sorry if I've not seemed very enthusiastic. You're the best granddaughter I could have and I appreciate you taking me this morning. I don't feel as if I'm alone in all this.' She reached for another sandwich. 'To be honest, I'm feeling grumpy because I'm right disappointed.'

I put down my cup. 'You didn't like it?'

Gran wiped her mouth with a napkin and stared me straight in the face. Her eyes looked a little redder than usual. The lids more hooded.

'I did. That's the problem. I don't want to. I don't want to move from Willow Court. I don't want somewhere else

268

to be suitable. None of this is fair.' Her voice wobbled. 'I was expecting to hate the place. The opposite has happened and has made the move feel all the more real.'

'I understand. Really I do. When I first moved in with you, I didn't want to enjoy a single second – I wanted my mum. I was determined to hate every minute, even though you and I got on. And the more settled I felt, the more disloyal I felt to Mum and the life we'd had together, even though it wasn't the best. Liking living with you... it made me realise I might never live with Mum again and it was hard. So I get how you're feeling.'

'Things turned out okay for you, didn't they?'

'And they will for you too. First off, did you see the exercise teacher, in the lounge?'

Her frown disappeared for a second. 'James Dean reincarnated.'

'I was thinking more Robert Pattinson.'

'I'd forgotten your sixth form crush on a vampire.'

'I do think it'll be lovely looking out onto the play area when the weather improves. Apparently it's a five-minute walk from a primary school and families head there at the end of each day.'

'I liked the sound of some of the activities. I've always wanted to try acting. And I noticed, as we drove away, there's a nice-looking pub and newsagent's around the corner.'

It was great to hear her sounding more positive.

'That care worker we spoke to in the dining room seemed very friendly,' I said.

'Joanne? Yes, she asked me what my favourite pudding was. Apparently they make sure everyone gets theirs regularly and one of the cooks is a trained pastry chef. It's just...'

I pointed to the Victoria sponge. Gran shook her head.

'I'm glad it's dual-registered – who knows, in the future, I might need more nursing care and I wouldn't want to move again. But I double-checked and there's no dementia wing. That means that Pan wouldn't be able to move there.'

The look on her face broke my heart.

'They said they had several rooms available. I'm sure some of your other friends might move in. And I can take you to visit Pan whenever you want. But it's early days... we can keep looking.'

Gran shook her head. 'No. I've got to be sensible. This place is highly rated. It's decent. And the not knowing, the living in limbo... that's harder than anything.' She sucked in her cheeks. 'Sooner or later I've got to make a decision.'

'How about we visit it again with Lynn? She offered to come with us if we liked the place, and she could ask any pertinent questions that we might have missed.'

'She's a diamond.'

'It's not too far for me and Oliver to drive to. Plus they allow well-behaved dogs into the lounge and what about—'

'I know. That swung it for me.' Gran took a slice of sponge and bit into it and for a second I saw a familiar twinkle in her eyes. 'Although Silver is a terrible name for a goldfish.'

'Its owner must have had a sense of humour so it suits you down to the ground.'

The person who'd had Gran's room had left behind a pet.

The care home hadn't liked to part with it. The manager had said they'd move it out unless Gran wanted it.

'Of course, we'd have to get it a bigger tank,' she said. 'Maybe you could take me shopping for a new underwater ornament.'

'I'll always help you clean it and buy the fresh weed whenever needed.' Maybe this was all going to turn out as best as we could hope for. The tea room emptied out as the lunch hour rush came to an end. I suggested we share one of the scones. Gran didn't reply so I took that as a yes.

'I... I just want it all over now,' she said. 'To move as quickly as possible. There's no avoiding it. I mean, what's the point in even having the party? Everyone should just accept the good times are over and cancel it.'

'Gran! Your friends are so looking forward to it. It's a final goodbye – a celebration of all the friendships and good times that you've all had.'

'More like a memorial,' she muttered. 'I won't be going.'

She didn't mean that. She couldn't.

'Well, I left my clipboard on your bed, listing everyone who's involved and the tasks we need to keep on top of... I... I thought you might like to look through it before Wednesday's crafting session.'

We sat in silence for a few minutes, watching the world go by outside.

'I could stay here all day,' I said.

'Stay as long as you like,' said our waitress as she came over to clear the plates. 'In fact, why don't I refresh those drinks?'

The rain-drenched street outside didn't look inviting so I nodded and thanked the waitress.

'I thought Oliver was coming today,' said Gran. 'Couldn't he change his shift? Not that I expect him to… He's a good sort to even consider coming.'

'He's very fond of you – you know that. No, he… he decided Buddy needed a long walk.'

Gran leant forwards. 'But it's been raining all day.'

'That's never bothered either of them,' I said brightly. Another teapot and cappuccino arrived.

Gran dropped sugar cubes into her refilled cup and her eyes narrowed. 'What's going on? You and Oliver… things have seemed strained between you these last few weeks. I know it's no business of an old biddy like me, but I worry about the both of you. I'd hate to see a friendship like yours break.'

'We're fine! I just thought we might want to chat privately. Two girls together and all that,' I said, giving her the excuse I'd given Oliver and trying to sound jokey.

'What about?'

'Nothing.'

Gran raised an eyebrow. 'Jessica?'

'Okay, okay…' I mumbled. 'I'd rather have told you somewhere more private, but as a result of that photo of you in the *Gazette* on Friday… I've received a lot of emails. The community has really been so generous. One party organiser company from Amblemarsh has offered to turn up early and decorate the lounge with snowflake shaped helium balloons and foil icicle chains. But there was one message a bit different from the rest…' I took another mouthful of tea but my mouth still felt dry when I put the cup down. There was no easy way to say it. 'I've heard from Mum.'

Gran stared. 'When did this happen?'

'Saturday night.'

'Why didn't you tell me immediately?'

'I wasn't sure what to do for the best.'

Gran's cheeks coloured up. 'I had a right to know.'

'That woman has messed our lives up enough and we've got this move to deal with. I didn't want—'

'You didn't think I could cope?' Gran snorted. 'I may be upset about Willow Court's closure but that doesn't mean I've lost my backbone. Is that how you see me? As weak, some sort of pathetic pensioner you are duty-bound to help?'

'No! Of course n—'

'In case you've forgotten, it's been me looking out for you all these years. Who sorted out those girls bullying you in Year 8 when the teachers did nothing? Who worked more than one job at a time to pay the bills? That's saying nothing about how I kept bailing out your mum until I realised that was just making her easier to do what she wanted. I had to draw on strength I didn't know I had to slowly let go. But now, years later, she finally gets in touch again and you decide it's none of my business. Were you not going to tell me at all?'

'I just needed to think about it, Gran, and find the right moment.'

'What if that hadn't arrived?' Gran took her gloves out of her bag. 'You know, I'm tired of feeling powerless – and now I realise that's partly my own fault.' She sat straighter. 'I've been wallowing in self-pity. I've lost sight of who I am.' She pushed back her chair. 'I'll be catching a taxi home.'

'Don't be silly.'

She gave me a sharp look. 'Please forward that email to me immediately,' she said stiffly. 'And I'll deal with Darkthorn House on my own, from this point forwards.' Unsteadily, she stood up. Looking a little confused, the waitress hurried over with her coat and helped her into it. Banging into a chair as she went, Gran shuffled outside, into the rain.

33

Gran hadn't spoken to me since Monday. I'd phoned but she didn't reply, so I texted, asking how she was. A two-word message came back: *Okay thanks*. I didn't look up when someone walked past me in the darkness outside Willow Court and their large bag banged against my leg. I hardly noticed the frosty air as I mulled over the chill between me and Gran. However as I approached the entrance loud voices jolted me back to the present. The door was held open by a man in overalls as two others carried the gorgeous welsh dresser that stood at the back of the dining room. Residents loved it, with its display of decorative plates.

'But I've made it quite clear to head office that no more removals are to take place until all the residents have moved out,' said Lynn. She was pacing to and fro. 'You can't take that. It's not right.'

'Sorry, love, we're only following orders,' said the man holding the door, in a gruff voice. He was texting with one hand into his phone.

'This is people's lives,' she said and looked at her watch. 'It's half past six. Head office won't be open now. They've done this on purpose.'

'We got held up in traffic.'

I stepped aside as the Welsh dresser was carried past. I hadn't even noticed the large van parked up outside.

Helplessly Lynn looked on. 'Jess. Come in.' I hurried indoors, welcomed by Bing Crosby's crooning. Lynn marched up to the man and grasped the door handle. 'Well, that's your lot for this evening. I'm ringing head office first thing. Now bugger off.' She yanked the door and pulled it close. We stood behind it and looked through the glass, Lynn glaring until he shook his head and left.

'They didn't even ask to see me,' she muttered. 'I'd just been checking a leak in one of the bathrooms, the emergency plumber hasn't turned up. I came back for the crafting session and those men were already here, door wide open, carrying out a box of the decorative plates.' She glanced into the lounge. 'Nik and Oliver said they'd keep everyone busy – try to lessen the blow.' I glanced at the entrance's silver Christmas tree with colourful fairy lights, twinkling intermittently. Lynn had been working so hard to give Willow Court an air of normality.

Oliver had managed to find thirty suitable sized stones in Springhaye Forest and was bringing them tonight, after cleaning them. He'd texted Nik who'd been chuffed. He'd got back from Paris last night. I'd had to stay a bit later, at work, to help with a stocktake. For a Wednesday we'd been surprisingly busy. I loved watching children becoming more excited as the season of Santa approached and was feeling more confident with the window displays. Our latest idea was one based around the theme of carol singing, with fake snow on the ground and toy dolls and plushies wearing beanie hats and standing around in a circle. We'd printed out sheet music and attached it to their hands. Then in the window we'd also placed our stock related to instruments such as a penny whistle, harmonica and a mini battery-run piano for toddlers. After that I was going to put Seb in sole charge of creating a new display – not to save myself work, but because he'd been brimming with ideas and deserved the opportunity. In fact, Angela had taken me to one side and said that showed true management skills. She said delegation was important but was also about making staff feel valued.

After those words I'd felt as if I was floating on air. Jess Jagger was a manager. Responsible. Independent. With Gran and Angela's support I'd been able to achieve the most important things I'd ever wanted.

Lynn headed off to find Betty. She had a scheduled video call with her daughter. Radiator heat and radiant smiles welcomed me into the lounge– along with a bark from Buddy who was with Nik as Oliver set out the stones on a table. I couldn't see Gran. Nik crossed the room.

'How was Paris? And Si Tu Veux?' I asked. My heart leapt a little. As Pan might say, he was so dashing. His striking looks and infectious charm had swept me away, on the plane. It was time for my feet to settle properly back on terra firma and forget about my love life for the moment. There was no time for getting close to a man – apart from Buddy. I crouched down to stroke him properly, took the lead and then stood up. Nik told me about Si Tu Veux's range of toys and the interesting chat he'd had with the manager.

'I don't need to visit any more stores,' he said. 'I'm coming to a decision about how Junior Magic might expand its customer base. I just need to research that a little more online. I video-called my colleague Lachlan this morning. He's finishing up the southern Europe leg of our research trip, in Italy, and likes my idea so is going to look into it as well. My neighbour, Rob, is lending me a spare laptop for the rest of my stay.' His face lit up. 'Hold on a moment – I almost forgot.' He went over to his coat that lay on another table, next to the one covered in stones. Seconds later he was back, one hand behind his back.

'Close your eyes,' he said.

'Nik. We've been here before. You're not holding a jar of Vegemite, are you?' I did as I was told and felt long fingers open up my hands. He placed a box in them.

'Wow. Mini bronze statues? I love the dog and the horse. And that frog is adorable.'

'Awesome, aren't they? They're actually chocolate and handmade by one of France's top chocolatiers. They had a section in a big department store I visited.'

I kissed him on the cheek, surprised to feel... nothing much. 'They look too good to eat.'

'I'd better polish them off then,' he said and reached for the lid.

I grinned and put the box onto a nearby chair.

'Did Alice like Darkthorn House? How's everything going with her? Are you going to contact your mum?'

'I told Gran on Monday about the email. It was a huge shock. Hopefully I'll find out today what she wants to do...' I didn't feel up to talking about our fallout. Buddy pulled at his lead, tail wagging furiously. I followed his gaze and gasped.

'Is that a King Charles Spaniel puppy asleep on Phyllis's

lap? She's not even fiddling with her activity apron. I've never seen her so relaxed.'

'It's just something I spotted in a department store.'

'It's not real?'

'No – it's an electronic breathing pet made especially for dementia patients. I had to walk through that part of the store to get to the toy section. It's meant to be especially beneficial for those sufferers who are restless. I remembered that Phyllis used to run boarding kennels. They had an offer on, so…'

'That's so lovely. She's never looked happier.'

Oliver came over. 'Could I have a quick word with you both?' he said and we followed him into the corridor. Lynn hurried past and went into the lounge.

'I just wanted Jess here, Nik, whilst I apologise to you whole-heartedly.' He rolled up his sleeves of his lumberjack shirt.

Nik's brow furrowed. 'What for?'

'That's decent of you to pretend you don't know. I… I haven't been exactly friendly. I've been suspicious of your intentions towards Jess and Glenda and I'm not proud of it.'

'Oliver, mate – it's okay. I understand.'

'You do?'

He looked from him to me for a moment. 'Sure, I'm a stranger from the other side of the planet. You wouldn't be a good friend to Jess if you weren't looking out for her. It's a cynical old world out there that's made us wary. I get it. But cheers for the apology. It takes a certain kind of person to accept they've made a mistake.'

'Right. Um, thanks… I'd like to explain…You see,

I've never told you this, Jess. I couldn't face it when I first moved in as the wounds were still raw, but meeting Krish...' He looked at Nik. 'A woman I've recently got to know... it's helped me open up because she's in business and understands.'

Didn't he think I would?

'I used to part-own a bar in Birmingham. I'd saved up. Money left to me by my grandparents helped. I went into partnership with a man who'd got a business degree. He had the intellectual know-how – I had the practical experience, have worked in bars since I left school... much to my parents' horror.'

'They didn't approve?' asked Nik.

'No. They are – or were, before they took early retirement – high flyers at the Foreign Office. Looking back, I think I rebelled against that and swore I wouldn't go to university, but as it happens that meant I fell into a career that I love. The business went from strength to strength very quickly. It was a relief as I invested everything I had into it. Three years in and we were making good money. Birmingham has the youngest population out of all the major European cities – forty per cent of people living there are aged under twenty-five. We struck gold, managing to appeal to both the huge number of university students and working locals.'

'What went wrong?' I asked.

'Josh swindled me, embezzling money once the business was doing well, and doctoring the accounts. I'd signed paperwork blindly over the years, thinking I could trust him. Turned out I couldn't. He just disappeared one day and never came back. I didn't have much legal redress because of how he'd stitched me up with the contract. I felt so stupid.'

'Oh Oliver, poor you.'

'Gee, mate, that's terrible.'

'He wasn't unlike you,' said Oliver. 'Tall. A way with words. So friendly. He acted as if he'd do anything for anybody. I guess you being you pressed alarm bells.'

'If it's any consolation, I have no intellectual power when it comes to business – Lachlan takes care of the more complicated paperwork.' He clapped Oliver on the back. 'You've done well to come out the other side of this and not be so bitter that you couldn't get on with your life. As someone who's part of an independent family business I couldn't be more sympathetic.'

Nik nodded as Oliver made some comment about male pride and explained how the police investigation never got anywhere.

'I hope that explains why I've been cool with you,' said Oliver. 'It's no excuse but…' He held out his hand. 'Friends?'

Nik hesitated then grabbed his fingers and pulled him close for a hug. I could have laughed at Oliver's surprised face.

'No worries. It's already forgotten,' said Nik. 'Well, almost – how about you shout me a couple of sherry cocktails in Misty's some time?' He winked and went back into the lounge as Glenda called his name.

I'm so sorry. I can't imagine how tough that must have been for you,' I said.

He shrugged. 'Just as bad was how I felt it must have confirmed, in my parents' eyes, that I was a loser.'

'Did they say that?'

'No, but at the time they were so wrapped up in their idea of living in France, we hardly spoke about what happened and it was as if that suited them. Krish is the first person I've spoken to about it for years.' He ran a hand through his tawny crew cut. 'Have you seen Alice yet? Has she had enough time to digest the news about your mum?'

I went to reply but Lynn appeared, her face drawn and white.

'What's the matter?' I asked.

'I can't believe this has happened. We've never lost a resident before.' Lynn wrung her hands. 'It's Betty – she's gone missing.'

34

Fifteen minutes later Lynn, Nik, Oliver and I met again by the entrance. We'd swept through the building discreetly checking for Betty, just to be sure she wasn't inside. Between us we'd searched the corridors, the treatment rooms, dining room and kitchens, and the laundry area.

'She can't have gone far,' I said.

'We have a protocol for this,' said Lynn. 'I've never had to use it before. First of all, I must organise a search of the grounds, front and back. If she isn't there, that's when I phone the police.'

We spoke in low voices and I glanced into the lounge. Fortunately, everyone was busy making Christmas tree decorations and crackers, with other care workers in there to look after those who needed help.

'Come on Nik, get your coat. Lynn, you wait here in case there is news – us three will check the grounds. I'm sure we'll find her.'

There was something about Oliver's voice that made me feel we'd resolve this. I'd noticed it before when anything went wrong: a lost purse, a flooded kitchen...

'Thank you. Thank you so much.' A tear trickled down Lynn's cheek. 'I should have been down here. I should have thought that one of the confused residents might have gone out whilst those damn removal men were here – especially Betty. To walk out of those doors is what she's been wanting for months. Maybe that's what has happened. What if she gets hypothermia or is hit by a car and—'

'Lynn, this is nothing to do with you,' I said as the men disappeared to get their coats. 'Those blokes turned up and bent all the rules about safety. If she did get out whilst they were here you couldn't have done anything about that or foreseen this. Willow Court couldn't want for a better or more efficient warden.'

'Well said.' Oliver was back and pulling on his jacket.

'What was she wearing when you last saw her?' asked Nik.

'Her usual – the raincoat. Slippers. Carrying her bag.'

'Oh God… I wish I'd looked up. I had a lot on my mind and didn't really pay attention when I came tonight,' I said. 'As I approached the entrance a passer-by almost knocked into me and their bag banged my legs.'

Lynn's hand flew to her mouth. 'You think that could have been Betty?'

'Well, you said you weren't here when the removal men first arrived – who knows how long that door had been held open?'

'She had her slippers on, you'd think they'd have noticed, although the man outside was on his phone for most of the time.' Lynn shook her head. 'I'm absolutely furious. Just wait until head office hear about this.' She exhaled. 'But getting angry can wait, first we need to find her. It's dark out there, goodness knows…'

Nik placed a hand on her shoulder. 'Oliver's right. Us three will bring her back.'

Lynn wiped her eyes with her sleeve and disappeared into the office. She came back carrying three torches and a space blanket. 'These have been packed away in case of an emergency like this.' She handed out the torches. I squeezed her arm, thinking I'd heard Gran's voice in the lounge. She must have gone in whilst I'd been looking in the laundry area.

I passed Lynn Buddy's lead. 'He'll be fine with Gran or Alf. I'll keep you posted with texts and try not to worry Lynn.'

We headed outside and scouted the grounds, looking behind trees – and bushes, just in case she'd fallen.

'I've found nothing,' Oliver said, out of breath, in front of the entrance again.

'Me neither.'

Nik shook his head.

'Okay. She must have gone into town.' I texted Lynn as we walked to the edge of Willow Court's entrance. Frost was already forming. We stood on the high street and I took out my phone again. 'I'll ask Lynn if she knows Betty's old home address. She used to be local. Perhaps it's within walking distance.'

'Fred once said she used to love going to The Silver Swan for lunch when she first moved in – the two of them would go together, before her dementia got worse. We should look there,' said Oliver. 'She could have ended up in the beer garden.'

He and Nik hurried off to the pub. Lynn's phone was engaged, so I texted about Betty's previous home address. I shivered and zipped my coat up higher. Without gloves and a hat Betty would be freezing. The men ran back, stopped when they got to me and stood panting.

'Nothing,' said Oliver as his chest heaved up and down. 'She's not out the back and the landlord hasn't seen her inside but checked everywhere, even upstairs in his private quarters.'

I stared at Nik. 'You know how she's been mistaking you for her husband, Jim?'

He nodded. 'Yes, almost every time she and I get talking, Betty mentions the video store where he worked.'

I raised an eyebrow.

'It's now the bookshop at the end of the high street, right?' asked Oliver.

'Yes,' I said. 'Come on. It's a long shot but worth trying.'

We turned left and dodging the last stragglers heading home after work we speed walked towards the end, past shops lit up with twinkling lights. I squinted as we neared the shop. There were two women outside. One was in her twenties and the other... I exhaled. She was wearing a raincoat.

'Betty!' I said.

The young woman stared at me. 'Is this lady a relative of yours? I thought she looked a bit lost and then I saw her slippers.'

Nik moved forward and positioned himself in front of Betty, crouching down a little. She looked at him. Confusion swept over her exhausted features.

'Jim... the children... need to get home,' she mumbled. Betty held onto just one of the bag's handles and it swung to and fro.

'Everything's all right,' he said, 'but yes, let's go home and get a nice hot drink.'

Oliver touched my arm. 'Well done, Jess. You've saved the day.' He and Nik wrapped the space blanket around her shoulders and then one of them either side, they accompanied her back down the street, her arm linked with Nik's.

I thanked the young woman profusely and she insisted on accompanying us for her own peace of mind, just to make sure Betty got back to where she belonged. I rang Lynn who choked up when I told her the good news. It was a short conversation as she needed to immediately update the police. When we arrived at Willow Court she gave Betty a big hug. Two of her team took Betty back to her room with instructions to make her tea and toast.

'I can't thank you three enough,' said Lynn before going into the office to fill in an incident form and ring Betty's daughter who would have been waiting for the video call.

'What a mess,' I said, the adrenaline wearing off and every limb suddenly feeling heavier. I stared at a blank space on the wall near the reception area, where a favourite picture had been removed. 'Perhaps Glenda was right – maybe this party is a bad idea. It's a distraction amongst unavoidable chaos and that could be dangerous.'

Oliver took my hand and led me into the lounge. 'You really think so? Just look around. I don't think Alice would forgive you if you cancelled it...'

I listened to the chatter, above which rose the voice of... *Gran?* She was walking out from behind the hatch, with Pan, holding court whilst reading from my clipboard. I pulled off my hat. We took off our coats and placed them on the chair where I'd left my chocolates. Most of the residents were sipping small glasses of sherry. Carers sat helping to make angel, bell and snowflake cardboard cut-outs. Nancy waved at us, silver glitter down her top. Gran and Pan stood wiping their hands on tea towels.

'That's the dough kneaded,' said Gran. She gave a thumbs-up to a couple of women who'd been waiting to go into the kitchenette. They got up. 'Now it's someone else's turn to roll it out and cut into suitable shapes.'

'I can't wait to try them,' said Nik. 'It's just as well we decided to leave the stone painting until Sunday – you all look very industrious as it is.'

'They aren't for eating and would taste right disgusting without sugar in,' she said.

'Beggars can't be choosers, I'm a poor, lonesome traveller making do with scraps,' he said and grinned. He clicked his fingers in time to the music, for a few seconds, and then placed an arm on Pan's shoulder, one around her waist, and started dancing with her as Bing Crosby picked up the beat. Her face lost the frown lines that had characterised it in the last week or two and she beamed as other residents began to join in. Fred stood behind Nancy and moved her wheelchair from side to side. My shoulders started to relax.

'Such a lovely bunch of people,' I murmured.

Gran hesitated. 'That's why I've told them there are places at Darkthorn House.'

We looked at each other. I helped her over to her favourite chair, with a straight upholstered back, and sat down nearby. Buddy rested his chin on her lap. She leant over and gently stroked my hair. 'I'm sorry, love, that I walked out on Monday – it's been a difficult few weeks and hearing about that email was the last straw. I appreciate that you thought about whether to tell me or not – I know you only had my best interests at heart. '

'I didn't mean it to come across as patronising,' I whispered, voice wavering.

'I know. And I love you very much. It's me and me alone who should apologise.'

Sorry wasn't a word I ever heard growing up with Mum – not in a healthy way. It was new for me when I moved in with Gran, an adult properly apologising, like for snapping when she was tired. I learnt to follow her example. Mum's way of saying sorry was to give me a big bar of chocolate from the pound shop. Yet even if I ate the lot it never seemed to fill an emptiness I felt.

'In fact, sweetheart...' She waved the clipboard in her hand. 'You did me a favour by delaying telling me about Karen's email... it made me realise how I've allowed myself to drown in a pity party since I heard this place was closing down, when the only party I should be focusing on is this Christmas one and making sure it's the best bloomin' one ever. In fact, I'd like to discuss a few pointers with you later. The buffet menu details aren't detailed enough for my liking, most us residents are a little particular – and we need to write an exact timetable of the big day, thirty minutes by thirty minutes, I'd say, so we know exactly what's going to be happening...'

I couldn't help grinning.

She caught my eye. 'It's time I took control of my life again. Darkthorn House is the next best thing to Willow Court and I'll accept the place there. I'd love fellow residents to move with me so I had a chat with everyone last night. Fred,

Nancy, Glenda and a couple of the others are interested in taking a look. Glenda's going to ask Nik if he'd mind accompanying her.'

My eyes pricked. Gran was back, taking charge.

'I've just got to get on with it,' she said. 'I've nursed my wounds for a while – and no shame in that, I wouldn't be human if I hadn't got upset… but now's the time to find that stiff upper lip Fred likes to talk about.' Gran fiddled with the cuff of her coral fleece. 'I chatted with Pan. It's hard knowing Darkthorn House isn't suitable for her – or won't be once her… her problem grows bigger. But I hope everything I said showed her that she just struck unlucky with the home she visited – and she really cheered up when I passed on what you said about us visiting each other.' She rolled her lips together. 'I can't help feeling disloyal – accepting a place when Pan's got no plans. She's my best friend. But I can't get sentimental about this. We've got to move out in three weeks.'

'No, you can't,' I said. 'But that doesn't mean you are letting her down. It's obvious how much you care.'

She nodded. 'So instead I'm going to do my best to help her find somewhere. We're going to go through the list in detail tomorrow. If my slow pace doesn't hold them back too much, I'm going to suggest I go on the next viewing with her and her son, if she wants – and if Adam doesn't mind. Pan deserves the best.'

'She does indeed,' said Alf, who'd just eased himself into a chair near us, notebook on his lap, a smear of glitter across his bald head. 'My Maisie would have loved listening to her talk about movies. She used to have a crush on Kojak. We used to joke it was just as well I lost my hair.'

'Did I just hear my name?' asked a breathless Pan as the dancing couple came to a halt in front of us. She looked ten years younger with her eyes sparkling and cheeks blushed.

'We were just saying what a wonderful person you are,' I said.

'And how we are going to find you a five-star place to live,' added Gran.

'You couldn't help me too, could you?' asked Alf and he groaned. 'Looks like I'm moving in with my daughter, for the time being anyway.'

Nik pulled a chair around to face us and pointed to Pan to sit in it, before he collapsed onto the arm.

'*Your daughter?*' asked Pan. 'Holly?'

'Polly,' he said and smiled.

'But I thought you and Maisie made some sort of pact about never...'

'Being a burden?'

'Yes. Like me and my husband did.'

Alf adjusted his rimless glasses. 'Things change, don't they? No point being pigheaded. Christmas is a busy time of year and it's more of a burden for my family to have to help me find somewhere to live at such short notice.'

Pan listened intently.

'What's more, I caught Polly crying when I went around for lunch yesterday. I managed to wheedle it out of her, just like I used to when she was a little girl and someone upset her at school. She said it was never a case of out of sight, out of mind with me – just the opposite. There wasn't a day when she didn't worry about me being in Willow Court, even though Lynn and the staff are brilliant.'

'I'd never thought of it like that,' said Pan.

'It's a huge decision to ask a relative to move in with you,' said Nik. 'I don't think people do that unless it's something they really want. My grandmother moved in with us eventually. Grams fought against it even though we knew she got lonely after Grandpa had died. Dad had a word in the end and told her how much Mum used to worry about her living on her own; how much happier she'd be if Grams moved in. He joked how much I'd love her cooking every day.' Nik stared at Pan. 'In my experience it's not a one-way thing – your family want to help look after you and it doesn't mean they won't get anything back.'

'They'll get peace of mind for a start,' said Alf and his eyes twinkled even though he pulled a face. 'Once Polly got over her upset, she was back to being just like her mum and told me not to be an old, stubborn fool, that it was the best answer all round and we could just see how it went. The grandkids have already left home and Polly's got a bedroom extension on the ground floor, that they built for their eldest.'

'How is Adam's house set up, Pan?' asked Nik gently.

'He lives in a sprawling bungalow. They have two teenage daughters but still have a spare room with its own ensuite – his wife's dance business has done very well. And there is a wonderful garden with a vegetable patch at the bottom and summer house.'

'Sounds very roomy,' he said.

'Santa Claus is Coming to Town' came on and Nik stood up as Glenda came out from the hatch, brushing flour off her smart cardigan.

He strode over and bowed. 'May I, Glennie?' Before she had time to disagree, she was gently swaying in his arms.

Pan and Gran were deep in a conversation about Adam's bird feeders. Oliver came over and jerked his head towards Nik.

'I can't compete. The man's got more charm in his little finger than I ever had in my whole body at my peak – which is nineteen for most men, according to Misty.'

'Wish I could remember that far back,' said Alf and he chuckled.

I got the feeling Alf talking about his daughter had really helped Pan. I mulled over what Nik had shared about his gran and the news that he'd be accompanying Glenda to look at Darkthorn House.

'He's an absolute saint,' I muttered.

'Funny you should say that,' said Alf. He pushed himself up, his breathing slightly better than normal today. 'It's no good. I can't keep this to myself any longer.'

'What do you mean?' asked Oliver.

'Let's go and sit by the window.' He patted the notebook.

Oliver and I accompanied him to the table where they normally played dominoes. The terracotta curtains had been drawn and gave the room an even cosier feel. I pulled up an extra chair and the two men sat opposite each other.

'What's this all about?' I asked. 'I've seen you jotting down notes about Nik.'

Alf rubbed his hands together. 'I've been building a theory, day by day. The evidence has stacked up and now there's no disputing it. I just have a few more things to find out before I'd say my case is concrete.' He undid the top button of his striped shirt.

'Case for what?' asked Oliver.

Alf looked over the top of his glasses. 'It's going to

sound damn crazy, but often the truth does… like… like a celebrity becoming president and talking to the world on that Twitter.'

'Alf! Don't digress!' I said.

'Not here,' he said in a conspiratorial tone. 'You'll both be here Sunday, right? And I need time to collate my notes so that they make sense. Let's meet at twelve o'clock in The Silver Swan on Sunday, before the next crafting session. Are you both off work?'

'I'm doing a late shift, starting at five,' said Oliver.

For once Seb had asked me to swap so I was just popping in for an hour to check up on things, late morning. 'I should be finished at twelve, but—'

'Okay, let's say half past. So that's Sunday the 29th November at twelve hundred hours and thirty minutes,' he continued in the same low voice, sounding like a spy. 'That still gives us an hour and a half before we have to be back here. Polly won't be seeing me this weekend, she and her husband are working flat out to set up my room before I move in.'

'I'm not sure I can wait that long,' I said and looked at Oliver's puzzled face.

He clasped the notebook to his chest. 'Trust me, young lady – it'll be well worth it. You're in for the surprise of your life.'

35

I gave a big yawn. It was Saturday night. I stood by the window and looked down onto the road and a couple bustling past under a streetlamp, laughing. They carried shopping bags with rolls of Christmas wrap sticking out of the top. Nik had been taken on a haunted London pub walk by his neighbour Rob. Oliver was on his second date with Krish. I thought back to the evenings Nik had come here and could almost not cringe now. What on earth made me think we'd ever be the perfect match?

For a start, I came out in prickly heat if I sunbathed – Oliver was the same. Last year we'd saved hard and gone on our hiking trip to Canada in autumn, both preferring that to a sweltering beach break. The Australian climate would have never suited me. Nik didn't like social media whereas, like Oliver, I was addicted to Instagram and Twitter, even though we knew it was a terrible distraction and he and I spend far too much time sending each other the latest silly memes. Plus Netflix was as important to us as oxygen whereas Nik laughed about how he'd first thought that word was a fishing term. His old school ways had made a refreshing change but his rejection had given me a new honesty and I had to admit they'd have pulled us apart once the initial passion died down. I needed to date someone who could talk Skype, hashtags and screenshots, especially if they lived nine thousand miles away.

I picked up the phone and dialled Gran's number.

'Hello?'

'It's me. How are things? Cold, isn't it? We may not need that snow machine next week.'

'Blimey O'Reilly you're right, sweetheart. I didn't put so much as a toe outside today once I saw how red Lynn's cheeks were when she got into work. Instead I started to sort through my things, ready for the move. Oh, and I've rung the catering company to check they're covering everyone's dietary whims. My mouth watered at some of their suggestions.' She went on to describe the finger foods that would be on offer, from chunks of soft turkey meat and soft, nut-free stuffing on sticks, to mini mince pies topped with whipped brandy cream.

'So… did you do it?' Yesterday I'd popped in after work and ended up staying for a couple of hours. 'You still think it's best to email and not phone?'

'Yes. After such a long time it could get emotional. I think writing to your mum is better to start with. So I sent the email after lunch. It wasn't very long, my fingers are more stiff with the chilly weather and couldn't manage much.'

'I'd have done it.'

'No. It was down to me. Shall I read out what I sent? Just let me find the piece of paper. I wrote it out first.' A minute later she cleared her throat. 'Hello Karen. Jess and I were both surprised to receive your email. You've got in touch now and that's all that matters. Yes, let's meet up. We'll fit in with where and when suits you. Love from Mum.'

'Is that okay?'

I nodded down the phone.

'I wasn't sure how to sign off. I do love her. She's my daughter. But after all these years...'

'No one would blame you for feeling conflicted. I do myself. Well done, anyway.' We chatted for a while, making pointless guesses about what my mum was doing now. How could we possibly all move forwards after such a lot of hurt? We both had so many questions. 'Better go and make my tea,' I said, looking at the clock. Half past seven. I suddenly realised how shattered I felt after a ridiculously busy day at Under the Tree – ridiculous and invigorating and stressful and crazy. I'd never get bored of a child's face light up at the sight of an exciting book or cute plushy. I felt as if I could sleep for a week but with Gran now helping out again, perhaps I could start really savouring this time of year. I hadn't been able to do that since the announcement of Willow Court's closure. 'See you tomorrow at the crafting session, Gran. Love you lots.'

I didn't tell her about the clandestine pub lunch with Oliver and Alf planned for beforehand because any conspiracy theory about lovely Nik was bound to be absurd. I yawned again and from the floor Buddy followed suit. I'd have a luxurious bubble bath with scented candles and then try some meditation, if I could focus.

The door buzzer rang. I went over and pressed the button. 'Who is it?'

'A special delivery,' said a voice in a weird foreign accent.

I felt too tired to go down. 'Okay, come up.'

Buddy's curls would be tidier than mine and I was still in my work clothes but didn't care. I had no one to impress now. A knock at the door. I opened it, wondering what I'd have for tea.

'Surprise!' Seb stood there holding a couple of bags and a bottle of wine.

'What's this?' I asked as Buddy barked and pawed him.

Seb ruffled his head. 'Aren't you going to invite me in?' He pushed past and went straight into the kitchenette, putting the wine and bags on the breakfast bar. He took off his anorak to reveal a denim muscle-fit shirt.

'Make yourself at home,' I said sourly, but couldn't help smiling.

'I will. In fact, I'll do more than that. I'll make you dinner and then we'll talk.' He looked in the cupboards, found two wine glasses, unscrewed the bottle and filled them. He handed me one. 'Here's to you.'

'What have I done to deserve this?'

'Turned up for work today – given it your all, even though I can tell that, for some reason, you're feeling down. You were diplomatic, as usual, with the parents that let their children come in eating sweets before manhandling the plushies with sticky fingers, and every time I turned around you were filling up the pocket money toy counter or demonstrating the latest electrical gadget. You even sang along to Angela's background Christmas music that I know you are already sick of. So you chill. I'll whizz up fajitas.'

I went over and gave him a one-armed hug. 'I don't know what to say.'

'How about… cheers, Seb for sacrificing your low-fat, sugar free diet for one evening.'

I couldn't help laughing. 'Right – like you're sticking to that at the weekend.'

He thrust a salsa-scented candle into my hand. 'This will really make us feel like we're in Mexico, it'll be like a little winter holiday for just you and me. I've even put together a Mexican folk music playlist.' He tapped on his phone.

An hour later we sat up the breakfast bar. A lime-green inflated cactus sat in the middle. My eyes widened at the spread. Tortillas. Chicken fried with red and green peppers. Shredded lettuce. Guacamole. Sour cream. Black bean and couscous salad. Tomato and herb rice. Refried beans.

'Bon appetit,' he said, 'although first things first.' He went over to one of the bags and pulled out two sombreros.

'Are you serious?'

'I'm here to put the fun back into your Saturday night. Now eat up.'

My mouth filled with the spiced flavours and textures of Mexico, with the sour cream contrasting the hot fried chicken and satisfying tortillas complimenting the light rice.

'Oh boy… that hit the spot,' I said when I finally finished. 'I had no idea you were such a good cook.'

'I always do better when I'm cooking for someone I care about.'

A lump formed in my throat as he cleared the dishes away and I hurried into the bathroom. I slid down the tiled wall and sat on the floor, covering my face. The hat fell off. I cried quietly, a habit I'd never shaken off from my childhood. Of course, I should have realised Seb would know. From outside the staff room door he could hear if anyone so much as opened a bar of chocolate. He knocked at the door.

'Jessie? What's the matter?' The door pushed open.

'Ignore me. It's been a long day.'

He picked up the sombrero and held out his hand. I took it. He pulled me up and led me back to the breakfast bar.

'Don't say a word, just eat,' he ordered and put a plate with the biggest brownie and squirt of whipped cream in front of me.

'Sorry, I—'

'I said not a word. Not until you've savoured every second of that moist chocolate.'

'You know I don't like the word moist.'

He caught my eye and we both smiled.

'Oh Seb. I've been such an idiot.' I told him all about Nik's rejection and how Oliver was out on a date and how I felt like the only person in the world in on a Saturday night. How worried I was about Mum getting in touch – that it might have a bad effect on Gran if she got let down again. Then there was the care home move and the increasing stress at work – I loved my job but with everything else that had been going on, I felt worn out. 'I must have upset Nik, upset Gran, Oliver too – recently he said he loved our flat, it proved that home was where the heart was… but in a rash moment I said he should move out and now it looks as if he might. To top it all off they've just cancelled my favourite Netflix series.'

'That last one is really bad.'

I rolled my eyes at him and sniffed. 'At least Gran is happy with her new place. I'm okay really. All the pressure should slowly ease off now.'

I went to stand by the window again. Seb joined me.

'I can't help feeling I'm partly to blame,' he said. 'I was convinced that Nik had the hots for you… I don't know how I got it so wrong. I pride myself on being astute when it comes to matchmaking and working out who suits you.'

It was true, Seb often came in on a Monday morning with news of how another dinner party at his place, with carefully chosen guests, had resulted in a new couple starting to date.

'We both did. You were only trying to help. Nik treats everyone as if they're special. I think that was our downfall, thinking he was only doing that with me.'

'What out of all those things is getting you down the most?'

'None of them. All of them.' Worry about Gran and Oliver the most. I gazed down at a car driving past with fake antlers fitted to the front lights.

'You know what Tim often says? Whenever someone is in a rut and feels like the world is against them, he reckons the way out is usually staring someone straight in the face. It takes an outsider to spot the obvious, so let's talk it all through.'

'I'm really worried about Gran and Mum – but am also still smarting a little after Nik turned me down and for some reason Oliver meeting Krish is making it worse. As for him moving out, I can't even... We've built such a comfortable life together, with Buddy and Gran, all this silly arguing, it's got out of hand...' A stab of pain went through my chest. The prospect of Oliver leaving was making me face just how much I cared about him.

'Okay... well, Alice has a new place sorted, so that situation is a little less stressful...'

I nodded.

'And your mum is an unknown entity, so there's not much

we can say about how it'll go meeting up with her. Instead, talk me through exactly what happened with Nik – he's the root of your fallout with Oliver, right?'

I took a deep breath and felt my ears turn red as I told him about the little things I'd misunderstood, such as Nik liking my short, tight dress.

'Yet he's invited you over to Oz.'

'Yes. I'm really glad we're still friends and as time moves on, I realise that's all we were ever meant to be. So why am I still upset?'

Seb tilted his head. 'How did the evening end?'

'We just chatted... I was surprised he liked Oliver so much as he was rude to Nik the night I'd invited him here for dinner. Nik asked me why I thought he hadn't been polite – I think Nik had his own theory but didn't like to say. I wasn't sure as Oliver is usually so thoughtful and kind but since then he's revealed he was suspicious because Nik reminded him of someone deceitful from Birmingham, so I guess that explains it.' I folded my arms.

Seb noticed my wrist. 'The bracelet he gave you...'

'That was another misunderstanding. I thought the heart was his way of letting me know he was interested.'

'What did he say about it?'

'Just that the heart charm wasn't about him.'

'Let me mull all this over whilst I do the washing up – and don't even think of offering to help, this evening's my treat.'

On the sofa I sipped the last of my coffee feeling decidedly better and picked up my phone, flicking through Instagram before taking a photo of Buddy. Seb finally finished and came over. He sat down.

'Tim's right. It is glaringly obvious. The heart charm.'

'Please enlighten me.'

'Oliver said it himself – home is where the heart is. You and him, I've seen how you are together – like a brother and sister. The way Alice treats him so fondly, the two of you have become his family, that's what the heart charm represents, the three of you, the unit that clearly also means the world to you. Unwittingly Nik was a threat to that – Oliver was worried you two getting together will break up the only secure, loving home he's ever had.'

'I suppose I did go on and on about the man on the plane.'

'It must have rattled him, a guy turning up out of the blue and the prospect of you being so smitten you might even move to the other side of the world. Your gran and mum, what happened with Nik, I think those things are on the periphery. Oliver and you, the flat, Buddy, that's the core of your life and has been for a while now. This is the first time a crack has really appeared in your friendship. Just give Oliver some reassurance and I'm sure he'll give it back that you and him are okay, whatever happens. Krish may be the one for him but it's incredibly early days, she may not. However, in time you'll inevitably both meet other people, but as long as you keep consolidating your friendship, it won't matter. You'll always be there for each other, whomever you are with, wherever you are living. That feeling of home between you isn't just about bricks and mortar.'

I gazed at the bracelet.

'Get your friendship completely back on track with Oliver and then you'll feel much better about all the rest.' He grabbed my phone and started to download the Tinder app. 'In the meantime, we'll find you a new romance.'

36

I woke up to see Buddy at the end of my bed, with half open eyes, watching me. The deflated cactus was between his teeth. I stretched and he moved up the duvet and lay his head on my stomach. I'd hardly slept last night. The thought of having hurt Oliver played on my mind. As the night had progressed and the pitch black morphed into dawn, as a chink of winter sun stole through the curtains, also stealing my ability to be in denial, I had to finally face one truth regarding why I felt so uncomfortable about Oliver dating Krish… I simply didn't want to be without my flatmate.

'Whaddaya reckon, Buddy? How about I make Oliver the best cup of coffee ever?' I showered and got changed. Oliver must have still been in bed. He'd left his bedroom door half open. I peered inside. It was empty. He'd spent the night with Krish. The bounce left my step as I went into the kitchen. A text popped onto my phone's screen. His train was getting in around twelve, so he'd just travel the extra stop to Springhaye and pick up Alf, to help him walk to lunch. They'd meet me at the pub.

After a lazy breakfast I headed into Under the Tree with Buddy. He'd be fine for a short while, ensconced in the office. I helped Seb rearrange the many stationery products

– the rainbow colouring pencil sets and Christmas-themed individual pencils and rubbers, the pretty snowman and reindeer notebooks and chalks for drawing outside. I also went through yesterday's mail. We didn't get much on a Saturday.

Just before half past twelve I entered The Silver Swan and my nose wrinkled at the smell of beer. If Seb had anything to do with it I'd be spending every free night from now on in a pub, meeting someone off Tinder. He was determined I wouldn't be single when the New Year started. I thought about Mum, and Gran's email. Maybe she'd already replied and was hoping to meet up at this time of year that was all about family. Perhaps I'd turn up to Willow Court finding a rendezvous had been arranged. I had a sudden urge to talk to Oliver about it, as he came into view. He sat with Alf. They were drinking halves of lager. I ordered myself a coke and went over. Buddy wagged his tail and immediately nuzzled Alf's trouser pocket.

'Damn me, you don't waste any time, do you boy?' he said and reached into his brown corduroys. The two men sat opposite each other. I sat in between.

'Nice shirt,' I said. It was floral. Not Oliver's usual practical style.

'Thanks. Krish's brother lent it to me this morning. He's a great bloke and called in to talk to her about his flatmate who, out of the blue, has up and left. He's now looking for someone else to rent with him.'

'Oh.' No.

'He doesn't live far from Krish and insisted on fetching me this to change into.'

'Oliver's just been telling me about the fine time he had

last night,' said Alf and he pulled a face. 'Bloody miss it I do, going out on the razz. Maisie and I used to love meals out, always followed by pudding and custard – until I had my heart scare. And Saturday afternoons were spent dancing at a hotel near us... bowling too and...'

The waiter came over and we ordered three Sunday roasts although I wasn't feeling very hungry. Alf sipped his lager and it inspired him to chat fondly about the old days, as if it were the elixir of youth, years falling away from him.

'Right, Alf,' I said when he drew breath. 'Don't keep us in suspense any longer. What's this theory of yours about Nik?'

His thick duffle coat was draped over the back of his chair and Alf reached into one of the pockets and drew out his notebook. He opened it.

'I've just got a few more things to find out before I have an open and shut case – but after hearing what I've got to say, I think you'll agree there's a lot of evidence. I've certainly done a blasted lot of research, but first... Oliver, Jess, do either of you believe in aliens?'

'I knew it. You think Nik comes from outer space – or that he's a scientologist.'

'Please, young lady, just answer the question.'

'Okay... well, not the scary green type with antennae and big eyes, but yes.'

'Agreed,' said Oliver. 'I think it would be arrogant of humans to think we were the only form of intelligent life in the whole of the universe.'

'So you both believe in something that can't fully be explained.'

'I guess so,' said Oliver.

I shrugged. Where could this be going?

He pushed his glasses further up his nose. 'Just to confirm, you first met Nik on an aeroplane?'

'Yes.' Why was that relevant?

Alf looked pleased and drew a tick in his notebook.

'Nik likes helping people and you mentioned some scheme he does to get presents to disadvantaged children. In fact, his whole life is dedicated to cheering up young 'uns, with toys.'

Oliver shot me a baffled look.

'It's as if he's come out of nowhere and brightened up everyone's lives at this festive time, just when that was needed this year. Selflessly he's worked to make our Christmas party happen, coming up with the theme of *It's a Wonderful Life* and having it early. He's been a welcome distraction from the serious business of moving and he's transformed Glenda into this new smiling, more tolerant sort of person. He came up with perfect idea of painting stones for our time at Willow Court to be remembered by. He always seems to have the right answer and more than once us residents have commented on how they feel as if they've known him for years.'

'I felt like that the first moment I met him,' I said.

'Well – what if we *had*?'

'What on earth do you mean?' asked Oliver.

Alf sat more upright. 'Consider these more simple bullet points. Nik is older than his years – he doesn't like social media. He has a basic phone and still carries around a camera. He has a gentlemanly-like manner that some might call old-fashioned.' He leant forward and his voice lowered. 'Nik is from Scandinavia. He has white hair. He always wears red. His favourite drink is sherry. Jess first met him flying through the sky. Can't you see the obvious?'

'You've got me, Alf,' said Oliver.

'Me too.'

'My Willow Court friends are always calling him a saint and I couldn't agree more.' Alf thumped his fist on the table. 'Nik said he had Greek heritage way back, as well as Scandinavian. I present to you Saint Niklaus – born in a Greek seaport. His mother's name was Joanna, just like our Australian's. Jess, Oliver, I know it must be one damn shock, but there's no doubt about it – Santa Claus does exist and we've been spending the last few weeks with him.'

37

We walked into the lounge, an hour late, Oliver and me in stunned silence. I hadn't wanted to laugh at Alf's announcement so I'd rambled at first, questioning all of his points, listening to his arguments. Oliver said lots of people liked red. Alf asked him to name one person he knew who wore it so often. Alf said he knew it was a lot to take in – that he'd not believed it himself but, as days passed, the evidence for his theory mounted up. He explained the research he'd done into Saint Niklaus and immortality – that cells not ageing due to a genetic mutation was being studied by scientists and who was to say some humans didn't already have that. I'd give him this – Alf was thorough. Before we knew it a couple of hours had passed. We'd walked back as quickly as we could, Alf's breathlessness allowing.

A smug looked crossed Alf's face as Nik strode over to us, wearing a red jumper, his hair seeming whiter than ever as he sang 'let it snow, let it snow' to that festive tune playing in the background.

'Sorry,' Nik said, and grinned before bending down to stroke Buddy. 'I'm just looking forward to the party – I can't believe it's just one week from today. I haven't seen snow in such a long time that even the prospect of a manmade version takes me back to being a little boy visiting relatives in Lapland.'

'*Lap*land?' said Alf and his jaw dropped. 'I thought you came from Finland.'

'I do – but Lapland specifically. It's a region that covers Finland, Sweden and Norway and my family come from the Finnish bit.'

'Of course,' muttered Alf, clearly thrilled. He pulled out his notebook and scribbled.

Don't meet Alf's eye, I told myself sternly. *Don't do it. You'll only laugh.*

Oliver and Alf headed off to the stone painting table. Next to that I noticed a table bearing a large triangular frame made of twigs, to mount the photos. Glenda was putting down a spray can. It looked fantastic. The smell of baked sugar wafted over from the hatch. Someone must have been practising making All American cookies. Lynn was in the far corner with a small circle of residents around a sturdy man holding a saxophone – he had the same shaped nose as her and must have been her brother, Geoff. He'd been due to come in to take suggestions for the party playlist of Big Band solos he was going to perform. Bursts of songs kept bouncing across the room, drowning out the background CD, and brought to mind lyrics such as chestnuts roasting over open fires. A group of scouts drank squash and ate cookies that residents were baking. They listened to Fred chat about his days as a firefighter. Their pack had raised over three hundred pounds to contribute to paying the caterers by doing bag packing at a large out of town supermarket, last weekend, and the tree was being delivered today. Gran thought it would be a nice idea to invite them in to help decorate it.

I was glad for the festive buzz, the bustle, the red and green tinsel Lynn had already hung across window frames, because despite continued protests Willow Court's owners had removed more things that made the place feel like home, albeit the smaller ones like the paintings of vintage scenes.

'How was your haunted pub tour?' I asked Nik.

'Fantastic! I never knew so many ghosts roamed London's streets.'

'You believe in them, then?' I poked him gently in the ribs.

'Just because you can't prove something, doesn't mean it doesn't exist.'

'Scientists might disagree.'

'I don't know about that. In 1974 Stephen Hawkings theorised that black holes eventually evaporate away. Yet this wasn't finally proved until 2019.' He pulled a sheepish face. 'Sorry. I'm a bit of a cosmic physics nerd. Don't you just find the sky and its contents fascinating?'

I thought about Alf and his theory.

'Hello, Jess. Lovely to see you.' Glenda didn't give me the usual suspicious peer over the top of her cat-eye glasses.

'You too... how did you find Darkthorn House?'

'Loved it, didn't you, Glennie?' said Nik.

Gran came over at that moment and I kissed her on the cheek. She held the clipboard with a pen attached to it. In the last couple of days, she'd started to draw up a final check list for the party and read it to me over the phone making sure she'd covered all the people who'd emailed me with offers of help. I'd been relieved that, as each day passed, her low mood over the home's closure continued to disappear.

'Did you mention Darkthorn House?' she said. 'Glenda has accepted a place there, so has Fred and I think Nancy will too after my recommendation. She's going to visit it tomorrow.'

'That's fantastic news!' I said.

'The staff seemed very efficient and everywhere was clean,' said Glenda. 'The other residents looked happy and Alice and I have been looking at the activities... there is a great choice but no book club. We thought we might set one up. It was Nik's idea.'

'I think Glenda is a little put out she doesn't have a goldfish though,' said Gran, eyes twinkling.

I waited for Glenda's offhand superior expression – a comment about animals not being hygienic.

'Maybe in time I'll buy one.'

'Really?' I raised my eyebrows. 'You've never struck me as pet person, Glenda.'

'Tell them about Gabby,' said Nik. I remembered him mentioning that name when I said she'd never talked fondly about a loved one.

Glenda took her hands out of her navy cardigan pockets. 'Gabby was such a good companion – although you are right, Jess... there was a time I never thought I'd own a pet. Especially a cat or dog that might shed hair or make a mess... However, Gabby chose me.'

'What do you mean?'

'She followed me home from the local newsagent's one night. It was soon after I'd retired. I would have ignored her but she was missing her back right leg. An old injury by the looks of it but…' She shrugged. 'I guess her following me brought back my happy life on the farm growing up and my favourite cow, Nettie, who would trail after me in the fields.'

'Did this Gabby belong to someone?'

'Yes, although you wouldn't have thought so. She was practically feral at the start and I had to handle her with gardening gloves. The Cats Protection League tracked down her owners who were only too happy to get rid. Such a pretty little jewel she was – a tabby with fern-green eyes and a white bib. Eventually I put a cat flap into my cottage's back door and after a couple of months she accepted I would never hurt her – that she would always be loved and fed. She was excellent company and used to talk back to me.' Glenda blushed. 'I suppose that sounds silly.'

'No,' said Gran. 'I had a nice chat with Silver when I visited. He came right up to his glass wall to say hello.'

The two women smiled at each other. I looked at Nik, admiring how he'd seen through the black and white outer image of Glenda that none of us could ever get past, revealing the more approachable shades of grey that were in all of us. Nik put an arm around her and they headed to a table covered in the photos she'd been collating. He stopped on the way to talk to Betty who, to everyone's relief, was no worse for wear following her trip to the video shop.

'It's all coming together, isn't it, Gran?' I said as she sunk into a nearby chair. 'I can't believe this party is actually going to happen.' I sat down too.

'Yes, and slowly but surely everyone has come to terms with the move afterwards. Even Pan.' She smiled. 'Even me.'

'Did I hear my name, darling?' said a voice. A wave of

pungent perfume wafted over me. Pan sat down on one of the leaf-patterned armchairs, wearing a magnificent flowing tie dye top over pink leggings.

'We're just talking about where everyone's going to live,' I said.

Pan wiped crumbs away from her mouth.

'Been sampling the cookies?' I asked.

'A very important job,' she said, beaming.

'So you've decided where you are living?'

'I'm moving in with Adam. I thought about what Alf said and his daughter getting upset. It changed my perspective a little, although the deciding factor was everything Nik told me.'

I glanced over at Alf who honestly believed Nik had magical powers of kindness that could only be attributed to someone like Saint Niklaus.

'He brought Glenda back after they visited Darkthorn House and came in for a coffee. I was eating dinner in the dining room. Glenda went to her room to get changed.' She flashed me a mischievous smile. 'I think she wanted to check her hair was all right, what with Nik being around. Anyway, he asked if I was leaning towards a decision. I said Alf had made me feel more positive, but it was different for him because there were no grandchildren. You see, my main concern, apart from being a burden to Adam and… and… Sus… I mean… Sar… his wife, has been that his teenage daughters would find it dreary having their gran around – even though we get on well. At that age you don't want to be talking medicines and nurses – you want to walk around singing to music, raving about pop stars, you want the world to be vibrant and… and romantic.'

'I don't see for one minute how you would detract from that, Pan,' I said.

'What did our Nik say to change your mind?' asked Gran.

'I didn't know that he'd been a teen when his grandma moved in. He said it was great – and not just because she was usually on his side if he got into trouble with his parents. He loved listening to her stories from when she was younger. Plus both working full-time, he noticed his parents used to get stressed with each other and having his grandmother there... it sort of created a new dynamic.' She shrugged. 'He was honest – said there were very difficult times, especially towards the end, but that his mum and dad had talked to him about it, before she moved in. They all agreed it would have been much harder if she'd been in a home and they were always having to to and fro and worry from afar.'

'So it's sorted and you're happy?' asked Gran

'Yes – although it's on the condition that if things get too... difficult, well, then they don't hesitate to put me into full-time care. I've made them promise me that. Taking in an older relative, it wouldn't work for everyone – but they have the room and I feel happier we now have this agreement that if things get tough, I won't be a burden.'

I took her hand. 'Well done, Pan. It can't have been an easy decision to make.'

Gran's stomach rumbled and we all laughed as Buddy pricked up his ears. 'I need a cookie,' she said.

I started to get up but Pan waved her hand. 'No. Allow me. Then I think you and I should paint our stones, Alice. I'm going to paint a willow tree. What about you?'

'A canal boat, if I can manage it.'

Gran watched Pan leave with a sad look on her face, then she turned to me. 'Just to let you know, Jess, your mum hasn't got in touch.'

'What a surprise.'

'Now, now… doesn't mean she won't. It must be daunting, the thought of facing us both. I was thinking, she might find it easier meeting us in a more relaxed environment, such as a party…' Her eyes shone with hope.

'You want to invite her on Sunday?' I thought for a moment. 'I guess there's nothing to lose. Okay. Whatever you think is best.'

Please don't let Gran down. I don't care about me. I've accepted the way things are but Gran's older and wants a sense of closure.

A commotion near reception revealed that the tree had arrived. The scouts jumped to their feet. Nik hurried over. The pine tree was even taller than him and had already been planted in a big red bucket. Nik helped them position it near the window. Lynn got out the stack of decorations the residents had made, all glittery and white, in the shape of bells, angels and snowflakes. Pan came over to us with a plate of warm cookies. Nancy followed in her wheelchair with a tray of what looked like cranberry vol-au-vents balanced on her lap.

I picked one up. 'Mmm. Delicious.'

Nancy offered me another. 'We used readymade puff pastry.'

'Really Christmassy. Now I could just do with a slice of turkey,' said Gran.

We all headed over to where Oliver was standing. The chairs around the painting table were empty now. He'd been helping residents with the trickier parts of their designs. My chest glowed as I observed his easy manner with the residents. Pan and Gran sat down and chose their stones and the acrylic pens they thought would suit their designs. I passed Buddy's lead to Gran.

'How was last night?' I asked Oliver as we stood watching, feeling oddly shy at the proximity. The urge I sometimes had to run my hand across his broad shoulders, just for a second felt overpowering.

'Good,' he said. 'We actually talked a lot about work and an idea Misty and I are considering, to bring in more income. I was going to ring but—'

'It's none of my business,' I said and forced a laugh. That didn't mean I wasn't keen to hear every single detail. Like what had she worn? Did they laugh much? How was the sex?

I pushed away that last thought.

'Are you seeing her again?'

'I've kind of invited her to the party. Lynn said it was okay. I hope you don't mind.'

'Gosh. Things are moving quickly.' I kept my tone jolly. 'In fact, it's quite inspired me to go on Tinder. It's about time I tried it – with a little help from Seb. Perhaps we'll soon be able to double date.'

'Sure,' he said, not sounding enthusiastic.

I couldn't blame him. We'd only ever been on one double date before and our partners decided they liked each other more than me and Oliver.

'It'll be great to meet Krish,' I said breezily.

'I only asked her because her granddad is reaching the point where he needs to go into a care home and I suggested her coming as it would give her an inside view. She said the family's really worried he'll feel lonely – I reckon this place, and the strong friendships everyone has made, and the amazing staff... the spirit of Willow Court will make her and her family feel much better.'

'Good idea. Right – I think I'll go and help decorate that tree. I can spot one of the scouts about to sink his teeth into one of Gran's decorative dough biscuits.'

Without looking at Oliver, I hurried away. I'd been so looking forward to the party with the good ole James Stewart vibe, the music and food, the fake snow outside and the residents forgetting their worries just for a few hours.

But now it would be an emotional event where Mum might turn up and where I'd be effectively saying goodbye to Nik – chuckle as I may about Alf's theory, a tiny part of me considered that he could be right. True saint or not, Nik was a one-off. Call it the pixie dust factor. And then there was Krish turning up, and the possibility of Oliver moving in with her brother – at this rate the party might herald the beginning of me also having to say goodbye to my flatmate.

38

Gran stood at the front of the lounge by the hatch with Lynn. The room was packed. It was Wednesday, the 2nd of December. The final preparations had been done and Nik, Oliver and I were about to head up to Pebble Rock to drop off everyone's painted stones. There wouldn't be another chance before Sunday. None of us felt goodhearted Nik should do it on his own, as he offered, and Oliver and I were both working until the weekend. We had torches and would take photos to show everyone. We stood in our anoraks and each had a rucksack. The collection of stones was quite heavy as the staff had painted one each, as well, and Alf insisted on decorating an extra one representing Buddy. However, the main reason for dividing them up was because if they'd all been bundled into one bag the paint might have chipped off.

'Right, everyone,' said Gran. 'Tell me if I've got any of this wrong.' She coughed and leant against the hatch's counter before squinting at her clipboard. 'The crackers are now finished – enough for one between two.'

We'd all agreed making nearly one hundred, what with thirty residents and two guests each, would have taken its toll on poor eyesight and arthritic hands! Foil had been twisted and wrapped and then – the most fun part – jokes made and one of the carers typed them up at home and printed them out. The gifts inside were individually wrapped chocolate bonbons.

'The decorations are done, too, and the scouts did a grand job of putting them on the tree. Glenda's twig frame is finished. How are you getting on with putting the photos onto it?'

'I'm doing a row every day,' she said. 'It's quite tricky using the clips Nik ordered for me online but I'll definitely be finished by Sunday.'

Gran wrote another tick on her list. 'Excellent. Right, Lynn, has your brother got his playlist together? The party kicks off at two – what time will he arrive?'

'Yes, everyone was really helpful on Sunday. Geoff will arrive before three and play for an hour – Nancy's Duke Ellington records can play until he gets here, along with the Big Band Christmas CD I bought especially.'

'Rose, Walter, Celia and… Nancy – you're going to bake the cookies on Saturday? And those little vol-au-vents, along with peppermint creams to have with coffee?'

'Yes,' replied Nancy. 'And at the end of this week the red and white candy canes we ordered should arrive.'

'The Springhaye Snacking Company that offered us finger foods at a discount price – and they do sound delicious – will set up their buffet at around one o'clock in the dining room, that's right, isn't it, Lynn?' Gran continued.

'Yes. Partygoers eating in the dining room will mean there is plenty of space in there and here in the lounge, for people to chat. And, if Geoff's playing gets too loud people can move. Oh, and the party organisers that offered to decorate the lounge with snowflake helium balloons and foil icicle chains will get here early too.'

'What about those American desserts we were promised?' asked Fred, rapping his walking stick on the floor. 'Damned delicious they sounded.'

Gran smiled. 'The American woman who emailed in? Cynthia will be dropping off her eggnog pie and spiced rum fruitcake on Saturday. Very generously she's made several of each. I can't wait to try them. I'm so glad she won the American cookie hamper that the *Amblemarsh Gazette* offered, for those emailing in with offers of help and tips.'

'We should write and thank the editor, again. I'll email him tomorrow, if you all like,' I said.

'I'll set up Misty's Minibar at the hatch, in here, right?' asked Oliver.

'Love the name,' I said.

He beamed. 'I'll make the eggnog cocktails and the Snowflake Martinis everyone liked, along with alcohol-free versions and a couple of Martini cocktails seeing as that's what most of you suggested. I'm working on a menu that will list all the choices. Misty's been great about donating ingredients and I'll bring along some of our most popular bar snacks.'

'Why don't we serve soft drinks and coffees from there too,' said Pan. 'That way both the dining room and lounge will feel really sociable all afternoon.'

With slow writing, Gran noted that down.

'The choir will turn up at five to sing carols,' said Lynn. They will perform in the corridor so that people can hear in both areas.'

'And things are winding up at half past five?' asked Nik.

Lynn nodded. 'The choir will make a nice finale. Our cooks will just put on a small Sunday lunch for residents, at twelve – perhaps soup and rolls. That way everyone will have an appetite to enjoy the buffet.' She looked around. 'Two until five-thirty is a long time and if anyone feels they need to retire to their room for a break, or bit of quiet, there's no shame in that.'

'Not likely,' said Alf. 'I don't think I've been to a party since last year's bash.'

'We don't mind if you need to take a break though, Lynn,' said Fred. 'We all know you youngsters can't keep up. There's no stamina these days.'

Everyone laughed, Lynn included, then her face turned serious. 'This might be the last time I can speak to you, all gathered together like this, just us...' She looked past Nik, Oliver and me standing near the corridor, and beckoned. Several of the carers came in and stood at the front with her. 'We just wanted to say... the closing of Willow Court, it's the last thing any of us wanted. You've all become our extended family.' She glanced at her colleagues who nodded. 'We're really going to miss every single one of you – Pan's stylish dress sense, Alf's skills with dominoes. We've loved hearing Fred's firefighting stories and Glenda's tales of travel...' On she went, mentioning people's names, demonstrating how her job was much more than just a way of paying the bills. 'You've given us all perspective...' Her voice wavered. 'About what really matters in life. You've taught us so much, sharing your life experiences. We wish you all well.'

A tear streamed down her face. Other carers dabbed their eyes.

'You've made a bloody big difference to our lives, that's for sure,' said Fred in a croaky voice.

'How about three cheers?' called Glenda.

'Hip hip...' Everyone else joined in with Alf.

'I'm so glad we're going to be all together forever, up on Pebble Rock,' said Pan.

'Talking of which, we'd better make a move,' I said. 'Oliver promised Misty he'd drop in to help with the last couple of hours of the Wednesday all-night happy hour. You normally work the whole of that shift, don't you?'

He nodded. The carers mingled with the residents, hugs and kisses were exchanged. Nik said goodbye to Glenda. Oliver and Alf chatted.

'I won't be long, Gran. Are you sure you're okay with Buddy?'

'Yes. He's good company. He never argues and is warmer than a hot water bottle.' She shot me a meaningful look. 'You haven't asked about your mum. You think she's not going to reply or turn up on Sunday?'

I didn't answer.

'She always was a last-minute sort of person. I'm not expecting an email response. Karen contacted us as soon as she saw that photo. There's no doubt in my mind that she's keen.'

'See you later. Whether Mum turns up or not we're going to have a fab time.'

Nik and Oliver were waiting. I joined them and we headed out, smiling at Betty who stood holding her doll.

'Has Betty got a new home sorted?' asked Nik as we strode out into the dark.

'Yes. Lynn's worked hard with her family and Social

Services. I think there are only five residents now, with uncertain futures and the council has found them temporary placements.'

'It's a miracle that anyone got sorted in such a short time frame,' said Oliver.

'I know, although Gran said some had been making enquiries at other homes for a few months, just in case, since the rumours started about Willow Court having financial problems. Has Krish's grandad got dementia?'

'No. Hearing and sight problems and he's had a couple of falls – he's living with Krish's family, at the moment, recovering from his latest,' said Oliver. 'They all work full-time and are worried about him being left on his own. Apparently he was a massive fan of James Stewart back in the day and *It's a Wonderful Life* is his favourite film. He's got a signed photo and has given it to Krish to bring, for the residents to look at.'

We turned left out of Willow Court and walked past homes and shops decorated inside and out with the reds, greens and golds of the season, then left again at the end by the book shop and over the bridge to the tarmac picnic area, talking about other old movies we'd all seen. The wooden tables glittered with frost. The recent rain had cleared to leave a cloud-free sky that offered no protection from the winter chill. Wishing I'd put on two pairs of gloves, I switched on my torch, like the others, and we headed up to Pebble Rock. The two men talked about a mutual love of hiking and Nik invited Oliver over to Sydney next year, like he had me, to go walking to the Mermaid Pools, whatever they were.

Breathing heavily, we finally reached the top and Nik

pulled me up to the plateau. I was shivering now. The three of us stood, looking out over the bench, down at the lights of Amblemarsh. We set down our rucksacks and chose a spot to deposit the stones. One by one we took them out, placing them carefully into a tight, tidy pile.

'Look at the one Alf painted for Buddy,' I said and shone my torch. It was a mass of yellow curls with two eyes in the middle.

'I love Alice's canal boat, on top of the stream,' said Nik.

'Fred's fire hose is, um…' Oliver looked at us both and we started laughing; for a second it felt like old times.

'X-rated, unless you look closely,' I said. 'Isn't Lynn's sweet – the blue forget-me-nots that fill the front borders every spring?'

'Kind of prophetic,' said Nik and we stood in silence for a moment.

My phone flashed as I took photos, making sure Pan and Gran's stones lay next to each other.

'I'd better get off,' said Oliver. 'See you Sunday, Nik.'

Nik saluted and grinned. He and I sat down on the bench. He put his arm around my shoulders. It felt comfortable. Friendly. I thought back to us meeting on the plane and me sitting in the wrong seat. Fate was clearly determined our paths would cross. I looked sideways at him.

'Thanks for everything, Nik. I'll always remember the winter we met.'

'Which you did, literally.'

'What do you mean?'

'Talvi – my surname. It's the Finnish word for winter.'

'Really?' I gave a wide smile in the darkness. Alf must never know this. It would totally confirm his theory.

'Thanks to you too, Jess, for welcoming me into your world.' He pulled me close and kissed the top of my head. 'And because the last few weeks have confirmed what I need to do to rescue my business.'

'Tell me more.'

He took his arm away. 'I want to set up a small sister company, to try something different. My – our – focus, at Junior Magic, has always been on the young. A sister company – Senior Magic – would do the opposite. I had the inkling of an idea for it before I left Australia.'

'Toys for adults? What, gadgets like drones and remote-controlled mini helicopters?'

'No – I mean activity items for people with dementia. I was amazed by Bill's little wooden workbench and Phyllis's activity apron and that doll obviously means a lot to Betty. Grams would have loved items like that for her restless hands. A few months ago I saw some featured on a television programme about dementia back in Sydney and it got me thinking.'

'That's why you got the electronic King Charles Spaniel for Phyllis! Oh Nik – what a brilliant idea.'

'Lachlan's really excited. It's a growing market but also the idea's got heart – his uncle has dementia and suffers from restlessness. I think this new project could be really rewarding for everyone involved.'

'You're going to leave Junior Magic as it is?'

'No. I'll pass on what I've found out about artificial intelligence to the design department and will discuss it with the board. I think we need to stick to our traditional principles of fun, education and quality, but bring in a modern aspect such as games that, say, focus on climate change and the world today, and recycling... So I'm grateful, Jess. I'm not sure I would have actually gone ahead with Senior Magic without meeting you.'

'I'd never have made a fool of myself if you hadn't been around.' I smiled sheepishly.

'Hey... there's no such thing as being a fool when it comes to following your heart. Talking of which... have you given more thought as to why Oliver disliked me at the start?'

'With Seb's help, yes, I know why now. Why didn't you just tell me?'

'I wanted to but wasn't one hundred per cent sure and reckoned if I was right, you'd figure it out for yourself.'

'It seems obvious now,' I said, 'after all these years of living together.'

'What are you going to do about it?'

'Ask Father Christmas to sort it out?' I said hopefully.

'My advice, for what it's worth, is to talk. Get things out in the open.' He stood up. 'Come on. I noticed a sign in The Silver Swan's window earlier – let's pick up Buddy and then I'll shout you a hot mulled wine before we both head home.'

39

The rest of the week at Under the Tree felt like the very best kind of Groundhog Day, helping customers choose the perfect Christmas presents for the little ones in their lives – and fighting over the last doughnut in the staff room with Seb. The evenings were a different matter, with Oliver working the evening shifts as companies' festive nights out started to take place. I'd missed his company, sitting on the sofa with my meal for one. It was hard to imagine a new flatmate replacing the banter and easiness between us. So I'd kept busy, ringing back several people who'd called who were involved in the party. *Thanks for letting me know and, agreed, it's probably best if choir members with sniffles don't turn up as the residents are especially vulnerable at this time of year. Sorry, I'm afraid your dog will have to stay in the car even if he is a great help to you, setting up decorations.*

Buddy kept being Buddy, laying by my side in front of the telly. Undemanding. Affectionate. A good listener. Why did everyone else have to change?

The only person I wanted to be different was Mum. I got up Sunday morning and stretched and padded into the bathroom. I switched on the kettle and looked at my phone as I did every morning. Gran had said she'd let me know if she'd got in touch. She hadn't, Gran had simply texted to say that Cynthia had dropped off the eggnog pies and spiced rum fruitcakes and they smelt delicious. Yawning, Oliver stumbled into the kitchen wearing jeans, and a T-shirt on back-to-front, his hair spiked up in all directions. I stared fondly at him, wanting to ask if he was moving in with Krish's brother but afraid of the answer.

'I can hardly open my eyes,' he said and collected Buddy's lead from the coffee table. 'Last night we had a nightmare of a Christmas party held by a law firm. One of the partners sat at the bar, on his own, giving me the gossip. They'd been out for a meal and were already loaded by the time they got to Misty's. We're talking married co-workers snogging and juniors telling bosses to eff off. It ended with someone throwing a punch.' He gazed at Buddy. 'Shall I take his Lordship out for his morning walk and pick up strong coffees and pastries on the way back, instead of us making our usual Sunday brunch? We'll be eating at Willow Court all afternoon.'

'Great idea. I'll take a shower. Is Krish meeting you there?'

'Yep. I can't wait for her to meet you.'

Telling myself it was nothing to do with Krish, I made an extra effort with my makeup and put on my best Christmas jumper – not the quirky pixie one with big gold buttons down the front and a matching hat, but the more sophisticated baby-blue one Seb had bought me last year, with a sparkly silver bunch of mistletoe down the front. Oliver wore his festive jumper covered in lines of Christmas trees. It was chunky, masculine and accentuated his sturdy frame. We went out into the chilly air, Buddy tugging at the lead as he headed to smell other dogs' signatures on a lamp post. We drove listening to Christmas music playing on a popular radio station, rather than talking. I parked up and Nik arrived at the same time and was able to help Oliver inside with the cocktail ingredients. I'd driven him to work yesterday evening and we'd loaded the boxes into the boot before his shift began and I'd brought them back to the flat so that he wouldn't have to worry about it at the end of a long shift.

Lynn let us in and the others headed over to the hatch in the lounge, taking Buddy with them, whilst I signed us in. Oliver had said something about them being *all men together* and Nik had shot him a conspiratorial grin. Her face broke into a smile.

'The last residents are just finishing off their light lunch – a suitably themed chestnut soup. Alice has finished and gone up to her room to change.' Lynn looked at her watch. 'The caterers and party organisers with decorations should be here any minute, it's almost one.'

I pulled off my woolly hat. 'Okay. I'll just pop upstairs to see her and then I'll wait down here for them to arrive. Pro Snow should arrive shortly afterwards. Normally they only keep snow falling for an hour when they are booked for a party, but they're bringing enough of the fluid they use to cover when people arrive, the hours of daylight and then they'll switch it on again for when people leave. So I thought they could come in for a hot drink and food around four, half four, before going out again.'

'People have been so generous.'

'Yes. The *Gazette*'s been brilliant and the local community.

The plight of the residents really seems to have struck a chord.' I walked past the lounge. Lynn's Big Band Christmas CD was playing.

'It's not right that you've been let in and I'm not allowed out,' said Betty.

I touched her arm. 'There's going to be a party today, Betty,' I said gently. 'Lots of people will be allowed in but that's to help us all celebrate Christmas.'

She stared blankly at me for a few seconds. 'I need to get home. My Jim needs his dinner and the children need their bath. They're always so scruffy after a day at school.' Betty walked towards the entrance door and peered out.

I passed the reception, turned left and walked along the corridor to Gran's room. I knocked sharply before going in. She was wearing her fancy rose gold striped trainers and...

'Oh Gran. I haven't seen you in a dress for so long! It's really pretty and matches your coral fleece to a tee.' It was long. Navy with big orange flecks with an embroidered neck – not her usual style at all.

'I feel like a bloomin' Christmas bauble in it but Pan does a lot of online shopping and she got really excited about this outfit. As soon as she saw it Pan said it had my name on it.' Gran sat down in her chair and looked out at the canal. 'Love Pan as I do, normally I'd have told her to bog off, but... I didn't have the heart, seeing as we won't be living together for much longer. I told her I'd remember her every time I wore it. But listen to me, getting morbid. I'm really looking forward to the party. Everyone's worked so hard for it.'

I sat on the bed next to her. Sunshine broke through the December cloud.

'I know what you're going to say – that I've been a fool to expect your mother to turn up.'

'No. And there's still a small chance, I suppose,' I said, hating her flat tone.

Gran turned to face me. 'No. Karen won't come and to be honest I've known that all along. But it's enough for me that she got in touch. It shows that she cares. She's obviously still having problems. Maybe one day I'll meet her again – maybe I won't.' She took my hand. 'Are you disappointed, sweetheart?'

'No, I'm not. I closed that chapter of my life a long time ago. You and me, Gran. The day to day. That's family. That's love. That's what gets me through. It's real. Whereas Mum – she's just become some kind of fantasy figure.'

Those words could equally apply to my situation with Nik and Oliver.

'She's never been there for the tough times. Not like you have. You've been more of mum to me than she ever was or ever could be. I don't need anything more. I know it's different for you, she's your daughter, you gave birth to her. It must feel as if a part of you is missing. But it's not the same for me. You've filled any mum-shaped hole in my life.'

We sat holding hands for a few minutes.

'Right, I'd better go and welcome the caterers and help them set up.'

Gran's eyes filled.

I rummaged in my coat pocket for a tissue and wiped her cheek. 'I'm sure you'll meet Mum one day again.'

'It's not that. Gordon Bennett, I've become a soppy old sod recently.' She blew her nose. 'It's been fun, as it always is, making the decorations and seeing the tree go up. I can't wait to see snow falling – the fake stuff is much better, as we won't slip on it tomorrow. And I'm looking forward to hearing the choir and Lynn's brother play. Cocktails and festive food – my mouth is watering just thinking about it. But...' Gran's stiff fingers covered her face. The hunched shoulders moved up and down. Drops of water fell onto the embroidered neckline of her new dress. 'This party is the last and first,' a stifled voice said. 'The last time we'll celebrate Christmas together and it'll be the first of many farewells. I feel like this year is coming to an end and the next one is creepily waiting around the corner – an unfamiliar void.'

My eyes pricked and I took her hands away, I removed her glasses and wiped them with another tissue. She blew her nose and I put the glasses back on her face.

'It is unfamiliar but not a void, Gran. We're going to arrange regular meet-ups with Pan and Glenda, Fred and Nancy are moving with you. Who knows what new friends you will make? There might even be a dishy man.'

'I don't want to laugh,' she muttered. 'I want to sit here and wallow. None of this is fair.'

'Life isn't, Missy. Get used to it. Years are like oysters. Some have pearls in. Some don't. The exciting thing is that we never know which is next. Who knows what the future holds?'

Gran raised her eyebrows. 'I'd forgotten that used to be my stock phrase when you were younger and having a hard time at school.'

I needed the reminder as well and felt a little bit braver. I'd had several great years with Oliver. Things were never going to stay the same forever.

'That's karma,' I said, hoping my eyes didn't look as wet

as they felt. 'You've got new responsibilities now, Gran. Silver's waiting over in Darkthorn House – you promised him a fancy new tank and Buddy's expecting you to introduce him to a whole new stack of friends.' I'd checked and, like Willow Court, they didn't mind well-behaved dogs visiting. 'Then there's that book club to organise.'

'I suppose,' she said and we looked at each other. 'And the first step to making my new room homely will be to put up that lovely little cuckoo clock you bought me in Germany.'

I smiled. Roles were changing but, as ever, we were there for each other. That was one constant I was sure of. I kissed her and hurried along the corridor. She said she'd join me in a few moments. The caterers were just walking through the doors, laden with bags. The canteen was empty now and staff were cleaning tables and setting out the bright foil crackers. I headed into the lounge. Fairy lights twinkled on the tree, and across the curtain tops, even though it wasn't dark outside.

I couldn't see Nik, perhaps he'd gone up to see Glenda, but Oliver was behind the hatch and I heard a woman's laugh. Hopefully that was Lynn. I didn't know how she'd coped with her workload these last weeks, continuing to supervise the care of thirty residents whilst fighting to keep the owners of Willow Court from starting to dismantle what they could, and also helping to organise this party. I stood for a moment, near to the entrance to the room. Glenda's twig photo frame had been balanced on top of table and leant against the wall.

'Moonlight Serenade' came on at that moment. It reminded me of Jimmy Stewart starring in the film of Glenn Miller.

James Stewart. Nik was like him. Tall. A perfect gentleman. Much loved. That would be just as likely a theory – that he was the reincarnation of that Hollywood actor and not Father Christmas.

I went over to the hatch, looking for Oliver there. It had a banner across the top saying Misty's Minibar in dusky pink, like the neon sign outside the bar. He'd set up drinks and a few of Misty's exclusive crisps and popcorn, and had made a professional looking menu describing the drinks available, all written in matching pink too. I was just about to go behind to the sink area when an unfamiliar woman's voice cut through the air.

'Oh Oliver, it's going to be so exciting. The date of the move is the 28th of December – you're sure that suits you?'

The hairs on the back of my neck stood up. That must have been Krish.

'That's fine. I can't wait,' he said in a happy voice.

My throat ached.

She laughed. 'Then don't look so nervous. You're going to love my brother, his friends are fun and the flat's got lots of room for all your stuff.'

I backed away and stood staring at the drinks and snacks. So it was really happening. Oliver was leaving our home and, by the sounds of it, as speedily as he could.

His face loomed into view as he came out from behind the hatch accompanied by a tall woman with lush dark hair and wearing jeans. She held Buddy's lead. He was making puppy dog eyes at her, clearly as smitten as my flatmate. He barked when he saw me and wagged his tail. A big cartoonish reindeer covered the front of her jumper with a silly red bobble nose, right in the middle. Suddenly I felt stupid trying to look sophisticated.

'You must be Jess,' she said and strode over. She held out her hand and on automatic I slipped mine into hers. What a firm shake. White teeth gleamed as she gave me a broad smile. 'Oliver has told me so much about you.' Posh London tones. 'It's great to finally meet.'

'Krish, I presume?' I said, sounding a bit too Sherlock Holmes.

'I'm so grateful to have been invited. My family and I couldn't be more worried about Gramps. From what Oliver says you're really close to your gran too. It must be such a weight off your mind to have found her a new home she is happy with.'

We chatted and I listened to her concerns about her grandad. She asked about Gran. Krish seemed nice. Oliver deserved that. I hoped the move would work out well for him.

I just had to get on with it now.

Lynn's brother, Geoff, arrived and set up in the far corner, before any of the guests arrived. Pro Snow did too and a member of staff showed them around outside. The party organisers turned up and began to transform the room with their snowflakes and icicle shapes. Gran appeared with her clipboard. Krish went over to her immediately, introduced herself and asked if she could help in any way. She offered to make the coffees later, seeing as she worked in the business. Gran patted her arm and said what a kind person she was. Slowly the lounge started to fill up as residents waited for their guests. Alf and Fred looked very dapper in jackets and ties and I'd never seen Nancy in a skirt before. Pan floated into the room, a suitable vision of green and red, in a kimono and scarf.

Oliver started handing out cocktails as two o'clock approached. Nancy put on one of her records. Duke Ellington crooned about jingle bells. I stole into the canteen just before the first guests arrived. Wow. What a buffet, colourful and bright with dishes of cherry tomatoes and clementine tarts. There were bowls of easy-to-manage finger foods made from light flaky pastry, the contents filling the room with smells of turkey, sage and onion and chestnut. The residents' vol-au-vents looked as professional as anything else on offer, next to pigs in blankets and mini slices of nut roast. As my stomach rumbled, I recalled the menu I'd been sent and looked for the mushroom and cranberry quiches and stuffed Brussel sprouts. Fresh batches of the cookies Nancy and the others baked had been set on plates, and I took them through to the lounge, putting them on the hatch. Nik appeared with Glenda. He'd taken off his coat and waved before disappearing into the throng. I caught Oliver's eye as he came over to me, wiping his hands on a tea towel. I tried not to look at Alf because Nik was wearing a jumper with a big Father Christmas on the front.

'I see you two,' said a gruff voice. Alf had appeared at our side, clutching his notebook. 'My suspicions may not ring true with you youngsters, but that jumper is more proof, like it or not.'

'Alf. Sorry, it just tickled me, given all the other bits of evidence you've listed. But this... it's just a coincidence, surely?'

'Like you saying how much your life improved once you started meditating? Who's to say listening to yourself breathe has any effect on mental health? You haven't got indisputable evidence.'

I sighed as the first relatives started to arrive. 'Trust me, Alf, I've a whole list of things I'd ask Santa for if he was here, right this minute. I really wish your theory about Nik was true.'

'What theory's this?' asked Nik from behind me and beaming, he came around and placed his hand on Alf's shoulder.

40

'Oh look! How beautiful!'
    'Damn well gets me in the festive mood.'
'Blimey O'Reilly, I wasn't expecting it to fall that thickly.'
'Bloody good show!'

Nik's question was thwarted by gasps of delight as everyone headed over to the window. Snowflakes tumbled down from the sky. I looked out, to the left, at the other side of the entrance way and watched a large cannon shooting the fake snow high into the air.

'I feel as if I'm back in Finland,' said Nik, holding back as he was heads and shoulders above everyone else. He stood, gazing over recently set perms and bald heads, mesmerised by the magical scene.

'Mum took me sledging once,' I said to Oliver. 'On a tray. It split as I sped down the local park's hill. I ended up in the river at the bottom. Luckily it was frozen.'

'Mine never let me out. Said it was too dangerous and the last thing Nanny wanted was to look after a child with a broken leg. Do you think your mum will come today?'

'No. Gran and I have discussed it and we're okay with that.'

'You sure, Jess?' he said, in a gentle tone.

'I've already got everything I need. Gran. Buddy.' You.

'Come on, Oliver – I'll help you make cocktails,' said Krish and she pushed him playfully. 'There's a queue forming.' He hesitated before leaving.

I went over to Nik and Glenda who were showing visitors the photo collection. The next couple of hours passed in a busy blur. The food was a big hit. I'd never tasted anything as delicious as the eggnog pie. People milled in and out of the dining room, listening to Geoff play in the lounge. I caught snippets of conversation. Pan sat with Adam and his wife, looking more relaxed than I'd seen her in weeks.

'I'd love to choose the colours for my room,' she said. 'I'm thinking bright purple.' She laughed at her son's horrified face. 'Your old mum can still fool you.'

Glenda chatted to Alf's daughter, Polly, about her bookkeeping business and outfit.

'I don't feel ready for work unless I'm dressed, made up and hair sprayed, even though I work from home,' said Polly.

'An excellent attitude,' said Glenda. 'I don't feel ready for anything unless I've got my lipstick on.'

They both laughed.

Nik sat with Phyllis who was stroking her electronic King Charles Spaniel. He stroked it too. Phyllis looked at him and her eyes filled for a moment. He nodded gently. No words were exchanged just some kind of intangible understanding like I thought I had with him.

A lump rose in my throat. This was what it had all been about – the hard work. The stress. The crafting sessions. Everything on the clipboard list. It was about bringing people together for one last time to create memories that would stand the test of time. Even in Pan's case because there would always be the stones up at Pebble Rock, the warmth in everyone's hearts.

The love.

Studying the photos collected by Glenda had also underlined why this get-together was so important. There were pictures of the residents as who they still were inside, the people behind the grey hair and wrinkles. The dashing firefighter, the stylish international business woman, the busy efficient and capable parents... It was so easy, in a care home, to forget the achievements of the resident – to forget that they had desires and hobbies and a purpose just like anyone else. The photos, their history, it all compounded the importance of Lynn's emphasis on treating them with dignity and respect. This party celebrated the lives they'd led in the past and, just as importantly, the lives they now had.

I swallowed and turned my attention to Krish. She was speaking to Oliver and Gran. Perhaps I was looking at the future in the wrong way. Oliver and me meeting partners may not mean our family would break up. Instead it could get bigger. Perhaps Krish or whoever he went out with next would take us from a three to a four.

I turned around. Lynn was tapping my shoulder.

'Going great, isn't it?' I said. 'Your brother's playing is fantastic and I feel we've all really pulled off the whole wintry feel, with the decorations. I can just imagine James Stewart walking into the room at any moment, covered in snow, and bells jingling because Clarence finally got his wings.'

'It's perfect and it's not James Stewart but there is a man

at the door and he insists he won't come in for something to eat. Seb – a friend of yours? He's asking if he could have a quick chat.'

Seb? Was everything okay at Under the Tree? What about Angela? I hurried out of the room and along the corridor where the choir were setting up.

'Is everything okay?' I asked.

'No. Annoyingly Tim has come up trumps again. He's always right and it drives me mad.'

'What are you talking about?'

Seb paced up and down. 'I know why Oliver never liked Nik at the beginning.'

My brow knotted. 'I really appreciate the interest, but couldn't this have waited?' I grinned. 'Or is this an excuse just to have some of the amazing food I told you about.'

'The last conversation you had with Nik, the night he rejected you, you thought he had his own theory about why Oliver had been rude to him, but he didn't say...'

'And that turned out to be because Nik reminded him of someone underhand from his past – and because Oliver was worried of our family unit being broken up... you and I have worked this out already. Nik didn't need to tell me.'

'But you missed the obvious. I didn't pick it up either. I think Nik's theory was to do with jealousy.'

'What?'

'That charm bracelet – the heart charm represents someone, not something, important in your life. So not Gran or Buddy as they already had charms of their own... *Heart,* Jess.'

'*Home is where the heart is* – we've already reached a conclusion about this.'

'Think of the word heart, Jessie. Try taking away the e.'

'Okay, okay…. H-A-R-T… Oliver's surname?'

'Exactly and it's nothing to do with that home and heart thing, that was a red herring. It's quite simple really – he was jealous of Nik, not because of his work or his jet-setting, or that infectious charm… but because this gorgeous Australian had *your* attention. Now can't you see what's been staring you in the face? You aren't happy with him going out with Krish not because you might be left alone, nor because it will change the status quo – it's because *you're* jealous back. You and Oliver are in love with each other!'

Silence for a moment. I burst out laughing. 'Don't be ridiculous,' I said unevenly. 'You… you said it yourself – we're more like brother and sister.'

'That's only because you get on so well. You're always there for each other. You're so comfortable in each other's company. All of those things could also apply to a very well-matched couple.' He slapped his palm against his forehead. 'I can't believe I missed it, Jess. You're meant for each other.'

'*You're wrong,*' I said firmly, pulse racing. 'He's a down-to-earth, forthright person and would have acted upon his feelings before now. Like the time we had noisy neighbours, who played music into the early hours. Oliver gave them a few nights, to see if it changed, and then went around. It didn't make a difference so he contacted our landlord. And when Gran mentioned in passing, last year, that she could do with more shelving for her books, the following weekend he turned up with several flat packs and he assembled them.'

To an outsider he might have looked laidback, working in a bar, not worrying about mortgages and promotions, but day to day he was decisive… a bit of an action man.

And his recently revealed past in Birmingham explained why he'd shied away from being career-driven.

Nah. If he'd developed feelings for me, I'd have known.

And the same for me. I mean, I did fancy him, when he first moved in but...

I bit my lip.

Seb looked at his watch. 'I've got to go – it's my turn to cook tonight.' He held me by the shoulders and stared straight into my eyes. 'Don't mess this up. From what you say Nik is pretty special person and he worked this out first. In my humble opinion you've been feeling crap because Oliver's the one you really want. The ball's in your court now.'

Then he was gone like a guardian angel of my very own. I couldn't breathe properly for a moment, and almost tripped over a chair's leg as I stumbled back into the lounge. Geoff was packing away his saxophone. I stood by the window and put my hand up to my chest. I'd compartmentalised my feelings for Oliver in a sensible box in my head and shut them away – but I'd still noticed things over the years. The curve of his mouth. The strength of his arms. The warmth of his hug. The hair that never lay down flat. The soft tone he used whenever Gran or I were upset.

'You okay?' asked a voice.

I saw Nik's reflection in the window. I didn't turn around. Instead I lifted up my arm and the charm bracelet, pointing to the heart.

'I've just worked it out... Oliver...' My voice wavered.

His brows knitted together. 'I thought you already had.'

'No... not until... you and I got our wires crossed... but now it's too late,' I said, still speaking to his face reflected in the glass.

An arm draped around my shoulders. 'Not going by the way he looks at you.'

'But Krish—'

'Have you actually asked him about her and where they are heading? Or has my very good English friend suddenly become telepathic?'

I blushed and turned around to face him but Glenda was calling him and he'd gone. The choir started up and tuneful words like Bethlehem and manger mingled with the residents and their guests. Krish handed out coffees. Oliver stood near her with a plate of cookies.

I went over, smiled and took a cookie. He smiled back. Sometimes I'd thought about what it would be like to kiss a second time. Yes, I'd been tipsy during that snog, but the memory wasn't blurred. Clearly, I remembered the softness, the warmth, the racing of my heart, a sense that I was truly home. I thought about the other men in my life. Seb was a great guy and good-looking and I hadn't known he was gay for a while but still never imagined the two of us together. As for the guys I'd dated, slow-burn was the best adjective for those relationships. Whereas I'd been drawn to Oliver right from the off, on that pavement, outside my flat – I couldn't peel my eyes away and that was the real reason I'd slipped in the snow.

I bit into the cookie, not sure what to say. Crumbs tumbled down my chin and Oliver brushed them away. It was such an easy, familiar movement, yet his touch sent tingles down my neck. He pulled his hand back quickly as if he'd made a mistake.

That sensible box in my head had well and truly flipped its lid open.

'Speech!' someone called. Gran, Lynn and I looked at each other. Somehow I made it to the front with the others. Gran beckoned Nik to join us. I cleared my voice and was about to try and assemble some words in an order that everyone would understand when a knocking came from outside. The entrance door creaked. Then footsteps. A tanned man with sunshine hair and open arms strode in.

'Nik Talvi, mate! I've come to take you home!'

41

'Mate? Is that any way to speak to your boss?' Nik grinned and hurried over. He and the man hugged and clapped each other on the back. 'But how did you find me? I thought you'd already gone back home?'

'Someone called Rob in the flat next to yours – he said you'd gone to a party, at a place called Willow Court.'

Nik looked around. 'Sorry everyone – let me introduce Lachlan. He's a colleague of mine who's also been travelling around Europe.' He shook his head. 'I had no idea you were coming to England.'

'Your mum told me to,' he said sheepishly. 'She knows what you're like.'

'Tell us more,' said Alf taking out his notebook.

Nik took Lachlan's coat and put it on a chair. Oliver headed over with a Snowflake Martini that had been left over.

'Cheers,' he said and grinned. 'Well, Nik has a habit of not knowing when to stop helping others. Once he's invested in a project he becomes fully absorbed and loses track of everything else.' He clapped Nik on the back again. 'Nik Talvi is one of the kindest, most generous people I know – but I'm guessing you've found that out for yourselves.'

Alf shot me and Oliver a smug look.

'Take the sponsored walks he does and Christmas shoebox appeals. They totally take over Nik's life to the exclusion of everything else. Joanna says you're needed back at the factory now – but more than that, I think she wants her son home for Christmas.'

Nik groaned and comically pulled a face. 'Mum's apron strings stay tethered even at nine thousand miles away.'

'I don't blame her,' said Glenda, eyes glistening. 'I think I speak for everyone when I say you're going to be deeply missed.'

'Damn decent man you are,' said Fred.

Nik's cheeks flushed. 'I'm no saint.'

'Really?' piped up Alf. 'I find that hard to believe. You see I've had this theory – it's as tight as a drum now – that—'

'No really. He's not joking,' said Lachlan and he chuckled. 'I've known Nik since we were at school together. Talk about drama.'

'It's true. I never studied. Was always outside the head's door. I even got caught shoplifting once.'

He and Lachlan preceded to laugh over some of the escapades he'd got up to in his youth.

Alf's face fell.

'Why, what's this theory?' asked Lachlan.

Alf put the notebook on the floor. 'Nothing. It sounds stupid now.'

But all eyes were upon him.

'If you must know… I thought… what with Nik drinking sherry, wearing red, coming from Lapland… what with him having the same name as Saint Niklaus and his charitable nature…' He sighed. 'I'm just a silly old fool, thinking

Father Christmas might really exist. Maybe I'm wrong about everything else. Perhaps man did land on the moon.'

Lachlan and Nik exchanged looks. No one laughed, not even Glenda.

'You're not a fool, Alf,' she said quietly. 'As you know, I've been more sceptical than anyone, over the years, when it comes to Christmas but this year – watching Jess, Oliver, Nik, Alice and Lynn... seeing how everyone has pulled together – the local paper, the community, the choir here, the caterers... it's made me believe that Father Christmas is a real thing, or at least his spirit. It's inside people at this time of year and makes them full of goodwill and charitable to others. I've never really liked the festive season with no family or children of my own and even though you've all always tried to include me in Willow Court, I've always felt like I've been on the outside looking in.'

That explained it.

'I don't think you're stupid at all, Alf,' she continued. 'Nik embodies the very best of that genuine Christmas spirit. He has a way of making people feel valuable, special, as if they are the only person on the planet and that their wish list, so to speak – their dreams – are just as important as anyone else's...'

That's exactly how he'd made me feel.

'And he's brought the Father Christmas out in everyone else,' she continued. 'Perhaps even me.'

'What a compliment,' said Nik and with a flushed face looked from left to right, across the sea of faces, smiling at every resident. 'You've taken me into your hearts and there's a place in mine for Willow Court. I think what Glenda says reflects the theme of this party. Every single one of you here will have made a difference to each other's lives, including all you party guests. Like George Bailey, we may have regrets, we may think ourselves not worthy, but if we each had a guardian angel they'd show us how, over the decades, all of us have positively affected others. It's a wonderful life even though, at times, it may not feel like it. I've been blown away about how strong you've all been at facing your recent challenge.'

I went behind the hatch and came out with a big bouquet of flowers and box of chocolates. 'This seems like a good moment to give you these, Lynn – from all the residents, to put in the staff room. Day in, day out, you and your team carry that goodwill throughout the year.'

Pan started clapping and one by one everyone else joined in, several residents and guests wiping their eyes. I gave Gran a hug and went over to the window. Snow was falling, on cue, as the end of the party drew near.

I was going to miss this place. So would Buddy.

Buddy! I hadn't taken him outside since we arrived. He was due for five minutes of fresh air.

I looked across the room, at Nik embracing Glenda. Lachlan was talking to Fred and Alf. Gran chatted with Pan's son, Adam. And Oliver and Krish... things would never be the same again. Come the New Year Willow Court would be a hotel. Nik would be back in Oz. Oliver would have settled into his new flat. Yet Buddy would always be by my side and I had a lot to be grateful for. The expansion of Under the Tree was exciting and if the residents of Willow Court could face the closure with such stoicism then I had no excuse not to show some determination.

I slipped on my coat, took Buddy's lead from Nancy who'd been fussing over him and slipped out to the front. Delicate snowflakes fell.

'Fantastic job. Thanks so much,' I said to the Pro Snow workers, before moving right, across the lawn, Buddy sniffing plants and happily stopping by a tree in front of the lounge window.

'Jess?' Oliver was heading my way, just in his shirt, sleeves rolled up. 'Everything going okay? I saw you nip out and wondered if you'd gone home. You can't leave without trying the trifle Nik made with that Spanish sherry he bought from the Birmingham markets... Hurry now and you'll get the last morsel.'

'I thought Buddy might be crossing his legs after all those treats Alf gave him.' I turned away, not wanting to see the etch of concern on his face, that only reminded me what a caring, loyal part of my life he'd become. 'You'd better not leave Krish too long.'

'I think she's taken a shine to that Lachlan, to be honest. Who could blame her with his surfer look?'

I turned around. 'But I thought... you stayed over.'

'On the couch. Why, did you think...? We're just friends, Jess. She's great but we've acknowledged there's no chemistry there.'

'Really? You seemed to hit it off – what with you and her both having experience of owning your own businesses, or, at least, her working with family.'

'Yes, it's been good to talk to her, really good, with that common ground. Birmingham – what happened – it had been too tough to talk about it with anyone on a personal level. If I could have done that it would have been with you.

Clinically dissecting what happened, with Krish – it's made me realise I've had trust issues.'

'Was there a woman? Someone you worked with? Did you break up with her just before coming to London?'

'It wasn't a woman. It was Josh, the guy who swindled me. At the beginning he wasn't just someone I met in a business capacity. We were best mates and did everything together, had done for years. That he could do that to me... it shook me to the core. It was all still so raw when I met you so I buried it and avoided getting close to anyone else – man or woman.'

'Right. It's just I thought... I sensed a spark between us, right at the start.' Inwardly I cringed but I had to tackle this. It was now or never. Willow Court closing so suddenly proved you never knew what was around the corner.

'You did? But all these years... the dates you've gone on... I mean, we're just friends, right – always have been?' He shivered and snowflakes rested on his shoulders.

'This is like our first meeting in reverse,' I mumbled. 'This time you're the one unsuitably dressed.'

'That split second when our paths crossed – it... it changed my life.' He stared at me for a moment and then started walking up and down. 'Okay – I'm going to say it, here goes...' He took a deep breath. 'I've regretted that things haven't gone further between us, that I never tried to tell you how I feel.'

What?

'I blew my chances, Jess. I know that.'

'You really *liked* me?'

He nodded vigorously.

'But... I don't understand... I overheard you and Krish

– you're moving out on the 28th of December and in with her brother.'

His eyebrows knitted together. 'No... no, Jess – it's Krish who's on the move. His place is much better than hers, with a balcony and communal garden, they both get on well and I sensed that she wanted to move in, so I made up some excuse about not being able to leave our flat for a while.'

'But the 28th?'

'I'm going around for a party they are holding, to celebrate the move.' His face broke into a smile. 'Meeting Krish and coming to terms with what happened in Birmingham... serving drinks today at this party... it's got me excited about work in a way I haven't felt for years. A while back I put forward the idea to Misty of the business branching out and providing pop-up bars and we've been brainstorming it whenever we've had time. Krish's move is when I'll test out Misty's Minibar properly. I'll be serving a selection of snacks and drinks and...' Eyes sparkling, he chatted for a moment.

'That all sounds amazing,' I said. 'Look at us both moving forwards – me being promoted, you being in charge of an exciting side venture...'

His mouth downturned. 'It is, Jess. New beginnings, and on that note, I need to up my search for other digs. You and Nik – it showed me I can't... I just can't do it anymore.'

'Do what?'

'I meant what I said – I really liked you when we first met. I always have and I can't pretend I don't want to kiss you on the lips. I can't watch you go out on any other dates. When we're on the sofa all I want to do is hold you tight in my arms. When you've done something great at work I want me to be the first one you call. I've got to move on with my life, Jess. The whole friends thing – it's been torture.'

Rapidly, I blinked.

'Your feelings for Nik prove—'

'Have proved to me what's really important. What love really means,' I stuttered. 'It's the being there when the sun rises and when it falls, whatever has happened in between.'

He stood still. 'What do you mean?'

'I don't want you to move out. I don't want you to ever kiss another woman. I want you to hold me tight on the sofa. I want to call you first if I have a great day at work. I want to watch the sun rise with you, and it fall. I want all of that and so much more.'

His face kind of crumpled and he came over and took my hand. 'You really mean it?'

'More than anything I've ever said,' I whispered.

'That night I came home early and Nik was there… I could deny it no longer – I wanted to be the one giving you red roses. When I first moved in, I thought dating other people might help me learn to trust again – it didn't. I just wasn't ready, it was to protect my own feelings because of Josh – and meeting you ruined my chances of ever feeling completely attracted to another woman.' He brushed my cheek with his hand. 'I love your tangled morning curls, the mole by your lip, the way the end of your nose tilts up at the end… but more importantly I can't stop thinking about you because of how much you care for your gran, for Buddy, the customers in Under the Tree, and how I've never laughed with anyone like I do with you. I've so much respect for the life you've carved out for yourself, after a difficult start. You make me feel alive, Jess. Accepted for who I am. Like I matter.'

'Same here,' I mumbled. 'All of this with Nik, it got me thinking about what true love really is. When he helped me write the article for the *Gazette* he made me feel as I was such an amazing person, and I decided it was that. But it's not. It's what we've got. With you I don't feel as if I've got to be anything but exactly what I am right now, with my mood swings every time of the month and my habit of never replacing the toilet roll.'

'I hate that,' he said with a shy smile.

'We haven't got a mortgage, high-powered jobs or pension schemes,' I said, my voice growing stronger as every atom of me tingled. 'The only pitter patter of little feet belong to Buddy here, but right now in my life, if we're together, I'm living the dream and it's real, no fairytale.'

'There's only one thing I'd change about the status quo...' Oliver stepped nearer. He glanced down at my mistletoe jumper. 'It would be rude not to, right?' he murmured.

I leant forwards and felt his lips on mine. I let go of his hands and ran one through his hair. I'd been longing to do that. His arm slid around my waist and eased me close. I lost myself except I didn't feel alone. All sense of time disappeared as if we'd never been without each other. Despite the winter chill heat coursed through my limbs. Buddy barked – and barked again. We drew apart, fingers intertwined, to see him wagging his tail and pulling towards the lounge window.

Cheers and clapping came through the glass. Gran had never looked happier. Pan beamed and theatrically drew a heart in the air. Nik gave a thumbs-up, one hand resting on Alf's shoulder. Nancy waved a bit of tinsel and Fred punched the air. Glenda smiled and nodded.

Oliver and I looked at each other with a new intimacy. He was my true Mr Winter and life really was wonderful.

Read on for a sneak peak of
The Christmas of Calendar Girls...

I

'You've got to be joking.' I pulled a face at Davina and Cara, my two best friends.

The cream sofa creaked as I shuffled backwards. Tea slopped over the side of my china cup and trickled onto the saucer. My curly hair and Cara's bright clothes always seemed out of place in Davina's orderly, elegant living room.

'There's just over a month to do it.' Davina shrugged. 'I think it's one of the Parents' Association's best ideas yet.'

'You would say that.' I couldn't help smiling. 'You came up with it.'

She gave me a flash of pretend offence. 'I've spoken to the Head and she agrees that a homemade advent calendar is a super challenge for Year Three.'

I groaned.

'And that it will develop the children's imaginative and motor skills.'

'Or rather those of the parents. Remember the paint-an-egg competition last Easter?'

Cara yawned. 'That Fabergé egg by little Tommy looked so authentic.'

'Mia probably used real jewels.' Tommy had only joined the class in September, with his lunchbox salmon bagels and tales of clay pigeon shooting with Daddy. And who could ignore his divorced mother, Mia, with her pewter Puffa jacket and pink jeep bearing her beauty salon's logo?

'This is to raise money for a worthy cause, remember,' said Davina. 'A reasonable entry fee will be charged and the winner gets a small prize.'

'Which charity?' asked Cara. She knelt on the laminate floor, stroking Prada, a Persian cat. 'I've not kept up to speed lately.'

Cara not up to speed? That was like saying Lewis Hamilton had been cautioned for driving too slowly.

'Cancer Research,' said Davina. In memory of...'

We all looked at each other. One month, Polly had been there. The next she hadn't. It must have been terrible for her husband. Indeed, I knew how that felt. And I'd tried to protect Lily but the school secretary's death was always going to make her think of her dad.

At the start, moving away from the centre of London – away from our memories of Adam – had diverted me. I envisaged cul-de-sacs where Lily would make friends and neat squares of garden to play on and Alderston village was just like that. The timing was perfect, as she was five years old and had just left nursery and started primary school. A new home. A fresh start. That's when I met Davina and Cara.

But three years later and the hurt still unexpectedly surfaced. Not as frequently as it used to but I'd never get used to that punch to the stomach. Like last week when Adam's favourite rugby team were on the television and won their match. Or yesterday when Lily laughed – blissfully unaffected by the fact she'd given the loudest, daddy-like snort.

I should have got used to it by now: the bedroom floor minus discarded socks; the bathroom cabinet missing shaving gel; the absence of off-tune whistling. Before his diagnosis Adam used to whistle a lot.

Our new home was very different to the London pad Adam and I had excitedly bought two years after we'd first met. Mum and Dad had given us a lump sum and said we could use it to spend on a honeymoon or a deposit for a house. We'd not even had to discuss which option to choose. Our relationship was like that. We agreed on the small and big things – like cream going on scones first and London being an exciting, vibrant place to bring up children. However, since his death, I wanted the quiet life. Somewhere to heal my wounds and provide a gentle upbringing for Lily.

Yes, things had changed. As Lily had grown, I enjoyed her arms round me instead of his. They were just strong enough to push me forwards in time when, now and again, I longed to jump back.

'But all those little doors – twenty-four!' I said brightly. 'Even Cara will struggle with that, and we know there's nothing she can't make out of a toilet roll and a cereal box.'

'Apart from a car that doesn't cut out in weather this cold. Now if I could create one of those…'

Playfully I pushed her shoulder. Dear Cara was ever modest. She'd warmly introduced her eldest daughter, Hannah, that first day in the playground, then beckoned over Davina with her twins, Jasper and Arlo. I was dressed up for a meeting to interview someone about the latest feature I was writing. Davina was dressed up just because. In jeans and trainers, Cara made some comment about herself never being a yummy mummy. I told her she looked

SAMANTHA TONGE

great but said being a chummy mummy counted for much more. We'd had to explain to the children that the word chum meant friend. Appropriately, Cara meant friend in Irish. Her great-grandparents had come over from Belfast and she'd often told stories of their legendary hospitality. She must have inherited it.

'I'm just a little worried for those of us who aren't so artsy,' I said. 'And what with me working full-time and Lily being more of an outdoors sort...'

'We've thought about that.' Davina put the coffee pot down onto the low gilt table.

'That's what worries me.'

Cara chuckled.

It would have been easy to write off the Parents' Association at Birchfield Primary as a bunch of people who had too much time on their hands. But it wasn't. Tease as we did, Davina did a lot of charity work and, having been an accountant, still did the books for her husband's building firm. The other members were either single like me and held down jobs, or, like Cara, they were busy stay-at-home parents.

And then there was redundancy, illness, divorce, caring for elderly relatives...

Everyone had a story.

Simply navigating the day to day was tough enough. Limiting screen time. Encouraging reading. Trying to make fruits and vegetables sound as appealing as chicken nuggets...

Davina proceeded to explain how she would design and provide everyone with a template made out of cardboard, her sleek, naturally blonde ponytail waving cheerily from side to side as she spoke.

'Just don't tell John's mum.' Cara undid her hand-knitted cardigan, its swirling pattern mimicking her wavy bob. 'Audrey has always bemoaned the fact that Christmas starts too early and is so commercial.' She'd lowered her voice as if her mother-in-law's hearing aids could pick up far-off conversations.

I studied the dark rims under her eyes, accentuated against the pale, freckled skin characteristic of redheads. Life for Cara had been hard since her widowed mother-in-law had moved in two months ago following a fall. Although, now she was getting better, Audrey seemed like such a help. She was always playing with the children and kept Cara company, what with my friend's husband, John, working all hours.

'Maybe she's got a point,' said Davina. She slipped off her shoes and tucked her feet under her bottom. 'Being involved with the food bank has really made me grateful for the life I have with Max, Jasper and Arlo.'

That's where I first met *him*. Kit. For just a few seconds I'd seen nothing but those warm chestnut eyes. The way they'd crinkled at the corners and made me feel like the only person in the room.

'Volunteering there has made me think about all the money we waste without even realising it,' continued Davina. 'One man was telling me that sometimes he has to choose between buying toothpaste or deodorant.'

'Imagine that,' said Cara and shook her head.

'So this Christmas I've told relatives we are to limit how much we spend on each other. Fifty pounds each should do it.'

Cara and I both looked affectionately at Davina. Her

attempts at budgeting were like born chef Cara deigning to buy ready-to-bake cake mix – one of Davina and my staples. Or like me complaining about aeroplanes flying over my semi, which was probably one of the quietest on the small estate, compared to Cara's terrace next to a drummer and Davina's detached house serenaded by a nearby cockerel.

Davina untucked her legs and rubbed her forehead. 'To be honest I've been worrying all week. Have you heard about it being under threat?'

I frowned. In the spring I'd grown to know Chesterwood's food bank well whilst researching a story on local unemployment. I'd met Kit's eyes across a stack of tinned tuna and was immediately hooked. The wild mocha hair. Tall toned frame. The surprisingly shy smile that caught me off-guard. I hadn't looked at another man like that since Adam, yet all this while I'd felt nothing but friendship for Kit – until our recent cinema visit.

'Up until now the warehouse it's based in has been charging minimal rent just to cover the rates. As you know, Fern, it's only small. The landlord inherited it and hasn't previously wanted the bother of doing much with it. But a developer has shown interest and made him realise he's missing out on some serious money.'

This didn't sound good.

'He had no idea the property had such potential and wanted to sell up straightaway but Ron who runs it talked him round.'

'So what's the problem exactly?' I asked.

'The landlord has said unless they can start paying a competitive level of rent, he'll have to evict them.' Davina shook her head. 'It's an astronomical amount. Not outlandish in terms of the market – in fact modest, by all accounts – but for a strapped organisation that previously has hardly had to pay a penny...'

'The news must have been such a shock,' said Cara. She sat a little straighter. 'The community should do something about this.'

I exchanged glances with Davina. It was nice to see a glimpse of the old Cara who always roped Davina and me into supporting her latest cause. Like the animal rescue centre last year that the council had stopped funding. She'd baked cookies with cat faces on to feed the demonstrators standing outside in the rain. However, she'd just not been herself lately.

'Yes. Ron looks even more tired than usual. With more wintry weather approaching volunteers can hardly cope with demand, as it is, and he's working all hours,' said Davina. 'The food bank's account can just cover rent until the end of December, but after that who knows what will happen? He's going to approach as many charities as possible in the hope that the place will be able to operate under their umbrella, and gain support and funding that way. Initial talks have made him feel optimistic that might happen but setting it up will take time. Max and I gave a donation—'

'That was good of you,' said Cara. 'I wish John and I were in a position to do the same but I account for every penny that we spend, and there's never much left over after the essentials each month.'

'Same here,' I said. Adam's death had paid off the mortgage but there were still living costs. Much-needed holidays to save for, along with university funds for Lily one day – and my old age. I never used to think much about things like that but Adam's death had brought my finances sharply into focus. I was now very aware of the fact that Lily was dependent on me alone, and that I needed to be completely self-sufficient.

Davina shrugged. 'There was only so much we could give, especially as our earnings haven't been as high this year. Ron really needs to cover January's rent, as well, to tide the food bank over properly until a more permanent rescue plan is in place – and to give the landlord the reassurance he wants that they are committed to paying long-term.'

The food bank couldn't close down. I'd seen first-hand how it changed people's lives, offering hope to those who didn't know where their next meal was coming from. And it benefited the community in so many other ways, bringing people together and reducing food waste. Local supermarkets, restaurants and hotels all donated goods they'd otherwise have to pay to store or throw away.

Not that I'd known any of this until researching my article. And I doubted many people in the community did. A food bank was one of those essential, highly important places that nevertheless existed away from sight, in the background.

She sighed. 'Anyway, enough about my concerns – Cara, has Hannah got over that nasty bug yet? Did little Lex catch it?'

I listened to Cara reply, relishing the relaxation. It was the autumn half-term holiday and the three of us had been keen to meet. I tried to plan my work so that I could free up days whenever the schools broke up. There was never enough time to chat in the playground. The children were currently upstairs in Arlo's bedroom practising a play they'd made up, about dragons, that they wanted to perform to us before lunch.

'So, Fern – what are you wearing on tomorrow's date?' said Davina briskly. 'I meant to ask yesterday, at the indoor play area.'

Cara stopped stroking the cat. 'Date? How come I'm the last to know?'

'Because it's not a date,' I said firmly and glared at Davina who had a gleam in her eye.

'Oh please. This Oliver guy has asked you out to dinner. And quite right too. You are giving his mindfulness venture a plug in your column.'

'It's business. And there's been nothing remotely flirtatious about our emails,' I said, thinking the sleet outside must be nice and cooling. The colder weather had come early this year.

'Gosh... this is your first, isn't it? Since...' Cara's voice softened.

Since Adam? It was. And my lack of enthusiasm towards Oliver didn't mean I wouldn't be ready to meet someone else if the right person came along. My thoughts flicked to Kit.

Last night we'd gone on one of our cinema trips. We both loved science fiction. The only seats left were in the back row. Kit had winked and I'd laughed. We sat down next to a young couple with their arms around each other.

'I've only got eyes for ice cream at the movies,' Kit had whispered, holding up two Cornettos.

Playfully I'd snatched one from him. It fell. As the lights dimmed, we'd both bent down to retrieve it. On straightening up our faces came the closest they'd ever been. I wasn't sure why but I couldn't help thinking about it now.

'She doesn't even know what this Oliver looks like,' said Davina.

'Actually, I did a bit of research.'

'You mean you've stalked him on social media,' she said comfortably. 'Perfectly understandable. Let's see what he looks like, then.'

I took out my phone and went into Facebook. 'Great blonde hair. Doting eyes. Could be a keeper, don't you think?'

Cara reached for my phone. A smile crossed her face. 'Perhaps you should be wary of a man who puts a photo of his dog up as his profile picture – although I do love terriers. Have you got a babysitter?'

'Young Megan, next door.'

'First things first, Fern,' said Davina. 'What are you wearing?'

I opened my mouth then shut it again.

'As I thought. Come with me. I've got a new green dress that will match your eyes perfectly.'

'It's really not nec—'

Davina stood up and gave me a piercing stare that only a mother of twins could master. She and Cara came over and waited for me to get to my feet. Then they linked arms with me, one either side.

Grumbling, I acquiesced, despite feeling sick. But it wasn't the thought of the date giving me nausea. It was the idea of the food bank disappearing. Cara was right. Something had to be done. The weeks I'd spent interviewing the unemployed made me realise any one of us could end up sleeping on the streets. When Adam died, I'd started drinking a bottle of wine every night – until the time Lily was ill. I couldn't drive her to hospital and had to book a taxi instead.

That was the wake-up call I'd needed. But what if I hadn't woken up? I could have lost my job. My home. Lost Lily. The sympathy of family and friends. Ended up as a rough sleeper, dependent on the kindness of others.

Keen to troubleshoot, my mind started racing. That came with the job. A journalist was used to working out speedy ways to find witnesses to corroborate stories or evidence to provide proof. I needed to come up with a plan to save the place that had saved so many people from going hungry.

As we walked up the stairs, an idea stormed into my head and demanded attention, inspired by Davina's talk of the Parents' Association and a foreign news article I'd read last year.

My heart thumped so loudly my friends could probably hear it.

It was certainly ambitious.

Some might say crazy.

Did I even have time to organise it?

Acknowledgements

Huge thanks to my industrious editor Hannah for helping me make this book the very best it can be and for bringing some added Christmas magic to the pages. I really appreciate the hard work she and the rest of the team have put in despite the unprecedented challenges of this last year.

Thanks to my agent, Clare Wallace of the Darley Anderson Literary Agency, for her fantastic perspective, vision, support and care.

Rachel Gilbey and all the bloggers who continue to be cheerleaders of my stories – you guys are the best and it's so lovely to connect with people who share such a passion for books. Thank you.

Martin, Immy and Jay I love you very much. Thanks for always being there.

A special word for my lovely readers: I know the last year has been difficult for all of us in many different ways. It's an honour to know, from reviews and by connecting on social media, that in some small way my novels may have helped. Good times come and go but books and escapist stories are always there, in the background, waiting for you when things get tough. Keep on going, one day at a time.

Sam xx

About the Author

SAMANTHA TONGE lives in Manchester UK with her husband and children. She studied German and French at university and has worked abroad, including a stint at Disneyland Paris. She has travelled widely.

When not writing she passes her days cycling, baking and drinking coffee. Samantha has sold many dozens of short stories to women's magazines.

She is represented by the Darley Anderson literary agency. In 2013, she landed a publishing deal for romantic comedy fiction with HQDigital at HarperCollins. In 2015 her summer novel, *Game of Scones*, hit #5 in the UK Kindle chart and won the Love Stories Awards Best Romantic Ebook category.

In 2018 *Forgive Me Not*, heralded a new direction into darker women's fiction with publisher Canelo and in 2020 her novel *Knowing You* won the RNA's Jackie Collins Romantic Thriller Award.

Hello from Aria

We hope you enjoyed this book! If you did let us know, we'd love to hear from you.

We are Aria, a dynamic digital-first fiction imprint from award-winning independent publishers Head of Zeus. At heart, we're committed to publishing fantastic commercial fiction – from romance and sagas to crime, thrillers and historical fiction. Visit us online and discover a community of like-minded fiction fans!

We're also on the look out for tomorrow's superstar authors. So, if you're a budding writer looking for a publisher, we'd love to hear from you. You can submit your book online at ariafiction.com/we-want-read-your-book

You can find us at:
Email: aria@headofzeus.com
Website: www.ariafiction.com
Submissions: www.ariafiction.com/we-want-read-your-book